THE
HOME PLACE

THE
HOME PLACE

CARRIE LA SEUR

WILLIAM MORROW
An Imprint of HarperCollins*Publishers*

This book is a work of fiction. The characters, incidents, and dialogue are drawn from the author's imagination and are not to be construed as real. Any resemblance to actual events or persons, living or dead, is entirely coincidental.

HarperCollins books may be purchased for educational, business, or sales promotional use. For information please e-mail the Special Markets Department at SPsales@harpercollins.com.

FIRST EDITION

Designed by Jamie Lynn Kerner

Library of Congress Cataloging-in-Publication Data has been applied for.

ISBN 978-0-06-232344-6

14 15 16 17 18   OV/RRD   10 9 8 7 6 5 4 3 2 1

For Esther and Jennie, keepers of the home place

Our native land charms us with inexpressible sweetness,
and never, never allows us to forget that we belong to it.
[Lat., *Nescio qua natale solum dulcedine captos*
Ducit, et immemores non sinit esse sui.]

Ovid, *Epistulae ex Ponto* (I, 3, 35)

ACKNOWLEDGMENTS

This book has been under construction for so long that it might be simpler to list friends and family who somehow managed not to be employed in this version of Tom Sawyer's fence-painting project. First, I am forever indebted to my parents and a host of dedicated public school teachers who taught me to write and to love books, and to Bryn Mawr College for investing in the scholar and writer the college believed I could be. The late Oxford don Malcolm Bowie held my writing and scholarship to the most rigorous standard, which is a very great gift.

Many people midwifed this book, from my law school friend Dave Grossman, who read a very early and probably painful draft and managed to say something sufficiently encouraging to keep me going, to neurologist Matt Rizzo, Billings police chief Rich St. John, and pathologist Michael Brown, who patiently answered questions about head injuries, police procedure, postmortem exams, and untraceable causes of death. If I got anything right about Native American life and culture, I'll put it down to the good influence of Eldena Bear Don't Walk and Chase Iron Eyes, attorneys and warriors. Montana poet and rancher Wallace McRae provided a full and thoughtful edit that fixed some clinkers. Of course, any mistakes and false notes are my own. My law partners Beth Baumstark and Derrick Braaten have been supportive and patient far beyond the call of professional duty. And the board and staff of Plains Justice, over the many years I was scribbling this book in stolen minutes, have been friends, family, inspiration, and comrades-in-arms.

Then there are all the unexpected and delightful friends in the publishing industry who taught this unworkshopped, self-taught, china-shop bull of a writer to navigate their world. Literary agent Michelle Brower at Folio, then editor Kate Nintzel, took my little book to boot camp and made a man out of it, or metaphors to that effect. It's been one of life's great pleasures getting to know them, as well as the brilliant, funny, creative team at William Morrow.

My husband, Andy Wildenberg, has done so much to make this book happen that he should have his name on the cover too. In neon. The fundamental things apply.

THE
HOME PLACE

Chapter 1

SUNDAY, 2 A.M. MOUNTAIN STANDARD TIME

The cold on a January night in Billings, Montana, is personal and spiritual. It knows your weaknesses. It communicates with your fears. If you have a god, this cold pulls a veil between you and your deity. It gets you alone in a place where it can work at you. If you are white, especially from the old families, the cold speaks to you of being isolated and undefended on the infinite homestead plains. It sounds like wolves and reverberates like drums in all the hollow places where you wonder who you are and what you would do in extremis. In this cold, you understand at last that you are not brave at all.

If you're Indian—a Crow or Cheyenne off the res maybe, a Shoshone, Hidatsa, Assiniboine, one of the humbled peoples of an unforgiving land—the cold will sound different, but still, it knows your name. It has no mercy for you no matter how long and intimate its relationship with your mothers and fathers. You of all people ought to know that it is a killer. How many of your relatives has it taken? More than wars and car crashes? Do your fingers and toes tingle in the cold because of some childhood frostbite, before you learned to cover up, or when the power company turned off the juice and your little back got pushed up hard against the cold rock of winter?

A woman in her midtwenties, too thin, with long, loose brown hair and smudged pink lipstick, has just stumbled out into the darkest, earliest hour of Sunday morning. Her hair needs a trim—a good brushing wouldn't hurt—and her eyes have settled into a distrustful squint at an early age. Every so often her lips come together in an expression that looks for a second as if she's about to complain about her bunions and a late Social Security check. Up close, her eyes can show a twinkling purple shade like northern lights, but to strangers they reveal nothing but mute, defiant gray. The length of her nose and width of her face evoke Gibson Girl prints, an old-fashioned beauty that wants elaborate hair and clothes to set it off. It hangs on her like an unkempt garment, ready to cast off soon enough as age and fatigue shred its fibers.

The woman's walk is stiff, even with her impaired condition. The prosthesis on her left leg moves mechanically, its knee joint rolling in a steel socket, supporting her well enough but not quite creating the illusion that there is a whole, real leg under her tight stonewashed jeans. The pointy-toed cowboy boots don't improve her gait. She weaves a little and burps. She fumbles in a heavy, stained canvas shoulder bag for a pack of Marlboro reds that turns out to be empty. She has forgotten her coat. Since much earlier in the evening, so early that most of the partygoers have passed out, she's been getting stoned and drunk in the barely furnished living room of a 1920s two-bedroom bungalow a few blocks south of the tracks. She's been staying there with a fat, alcoholic Pole named Garfield Kozinsky, after the Montana county where he was born. He's not her boyfriend, she tells people, but she sleeps with him and he doesn't ask for rent.

This part of town has been the wrong side of the tracks since they went in, spanning North America back in the 1880s, when Frederick Billings the railroad man came blustering across the northern plains with a load of cash and dreams. The cash has long since dried up, and who would have a dream around here? Who would be that stupid? The ones with dreams have left, abandoning the others to their cryogenic stasis. It's a neighborhood of vacant lots, chain-link fences, and wide, dented siding, where broken-down cars sit like ships run aground in this ancient inland sea. The oil and coal money lubricating the rest of town only makes the dry rasp of need more pronounced. The derelict shopfronts out on Minnesota Avenue reflect the ashes of prosperity in dirty, cracked windows and urine-soaked doorways.

There's an old bakery on the corner, dating to the days when horses pulled bread wagons on local routes. When you peer into the boarded windows, through the cracks, the dust on the long counter looks as if someone has been kneading dough again, getting ready for another early morning's baking. The old delivery truck is on blocks out back, stripped clean and sun-bleached. Cars and other abandoned machines inhabit the yards of houses that would be called shacks in warmer parts of the world where nobody would bother to finish or heat them. Ragtops and upholstery are shredded and the door and window levers don't work. They suck up gas and run on duct tape, baling wire, and desperation. Here and there is a creative attempt at auto body repair. An old Chevy just up the street from Kozinsky's has a headlight reflector fashioned out of a pie tin with a hole cut in the middle for the lightbulb. The slightly crumpled fender has been pulled out a bit with muscle, not proper tools, and the uneven surface is mottled by a patchy putty-and-paint job. There is dignity, even elegance, in this, a fuck-you ingenuity that takes pride in the homely fix.

They say the cold keeps out the riffraff, but it may just keep them out of sight. The wind comes barreling out of the

Beartooth range to the west, pinballing off the Pryors, the Crazies, the Bull Mountains, gathering force in the foothills and across the plains, shivering down the Yellowstone, the mighty Elk River—howling, hunting tonight. The leafless trees bow over before it, but the pines, the native ladies, merely part their heavy skirts and let the wind come through, lifting the featherweight of snow from their boughs, dispersing it in breathtaking little blizzards that sweep down the street, one after another, like guerrillas advancing, attacking, and taking cover.

Brittany is eleven years old. Her mother believes her to be asleep under the coats in the back bedroom, which is really a walled-in, icy back porch, but Brittany has stayed awake and dressed, passing the time by imagining the living room populated by talking animals rather than growling humans, waiting for people to quiet down and pass out. Those who haven't gone are mostly unconscious when her mother decides to go find her ex, Dennis, to see if he's still good for a little pot. From the crack where the bedroom door doesn't hang flush, Brittany watches her mother stagger out, then come back for her bag. Brittany leaps back into bed, expecting her to come looking for her coat in the pile.

But she isn't coming back. Instead, the front door slams. Brittany hurries to the front room and hops over sleeping bodies to climb onto the back of the gray velour couch and wipe a hole to peer out the fogged, frosted window. She sees her mother find her keys and follow an indirect, tacking course through gusts of wind toward their car. She fumbles at the car door, then gives up and starts to walk toward the lights blocks away on Twenty-Seventh Street. Nobody on this street bothers to shovel the sidewalk. The thin layer of snow on the ground has hardened in the recent cold snap into a layer of ice you'd need a chisel and hammer to crack. Brittany watches her mother meander down the middle of the street, coming in and out of focus as she appears in the pooling illumination of one streetlight after another.

Dry snow pellets rush before the wind in a steady current. Brittany clambers along the back of the couch to drop onto the cold patch of floor next to the front door. Even with the overheated living room behind her, Brittany inhales hard in the doorway as the cold slaps at her. "Mom!" she cries, but the wind throws the sound back down her throat. She tries again. "Come back!" A gust smacks her chest so hard it knocks the wind out of her.

Her mother is making uncertain progress up the street, oblivious to the calls behind her. Brittany navigates through the bodies in the living room on tiptoe. A greasy-faced, long-haired guy half awakens from the spot he's nabbed near the heat register and grabs her ankle.

"Hey, sweetheart, get me a beer, will ya?"

Brittany nods and yanks her leg free. *Fantasy Island* is starting on TV. Ricardo Montalbán intones something heavily accented about the dangers of getting your heart's desire as she finally reaches the yellow phone on the kitchen wall. Sometimes there's no dial tone. Tonight there is. She exhales and begins to dial all the numbers she knows. Her father, her great-grandma, her great-aunt Helen, her uncle Pete. Dad doesn't answer. He never does, but she always calls him first. She dials Great-Grandma wrong and gets an angry hang-up. Great-Aunt Helen answers the phone and tells her no, Uncle Walt won't come, and quit bothering people in the middle of the night. Last, she calls Uncle Pete, the most likely to say yes, the one they've cried wolf and wild goose to over and over, the one she least wants to bother again. He sleepily agrees to come.

Brittany peeks around the doorjamb toward the beer drinker, who has fallen asleep again. She creeps along the edge of the living room back to the bedroom, where she finds the heaviest coat in the pile. Then she sneaks back out to the living room and again maneuvers herself onto the back of the couch pushed against the front window. The chill comes straight through the single pane. Brittany wraps the coat more tightly around herself and stares out for as long as she can stay awake. She thinks she sees headlights down the street, but they don't come as far as the house. If it were Pete, he'd come for her, jog up the steps in his businesslike way, sweep into the house with that steadiness like he's on land and Kozinsky and all his pals are swaying on a ship's deck. If she can't have Pete, Brittany wishes that her invisible dog, Burro, were here, climbing up the way he used to, nearly unbalancing the couch with his weight, to lie down along the length of its back next to her. She can almost see him, almost feel his smelly, doggy warmth. For just a moment, Brittany allows herself to caress Burro's head and ask him to shift her mother's steps, just enough, toward safety. Brittany is too old for Burro—people have made clear that this is childish foolishness. Burro padded off when she was seven or eight, but she still thinks of him, still knows that he's real, even though she doesn't talk about him anymore. Tonight, unexpectedly, here he is. Burro lifts his head to show his empathic brown eyes and nudges his licorice-black nose into her hand. The warm solace fills her, makes her sleepy.

Sunday, 7:45 a.m. Mountain Standard Time

Some early riser has just found a woman facedown in a front yard three blocks from Kozinsky's house. She has her keys clenched in a bloodied fist, as if she cut herself falling or struggling with a car lock. Her old wool sweater is twisted around her, and her bag has spilled with her wallet still inside. Her nose is bloodied. A small amount of blood from her nose and a gash on the side of her skull is pooled under her head, frozen so quickly that its color hasn't changed from red to brown. It looks fresh and urgent on the ice, as if she needs only to be bandaged and sent home, but against the bright blood her skin is already changing from no color at all to a morbid shade of blue. On the solid sheet of snow and ice, her body leaves no mark. To fall on such a surface would be very painful, but the expression on the woman's icy face is not a grimace. It's a childlike look of disbelief, as if she was taken utterly by surprise when death leaned in with rattling bones and trailing robe to take her breath.

This morning the cold has crept away on padded paws and left only this. The wind that was so angry and vicious the night before has slackened and temperatures are back above zero. The Billings PD patrol officer who answered the call stands huffing warm breath over his first cup of coffee, staring down at the woman. "I get real tired of seein' this shit," he says, perhaps to the fire department paramedics, who have brought out their equipment to check vitals on a body already turned blue. "If she'd wandered out in July she'd be sleepin' it off instead of ridin' away in a fuckin' bag. Makes you sick."

He looks up in time to regret his cussing as a little girl in a very large coat comes padding around a high wooden fence at the edge of the lot. She sees the body and the paramedics who have set aside their lifesaving tools and are unfolding a body bag and a stretcher. The officer comes toward the girl, positioning his body between her and the ugliness behind him, stretching out a hand, beginning to speak calming words, but as the crew lifts the body onto the open body bag, the head turns enough that the girl can be sure who it is. Her arms stretch out to her left, as if reaching for something, but there is nothing beside her. Before the officer can get to her, she begins to scream.

CHAPTER 2

SUNDAY, 6:45 A.M. PACIFIC STANDARD TIME

At dawn on Sunday morning, Alma picks up a protein shake from her granite countertop. With her other hand she smoothes several newspapers: the *Seattle Times,* the *New York Times,* the *Financial Times.* She's dressed in head-to-toe cycling gear, from her aerodynamic helmet to the pedal clips on the bottom of her shoes. She glances at the time on a heart-rate-monitor watch.

The view from Alma's kitchen sweeps over a broad expanse of water to low, blue islands still dark and indistinct along the western skyline. Alma steps toward the hall and gazes into the bedroom to where Jean-Marc lies facing the door. His eyes open at the sound of her pedal clips clicking on the tile.

"Off so early?" he asks, propping up on an elbow. "Stay awhile, let me make you some breakfast before you go in."

"No thanks." Alma smiles and comes to the bed to kiss him even as she's grabbing her phone and keys from the dresser next to the bed, tucking them into the back pockets of her jersey. "If I get in early this morning we can still do something together this afternoon. Go back to sleep." She slips away toward the front door, shrugging on a fitted jacket. In the lobby of the condo building, the pedal clips click faster as she wheels a titanium racing bike toward the glass doors. Outside she clicks into the left pedal, pushes off, and swings her right leg over as the college student opening the coffeehouse across the street pauses to watch. A runner coming down the sidewalk spots Alma and nearly collides with the coffeehouse guy as they both stare after her swift departure. Alma notices out of the corner of her eye and allows herself a satisfied smile.

She rides with a fast, practiced cadence through the hills of north Seattle, moving south with purpose, checking the display on the handlebar-mounted computer: speed, cadence, power output, heart rate. She'd program it to display stock quotes if it had an app for that. She dodges potholes without looking and catches lights by pausing or speeding up. Traffic is very light, but Alma's body is alert to every variance in the familiar route.

She should be thinking about the upcoming deal. For the last few weeks, the thrill of working out points of conflict in the merger agreement and bringing off this coup for her client has occupied Alma's every waking moment—but now, instead of thinking business, Alma is watching the sky. Her nose twitches with the distantly familiar smell of snow. Her deep-frontier instinct is to look for sun dogs and follow clouds for the heavy kind that bring the storm, but the skies here are smaller and speak a language that Alma cannot easily read. She shakes her head and hunches her shoulders against the thickening cold, tugs at the snug collar of her jacket, and shakes out her hands. After more than a decade, they still itch for reins, not handlebars, but this is her mount now, a bike called Shadowfax.

"Show us the meaning of haste!" Alma murmurs with a smile in her cold cheeks.

The backlit eastern sky is dove-colored this morning. Too wrong, those mountains to the east. They confuse everything for Alma, turn the sky upside down. She crosses the Fremont

Bridge, watching a few hardy rowers paddle out from the docks with quick warm-up strokes, matches the Zen of her rhythm to theirs, and examines the angle and acceleration of the blades with a knowledgeable eye. On the far side of Lake Union she heads downtown, spinning through the quiet with occasional smells of baking, coffee, and exhaust, relishing the speed and the cold in her hands and feet, breathing in the sense of purpose she feels every time she approaches the glass and steel towers of the city. In these buildings there is work enough to keep her out of trouble, to stop her from reliving past mistakes.

Alma secures her bike in a locker and strides into the gym, where the Latina attendant greets her by name—enunciating the Spanish word with relish—and hands her a thick white towel. She showers and changes into clothes waiting in her gym locker. Everything is here: makeup, jewelry, shoes, freshly dry-cleaned clothes. There is no official reason to dress formally—there will be no clients to see—but the habit is fully formed. She has an image to project, as does the firm of Presley, Moi and Torvalds. Alma sighs and rubs her right temple as she enters the elevator block of her office building and the sun breaks over the hills of Bellevue. An obsessive-compulsive lawyer is a productive lawyer. She checks the elegant gold watch she's traded for her training watch: 7:53 A.M.

Her cell phone starts to play a Cajun waltz—Jean-Marc's idea of a joke—as Alma crosses the threshold of her office, sipping the Starbucks that the firm provides. There are three coffee shops within a block of the office, but Alma will not pay for what she can have for free. Her great-grandparents saw the topsoil blow away and the livestock starve, and finally sold everything—even the pump head from the homestead—to make ends meet in town. They saved tinfoil when the world wars had been over for years. Her parents never bought another car until the old one could hardly be sold for scrap. Even now, with far more money than time, Alma can scarcely bring herself to buy something that isn't on sale. After nearly two years together, Jean-Marc has learned to take care of that. He tips the doorman, orders the fine wines, buys the first-class seats. She would never.

Alma drops the phone on her desk and taps the speaker button with one finger while automatically switching on the computer, juggling her coffee from hand to hand. "Good morning—Alma Terrebonne."

"This is Detective Ray Curtis of the Billings Police Department," a reluctant voice answers.

"Billings? You're calling from Billings?" She snatches up the phone and clicks off the speaker.

"Yes, ma'am. I'm sorry to call so early on a Sunday, Ms. Terrebonne."

"Has something happened?" Alma stands clutching the phone to her ear, holding her breath.

"I'm afraid I'm calling with bad news. There's been a death here in town. I think the woman may be your sister—Vicky Terrebonne?"

"Yes." Alma exhales and sits down hard, grabbing at the arm of the ergonomic chair as it rolls away from her swaying center of gravity. Coffee splashes onto her hand and wrist and she swears, trying to shake it off. "Vicky's my little sister. What happened?" This cannot be. She will not believe it until they show her a body.

"Well, it— To tell you the truth, it looks like a bad fall and exposure, but we have to investigate it as a homicide since it was an unattended death. The coroner will do an autopsy. I'm sorry, I would have called someone local but we've got Brittany here and she had your business card on her. It's the best contact I have right now. I'm so sorry to break the news to you this way."

Detective Curtis's voice is soft, contrite, and marked with the soft-shoe rhythms of a native Crow speaker. *Ka-hay. Sho'o Daa' Chi,* Alma thinks, the greeting all she remembers of the language that floats unseen through the city like water in the irrigation ditches, dust underfoot, ever present, barely acknowledged.

"Brittany was there? She saw what happened?" Alma pushes up her sleeve to wince at the light burn.

"No, not really. Well, she—" Detective Curtis's voice gets higher and, if this is possible, even more uncomfortable. "She saw the body, yes."

"So you're sure it's Vicky?"

"Well, she hasn't been positively identified. We'll need an adult to come in and do that. Her wallet was still on her, but the best piece of ID she had was an old library card, and those just have a signature on the back."

"So this could be a mistake. It might not be Vicky."

A pause and a sigh in Billings. "Yes, ma'am, there's always that possibility, until she's been positively ID'd."

"Is Brittany there with you?" Alma dabs at the spilled coffee with a pad of sticky notes. She glances out the door for her assistant, who of course isn't there.

"With me? No. She's down the hall with the social worker. She doesn't want to talk to us." At least that explains why Alma's business card is the best contact they have. It's been generations since Billings was the sort of small town where everybody knows each other.

"Who found the body?" Alma follows up, her lawyer's instincts kicking in. She wants to interrogate Curtis, find out everything he knows, get to the detail that proves that this is all a mistake.

"Somebody drove by early on their way to work and called it in. She'd been partying at a house up the street with a whole crowd of the usual suspects. Your sister had a list of priors, you know. Three DUI convictions and an assault charge that was dropped. These folks she was with—we're holding two of them on outstanding warrants, to give you an idea."

"What for?"

"Oh, nothing all that surprising. Possession, distribution, simple assault—bar fight—driving with a suspended license. I could pick up half the county for that. But in the right circumstances I think any one of them could cross the line. They're a rough bunch. The tenant, a"—the shuffle of a notepad comes through the phone, then the detective continues—"Garfield Kozinsky—looks like he'd been dealing too. All I'm saying is, we're carrying out a complete investigation, ma'am. We'll find out what happened to your sister."

"I see." Alma is braced on the very edge of her chair, one hand on the phone, one hand clenched on her desk, feet planted. "Tell me what I can do to help."

"I need names of any family members or friends who might have been in touch with her recently, people who would know about her life. And the social worker needs to know who we should call for—your niece, I assume? She won't give us any names. All we have is this one thing she said to the patrol officer about how she 'called and nobody came.'"

"You can call our aunt and uncle, Walt and Helen Terrebonne." Alma reels off the number. "Or our brother, Pete Terrebonne. He owns a coffeehouse called the Itching Post, up by MSU-B."

"Oh, sure. Nice place." Detective Curtis's voice moves a few steps back down the octave.

"There's our grandma Maddie Terrebonne, and then all kinds of cousins and shirttail relations. I don't know who Vicky might've been in touch with lately. We weren't what you'd call . . . close. Other than what the rest of the family told me, I don't know much about her life the last few years."

Throat clearing. A gulp and hiss like a man drinking hot coffee too fast. "When was the last time you saw her?"

"Me? Oh, it would have been . . ." Alma pauses and stares up at the glossy green volumes of *American Jurisprudence* at the top of her bookcase. She hadn't expected a police interrogation about her most recent abandonment of her sister. The picture is coming into focus: Brittany alone in the police station, the family dithering as they do until chaos reigns. Alma will have to go. She will have to handle this, whatever this is. "Nearly five years ago, when our grandpa died. But we hardly talked then."

"I see. If you don't mind, I may call you again if I need to ask more questions about the family."

"Okay. But I'll be there. I'll catch the next flight. May I talk to Brittany, please?"

"Hang on, I'll go get her." There's a long pause, then Curtis's distant voice. "Here she is."

Silence fills the line.

"Brittany? Are you there?"

Nothing.

"It's me, honey. Are you okay?" Alma tries again, leaning forward as if Brittany were there in front of her. "Are you there? Brittany, listen to me. I'll be on the next flight. You have the police take you to Great-Grandma's or Pete's house and I'll be there as soon as I can. Okay?"

Another moment passes and Curtis is back.

"She hasn't said anything since right after the patrol officer found her," he explains. "She gave him her name and said something about how she'd called people and nobody came, and then she just clammed up. The social worker says she won't say a word."

"Have you spoken to anyone else in the family? Do you know where she tried to call?"

"No, I don't. And I haven't spoken to anyone else. Thought I'd start with you since Brittany had your business card with her."

The picture comes to Alma again of her niece huddled in Ray Curtis's office, the Sunday morning quiet of the police station around them. Brittany is so small. Alma tosses the soggy notepad in the trash and covers her eyes. She can imagine Brittany's feet not quite reaching the floor as she sits lost in the well of a big chair. And then, before she can help it, she is overcome by memories. Arcs of sweeping floodlit luminescence split the darkness. Alma is pinned down. Somewhere a child is crying.

She uncovers her eyes abruptly. The recirculated office air smells stale and stifling. If she could only get a breath of fresh air, things would be better. You can never get a breath of really fresh air in this town. She refocuses on the phone to mumble an inarticulate goodbye, then hangs up and begins to dial numbers starting in 406. Right away she gets Helen, who almost doesn't let Alma get the words out—*found a body, they say they think it's Vicky*—before broadcasting a horrified shriek down the clear fiber-optic line. Alma holds the phone away from her ear until Helen's exclamations quiet down.

"Brittany's at the police station," Alma begins again. "Do you think you could—"

"At the police station! I have to get down there." And the line goes dead. Alma rolls her eyes and dials her grandmother Maddie.

"Oh, honey," Maddie clucks. "You'd never call me so early on a Sunday unless something was wrong. Are you okay?"

"I'm fine, Grandma. It's not me, it's—"

"Vicky." Maddie's voice is resigned, heavy.

"Did somebody already call you?"

"No. I just know that if there's going to be trouble with any of you kids, it's going to be her. Is she in the hospital?"

"Are you sitting down, Grandma?" Alma asks. Maddie walks with a cane. Falling is a serious consideration.

"I'm in my chair," Maddie answers, her voice growing hesitant. "What is it?"

And Alma tells. Then there is silence on the line, so much that Alma grows fearful.

"Grandma? Are you okay?"

"I'm here," Maddie whispers. "You're coming, then?"

"I'm coming," Alma confirms. "Can I stay with you for a few days?"

"Of course, as long as you want to," Maddie says, then holds Alma on the line to give her specific instructions about the funeral, as if she's been reflecting on such things. Nobody in the family but Alma will be willing and able to afford a funeral, and not for a moment will Alma consider shirking this final duty to her sister.

"You're gonna stay awhile, aren't you, honey?" Maddie asks in the same nonnegotiating voice Alma has heard her use to order around ranch hands. "We're all gonna need each other at a time like this. Brittany's gonna need you. You can take a few weeks off work, can't you?" Arguing with Maddie Terrebonne's gentle suggestions is generally about as fruitful as cultivating a cactus garden in Seattle.

"I guess I can stay the week, Grandma, but that's all. I already told Brittany I'd come out, but I'm in the middle of something big here and I can't afford to be gone. Maybe I can come back over the summer if things lighten up a little." Maddie makes a contrary little noise to indicate that the issue is not settled, then leads the conversation into what Alma would like to eat, where Brittany is, who will fetch her things, all the details that Maddie likes to know and manage. After talking for longer than she'd normally allow anyone to detain her, Alma gets Maddie off the phone.

Alma pushes another button to get her assistant's home number. Amanda takes several rings to answer. "Alma—yes— what can I do for you?" Half-asleep but unsurprised. Alma rushes into the next of so many awful, necessary words, explaining as succinctly as possible.

"Oh my God." Amanda's voice switches to professional like a computer screen lighting. "I'm so sorry. Don't worry about anything. I have your whole schedule on my phone, so I can reschedule everything right away."

"You're the best. Thank you. I knew I could count on you. I'll call you every day and keep tabs on e-mail. Whatever you do, don't let Duncan into my office. I'll lock the door behind me. Anything they need, I can e-mail, but I do not want him having access to my hard drive. Unplug it and hide it if you have to."

"Done." Alma knows that Amanda will take care of the spoken and unspoken issues. She'll keep Alma's work schedule ticking along, report in regularly, and stand like a perky, well-groomed watchdog over her client files and computer. The generous bonuses are worth it for someone who understands loyalty.

After a few more messages for colleagues, Alma books her flight to Billings. She hopes not to be able to get out until later in the day, but there's an early flight and just enough time to cab home and get down to Sea-Tac. There's work waiting, but there's no helping it.

The final call, to Jean-Marc, wakes him too. "I can go with you if you want," he offers. "It sounds . . . complicated." Jean-Marc Lacasse is Québécois *de souche,* old stock, and in any discussion involving emotion he tends to revert to Anglicized versions of French words, before code-switching entirely back to the mother tongue, the musical language of Molière. *Compliqué,* she hears him thinking. *Bouleversant.* The French meanings well up in his words, more foreign for the flawless mid-Atlantic English in which Jean-Marc pronounces them. The language is largely lost to the Terrebonnes, for as much as they carry it with them as a marker of ancestry. Part of Jean-Marc's appeal is the concrete link to those roots—the *coureurs des bois,* the *voyageurs,* the Métis—that hardwire her into centuries of North American history so bitter and complicated it borders on Middle Eastern.

"No, you can't afford to be out of town right now, not with the Parker deal going through. Think of the bonus you'll get for that," she reassures Jean-Marc. He's a Pacific Rim investment banker, fluent in Mandarin and conversational in Japanese. His bonuses shock Alma deeply. All those zeros, for what? She's never told him how the open-throttle flow of cash disturbs her, seems almost an insult to the kind of labor she was reared to understand as earning a living. She just lifts the champagne flute and swallows it all silently.

"I'll take you to Kaua'i for a few days when it's all over. First-class."

"That sounds fantastic," she enthuses. There will never be time for such a trip, but it's a nice thing for him to say, a warm fantasy to carry with her on this direct flight to cold reality.

"Are you sure you don't need me? You'll get sucked in. I am very useful in chaotic situations. I'll arrange everything in twenty-four hours and you won't have to muddle with the grandmother." Muddling—a very halfway English, Jean-Marc thing to say. He uses it to mean something like fussing, as Alma understands him.

"No, really, Jean-Marc, it's better for me to do it myself. It's going to be complicated enough without you giving my lunatic family the *Art of War* treatment. I'll be back to pack a bag. I'm going to have to be there most of a week. No way Grandma will let me get away with less, and we'll have to figure out what to do for Brittany."

"Very well. But if it becomes war, you know whom to call."

"I hear you." Alma feels the shadow of the moment in which she should tell Jean-Marc that she loves him. It passes and is gone. He doesn't say it because he knows she won't. "I'll see you soon," she says and hangs up.

Gathering papers and her laptop in a bag with the firm's logo, Alma lets her eyes fall for a moment on the view she rarely notices. To the southeast, lit by impeccably clear morning light, Mount Rainier reveals herself in her true form: Tahoma, the mountain that was God. Alma inhales at the sight and pauses. The snowy flanks of Tahoma evoke Billings, the magnificent

Absaroka-Beartooth range, and chilly afternoons when she, Pete, and Vicky flew down the slopes of Pioneer Park. Vicky was never satisfied with the safe runs that flattened out toward the playground equipment. She wanted the steep, dangerous lines on the western side, angling toward the creek. Alma recalls bailing from the back of a sled more than once while Vicky held on, shrieking and laughing, as she soared off the bank and splashed down in icy water. Vicky would clamber up undeterred, wet and muddy, ready to ride again, and Alma would have to go all bossy and march her home, bundled in Alma's coat, to forestall hypothermia. Alma hasn't thought of those days in years.

In the distance is the faint peal of church bells. How many years has it been since she last slipped into the cushioned pews of First Congregational Church in Billings, where her parents and grandparents once stood to sing the good old hymns, shoulder to shoulder, now thank we all our God? Who is there now, mouthing the joyful joyfuls and passing the collection plate, standing in the shadow of that fearful father God who takes and takes, thy will be done? Alma can still envision the massed troops, row after row of stalwart old Protestant ladies descended from New England families gone west, the Masons, the Eastern Star Worthy Matrons, the deacons, the choir, her grandmother's side of the family, the old Yankees' great-grandchildren who still fill the pews, as if bound by their ancestors' habits and vows.

Down on the street, Alma grabs her taxi north, charges up to the condo to throw a few things in a bag, kisses Jean-Marc, and rushes south to catch the 9:50 Alaska Airlines direct flight to Billings. It's good timing, dying on a Sunday morning, Alma reflects with a morose half smile as they race down I-5. Any other day of the week and she'd never have made the flight.

CHAPTER 3

Billings lies in the Yellowstone River valley, framed by vertical Sacrifice Cliff and the stunning outcrop known locally as the rimrocks, which together give the city a broad canyon feel. The south side, along the river and the interstate, is a fortress of refineries and industrial space. The sweet spot is farther north, where many visitors never penetrate—the quaint older neighborhoods, the gracious parks, the colleges. In her memory Alma forgets the rough spots and remembers only the sunny hometown embrace.

The plane comes in low toward the rims. Alma looks for landmarks. She learned to drive down there on Black Otter Trail. No guardrail, no pavement, just an old Jeep with a stiff manual transmission, that was Grandpa Al's idea of a proper initiation. The fairgrounds and the downtown towers, the river and the south hills, the Beartooths snowy and radiant in the distance, it's all as it always has been. She could trace the geography and the architecture with her eyes closed. The wheels touch tarmac and the peculiar thrill of coming home to native ground rivets Alma. She is oriented once more.

She lets out her breath and wonders when she began to hold it. It's been a very long time. Here her dead are buried—and at the moment, unburied—her many kin are living, her ghosts stand vigil, and she is known, she is home. When she turns on her phone, there's a voice mail from Detective Curtis asking her to visit the Billings Clinic morgue.

Nobody greets her. After five years the airport is different, more upscale, but without the god-awful western kitsch Alma associates with ski resort towns. In the new service economy that relies on magnificent mountain views, high-speed quads, and destination spa ranches, Billings is inconveniently placed. The city turns more naturally toward the east and the south, farms and ranches, oil and gas, the parts of the state only a real Montanan could love, where the magnificence of the Rockies gives way to sugar beet fields and sagebrush buttes. The land of Custer and the Crow, where in the worst weather the state troopers shut big steel gates across the on-ramps, because now as in earlier days this country is sometimes too dangerous to dare.

The Terrebonnes have survived for centuries in the North American wilds on wits and kinship. To cross the territory of the warlike Lakota, they traveled at night, took the white canvas off their wagons, and carried tobacco for trade and bribery. The old man, Alphonse Terrebonne, took pride in never carrying a gun and spoke Indian sign language well enough to get himself invited to join camp. The story Grandpa Al told Alma was of his own grandfather, Alphonse's son, who nearly opened fire on a group of mounted Lakota who surrounded the wagons one morning, shouting and firing into the air. But Alphonse grabbed his arm. "Look," he said, "they're not in war paint. If you want something to do, go join them." The younger man mounted up and rode into the circle, to the delight of the Lakota, who invited the Terrebonnes' party to camp with them that night. Alphonse handed down through the generations the code of the voyageur along with a stern lesson: *Never fight an Indian. He's defending his land, and considering who we are, he might be your kin.*

Alma's red Mitsubishi rental sedan has antilock brakes and front wheel drive, for which she is immediately grateful as she downshifts to take the steep hill to the valley floor. The view hasn't changed, coal plant and refineries puffing in the middle distance, MSU-Billings standing steady in brick against the backdrop of the rims, the breadth of Twenty-Seventh Street cutting straight to the river.

Alma heads the car toward the massive hospital complex growing inexorably outward from North Twenty-Seventh Street, consuming a charming old neighborhood. This is the place she came in the ambulance with Vicky, right after the accident, Alma's scrapes barely meriting notice next to her sister's crushed leg and internal injuries. She remembers family beginning to arrive as she sat in the corner of a surgical waiting room, wrapped in a blanket, resisting the attentions of a hovering nurse. She remembers a uniformed police officer inquiring in a low, tentative voice about what she'd seen. She refused to say a word, or even look at him. Tense conversation hummed around her, but her mind was still out on the interstate, wandering, terrified. "Man up," Alma whispers to herself. She parks, squares her shoulders, and marches in.

The main reception atrium is full of glass and light, with a grand piano where an elderly volunteer is playing Sinatra. She should have called Pete, she realizes now, but it's too late. She's been spotted. A heavy blonde wearing a name tag is sitting within a circular reception desk. "Alma? Alma Terrebonne? Well hello there! Don't you remember me? It's Sarah Marquardt, or Sarah Jessup now." She gestures at the name tag. "We were in speech class together. I joined the navy, remember?" Sarah is wearing head-to-toe surgical scrubs with the top printed in Hawaiian Mickey and Minnie Mouse figures.

"I— You— Do you work in pediatrics?" Alma fumbles for words.

Sarah blinks. "What? Oh, my scrubs, you mean—no, I just think they put people at ease. Everyone's so tense walking in that door. I like to give them something to smile at."

"Oh, sure." Alma nods. This is what always throws her about Montana—being recognized, remembered, everywhere she goes, like a lesser celebrity. But Sarah's good people. They were in marching band together too. Sarah could always be counted on to know the routine. "Good idea. What happened with you? You got out of the navy and came back here?"

"Yeah, I married Scott Jessup. He was two years ahead of us." Alma remembers Scott dating a mean little cheerleader named Shelly. He's better off with Sarah. "He's farming his folks' place east of here, and I'm working until the next baby comes." Sarah rolls her chair back to reveal a rounded belly on an already substantial frame. "We've already got one, little Micah, so after this one it's full-time mom duty for me! Are you visiting someone? Can I look up a room number for you?"

"No." Alma feels an awkward silence rise between them before she figures out what to say next. "I have to go to the morgue. My sister died last night." Her throat constricts as she admits this. Is there still some chance they could be wrong? Shouldn't she feel different—*know* somehow—if Vicky is really dead?

"Oh my God!" Sarah pushes back her sandy blond hair with both hands. "Oh God, I always put my foot in it. I'm so sorry. Hang on, just hang on and I'll find someone to take you down." Sarah picks up the phone and speaks in a low, urgent voice. Alma backs away a few feet, but Sarah holds up a hand to stop her. "Wait, wait! Someone will be right down. Alma, don't take this the wrong way, honey, but you look like hell. What can I get for you? Coffee? Tea? Nice shot of whiskey?"

Alma raises her eyebrows.

"Kidding. Although I've thought about keeping a bottle in the bottom drawer." Sarah's conspiratorial laugh turns into a little sigh. "It's what a lot of folks really need."

"A coffee would be nice, thanks." Alma offers up a smile in recognition of Sarah's kind humor. "Black, no sugar."

"Sure thing. And hey, I don't mean you look *bad*. You look great, actually. I love that scarf. Just . . . like you've been hit by a truck, you know? In shock. You can have my chair. I'll be right back."

Sarah rises and hurries toward the coffee shop in a corner of the atrium. Alma sinks into the desk chair. A middle-aged couple walks up to the desk. Alma gestures vaguely in Sarah's direction without making eye contact. The pair look around, confused, but too rural polite to demand attention from someone unwilling to offer it. Sarah is back in nearly superhuman time with coffee and gestures urgently at a candy striper who's just appeared from a long hallway to their left.

"This is Jennie. She'll show you down to the morgue. You know the way, right, Jennie?"

Jennie is a high schooler with badly cut short blond hair and glasses. Her red and white pinafore is too big for her and held in place with safety pins above her scuffed white Crocs. "I think so," she says, biting her lip. "I mean, it's only my second day, but I looked at the map."

Sarah looks concerned. "Maybe I should take you down, hon," she begins.

Alma shakes her head. The last thing she wants is hometown interrogation in the key of effusive blonde. "No, Jennie and I will be just fine. Thanks for the coffee."

They set off at a quick pace, Jennie's Crocs making squeaking sounds on the linoleum. They descend in the elevator and begin to traverse a part of the hospital that looks like original construction. Alma forces down the bitter coffee, one long swallow after another, wishing the cup were bigger. She feels sleepy, ready to lie down in the corridor and nap curled against the wall.

"It's only my second day," Jennie repeats as they take turn after turn without arriving at any destination. The heating pipes overhead make the air oppressive and the walls are a yellowish block that sweats. When Alma brushes up against a wall, it's slick and slimy. She feels sweat break out on her lower back and takes off her coat and scarf.

Jennie grows agitated as they wander through serpentine basement corridors. At last, through retracing their steps, they find a locked steel door with a telephone beside it and a tiny plastic plate that reads MORGUE. Jennie calls in to announce Alma, then flees. The hot, damp corridor returns to perfect silence.

The door opens after a long minute to reveal a short, round, cheerful man, the sort of character who'd be better cast as a satyr than as Charon. He wears a bright yellow disposable smock and purple latex gloves, making his appearance all the more a clownlike non sequitur. "Hi there, I'm Larry Sears," he announces, and peels off a glove to shake Alma's hand. "I'm assistant to the coroner. I'm really sorry you had to come down here for this. I'll try to make it as quick as possible."

The room he lets her into is nothing but a small antechamber to an office with an autopsy room beyond. Alma tries not to look through to the steel examination table and the instruments arrayed beside the sinks and along the walls, but they draw her eyes. It's impossible not to feel like a voyeur. She wants to look everywhere at once, to stare. Larry seems not to notice. He offers Alma a low plastic chair, then unlocks the heavy steel door that guards the cooler. As he swings open the door, a smell drifts out—like Alma's high school biology classroom on the day they dissected frogs, not strong but evocative. She threw up

in one of the lab sinks that day. Now she sits still and is thankful
for the chair.

Larry rolls out a steel gurney with a thick black pad. On top
lies a heavy blue bag. He locks the gurney wheels, stands next
to the head, and gestures for Alma to stand opposite him. "I'll
unzip the shroud enough to see her face, and all you have to do
is nod yes or no," he says. He waits until Alma is in position,
looks her over to be sure she's steady, then opens the shroud.

Vicky's face is clean. Someone has wiped away the rest of
the blood that still crusts at the edge of her mouth and combed
her long, dark hair. Her features are a little puffy, bruised by
postmortem lividity, but it's definitely her, all the Hopkins and
Terrebonne genes pooled in her high cheekbones and long
nose, so like Alma's that sometimes they could pass as each other
with strangers when they were younger, even though Alma is
five years older. The resemblance is strongest beside a camp-
fire, when the low light draws out their bone structure. This
is Alma's face, her*self*—the but-for-the-grace-of-God scenario.
She mouths the words: *There but for the grace of God go I.* She
has repeated them to herself many times as a talisman against
hubris, and always when she says them she thinks of Vicky, that
other self, living out the bitter, addictive abandon that is the
flip side of Alma's compulsive work ethic and white-knuckled
self-control.

Alma wants to grab the gurney with both hands and howl
her anger until Sarah hears her upstairs. Is this what had to
happen, this brutal last moment together, the face of the living
looking into the young, bruised face of the dead? From a place
detached from her body, Alma feels herself go cold. She puts out
a hand toward a scrape along the side of Vicky's face, where she
must have fallen on the ice, and lets her fingers rest on the cool
skin. The scrape still looks raw and painful, although Vicky of
course no longer feels anything. Her reckless heart is finally
still. She used to call Alma early in the morning—Alma off at

college or in law school, Vicky an angry teenager who blamed their parents for everything and for dying most of all, then a high-school dropout living in a Section 8 basement apartment in Billings with a colicky baby and passive, minimum-wage Dennis on the night shift—to talk about the nightmare she'd been having when Brittany woke her up. Maybe she woke Brittany with her own screaming, she wasn't sure, but Vicky remembered the nightmares in every disturbing detail.

Vicky was running across a dark college campus, among dark Gothic arches and gargoyles, trying to get to Alma's dorm room. She'd be safe there, and more than that, in the dream she was sure that everything she wanted was there, if only she could find the place, get inside, and bolt the door. But where was Alma? Alma knew the way. Why wouldn't she help? Or the water dreams: Vicky was underwater and couldn't get to the surface, didn't know which way was up. It was dark and murky in the depths of Vicky's dreams and she didn't know how to swim, this girl who'd spent summer afternoons with Alma retrieving pennies from the bottom of the diving well at the pool and cannonballing until the lifeguards made them stop. Sometimes it was Alma herself holding her down, Vicky said, clambering over her to the surface, kicking free of Vicky's grasp to save herself.

Vicky talked about college once in a while and said maybe she'd finish her GED and enroll in a few classes, get started. How was that going to happen, Alma always wondered, with the baby, the job, rent due, constant child care problems, and the gang of hard-partying friends Vicky was still hanging out with? Who was she kidding?

Alma grew exhausted with the calls. The nightmares were so similar, and there was nothing Alma could do, no words of comfort that would mean anything from a thousand miles away. What did Vicky want from her? Didn't she understand how hard it was for Alma just to keep her head above water at a place like Yale Law, then at the firm, without answering these panicked phone calls every few nights?

Then one night in the middle of a huge work crunch, when Alma had been pulling repeated all-nighters on a deal and was trying to get some solid sleep before an important presentation to the firm's managing committee the next morning, the phone rang. Alma knew who it had to be and answered anyway. It was another of Vicky's nightmares, followed by the dramatic tale of a recent breakup. Halfway through the predictable description of an alcoholic, adrenaline-junkie boyfriend with commitment issues—was there any other kind of man in Montana under the age of thirty?—Alma just couldn't do it anymore.

"Vicky, isn't there someone else you could tell this to? I've got to get some sleep," she muttered in frustration, face half buried in a pillowcase that needed washing.

A long silence followed. "No." Vicky's tone sounded accusatory. "There's nobody." She hung up. It was the last really open conversation they'd had, even in the intervening years when Brittany had come to Seattle several times to visit, with tickets Alma bought. A wall had gone up.

Alma has a detailed memory of how, at Al's funeral, Vicky slipped out to her car with Brittany the moment the last hymn began. Alma jogged out of the church after her, trailed by Greg Severson, her own boyfriend at the time, and trapped Vicky at the curb by planting herself at the driver's window. Vicky never got out of the car, never turned off the music, never looked Alma in the eye. Greg waited on the sidewalk, staring back and forth between them as if he didn't trust his eyes at Vicky's eerily familiar profile.

"I've been looking forward to seeing you," Alma pleaded. "Can we talk a little?"

"What about?"

"Anything. How you're doing. Brittany's school. Bad boyfriends." Alma tried to make a joke and winked at Greg. A little family foolishness, nothing abnormal, nothing to see here.

Vicky sneered. "You don't get to care about our lives every couple of years when you have a few minutes free." She threw a contemptuous glance at buttoned-down Greg.

"I always care about your life, bug." The old nickname slipped out. "Most of the time I'm just trying to keep my head above water."

"Fine. Go. Swim. Do whatever it is you do." Vicky tapped a pack of cigarettes against the steering wheel. Alma wanted to snatch the pack from her sister's hands, slap her face, do anything that would snap Vicky out of the snide drawl. She went with a different tack.

"Can Brittany stay with us the rest of the afternoon? I haven't seen her in so long."

"Go play your do-gooder act somewhere else. I'll get by just fine on my own. I have to get to work." She spoke staring straight ahead, spitting out the phrases between puffs on her cigarette. And then, without warning, she pulled away fast like always, in a cloud of angry blue smoke, Alma careening out of the path of the car. Brittany twisted in her seat to watch her aunt recede.

Now Alma looks down at Vicky for the last time. There will be the funeral, but this is the last time together, the only opportunity to speak whatever words Alma has for Vicky's unhearing ears. Alma has always imagined the eventual reconciliation, how they'd sit down together one day at Pete's coffee and pool house up by the college and laugh about growing up. Their estrangement was never meant to be forever, only a little hiccup. The silence between symphonic movements. Alma glances at Larry, but he has folded his hands and is looking at the ceiling, letting Alma take as much time as she likes.

Alma uses her left hand to wrench her right away from

Vicky's face. When she speaks, her voice is far louder than she intends and echoes off the cinder blocks. "This is my sister."

"Thank you," Larry says. He moves a hand to close the shroud, then pauses. "The tattoos are beautiful," he adds with some reluctance, as if he knows he's crossing a line but needs to reach out to her somehow.

"What tattoos?"

"Hadn't you seen them? She has a tattoo of a wing on the back of each shoulder—like angel's wings. It was . . . oddly appropriate. I'm sorry, I shouldn't have said anything."

"Can you—are you allowed to show me?"

Larry glances down at Vicky's body, judging the easiest way to roll the corpse. Without hesitating, he unzips the shroud a little and reaches across to put one hand on Vicky's right arm and the other on top of her right shoulder, rolling her toward him enough to expose her upper right back to Alma. "She fell face-first, you see," Larry mentions in a tone of professional appreciation, "and they didn't find her until morning, so there's no lividity on the back. The tattoo is remarkably clear."

He's right; the tattoo is beautiful and detailed. It must have taken a long time, by someone with talent. "And the other side is the same?" Alma asks. She wonders when Vicky had them done, how she paid for them.

Larry nods. "Perfect matching set. The only ones she had. It's unusual, because they're so big. Usually a person who goes in for that kind of body art will have it all over, but she's completely clean except for that."

"I never knew about it," Alma says. She reaches out to touch the fairy pattern on Vicky's back, but the cold of her sister's skin is too much this time.

Larry clears his throat, as if suddenly aware that he's said too much, and offers a form verifying the identification, then another authorizing the release of the body to the funeral home.

As soon as she's scrawled her signature next to the Xs, he steers her back into the hall as quickly as possible.

It is only when the steel door latches behind her that Alma slumps against the slippery wall and braces her hands against her knees. She takes a few deep breaths. Vicky's wings seemed inexplicably familiar—and suddenly she knows why.

She and Vicky are back in the hall outside the sanctuary at First Church, getting ready for some long-ago Christmas pageant. Alma is the angel of the Lord who appears to Mary with glad tidings, and little Vicky—Victoria Rose, as the choir director liked to intone to get her attention—has been relegated to some shepherd role in a towel and headband. Vicky is distraught. She wants with all her fierce little heart to be an angel, and Alma wears the biggest and most beautiful pair of wings.

"Please," Vicky begs, lower lip beginning to tremble in a way she knows affects Alma, "let me try them on?"

Alma's entrance is coming up in just a few minutes, but she's afraid that at any moment the congregation will hear Vicky's wail louder than the angel chorus if she's denied. "Just for a minute," she concedes. "And be very careful." She shrugs the wings off her own shoulders and helps Vicky pull on the straps. Vicky spins in delight, brown curls bobbing, then on impulse runs up to the first landing of the stairs to the old offices. Light shines through the wings from above, backlighting Vicky in a pose of divine exaltation as she stands on tiptoe at the top of the stairs, raising her arms.

"Hold on to the rail!" Alma hisses, trying not to raise her voice. It's too late. Vicky is tumbling from her precarious pose, sliding hard down the steps on one side, shredding the left wing, while Alma watches, unable to stop the bruising descent. Alma gasps at the destruction of the precious wings that she herself has longed to wear for several years. At the bottom, Vicky raises herself on one hand and twists to look at the wings. Her movements show that she isn't badly hurt, but at the sight of the wings, she begins to sob, a discordant, broken lament audible all the way to the choir loft. Alma sets aside her own stabbing disappointment and kneels to put her arms around Vicky and shush her. "It's okay, it's okay," she murmurs. "We can fix them."

Vicky only cries harder. The choir director, Mrs. Thompson, runs up, heavy bosom bouncing, to tell Alma that it's time to make her entrance. Her face falls at the sight of the wings. "Oh dear," she says. "Well, they'll know you're the angel even without the wings. Just get in there, Mary's waiting!"

Alma rises to take her cue, leaving Vicky alone and weeping on the floor. By the time she comes back, the wings are abandoned in a pile, trampled by the other characters coming and going from the sanctuary, and Vicky is playing some sort of hand game with a girl in a pair of donkey ears.

Alma thought the moment had passed without any real damage to Vicky, but now the tattoos have revived the little girl poised at the top of the steps, glowing like a cherub, just before the fall. Grown-up Alma, alone in the corridor outside the morgue, wraps her arms around herself and fights for control. She pulls her mind into the present, but the effort leaves her trembling. Her breath comes in gasps. She shuts her eyes, but vertigo nearly takes her, so she opens them wide and slams her hands against the wall. Slowly, the world rights and stills. Her breath slows and deepens.

In a moment, Alma begins to move her feet, bolstered by the steady click of her high-heeled boots along the corridor, growing faster, seeking the sunlit world above. She finds a side door and plunges back into the bracing cold.

CHAPTER 4

SUNDAY, 2 P.M. MOUNTAIN STANDARD TIME

Without thinking much about where she's going, Alma steers the car the few blocks to the Itching Post, Pete's place. As on any afternoon during term, its sofas and big upholstered couches are full of students nursing coffee and trying to study. The pool tables in back are hidden by the usual crowd of ringers and procrastinators, playing for what each desires most: money or the passage of time. It's a commuter campus mostly, so Pete's endeavor wasn't an instant success, but he's been in business for several years now and the place has developed a loyal and jittery following. Volume, Pete told her once over the phone, is the secret. Get the hospital workers coming in every day, get the standing orders going, give them what they need faster and better than the competition. Encourage the regulars, the coffee groups and book groups, give them a few specials to keep them happy, learn their names. Until this coffeehouse thing, she'd never realized her older brother had such a head for business. In high school, she would have picked him for Most Likely to Move Back Into the Family Basement.

She remembers a late-night call at the office, nearly seven years ago now, Pete's bright voice on the line. "I wanted you to know," he said as she scrolled through a document she was editing, "I got a job. I start on the morning shift tomorrow. There's a little training, then I'll be managing a coffeehouse downtown." Pete had tried going to college on his GI benefits and wound up spending more than he could spare of every check at the nearest bar. After he flunked out, he ran through a series of minimum-wage jobs. This was the first time in many months that his words didn't seem a little slurred on the phone, regardless of the time of day.

"That's great, Petey," she enthused, wondering how long this job would last.

"Alma, listen. This time is different. I'm sober. I've been sober nearly a month. My new sponsor helped me get this job." There was a light in Pete's voice that she hadn't heard since before their parents' accident. It came down the line with a warmth resembling hope.

"Aw, Pete, I'm so glad to hear that," she answered. And she was, but the preceding years had been teaching her not to trust Pete's recoveries. They were shorter and less frequent each time. "Who's your sponsor?"

"His name is Shep. He's a vet too. We can . . . talk about things."

"I'm glad," she said. Glad he could talk to someone. Pete was resolute in refusing to tell Alma about the things rotting in his soul, a big-brotherly gesture of protection that had cut him off from the person most likely to hear and understand. Maybe talking things through with Shep would make Pete somehow, someday, better able to talk to her again.

Now Pete is behind the coffee bar, looking very much at home in a bartender's apron and an Edmonton Oilers cap over his balding head. "Little sister," he calls, waving with a rag in hand. "Good to see you. You look like hell." He comes around the bar and Alma steps into a bear hug that picks her up off her feet, as always.

"I'm glad everyone in town is in agreement on that." She laughs into his flannel shoulder. Pete is several inches taller than Alma and broad, a man who looks more like he should be cutting trees than pushing espresso. He got his size so early that he worked summers during high school doing ranch work, which he always says taught him that castrating bulls and mending fences is no way to make a living. His fine hair is half gone, but his eyes are the same soft brown that skipped a generation from their grandpa Al, against all laws of genetics.

"Can you believe it?" Pete says into her ear. His voice has a deep growl that's a little Johnny Cash and a little Elvis. Alma smiles at the beloved sound. "I keep thinking I'll wake up and it won't be real. Grandma said you were going over to identify the body. I'm sorry, I just couldn't do it. You okay?"

Alma nods and explains to him sotto voce about the coroner and the police, the way Vicky was found, the planned autopsy. Pete shakes his head.

"No surprise there. She was messed up with some bad folks."

"Do you know any of them?" Alma holds Pete's eyes, feeling the irresistible draw of suspects to pursue. She wants something to offer Detective Curtis. Whatever happened, she wants it resolved—and quickly, before anything in Seattle goes off the rails.

Pete thinks a minute, then pulls a few stools behind the bar so they can sit away from the customers. "A few. Nobody I consider dangerous, except maybe this one guy, Murray something. Bad news. I'm not sure about now, but Dennis used to have these friends who went back and forth to Salt Lake, running drugs. Hard stuff. It all comes through here. If I were the cops, I'd look into that scene."

Alma skates a hand across the slick surface of the counter. "I knew about that. She let a few things drop about Dennis, back when she was still talking to me."

"She got to know them through him. She comes in here now and then." Alma notices Pete's use of present tense. How odd that he hasn't digested Vicky's being dead, while Alma has begun to feel as if Vicky's been gone a very, very long time. On the other hand, Pete didn't see her body on that gurney.

"Yeah," Pete goes on, "there was a while when I felt like I was her best friend. She'd come in here strung out or working double shifts and I'd give her mugs of coffee to bring her around, listen to her problems, that sort of thing. Tried to get her into the program, but she didn't want anything to do with it. I never asked where Brittany was or if she should be at work. I wanted her to come back."

"And she talked about this Murray? You know him?" *Explain this to me,* she wants to demand. *Tell me how this could happen, who could do this to our sister.*

Pete raises an eyebrow at her eagerness. "I could pick him out of a lineup, if that's what we're talking about. We aren't exactly buddies but, yeah, I met him." Pete keeps moving as he talks, arranging pastry trays, stowing supplies, straightening tea boxes, coming back to rest lightly on his stool until he notices another task to be done. Somewhere, he's recovered the sort of hummingbird energy he had as a small boy. "Came up here from Vegas a few years ago, I guess. He used to be mostly a small-time meth dealer, but she owed him money, and I got the feeling he was expanding the operation. She let him use the home place a few times to get him off her back, and then of course he wouldn't leave."

"She let him use the home place?" Alma hears how her voice sounds, just like Grandma's when one of the neighbor kids gets a new tattoo, but she doesn't care. This *is* shocking.

"It's so far from anything, and those big barns. It's perfect. I tried to get rid of him a few times, but I didn't want to involve the police for fear it would lead back to Vicky and she'd lose Brittany. She did once, you know. They put her in foster care for a few months a couple years back, before Vicky pulled it together again."

"You never told me." Alma knows that Pete has been a source of support for Vicky and Brittany in ways she couldn't be, but this—this angers her. How could he see Brittany almost lost to the family and not tell her? How could he let the home place—their common heritage—become part of Vicky's games? And why the secrecy about such important things? No matter how often she calls or e-mails, as long as she's in Seattle, she's an outsider. She fingers the edge of the counter, exploring its hard edge and rough underside, pressing the texture against her fingertips until it hurts.

Pete blows his breath out and stands again, like he's on a spring. "Nothing you could have done. Anyway, finally Murray pointed a gun at me and I just said okay, cowboy, have it your way." Pete stretches out his arms in a gesture of capitulation. "God grant me the serenity, you know? So I just walked away."

Alma keeps her eyes down, following her fingers. He'll read her if she looks up, and she doesn't want to fight. Walking away is certainly an improvement on Pete's natural tendency to respond to any slight with a full-on bar brawl, but she finds herself wishing that he'd made an exception for Murray. "So tell me what happened when Brittany called."

"Ah, she told you." He shakes his head. "And now you expect me to come up with an explanation too."

At this, Alma looks up. Damn straight she expects an explanation, although she can hear Pete's side of the argument in her head: she has no right, wasn't here, hasn't been here for anything that mattered in years. Who is she to come back and demand explanations? She looks down again, retreats, becomes smaller on her stool.

"Maybe I don't have one." Pete leans back on the counter and folds his arms. "Maybe I just didn't go this time, and it turned out to be the one time that really mattered." He finishes a coffee the barista started, takes money, makes change, turns back to her. "Look, for what it's worth, I was going to go. I was in the car and then I thought I saw Walt's GMC go by out on Twenty-Seventh, so I thought he was taking care of it. I guess I was wrong. But do you have any idea how often someone or other in this family calls me expecting me to rescue them? Just because you got out doesn't mean they've stopped being needy as hell, and I'm Johnny on the spot. Sometimes I just say no, and sometimes I make the wrong call." He starts attacking the counter with a rag.

Alma sits beside him, trying to form the words to ask how this can possibly apply to Brittany, how he could ignore a child's call for help. But it will only start a fight, and she can't afford to fight with Pete right now. It would cost her too much, from an account drawn way, way down.

Pete takes up his monologue again, leaning over her, speaking into her ear, every muscle tense. "Look, Vicky's been relapsing for as long as I can remember. Nothing's ever made a difference. How many times has she been in rehab, court-ordered or otherwise? I lost count. It got to the point where she knew I wasn't going to come running for her anymore, so she started having Brittany call. Do you have any idea what it's like getting frantic calls from a little girl saying there's no food in the house? Of course you go. There's nothing else you can do. And you get there and Vicky's sitting on the couch watching *Days of Our Lives,* laughing at you like you're the fucking Sucker Delivery Service. I still came most of the time. And the one night I decide I'll just let Walt take care of it, since he seems to be doing something for once, she goes and gets herself killed. And Brittany blames me. You blame me, and you were in Seattle! It's not like anyone's called you for help in the last ten years, is it?" Pete's voice has been gaining volume, but with that last sentence he stops, leans on the bar, and sighs. "I'm sorry, that was a cheap shot."

Alma slumps onto the bar next to him. "No, it's true. But what would you have had me do, Pete? I was in no shape to take care of anybody when I left."

They're silent together like that for a few minutes. It is good to be quiet together. Her parents had that between them too, Alma reflects, that calm that was a refuge. After their deaths, the calm got lost for many years. To feel it settle between them again is a rare benediction. After a few minutes, Alma rouses herself to ask a question she's been pondering for some time. "What ever happened with you and Walt?"

Pete startles. "What?"

"I know Walt said something, or did something, when he found out about you and Shep. Something bad. No one ever told me what."

Pete looks down. He begins to nod, slowly at first, then more vigorously. "Yeah," he answers, his head coming up. "Yeah, you're right. Why do you want to know?"

Alma stares at the ceiling for a moment, but the answers are nowhere on the stamped tin.

"Maybe I want another chance to be there for you," she says. "Can I have another chance?"

Pete settles his arms more comfortably on the counter and laughs. "All right. Fine. Jesus, what a story. I've tried to forget." He lowers his voice and Alma settles in. "I guess it happened because I'd borrowed some tools from him—this is three, four years ago now—and he came by to get them. We were in the garage working on Shep's pickup with the big door closed, but the side door was open. Walt came in that way and we didn't hear him. I was fitting some new plugs and Shep was handing me the spacer. I still have no idea what he did—something about the way he touched me, I guess—but Walt knew right there."

Pete's voice drops even further and he glances around before continuing. "He started screaming and coming at us. I had his tools sitting by the door and he grabbed a monkey wrench, started swinging it around, screaming faggot this and faggot that. I never thought he'd do anything until the wrench came down on my head. Next thing I knew I was staring into bright lights in the emergency room. Shep says the sight of blood made Walt reconsider and he ran off. Never did ask for his tools back from us. Cooties, no doubt." Pete smirks. "Look."

He leans forward and lifts his hat to reveal a long, raised scar stretching back from his left temple.

"Jesus, you're lucky he didn't kill you. And you never pressed charges?" Alma is incredulous. The whole family has thought of Walt as a loose cannon ever since he came back from Vietnam, got raging drunk one night, and told his father to go to hell and take the ranch with him. Al could have forgiven the insults, but rejecting the land was a mortal sin in his eyes. Alma had believed—hoped, rather—that time had mellowed Walt's uncontrollable anger over whatever happened in the southeast Asian jungle, but it hasn't.

Pete shakes his head. "Glancing blow. Wasn't even a concussion, just a lot of blood. We didn't want to get into it."

"Not even aggravated assault? They could've tried him for attempted murder! Did you tell Helen?" Alma leaps to the suggestion of criminal charges without reflecting for a moment that this is her own uncle she's talking about. She is fully able to imagine such an outcome. That reality—this veil drawn from what she really believes about Walt—shivers through her. And then she remembers that Brittany is at his house.

Pete tosses his rag on the counter in a contemptuous gesture. "Come on, what for? She'd never hear a word against Walt. Plus we didn't want to get into the faggot part, and besides, Montana's hate crimes law doesn't cover that. We told the cops it was an argument over the tools. Then they just thought we were all stupid."

"You could've called me for a second opinion." Alma reaches up to pull Pete's scarred head down to her. She kisses the wounded place and replaces the hat. "I don't think you're *all* stupid. Shep's pretty clever."

"Thanks, sis."

"Anytime." The ease between them is back, like a gas that circulates in and out of the room. Alma unbuttons her coat and Pete resumes his bar tasks.

"Is Brittany doing okay?" he asks over the noise of the espresso machine. "I haven't talked to her yet."

"I don't know. She's not talking."

Pete waits for the noise to stop, watching Alma all the time. "Not talking? You mean, not at all?" he says.

Alma shakes her head and cracks the knuckles on her right hand. The sound startles her. She can't remember ever cracking her knuckles, but somebody else did. Who was it? An ugly memory crouches down there, muddled dirty and deep in the black swamp that holds the days after their parents died. She doesn't want to remember. She shakes her hands out and stands. "Not at all. Not to the cops, not to the social worker, not to me on the phone this morning. I'm going over to Helen and Walt's after this. Hopefully it will have passed by now. I've got to get her out to the home place." She doesn't have to explain this refuge instinct to Pete.

"You're picking her up, right? She's staying with you?" Pete demands.

Alma nods. "Of course," she answers, a little surprised at his vehemence.

"I worry about Brittany." Pete hesitates and ducks his head, drawing Alma back toward him with a look. "There was a night several years back when Vicky came by here in the middle of a hard night of barhopping. She was a mess, so I took her back to our place after I closed. She got started crying on the couch, so I said maybe I should take her over to Walt and Helen's. I mean, have mercy, I don't know the first thing about crying women. Well, I no sooner got it out of my mouth than she just turned off. Curled up on the couch like she was catatonic or something. Refused to talk. Scared us both to death. I wanted to take her to the hospital, but Shep said just to put a blanket over her and let her sleep it off, and so we did. She woke up the next morning and acted like she couldn't remember what happened." Pete's pupils are dilated in the dim light, giving him the disconnected aura of a shock victim. "It sure makes you wonder what's gone on with her. I tried to talk to Brittany a little, make sure she's okay, but you know that kid. She can be a sphinx. And Vicky watches over her like the Secret Service, when she's clean. I would have done something, you know, if I knew anything for sure. But as soon as she's sober Vicky shuts me out again."

Alma rubs his shoulder as he leans over her, braced on the counter. She feels hysteria rising and breathes in the strong smell of coffee with all her strength, to hold it down. This is what she ran from, what ultimately took Vicky. If she were ever to come back to stay, there would be things she'd have to know—to acknowledge—that are beyond her capacity to survive. Her cultivated control is black, groaning ice underfoot. "Petey, I can't take any more of this. Can we just . . . sit for a few minutes?"

He pats her hand, still resting on his shoulder. "Tell me about Seattle," he says, "or your flight. Something different." His eyes hold hers, bearing her up, as always, as Alma relaxes back onto the stool and firmly changes the subject.

CHAPTER 5

Back in the car, she turns her wheel toward Helen and Walt's house, where Brittany will be. The route takes her past the ballpark where her parents used to sit with her and Pete and Vicky in the creaking outfield bleachers on firefly nights, before the fancy new stadium went in, heckling the opposing batters. Helen and Walt have moved to one of the newer subdivisions out by Alkali Creek Road since Alma's last visit, and Alma has only an address to guide her through the cookie-cutter streets. Her GPS circles aimlessly, confusing similar street names. She drives up and down a few unfamiliar cul-de-sacs before spotting Helen's old minivan and Walt's pickup in one of the evenly spaced driveways. She parks across the street, steps out of the car, and examines the house.

It's a suburban special, a snout house, all garage, so that you'd hardly know there was a house attached until you wandered around the side and stumbled upon a front door. Maybe the layout makes things easier for Helen somehow, as she gets sicker. It certainly suits Walt. On their annual birthday phone calls, Alma remembers Helen mentioning that Walt has taken over the entire cavernous garage for his woodshop and leaves their cars in the driveway. Staring at the GMC, Alma unconsciously raises her hand to rub her temple.

In spite of the lack of windows onto the street, Brittany somehow knows that Alma has arrived. She runs around the edge of the garage like an angry Rottweiler that's just noticed trespassers in the junkyard. When she sees her aunt, Brittany bullets down the driveway and across the street without any pause to look for traffic in the empty street.

"Brittany! Be careful!" Alma shakes her niece in a quick-passing fury, then clings to her. Brittany looks up and pushes long brown hair out of her face, with an innocent look that says "I'm okay" but offers up no words.

Brittany's face is round with a little leftover baby fat, probably from a diet of dollar meals and cereal. She's in skater clothes, baggy, no labels, that make her look smaller than she is. The little girl who a few years ago would have grabbed Alma's leg and shut her eyes has given way to a keen-eyed person who steps back and examines her aunt. Alma has changed very little in the year since she sent Brittany a ticket to come down to Los Angeles for a few days to see Disneyland and walk carefree on the beaches while the winter winds howled up north. The firm had transferred her temporarily to the L.A. office to assist with a major deal, and at the end she had a few days free in an executive condo. Short, impromptu visits are the only way she gets to see Brittany. It's less complicated than coming home to Billings.

Brittany is nothing like the same person. The child who chased any ball on the beach to return it cheerfully to its owner now looks only straight ahead, long hair blinkering her regard, which focuses on Alma—highly charged, electric. The eyes that reflected infinite Pacific sunlight on surf have turned opaque and swim with dark questions, the sort of questions that Alma was asking herself at seventeen, not eleven. She's run far and hard to avoid them, and here they are again, glinting up at her from the face that trusts her most in the world and requires of her all the honesty she can dredge up.

Before her eyes can show Brittany fear and uncertainty, Alma looks away. The fact that she has lived this story does not make it hers to explain. Instead, Alma takes Brittany's hand firmly before crossing the street. The answering grip is proprietary: Alma is hers now. Brittany wants her to know it. Alma lifts the small hand to her lips for a kiss. As they reach the driveway, Alma notices that the small windows in the garage door are lit. "Walt?" Alma asks, tilting her head toward the garage. Brittany nods. "You go on in. I need to talk to him for a minute. I'll be right there."

To this day, Alma can't look at Walt without remembering the words he spoke a few days after her parents' deaths. "It all belongs to the government now," he snapped at Pete and Alma, while Vicky still lay recovering at St. Vincent's. He was so angry—at his little brother Mike, Alma realizes now, although at the time she took every word personally—and he wanted the house cleared out almost overnight. Their father had been cooking the books at his shop for years, doing jobs for cash, paying employees under the table to avoid payroll taxes. If he'd lived, he would have wound up in jail for tax evasion, according to Walt, who had clearly known all along. Mike, the good brother, the one who had it together, not like his crazy screwed-up Vietnam-vet big brother. It couldn't be true.

Mike Terrebonne was Walt's younger brother who missed the draft. Anne Mendenhall Terrebonne came from outside Bozeman, where she had two bachelor older brothers, the old-fashioned kind who wouldn't know what to say to a woman if she showed up at the door of the ranch house with a giant check from Publishers Clearing House. They met in the seventies at Montana State, where they seemed to have missed anything resembling counterculture. Mike was going through college in

ROTC, ready to be a soldier like his big brother. He dropped out halfway through. The university, he said, wasn't telling him anything he needed to know. He was making more money than the government check doing bodywork on cars and pool shark-ing. He wanted to marry Anne, go home, and forget he'd ever left. The specter of Walt, utterly undone by his tour of duty, must have been an influence.

Mike owned a machine shop, did metal work and all variety of odd mechanical jobs for local businesses. Anne had finished her nursing degree, but she cut back her schedule to part-time after the kids arrived. Add to that the fact that Mike had no stomach for collecting on debts—*I'm sure they'd pay if they could,* Alma remembers him saying more than once—and the ar-rangement left little money in the house.

"You're lying! You always hated him!" Pete shouted at his uncle on the chilly day when Walt laid out their financial re-ality, sitting in a bare kitchen, cracking his knuckles over and over in the mortuarial silence, at the table where their mother used to lay out sewing and quilting projects. It happened to be the Ides of March. Alma isn't sure if she knew that at the time or figured it out since, but her mind clings to the fact. She opens the side door to the garage and steps into Walt's man cave. It's a little cold, but not freezing. Walt is in his parka but working without gloves on some kind of rail.

"It's for the front steps out at the cabin," he answers without expecting any question or offering any greeting. "I'm getting to be an old man." Yes, the cabin. Maddie's great-uncle surveyed the high country up the Stillwater canyon back when the gov-ernment first claimed it. He got a little chunk in payment. It's the only private parcel around there, and Walt laid claim to it many years ago.

"Ah," says Alma. She moves toward the table saw and lathe in the middle of the garage and studies the elaborate vacuum system suspended above.

"You talk to the police?" Walt inquires.

"Yeah. And I went by the morgue."

Walt huffs. "They wanted me to identify the body. I told them to go to hell."

Walt left the dirty work for her. What else is new? Alma breathes with concentration, focusing on the smooth planes of hickory stacked in front of her, the order and symmetry of woodwork. "How has Brittany been today?" she asks.

"Seems okay. I haven't been in there much." Walt sniffles a little in the cold and wipes his nose with the sleeve of the parka. Alma wonders if he could actually be crying, then dismisses the notion as absurd.

"Pete said he thought he saw your pickup heading down Twenty-Seventh last night. That's why he didn't go."

"My GMC?" Walt's bushy, graying eyebrows sweep toward her almost independently of his face. "I ain't had it out of the driveway since Friday."

"Brittany said she called people last night, when Vicky went outside. Did she call here?"

Walt moves across the bench and comes up with a small hand sander. "She called all right. Middle of the night, woke us both out of a sound sleep. I probably would've gone down, but Helen told her to call the police if she had to call somebody."

Alma can believe that. Helen once told her that if she wanted to come home for Christmas, she should get off her butt, earn some money, take Amtrak from Philadelphia to Denver, and get a bus to Billings—more than a two-day trip. *Nobody ever gave me anything.* Helen's tight voice sounded economical even over the phone, like she was using the fiber optics at maximum efficiency, not expanding into unnecessary bandwidth. "Brittany must have been very worried to call," she says at last, trying to draw Walt out a little, feel for some of the human emotion he shows so rarely. The last time she remembers seeing any warmth from him, it was directed at her father, on a riverbank on a kindling-dry summer day, as they remembered some childhood fishing trip while baiting hooks for the kids. Mike had never accepted the darkness that came back from Vietnam with his big brother. To him, it was only a passing struggle from which Walt would one day emerge, whole and reborn.

"I know," Walt admits. "Alma, I just—I've loved them both the best I know how. I think we all knew what would happen to Vicky in the end. I get no joy out of it." He glances at Alma, a look she knows well. As long as she's known him, Walt has had trouble holding eye contact, as if connecting that much with another person causes him pain. He turns on the bench sander briefly to smooth the top edge of the handrail.

Alma is so empty inside, so hollowed out with the searing immediacy of new grief—barren, blackened prairie after brush fire—that she has to scrape around for any emotion to respond to Walt. She has tried to hate him, God knows she has, but he's still her daddy's brother, the closest thing left of him, and he took Vicky in when there was nobody else. Her evergreen love for her father is enough to let her reach out to Walt one more time.

"She was my sister," Alma says when the machine turns off. She is careful not to speak loudly, but with all the intensity she can muster. "Whatever she was, you had a big part in making her that way. When I left, I asked you to keep a close eye on her. Do you remember? She and Dad were so close, and she was so young. It was harder on her than anybody not to have him. To help with homework and take us fishing and stuff. He really loved us." Alma chokes on a few of the words, feeling like a tongue-tied girl again, but she gets them out.

"Loved you? Tried to kill you, that's what he did," Walt grunts, hunched over the massive saw that looks small next to him. "Probably would've been better off if he'd succeeded. Pretty rotten life he left for you kids."

"Tried to kill us?" Alma is dry-mouthed at Walt's words.

How dare he say something like that to her? How dare he *think* it? Her father's love has always been an absolute to her, an element to chart on the periodic table.

"There were no skid marks. I saw the police report. He never put his foot on the brake. He ran you straight into that truck. That's a man who loves his family all right." Walt lowers the saw to finish an edge, as if he isn't even distracted by what he's saying. Alma wants to throw herself at him and pull out his hair.

"You're lying! Even if there were no skid marks—it happened so fast, and it was icy. You weren't there! You don't know anything!"

"Don't be stupid, kid. His business was going under and he was going to jail. He figured he'd rather be in Mountain View than Deer Lodge, that's all, and he thought he'd take the family with him. You're better off without the selfish son of a bitch." The cemetery rather than state prison. The phrase echoes in Alma's mind. *Rather be in Mountain View than Deer Lodge.* Is that really what her father chose? This is the root of her hatred of Walt—that he made her doubt her father, on that long-ago day in the kitchen. The hatred and doubt remain real, just paler now, like upholstery left in the sun. This new accusation pumps up the colors to vivid, real-life shades.

"Stop it!" Alma clamps her hands over her ears. "Stop it! I won't listen!"

"Suit yourself." Walt pulls a half-smoked cigarette out of the ashtray and relights it, sawdust hovering around him, recklessly inviting combustion. His actions are slow and purposeful, daring her to challenge him. Her parents had never let him smoke around the kids, and now he makes a point of lighting up whenever he sees Alma. This is deliberate provocation.

"If you ever say anything like this to Brittany, I'll—" Alma has to let her threat hang embarrassingly unfinished in the air. She'll do what?

"You're just like your mother. She always thought she could boss everyone around." Walt's voice is so moist with contempt that spittle forms around the edges of his mouth. "All the women in that family. At least I found a woman knows her place."

Alma knows the answer to that one. Her mother had said it enough times. Alma wants very much to borrow Anne's muttered phrase and snap back at Walt "Because you keep her in it," but she doesn't say it. When Walt turns toward her, Alma realizes not only that he's closer than she thought but also bigger than she remembered. Her mind has shrunk him in the years she's been away, made him less terrifyingly like a force of nature, an avenging, red-bearded Norse god, hammer held high. He's looking at her with a strange curiosity. Something in her eyes has given away her furious thoughts. Now he comes at her faster than she would have thought he could, twice her size, bearing down on her as she backs away. A hinge slams painfully into her shoulder blade as she miscalculates and steps hard into the overhead door. His eyes, close to hers, are dilated and anguished. She expects him to shout, but instead his voice drops into the lowest register his massive form can rumble out. She breaks the eye contact herself as Walt begins to speak.

"You go back to Seattle and leave us the hell alone," he spits out, backing off with an abrupt gesture of dismissal and contempt. Alma looks from side to side and chooses the door she came in through as the quickest exit. She bolts for the relative normality of the house with Helen and Brittany.

After the shock of cold between the heated garage and the front door, the smell of Helen's macrobiotic cooking permeates a humid atmosphere, filling Alma's lungs with air too swampy to breathe. Walt's overengineered woodworking projects cover every surface: bookcases, shelves, an elaborate oak entertainment center, even a bizarre hanging bridge for the cat from one side of the living room to the landing of the staircase. Cat hair upholsters every surface, and one corner of the living room

couch is shredded down to the frame. Dominating every remaining vertical surface on the first floor are Walt's glass-eyed
hunting trophies: mounted heads of elk, moose, mountain
goats, bighorn sheep, a black bear rug in full growl, even a
perfect prancing fox in a glass case on the coffee table. A white
cat sleeps on top of the moose head. The psychological effect
is sensory overload, like being in the front aisle of a box store,
confronted by end displays, neon, music, traffic, and fluores-
cence all at once. Alma shuts the door and leans against it.

In a disproportionately small kitchen for the size of the
house, Helen slides a pan out of the oven and strains to lift it
to the stovetop. She was diagnosed with MS nearly four years
ago. The disease has advanced, but Helen was able to carry on
normally for so long after the initial diagnosis that it seemed
like a false prophecy. Little things here and there went wrong,
she has confessed to Alma over the phone: shaking, weakness.
The symptoms came and went, then eventually came back to
stay. Alma hasn't seen Helen since Al's funeral, and the shock of
seeing all the change at once is severe. Alma hurries to take the
tray of grilled vegetables.

"Hello there, sweetheart!" Helen cries, throwing her arms
around her niece. Her embrace is weak, her limbs like tree
branches brushing up against Alma without human warmth or
grip. Helen has a little of the off smell of the irrigation ditches in
late summer, an aura of decay. Alma masters an instinct to pull
away and hugs back. Her mind registers the roar of the GMC
pulling away. Walt will be headed to the cabin. That figures.
Any time somebody might need him, Walt retreats at highway speed. The flipside of frontiersmen who can survive any
extremity of weather or personality: they don't want anybody
thinking they can be counted on.

Alma lets Helen go and refocuses. "Hi, Helen. It's good to
see you again. I wish it were under better circumstances."

"This is how we see people these days. Funerals. Not many

weddings to speak of." Helen's voice is resigned as she pulls her head back to look at Alma, who used to be shorter but now looks Helen in the eye, so bowed is the older woman with the weight of illness. Helen was the tallest girl in her high school class. She defied her Mormon parents to marry the only man who looked like a reasonable physical match for her: great lumbering Walt Terrebonne, whom the draft would shanghai to Vietnam before his young bride had figured out how he liked his coffee. What irony, Alma reflects, that marrying Walt was one of the last shows of defiance that life with Walt would allow her.

Walt and Mike were older baby boomers, born in the early fifties after the first rutting of returned troops, as relief and normality went down like a tonic into the small towns and ranches of Montana. The teenage pictures show the brothers side by side in all things—sitting on fence rails, astride green horses, half hidden beneath cars, hulking Walt protective of smaller, wiry Mike. Then, after one poorly framed wedding day snapshot of Walt and Helen on the courthouse steps and a few pictures from the years immediately after the war, no photos at all, the rest of the album empty all those years.

Alma reaches back into her memory. "Emma got married a few years back. That's a wedding for you."

"That wasn't a real wedding," Helen huffs. "That was a couple of people at a courthouse. Emma deserved better. We sure don't see them much anymore, now that they've moved to Roundup."

"I thought Emma was still working here in town."

"No, she quit that job. Said the drive was too dangerous in winter, and she never did have a reliable car. Lou says he can fix things, but he sure can't keep that Ford working. I don't like her up there without any way to get out if she needs it. Lou gets wild sometimes." Helen hands these quiet words to Alma alone as Brittany carries a plate to the table.

"Gets wild how?" Alma shifts around the kitchen, trying to help without hovering or condescending. Nothing in the house seems to be modified to compensate for Helen's disintegration—Alma moves to open a can of olives after watching Helen fight to clamp a manual can opener onto the lid.

"Oh, he's like all those good old boys up there. Drinks, parties, gets in fights." Helen pauses at Alma's glare. "Now don't look like that. I know what you're thinking, but they seem happy. No relationship is perfect."

"At least in mine nobody goes to the emergency room," Alma mutters. This isn't the first time Helen has mentioned their cousin's volatile relationship. Domestic violence is almost the default around here. The story is more familiar than shocking, but it has the same effect on Alma every time. Helen turns away.

When Alma uses the bathroom, she notices the metal folding chair sitting next to the toilet as a makeshift grab bar. Walt has every power tool known to mankind out in the garage, but nobody has mounted grab bars in the bathroom or a second bar along the stairs up to the bedrooms, or acquired any appliances or tools to compensate for Helen's weakness and pain. Alma sits on the toilet and sifts through magazines in the handmade rack mounted on the end of the vanity. Woodworking, hunting, *Reader's Digest,* a few old *Better Homes and Gardens.* All the props speak of a traditional home, where everyone takes care not to mention or notice that someone is dying.

Brittany is taking a salad bowl from Helen and carrying it to the table as Alma comes back into the room. Alma hangs back for a moment to watch as Brittany carries everything to the table without being asked, helps Helen walk and sit, then serves out the meal.

As they all begin to eat, Helen says, "I'd invite you to stay here, but I can't take very good care of the house these days. I think you'd be more comfortable with Maddie."

Brittany looks up expectantly at Alma.

"Oh, that's no problem," Alma affirms, nodding back at Brittany. "Grandma expects me to stay there. I spoke to her earlier."

"But Brittany can stay here for now," Helen says firmly. Brittany's eyes, fixed on Alma, widen in dismay. While Helen carefully sips from her water glass, Brittany directs a tiny, fervent headshake toward Alma, eyebrows high. Alma's eyes move briefly to Helen, who is now trying to cut a piece of steamed broccoli with the edge of her fork. Finally she spears the entire chunk so that she can gnaw on one end.

"I'd like to take Brittany with me," Alma tells Helen. "I need to get out and check on the home place tomorrow. Besides, I don't want to put her back in school right away. I want to spend some time with her," Alma says as she reaches over to squeeze Brittany's hand, then turns back to Helen. "Is Dennis still in the picture?"

"Dennis." Helen scoffs at the name of Brittany's father. "The way I hear it, he almost got kicked out of his apartment last time he got fired. And you know, Maddie can't drive anymore. She's got cataracts. She won't be able to run Brittany anywhere after you go back. I still have my license."

Alma lets a forkful of quinoa fall at the image of Helen operating a motor vehicle, then takes hold of herself. "We'll cross that bridge when we come to it. I'd like to spend as much time with Brittany as I can while I'm here." Under the table, Brittany's fingers find Alma's and squeeze them in a fleeting touch.

Helen's lips thin out and her hand tightens on her fork, but she stays quiet. Alma recognizes the look on her face as the exact one she wore in pictures from after the war, when Walt came back just about mute and took a job shepherding. It was a thankless, low-man-on-the-totem-pole job if ever there was one, babysitting sheep on isolated high-country grazing allotments through the mild summer months. A job for the artistic, the insane, and those who don't know better than to follow them. Helen went into the mountains with Walt out of sheer bullheadedness, without invitation or backward glance by her husband. Alma has a few of those early-seventies square Brownie photos, colors all gone pastel, of Helen and Walt beside their sheepwagon, with their dog, Bobcat. Walt's eyes are unfocused, wandering off toward an unseen horizon. His body is turned slightly away from Helen, not even acknowledging her there in the frame with him, and Helen is right up beside him, a fixture like the shotgun, immobile and immovable. Her determination to stick by Walt, no matter what it does to her, has been the transforming fact of her life. What took place between them up in those high ranges, where he wanted to forget the world or end it and she would not let him abandon her, is a secret for the ages, kept in Helen's steel-gray eyes.

"Where's Walt?" Helen wants to change the subject. "Isn't he coming in? He gets upset if I interrupt him, but he knows when suppertime is."

"He took off a few minutes ago. He . . ." Alma glances at Brittany and stops herself from saying what Walt's words were. "We argued."

Helen inhales sharply. "Not here fifteen minutes and you're causing trouble. Sometimes he disappears out there for days now that he's semiretired. Now what will I do?"

"If he doesn't come back I'll have to go after him," Alma answers, "or he'll miss the funeral."

"You know he doesn't like public events. Besides, he and Vicky never got along very well," Helen says in her resigned, inward way. "Maybe this is all a blessing in disguise, anyway. Vicky was an unfit mother. We want Brittany to live with us. It's our duty to look after her soul." Helen glances at Brittany, who withdraws into the oversized hoodie under her coat.

"She was his niece, for heaven's sake," Alma says. "He helped raise her." Alma looks back and forth between Helen and Brittany, the lost child still wearing her coat at the table and the frail woman inhabiting a body bigger than what's left of her strength. It's clear who would take care of whom. Is this Walt's idea, to acquire a caretaker so that he can go off hunting more easily?

"He didn't come to Daddy's funeral, and he knew how much that meant to me." Helen's gaze is absorbed in the quinoa she's pushing around her old-fashioned Desert Rose plate, a wedding gift from Al and Maddie. "He won't do anything just because somebody else wants him to. That's the life lesson he took away from Vietnam."

Alma throws her head back in exasperation. "Vietnam! If that war caused half the problems that get blamed on it around here, it really would be the root of all evil."

Helen looks at her with narrowed eyes. "You weren't there. You have no way of knowing. And you didn't know him before."

"Grandpa always said he was the same way before the war."

Helen slams down her fork, or tries to. Her hand is curled awkwardly around the implement, so that her hand bangs the table instead and she must disengage her fingers deliberately, one at a time. "Don't you quote my father-in-law at me," Helen mutters, distracted by the fork and her noncompliant hand. "I know good and well what he always said. He wasn't a saint either. I won't have my husband talked about like that in my own home. Not by you or anybody."

With effort, Helen rises and carries her plate and glass to the counter separating the kitchen from the dining area. At the table, Alma and Brittany sit in silence, swallowing hard on their undercooked organic vegetables. Brittany's shoulders slouch toward the table along with her head. Alma has a sudden Mary Poppins urge to make her march around the living room a few times with a book on her head. She pushes away her plate and Brittany quickly imitates her.

Helen turns back to them, her face newly composed. "Just

take things right to the dishwasher, girls." She crosses the threshold into the kitchen and begins to drag pans across the counter from stove to dishwasher. Without hesitation, Brittany rises and starts stacking dishes.

The doorbell rings. Helen is loading the dishwasher, very slowly, so Alma answers the door. A man stands before her in a knee-length parka, the fur hood pulled so far up that his face is barely visible in its recesses. He pushes the hood back just far enough to reveal his eyes. "Howdy. I'm here to speak to the man of the house."

Alma stiffens at the request. "I'm afraid I'll have to do," she says. What kind of crazy door-to-door guy would be out in this weather? But this is no salesman. He wears an aura of entitlement that is already prickling at being kept on the doorstep this long. This man is used to people being just a little afraid of him. "And you are?"

"I'm the ward secretary. I came to bring condolences on behalf of the Saints and offer guidance on the funeral service."

Alma's mind races. *Saints?* Catholic iconry, football . . . then she realizes: *Latter-Day Saints.* Mormons. Helen's church. *Christ.* Can't they leave people alone at a time like this?

"Ah, thank you," she manages. "I'll tell Helen you stopped by." She starts to shut the door. No way is she letting Mormon parka guy in to preach at them for the next hour.

He sticks his foot in the door. "Actually, I got a call from a brother who saw Walt leaving town again just now. I know how difficult this must be for Helen. We want to be sure that Victoria has a proper service with the bishop presiding."

Alma smiles at him with only the edges of her mouth. No teeth. No eyes. "How did you find out about Vicky? The police only called me this morning."

"The bishop's second assistant has a police scanner, to keep track of developments in the ward."

To fucking spy on us, you mean, Alma says to herself. There's bad blood between the Terrebonnes and the Mormons dating to a stolen homestead claim a hundred fifty years ago, and then Walt had to go and marry one of them. "Vicky wasn't a—uh—Saint, you know," she answers instead. "We've already made the arrangements with my grandmother's pastor at First Church." White lie, but told to a Mormon at the door—probably a wash, sin-wise. "But thanks again for—"

The ward secretary interrupts. "I don't think you understand me, young lady. Victoria was baptized with her father's permission in the Temple."

"Our father's permission? That's a lie. He would never have done that, and besides, he's been dead fifteen years."

"Who's that, Alma?" Helen calls. "Shut the door!" Alma steps outside and pulls it shut behind her, forcing the ward secretary to back up from his position on the welcome mat.

"I see." He licks his lips, which are chapped and raw. "You must be Victoria's sister. Walter became her father in the eyes of the church when he became her guardian. At Helen's insistence, he agreed to her baptism soon after your parents' deaths. I performed the ordinance myself."

"He did *what*?" Alma wants to shove the ward secretary onto his roly-poly back and watch him slide down the slope of the front yard. "But I was here for months after they died. Neither of them ever said anything. Vicky hated the church. Why would she do that?"

The ward secretary's Play-Doh face morphs into a squeamish look, as if some minor demon has taken corporeal form in front of him and started oozing slime on the mat. "Perhaps they did not share this special event with you because of your obvious . . . hostility toward the Saints. If Walter isn't present, it is my duty to see that things are handled properly according to the dictates of the Church. You are . . . Alma?" He's got her on file somewhere, the little weasel. He's looked her up. Her hands, stuffed into her armpits, form into fists.

Alma doesn't bother fake-smiling again. "I don't believe you've introduced yourself," she says.

"Fred Winters." He offers a gloved hand.

"Alma Terrebonne." She puts out her hand to have it crushed in Fred's grip.

"We were worried after last night, the way Walt . . ." But Fred trails off, his mouth open, blowing clouds of warm air down onto the welcome mat.

"Walt what?" Alma prompts. What did the Saints see that Fred wasn't supposed to mention?

"Oh, I— I misspoke. I meant the way he took off just now."

"Someone saw him last night? Where?" Alma takes a step sideways to get more squarely in front of Fred.

"Just the pickup. He could have been mistaken. I shouldn't have said anything." Fred rubs at the freezing hairs in his nose with one hand and comes away with a slick of snot on the leather. He gamely changes topics. "Now, don't worry about a thing. We'll arrange the service and provide refreshments—"

"No." Alma shakes her head, lawyerlike. "You won't. You won't do anything. If Walt comes back and makes his wishes known, then we'll talk about it, but otherwise we'll do things the way I've arranged them, and if you and your ward want to come, that's up to you. I'm the next of kin and I'm making the decisions."

Fred's face is already red from the cold. Now it tints toward purple. "That's what's always been wrong in this household. Your uncle has never taken a firm enough hand with the women, and from that seed he reaps this kind of contempt and disobedience. Victoria never would submit herself to her father's rightful authority, and that's why the Lord struck her down. I fear for your future, young lady. I fear for your soul!" Trembling in his Michelin Man outfit, Fred pivots and heads down the driveway to his diesel pickup, chugging at the curb.

"I bet you piss off even God," Alma says to herself and hurries inside.

"Who was that?" Helen wants to know.

"Mormons."

"Who? What did he want?" It's always a him with Helen's church, Alma remembers, always an overstuffed man in a tie.

"To run our lives, as usual. I got rid of him."

"It's a good thing your uncle's not here." Helen's eyes meet Alma's. It's always a good thing if Walt isn't here when Mormonism comes up. Helen drops her eyes and withdraws from Alma's gaze.

CHAPTER 6

SUNDAY, 9 P.M. MOUNTAIN STANDARD TIME

After leftovers are put away and Brittany is bowed over the second Harry Potter book, dug out of her ridiculously small bag of belongings, comes the last trip of the day, to Maddie's. Brittany is quiet on the long drive to the other side of town. They speed along the rims with the dim, snow-laced city below, the refineries beyond twinkling like Christmas trees. Alma can just make out the dark line of the Yellowstone, where her parents let all three of them get as filthy and muddy as they wanted to, even as other parents pulled their children back from the river's edge to warn about currents and ruining their shoes. In her childhood, there was never much worry about staining a shirt or breaking a plate. Those things had no real value. The family was what counted. And then there was no family.

Alma looks up just in time to steer back across the center line. She shakes off the memory and starts to contemplate what she knows about the people who could have been near Vicky the night before, if this horror turns out to be murder instead of the perpetually cruel hand of God reaching out to take her sister. Vicky hardly seemed to need help to do herself in. The thought of murder—someone putting hands on Vicky to end her life—feels like a vulgar joke. Too much, from a universe that has already asked too much of this family.

Brittany has fallen asleep in the passenger seat as Alma drives, taking Alma back to winter nights when her little sister crept into her bed in their shared room to cuddle close for warmth and ask for tales out of the well-stocked family larder of wild-life stories. "The one about the bear in the car," she'd say, or "The one about the camp coyote," or "The one about the big-horn sheep in the fog." Alma almost smiles at the warmth the memory still holds. Vicky would fall asleep on Alma's pillow every time. That image—not the cold, bruised body on the gurney—is what she will hold close.

Maddie's place is a double-wide trailer in a nicer trailer park on the west end, bought after her stroke but before Al died. She and Al moved into Billings off the ranch to be near family and medical care. She gets around with a cane, her left side weak but not useless, and from her flowered recliner watches her shows. Alma glances through the front windows into the living room and sees that the television is tuned to a new game show she doesn't recognize. Off to Alma's left, almost obscured by the darkness, are the raised garden beds that Walt built after his father died. Maddie had called Alma just to tell her. Now that death had ended Walt's long feud with Al, Maddie could make coffee for her only surviving son in her own kitchen, pat his shoulder, send him home with bread or pie. He didn't come around all that often—he was still Walt, after all—but he did little things for her, and Maddie was exultant.

Alma opens the storm door and pecks at one of the three small rectangular windows in the door. Maddie startles and looks up fearfully, then smiles and reaches for the cane. "I'm comin', honey!" she shouts. "Just give your old grandma a minute."

Alma tries the door, but it's locked. This is new. Maddie and Al never used to lock their door. In fact, they had trouble finding the house keys to lock up when they went to Arizona to overwinter in the Airstream.

After a slow progress from her chair, Maddie unfastens a chain and turns a dead bolt. "Well, look at you! Skinny as ever, I guess. Still workin' too hard out there in the big city. And ain't you pretty. You look just like me when I was your age!" As Maddie reaches up to hug Alma, who's at least six inches taller, she gets a good grip on her ribs to measure the extent of the skinniness. "Good Lord, don't you eat? Come on in—you too, Brittany, get out of the cold, girls—and have some brownies. I made a pan when you said you was comin'. You can tell me about your trip." Alma exhales in relief. She should have known that there would be no emotional scene with Maddie, especially with Brittany present. At some point, they will talk about Vicky, but first there will be welcoming food and the calm of her grandmother's house. They will reveal as little pain as possible, and in that way overcome it.

Maddie is already moving at her deliberate pace to turn off the TV. The house smells of dust in unreachable places; meat and potatoes cooking; a little white cockapoo that has left behind its hyperactive days and now wanders in a senile daze, peeing occasionally on a potted fern in the front window; and the homemade lilac potpourri that Maddie has always used in overabundance, like incense. There's something else that Alma doesn't remember and takes a moment to place: not the decay she smelled on Helen, just age, perhaps, settling over her grandmother like a shroud.

"There's not much to tell, Grandma. It was an easy flight. Much better now that they've stopped crossing the mountains in turboprops. Listen, you don't need to bother, I ate at Helen's."

Maddie snorts. "Sprouts and organic carrots, that's all you'll get over there. Supposed to be purifying her system and all it does is make her crabby. You need something that'll stick to your ribs. I'll fry up a few pork chops." Maddie ignores Alma's protests and takes out plates and cups. "I sure am glad you came out right away. And Brittany, I'm so happy you're here, hon. I would've brought you right over here if I still had my license. I don't know that Helen's in any better shape than I am, but the state of Montana thinks so and that's what counts."

Maddie's words flow together in the patterns Alma learned as a child—little grammatical glitches, dropped or added consonants, a twang and a drawl. The slow, John Wayne cadence affects her like the sweep of sky visible from the airport. Hearing it, Alma knows she's home. Maddie's voice speaks of place almost as much as the place itself, not the word but the land made flesh. Maddie herself is a child of Big Horn County, who grew up in town as the sheriff's daughter, just a generation removed from ranch life. She dropped out of high school to get married, as you did back then when a landholding man like Al Terrebonne proposed. The transition to the Terrebonne home place held few surprises for her. It was a stretching out of what had been contracted in Hardin, relearning the deep textures of place, the intimacies of soul-mapped land, every rock named, every season a new geologic layer of meaning.

Brittany cuts herself a large brownie and disappears into the guest room down the hall. Her watchful, withdrawn silence is starting to feel like a ghostly presence, almost—but Alma rejects the thought as soon as it crosses her mind—almost like Vicky with them, waiting to see what Alma will do.

At the table with her hands on the worn vinyl tablecloth, Alma pushes her hair back and turns her face toward Maddie. If only it were as easy as dropping a decade of training to speak to her grandmother in the same dialect, the song of that soft western voice. She made such an effort to lose it in college out east, where they made fun of the way she talked and dressed, and laughed at her for being so proud of being from Montana. She wonders what kind of woman she would be if she still talked like that. Not the same person at all. Would it be someone she'd want to know? Someone she'd like better?

Alma tries to think of something positive to say about Helen's condition and fails. "Helen doesn't look good to me. I mean, I'm sure she's reeling from the news, but physically she's deteriorated a lot since I last saw her. Do you see her much?"

Maddie pauses in slicing the rest of the brownies. "Well, I— You know I try to see her, but we've been distant so many years now, and Walt, my poor sweet boy—he was like a stranger since he and Al fought after the war, until he started to come around a little these last few years. They bought that house up in the Heights, you know. None of our family has ever lived out there. It's so far." With her infallible country girl's sense of direction, Maddie stares at the northeast corner of the living room, facing the Heights, as her face slips momentarily into sadder lines than the ones imprinted on her face. Her resemblance to Walt is suddenly very strong. Her voice grows soft, barely a whisper. "Al was so harsh with them, you know. It's the way he was raised. It just rolled off Mikey, but Walt—he always took everything to heart."

To Alma, this is a new window into Walt's dark, surly character. Her dad never spoke much of his childhood, but his bond to the home place and his father was unquestioned. Alma remembers Grandpa Al as a benevolent patriarch, ever ready to pull a quarter out of her ear.

"Did Vicky and Brittany spend much time with them?" she asks. "Walt and Helen, I mean." This is history Alma doesn't know well, beyond the time when Vicky cut her off. Their mother's dislike for Walt was catechism, but to listen to Maddie is to hear another story altogether. Alma realizes with a sudden, disorienting shift in perspective that Maddie remembers only the gentle giant she raised, the sensitive boy who never came home from the war. She recalls for the first time in years how Maddie used to have a special place next to her good china for Walt's Silver Star and Purple Heart, dug out of the burn barrel at the home place where Walt threw them years ago. Glancing over at the cabinet, Alma spots the boxes behind the glass.

"Walt had a soft spot for Vicky, and now Brittany. He tried to look after them, I'm sure he did, but Helen took a dislike to Vicky early on, thought she was wild, didn't want her around. I wanted to bring her out to live with us, but you know how things were between Al and Walt. They couldn't even discuss it. I remember Helen talking about how Vicky lied before anybody else noticed it. Sometimes I think Vicky just fulfilled Helen's prophecies about her. I never trusted Helen. I know she's failing, but I think she milks it a little, trying to keep Walt close this way when nothing else ever worked." She gestures with the knife, seeming unaware of its threatening flight as she talks about Helen, then slides a brownie onto a paper napkin decorated with red and green bells and hands it to Alma. She glances down the hall, where Brittany has shut herself in the guest room. "That poor, poor child. I—I just don't know what to say about Vicky, honey." Her tears come down quickly and copiously, as they always have. "It sure ain't the world I grew up in. As much as I worry about you out in Seattle and it's right here in Billings that . . ."

The whistling teakettle saves Maddie from further words. She gets out the jar of Taster's Choice and makes them each a weak cup, then remembers and opens the jar to add another heaping scoop of brown powder to Alma's cup. "I wish I could have done more," she says as they sit. "It never seemed like that girl got a fair shake."

Alma folds her hand around the thin porcelain coffee cup, feeling the heat leaching out in a vain attempt to take the chill from her hands. "Everyone was always trying to help Vicky. It never did any good. She was so angry all the time." She wonders briefly where her own anger is hiding, in what tense body part it has taken up residence.

Maddie lets her coffee sit, cooling, while she examines Alma, pausing on the diamond earrings, the bare ring finger, before going back to the subject of Vicky. "She was trying to get things together this last year or so, you know. She's been helping me out, coming by to fix meals. She took me to the doctor a few times for checkups too, and she'd go out Sarpy once in a while to check on the house. Of course Pete's always helped out a lot, but Vicky was trying, she really was." *Which means,* Alma says to herself, *that Vicky's been doing her grocery shopping in Maddie's kitchen and helping herself to Maddie's prescriptions.* God knows what's going on out at the ranch. The house. The home place. The land. Even the Circle E—the brand Charles bought for Eliza as a wedding present, still owned by the family. Like the Inuit with their dozen words for snow, the Terrebonnes name and rename the most important thing.

"I'm sure she was, Grandma," she affirms as she sifts through the Sunday *Gazette.* If the paper is still as doggedly reliable on local crime as it used to be, the story on Vicky will show up tomorrow. Alma hopes they won't say much. They'll repeat the ugly verities the police have given out: unattended death, autopsy, automatic homicide investigation. It might not hurt to call the paper and ask for a little discretion, for the family.

"These last few months, though, there was something going on," Maddie interrupts the reflection. "She was upset, didn't want to talk about it. She used to talk to me when she was little, but lately she'd just get all cutesy and say, 'Don't you worry, Granny, I'm a big girl!' Huh. She never was a big girl. You knew that. Never could take care of herself like you were born doing. It all would've been different if the kids hadn't died like that. Terrible thing." For a second, Alma is confused: *The kids?* But Grandma means Mom and Dad, of course, her lost son and daughter-in-law. Maddie grips her cup and stares into the dark liquid, looking for something that isn't there but should be. With a grunt, she presses both hands on the table to force herself upright. She picks up her cane from the back of her chair and moves to the refrigerator. "And she'd talk about the home place. She had this idea maybe we ought to sell out, after all this time."

"Sell the home place?" Alma gasps. "How could she . . . Grandma, are you sure? Could you have misunderstood her?"

Maddie doesn't open the fridge, but puts a hand on it for support. "She didn't make no sense sometimes. She'd say one thing, then another. There's this fellow who wants our mineral rights, so they could mine right up near the place. I told him no way no how, but then Vicky, she thought since nobody's out there now, maybe we oughta go ahead. She says they put it all back the way it was after."

"*Grandma . . .*" Alma's voice is low, scandalized. Such a thing is beyond imagining. She's terrified that next Maddie will say that she's already signed.

"But I just don't see how that could be so," Maddie continues, straightening up with the support of the fridge and the cane. "We lived out there so long. All you kids know every ridge and coulee. I just don't see how they could come through and put things back like they was. And where do all the animals go while they're at it? We've got winter range for elk out there, sage grouse leks, even those black-footed ferrets, they say. They can't graze and nest and mate in a big hole full of dump trucks. So I told her that."

"What did she say?"

"Well, she come back a few times with different ideas, how they could mine different parts of the place to move across to Crow land. That's what they want, I guess. But then she started to talk about the other families out there, how she didn't think it was right the way the land agent was pushing them around. She had all these notes of stories they told her, people I've known all my life getting threatened. She started saying she just wanted to get the company to leave us alone."

"Really?" A chill hangs on to Alma in spite of the hot cup in her hands. "So she changed her mind about signing?"

"She was a good girl, Alma." Maddie smiles, opening the fridge at last, as if the subject is settled. "I don't want you to think bad of her. I just wanted to tell you about that business with the coal company in case—in case it turns out to matter somehow. I think she might've hatched some plan of getting them to pay her off to keep quiet about their methods of getting folks to sign. She always had some kind of fool notion about getting rich, always playing at something. I'm afraid of what might've happened if she crossed the wrong person. I tried to look after her, Alma. I sure wish I knew what I should've done different." Maddie's eyes are very like Alma's, clear and bright and green. Looking at her is like staring into the funhouse mirrors that show your eyes in a different face, Alma thinks. But when she speaks of Mike, or Walt, or Vicky, the undertow of sadness in those eyes is nearly too much to resist. Alma averts her gaze to take in the rest of her petite grandmother. Maddie's carefully styled and colored hair is a late-blooming, endearing vanity in a woman who spent years many miles from the nearest salon, but her neat, matched outfit is vintage Maddie. At the home place she was always at breakfast in a tidy housedress, hair combed, even if she'd been up half the night pulling calves in Al's bibs. The hand she stretches out toward Alma across the counter is knotted and spotted, but when Alma goes to her and takes it, the grip is powerful.

"I don't think there's anything any of us could have done," Alma says. "As hard as anybody ever tried to help Vicky, she just pushed us away harder. I don't know how many times I've called her since Grandpa's funeral. If she even picks up, everything is always fine fine fine. She'll tell me about a concert she went to or some joke she heard but not that they're about to cut off her phone, so I have to find out by getting the disconnect message."

"Oh, that was Vicky all over," Maddie says with the beginning of a laugh that dies. "Never admitted anything was wrong, and always thought everyone was out to get her. She used to drive me plumb 'round the bend sometimes." Maddie is pawing through the freezer now, tossing Tupperware and aluminum foil packets on the counter.

"What are you doing, Grandma? Do you need help?" Alma asks, fielding frozen items that threaten to sled onto the floor.

"I'm making you pork chops. They thaw out quick in the microwave and I can fry 'em right up. You haven't had a decent meal all day. Got some string beans in here too somewhere, that I froze last summer. Here we go." Maddie shuts the freezer, tosses the bag of garden beans onto the stove, and moves to the microwave with the chops.

"Really, Grandma, I'm fine." It's not the time to tell Maddie that Alma is a vegetarian now. Besides, the girl who learned how to field dress a moose isn't squeamish about the origins of meat, just scrupulous about what she puts in her body. Maddie's meat has always come from some friend's hunting trip or farmyard. "I was just going to do a little work before I go to bed. There's a lot to keep up with."

"Mm-hm," Maddie mutters. "I think I'll make up some mashed potatoes too. You always like that pork gravy I make. Go see if Brittany wants some."

Alma smiles and shakes her head as Maddie pushes the canister of flour along the counter toward the stove. The word *no* won't do any good now. Alma bends to get out pans and utensils, saving Maddie the effort, then pads down the hall to check on Brittany.

"Sound asleep," Alma announces, reemerging from the hall.

"I'm sorry about the instant potatoes," Maddie says. "It's easier for me with the bad hand, but I know it don't taste the same."

"It'll taste better than takeout, I guarantee."

Alma takes over the mashed potatoes, and together they soon fill a plate with the classic Terrebonne homecoming meal. Alma sits down over the food and breathes in its moist warmth, the erotic smell of her grandmother's thick pork gravy. God it's good.

"Listen, Grandma, I'll go out Sarpy tomorrow and make sure everything's snug around the home place, okay?" Alma breaks the silence as she finishes off the second chop. She hasn't eaten like this in months, and she hadn't realized that she was hungry.

Maddie nods. "That'd be nice. I always liked it out there this time of year. Real peaceful."

"You ought to come with me then, along with Brittany. It'll be good for her to spend time with you too. We can have lunch in Hardin like we used to. If we have time we can stop and see some of your friends."

Maddie reaches out and pats Alma's wiry hand with her scarred, wrinkled, soft one. Her agate rings glitter even in the low-wattage glow of the dusty overhead fixture. Grandpa Al's hand-polished stones still speak to Alma of days on the river with him and his bamboo fly rod, standing thigh deep in rushing water, casting into dark, glowing pools. They all slept in the camper on the back of his old blue Chevy, or in an army surplus pup tent if he wasn't too worried about bears. Grandpa knew how to keep the rain out of the tent in a spring storm, clean fish without attracting bears, start a fire in any conditions, and, if necessary, kill a charging moose with a low-caliber bullet through the head at close range, which Alma saw up close once.

Pete and Vicky were farther downstream, but she'd wandered past Grandpa, almost around the upstream bend. The moose came charging past a shelter of thick pine, suddenly upon her at full speed, and Grandpa, flying faster than the moose, grabbed his old Winchester from shore and downed the massive beast with a single shot. The crack of the rifle ricocheted over the water like thunder after a close strike of lightning. The moose dropped to its front knees in shallow water ten feet from her, let out a long, echoing groan, and died. Blood ran out of its head with the water and she felt the sticky warmth engulf her bare calves.

Grandpa walked out in his waders and stood over the animal. It was a full-grown bull with a rack on each side wider than Alma's arm span. It would have killed her. She wanted to go to Grandpa and feel his protective arm around her, but she couldn't move.

"It's a damn shame," Grandpa said. He levered another bullet into the chamber and walked up around the bend, just to be sure, then came back to pick up Alma and carry her to the pickup. "What did you do to make that moose so mad?" he asked.

"I don't know, Grandpa. I'm sorry," Alma didn't entirely understand what had happened, but she felt Grandpa's sadness. "I'm sorry you had to kill him."

"I didn't have to kill him. I chose you."

Grandpa fished avidly, but he didn't hunt for sport. He'd hunted as a child, for food, out of genuine hunger. For him, that was the only ethical justification for killing, aside from self-defense. He'd grown up a rejected, beaten-up white boy on the Crow res. For a white man he had an exceptional sense of the sacred, along with a vicious uppercut.

As Alma and Pete helped Grandpa cantilever the carcass out of the river with ropes and the winch on the pickup's front bumper, she felt unworthy. Something was born in her that day, a small knot of determination that would one day change the course of her life. They ate moose steaks, sausage, jerky, and stew all through the coming winter, and Alma had to choke down every bite.

After clearing up, Alma helps Maddie to bed. The bedroom hasn't changed from the old ranch house, right down to the faded prairie rose sheets that match the china pattern. Maddie gets into her button-down polyester nightgown and sits down on the bed for Alma to unbuckle her leg brace. Alma picks up the hairnet and thick foam headband from the bedside table and settles them around Maddie's salon-golden hairdo.

"Grandma," she says as they struggle, laughing together, to do up the Velcro closure, "what in the world do you do when I'm not around?"

"Brad Pitt comes by most nights to help me," Maddie dead-pans. "He's such a nice boy."

"Brad Pitt, you don't say?"

"Oh my, yes. Your old grandma's still got it."

After leaving Maddie, Alma tiptoes to the door of the tiny back bedroom. The door is shut but not latched. It opens on well-greased hinges to reveal Brittany asleep in the bright light of a waxing gibbous moon. Even in her great-grandmother's warm house, Brittany has gone to bed in her stained army-navy surplus coat. Alma kneels to help her out of it. Brittany is limp as a baby, allowing Alma to move her limbs without the slight-est protest.

"Poor thing," Alma murmurs, "no wonder you're worn out." As Alma settles Brittany's arms under the blankets, she notices that even in deepest sleep, Brittany clutches something under the dirty fingernails of her right hand. Alma peels the fingers back enough to see a faded photograph, torn in half but reattached with tape that has begun to dry and yellow, clutched against her own dog-eared business card. She recognizes the photo. It's Brittany as a toddler, in a Sears portrait paid for by Alma as a Christmas present, posing with Vicky and Dennis, like the cozy nuclear family they never were. They're all in Christmas sweaters knit by Maddie, scrubbed and combed, a smiling catalog family. Alma claps one hand over her mouth to muffle her sigh. With the other hand, she closes Brittany's fingers back over the precious photo.

Settled in the guest room at last, Alma gets out her laptop and begins her day's work. Her inbox has accumulated dozens of messages just in the last fifteen hours, on a Sunday. She's been hearing odd things in interviews with administrative staff at the merger target, and follow-up queries aren't easing her mind. Her fingers fall to the keyboard.

CHAPTER 7

MONDAY, 7:30 A.M. MOUNTAIN STANDARD TIME

After a morning jog cold enough to sear her lungs and freeze her nose hairs so solid they tickle, Alma comes around the last corner to find a strange pickup in the carport. Through the windows she sees an unfamiliar man the size of a linebacker emerge from the hall and open the fridge. Alma snatches her cell phone out of the pocket of her jacket, rushes in the front door, and shouts, "Hello!" as forcefully as she can.

The linebacker comes around the dividing counter between the living room and kitchen with a smile. "Oh, hi there. You must be the other granddaughter. Mrs. Terrebonne is really excited you're here. I'm Brad, the home health assistant."

"Oh!" Alma is already moving across the room with great momentum, so she bounds up to Brad and shakes his hand with vigor to hide the fact that she'd been considering breaking a lamp over his head. "Hi, nice to meet you. It's not— It's not Brad Pitt, is it?"

Brad barks his laugh. "Brad Pittman. Your grandma thinks it's quite a joke. Listen, I'm making some real coffee if you want.

It's in the pot. And I brought over those whole-wheat cinna-mon rolls from Stella's. Mrs. Terrebonne loves them and she needs more fiber in her diet. She told me you were coming in yesterday, so I thought I'd stop by to make sure everything's okay. I'll just finish helping her get dressed and check her blood pressure and leave you two to start your day." Brad speaks in a booming baritone, as if he's addressing the defensive line. He seems accustomed to people who don't hear very well and re-quire motivational support. Alma is overwhelmed by his pres-ence and at the same time reassured. She had forgotten that Maddie has help.

"Sure. Thanks." She edges toward the kitchen. Brad starts a purposeful charge toward the bathroom to help Maddie, then turns back.

"Listen," he says in a more subdued tone, "I'm really sorry about your sister. I don't know what to say."

"It's okay," Alma says. "Thanks."

With Brad's help, Alma gets Maddie into the car for her first trip to the ranch in months. Maddie wears a bright red coat with a matching knitted hat and fairly dances outside. Brittany settles into the back to play games on Alma's phone. There are a few stops to make before they can leave town. First, Alma pulls into the lot next to the Denny's on Twenty-Seventh Street, where Vicky worked. The hostess is so young that Alma can't believe she's not in school. As they move toward a table, Alma asks in a low voice who would have known Vicky best.

"We're all running around all the time. I only really saw her on breaks, and then she was outside with the smokers. I don't smoke." The child-hostess twists her freckled nose in distaste. Her light manner makes it obvious that she doesn't know what's happened. Yet it's odd that the girl refers to Vicky in the past tense. Alma moves away from the table with her as Maddie and Brittany sit.

"Vicky died this weekend," Alma says in a low monotone.

The words feel like something she swallowed accidentally and needs to spit out, fast.

"Oh my God!" the girl exclaims and bolts for the kitchen. With a quick word to Maddie, Alma follows the flapping tails of the girl's apron.

"I know," a short white cook with a buzz cut is saying to the hostess as Alma enters the kitchen. "The cops were here yesterday. They interviewed everybody. They'll be back, I figure. Who are you?" He nods in Alma's direction and she explains who she is. Mumbled condolences rise from the staff like steam off the grill. Nobody stops moving even as they offer sympathetic looks, subtle gestures of condolence over plates and tools. She looks them over with quick, surreptitious glances, hoping for no awkward moment where she recognizes some high school classmate still waiting tables. Luckily, they're all strangers. The servers leave quickly, carrying plates that cannot wait, but the cooks and prep staff remain, eyeing Alma.

"Were any of you friends with her?" Alma asks over the noise of pans and the hot dish machine in a doorless room to her left.

The cook looks up. "Nobody here knew her very well. She didn't try to make friends unless she wanted something, and the last couple of months she had sketchy guys coming around asking for money. She owed everybody money." The cook snorts and turns his back to Alma.

"Including you?"

He flips a row of bacon as he talks, as casually as if he were playing table tennis. "Yeah. I loaned her a hundred bucks her first week here. She said she needed it to cover until she got her first paycheck. That'll teach me. Never saw a dime of it back, and she got money out of most of us before we caught on. Nobody who works here has a lot of cash to spare, if you know what I'm saying. Tyler, the manager, suspected her of stealing food, but he could never prove it."

"Was there anybody who was really angry at her?"

"Enough to kill her, you mean? Look, the police are getting into it with everybody. They're here all the time anyway. They all knew her. I don't know what everyone's saying, but I don't figure it makes much sense to kill somebody who owes you money. That's a surefire way never to see it again. Besides, she was mixed up with a bad crowd. She had a lot more to worry about with them than us. We're just working stiffs."

"Do you know their names, this 'bad crowd'?" Alma feels unbearably hot in her long coat, this close to the bubbling grease and dish room. Her skin itches and crawls under the smooth merino sweater that's never bothered her before. Stealing food. Borrowing money. Doing drugs. Hanging around every lowlife in town. It sounds like a minor miracle that Vicky survived as long as she did. Alma shifts from one foot to the other and fights an urge to run for fresh air as she waits for the cook to answer.

He fills a few plates, sets them under warming lights, and hangs the tickets before turning to get a better look at Alma. He takes in her long cashmere coat and scarf, shiny boots, and the soft leather bag on her shoulder. "She was your sister, you say?"

Alma nods.

"Well if that don't beat all."

"What do you mean?"

"Just—well, you look like her, but I'm surprised she even knew somebody like you. She was just a girl from the wrong side of the tracks who was gonna meet a bad end pretty soon, and sure enough she did. I could pick out a couple of the guys she hung around with, maybe. There was a guy named Murray—skinny, long hair. They call him the crank pimp."

"Crank pimp?" Alma is sure she doesn't want to hear this. It's like the moment when a business client mentions that oh, by the way, he's been embezzling, but he knows she has to keep his secret because she's his lawyer. Lawyers are paid well to keep secrets, to be sealed receptacles of other people's evil, and here is more, offered to her freely. She shrugs off her coat and hangs it over one arm as the cook plates a few orders.

"He gets girls hooked and then gets them started turning tricks to pay him. Real prince. He picked her up here a few times. I warned her to steer clear."

"Is that what happened? Was he her pimp?" At enormous cost, Alma manages to get this out like a normal question, like asking the price of the lunch special. Sweat is trickling between her breasts, starting to soak the lace of her bra.

"Nah, she cut a deal. She talked about letting him use some place her family has out of town, to get him off her back. You probably know what I mean." He takes a look at Alma over his shoulder, never pausing in scraping the grill with a long metal spatula.

"I think I do." It can only be the home place.

"And her baby daddy—what's his name? Dave? They met in the parking lot when she needed him to babysit. Lot of scream-ing matches over money he owed her. He was all mixed up with that scene. And that guy she lived with. I never met him, but they say he was running a medical marijuana dispensary for a while. It all got shut down when the law changed. You know the type: fancy car, house is a dump, you can smell weed from halfway down the block and that's for sure not all he's selling. I don't go near that scene since I got home from the military. I've got too much to live for." The cook wipes his hands on a towel and fishes his wallet out of his hip pocket. He flips it open to show Alma a picture of a smiling little girl.

"Your daughter? She's beautiful."

"Thanks. One day at a time, you know."

Alma turns so that the rest of the kitchen staff can't see what she's doing and reaches into her purse to count out five twenties from her wallet. She slips them to the cook, who tucks them into his wallet with a whispered "thank you" as he puts it away. Alma starts to ask his name, but the cook turns back to his tasks as the Indian dishwasher steps out of his steaming alcove. At first he says nothing, just stands there a few feet from Alma, looking uncomfortable, drying his hands more than necessary on a dishcloth tucked into his apron. Alma waits for him to speak, but the silence gets too long.

"Did you want to tell me something?"

"Your sister walked on?" he asks. Alma feels her face changing as her mind shifts to take in those words. *Walked on.* Yes, Vicky has walked on, into the spirit world, where the ancestors are waiting. Their parents. Grandpa. All the grandmothers and grandfathers, long skirts, hard hands. That's right. Those are the words.

"Yes," she answers. "I'm Alma."

"Arnie. She was a singer, your sister."

"A singer?" Alma remembers Vicky as a little choir girl in a blue robe. "Yes," she agrees.

Arnie tosses the rag in his hand onto a big dish rack. "She sang for the whole crew while we were doing prep each night. She knew the lyrics to any song we could name, and all these old country songs I'd never heard. Hank Williams, Patsy Cline. She loved that George Strait. The ladies all love him."

"My dad loved those songs," Alma says. "He taught us."

She remembers family car trips, singing Johnny Cash and Dolly Parton songs, led by their father's rich baritone, so like Pete's, with Vicky's clear soprano like foam on the waves of their common sound, carrying the high, pure melody. For Alma, since the accident, those songs have always brought tears, because then she was so secure in the riches of her family, their love, their golden circle, no matter how little they possessed. She had no premonition of what would come after, of how quickly and irrevocably the circle could break. To think back on the time before the circle shattered requires more courage than she has at the moment.

Arnie coughs and turns a little to the left—choosing the proper direction—lifts up his hands, and without warning starts to sing in Crow. His voice rises above the noise of the kitchen. Surely it can be heard out in the restaurant, Alma thinks, and within seconds a man in a tie comes rushing into the kitchen. He halts at the sight of Arnie, singing loud with his eyes closed, and Alma watching him, transfixed. They both stand still until the song is done. Arnie opens his eyes and turns to Alma. "A travel song, for your sister's journey to the other-side camp."

Alma swallows with difficulty and squeezes his heavy arm. "Thank you. *Ahó.*"

Then the manager steps forward to recite health codes and ushers Alma out of the kitchen.

They're only a block from the police station. Alma carries out coffee and rolls for the ride, secures them in the backseat just as her parents used to do on Saturday-morning rides to spend the weekend helping out at the home place. Then she directs her slow-moving posse toward the waiting lawman. Might as well get this interview over. What could Alma tell him that would be any help? The Terrebonne family is dysfunctional but not homicidal, and she doesn't know Vicky's friends. What she just heard about Murray and the home place is worth discussing, but what she knows about Dennis's Salt Lake drug supply is at least five years old, and she doesn't relish the thought of testifying against Brittany's father. Brittany's phone calls, Walt's apparent outing late Saturday night, Pete's lamely excused failure—what does she really know? Alma herds Brittany and Maddie across two intersections and up to the glassed-in front desk at City Hall, where a short-haired woman in a snug pink polo shirt calls Detective Curtis to meet them. When the heavy metal door to the offices swings open, Alma realizes that she knows him.

"Ray, hello." She offers her hand. "You look familiar. Remember me from school?" Ray is only slightly taller than Alma, but solidly built under his well-pressed detective's business casual. She is surprised to see his hair braided down his back—the police dress code must have relaxed, and Ray himself has changed from the skinny, buzz-cut kid she knew. Everything else about him is perfectly regulation, down to his well-groomed fingernails and shiny boots. His dark eyes are guarded, but he smiles readily enough when he recognizes her.

"I was a few years ahead of you at Senior." He takes her hand and gives it the gentle press with which Indians interpret this foreign gesture. How interesting. He will have shaken enough white hands to understand the cultural expectation of a firm handshake, and he is either rejecting that altogether or making some sort of exception for her, either personally or because of her gender.

"Were you ROTC? Very clean cut?"

He ducks his head with a little acknowledging smile. "Coming off the res that's pretty much the only way to get through college. I did criminal justice here at MSU-B."

"Your family must be proud." At the mention of family, Alma remembers her own. She steps to the side to show Brittany and Maddie to Ray.

"My family, yeah." Ray laughs like she's cracked an inside joke. "They call me Apple."

Apple—Alma knows that one: red on the outside, white on the inside. Red, white, it doesn't matter; this is what the place does to anyone with talent and ambition. It slaps them down and mocks them until they get out or give up. Ray will be heading one way or the other himself by now. She looks at him more carefully. There's something else she knows about him, a thing she can never say. Ray is Mountain Crow. His ancestors roamed the high country of what are now the Big Horns and Absaroka-Beartooth range. When they were driven out by the whittling of the reservation—removed from the place now called Absarokee after the people forced to abandon it—there were white settlers waiting to move in, and Alma's ancestors were among them. Alma has the homestead patent in her files. The story has come down to her through journals written in a tight cursive, with careful line drawings.

These are things that are never said among white and Crow in this town. This is the history lying under thin, angry skins, separating people who ought to be united by a common love of fried food and ritualistic spectacle: fairs, powwows, and rodeos, the deliberate enactment of culture, the heartbeat of ceremony.

Alma offers up more recent history instead, less charged common ground. "Yeah, I remember you now. The rest of your class was the original cast of *Dazed and Confused*, and you were a straight arrow. The younger kids looked up to you."

"Did they?" Now Ray looks surprised. "I never knew that. I was the dork who had to go home with his grandma after every game." A man in cargo pants, a wrinkled shirt, and a day's growth of beard passes them on his way out. He and Ray exchange respectful nods. "Detective," each says to the other, and Alma takes in how carefully Ray grooms himself, compared to his white colleague.

"Yeah," Alma acknowledges. "I wish there had been more like you. It might have helped my sister. You've met Brittany, my niece. And this is my grandma Maddie Terrebonne."

Ray nods to Maddie and Brittany as he moves to offer an arm to Maddie. "Mrs. Terrebonne," he acknowledges with a respectful nod. "Brittany, I'm very sorry about your mom. I realized I've seen her waitressing the last few years—cops and Denny's, you know. I'll do the very best I can to find out what happened to her. We'll let you hang out and watch some TV while we talk, okay?"

Brittany doesn't respond, just follows as Alma holds the door for Ray to escort Maddie and they begin to walk down a hallway lined with closed doors. Ray opens one into a small meeting room with a television and ushers them inside. He hands Brittany the remote.

"Can I get you water or something? I might be able to scare up a doughnut around here. Or if you'd like to talk to one of the social workers again, I think—"

Brittany's eyes find Alma's, giving off the same silent alarm she used when Helen suggested that Brittany stay with her.

"No more social workers," Alma tells Ray. "But water would be nice."

A complicit glance passes between aunt and niece. Alma puts an arm around Brittany, who tucks into the safe place under her aunt's collarbone. Ray steps out for a few minutes and comes back with a ceramic coffee mug full of water. He closes the door as he, Maddie, and Alma back into the hall and keep moving.

"She always like this?" he asks, tilting his head toward the door.

"Mute, you mean?" Alma shakes her head. "She's quiet, but not like this. As far as I know, the last she spoke to anybody was whatever she said to your officer."

"It wasn't much," Ray replies, returning his arm to Maddie, who takes it with a sweet little smile. "It's all in his report, but she only said a few words. She said she called and nobody came. Have you found out anything about who she might've called?"

Alma hesitates, glances at Maddie, exhales. "Yes. She called my brother, Pete, and our aunt and uncle, Helen and Walt."

"*What?*" Maddie cries out as if bitten and stops, clinging to Ray's right arm with both hands, the cane dangling from her arm by its crook. "She called them? Alma, what happened? Didn't they go? Why wouldn't they go?"

Alma turns back to Maddie and reaches for her arm. "Yes, Grandma. I'm sorry. I'll explain later. They didn't—"

"But why wouldn't she call me?" Maddie looks from Alma to Ray and back, wide-eyed. Ray looks down at Maddie's fierce grip on his arm.

"You can't drive anymore, Grandma," Alma soothes, loosening Maddie's hands from Ray's bicep before they leave a bruise, tucking one into her own arm and taking the cane. "She knows that."

Maddie moves along more slowly now, putting more weight on Ray while Alma balances her from the other side. Ray points at a door to the left with only his eyes and lips, a Crow gesture that Alma recognizes. They step into a small office piled high with files on every available surface. There are no identifying items, not a degree on the wall or a photo on the desk. Alma pictures Brittany perched on the utilitarian orange office chair in front of the desk, tiny in this impersonal space, collapsing inward, staring at the telephone receiver, unable to respond to Alma's insistent, distant voice. The void expanding inside Brittany is all too familiar to Alma, an infected vestigial organ.

Ray follows and shuts the door. "What did she tell them when she called?"

"You should ask them. I'm not sure." The lawyer in Alma balks at hearsay. Ray helps Maddie into the office chair and turns to where Alma leans against the wall next to the door, poised to escape, both palms flat against the drywall, her breath coming faster as she flashes back to the morgue.

"I talked to all of them yesterday," Ray says.

"Then what are you asking me for?" Alma's hands ball up beneath the cashmere folds of her coat. She is embarrassed by the inappropriate antagonism in her voice, but she hates everything about this: the fluorescent lights, the gunmetal desks, Maddie sitting very straight on the edge of that ugly chair, ankles crossed, looking around with a vague sort of terror as she takes in the inside of a police station for the first time in her life.

Alma wants a rewind, a repeat of yesterday morning's serene bike ride that doesn't end this way. It's not Ray's fault, but here he is in front of her, asking questions he's already got answered like she's under cross-examination. She drops her chin and faces him like a cornered animal.

"I need to know if they told you something different," Ray says in that calm, lightly accented voice that came over the phone so powerfully. Alma tilts her head and reconsiders. After a long breath, she starts over in a steadier voice.

"Pete said he thought it was just Vicky using Brittany to manipulate him again. I guess he's had a lot of calls like that. And he thought he saw Walt's truck heading that way. But Walt says Helen told her to stop bothering people in the middle of the night. He never went. Walt and Pete, they've both done a lot of running around to rescue Vicky. And then the one time—" Alma stops as the words stick, caught up in her throat.

"Honey," Maddie says, holding out a tissue. Alma reaches over to take it but finds she doesn't need it. She shoves it into her pocket.

"Then the one time . . ." Ray sets his hip on the desk and leads her back to the sentence.

"Then the one time they don't show up, this happens. It's . . . It's cruel." Alma blots her nose with the tissue, then hides it again. "I talked to the staff at Denny's this morning. I wanted to know what they'd say about her."

Ray steps behind his desk but doesn't sit. He's looking her over now. She notices how few gestures he makes, standing there with his arms at his sides, not allowing his body to communicate at all. Did he have to practice that, or is it natural?

"And did you find out anything you didn't know?" he asks.

Again she hesitates. There's no point in hiding this from him, but it still pinches her, somewhere in her gut, to be the one revealing such dark things about the family. Maddie hasn't even heard this. Alma's eyes drop to Maddie, who is folding tissues in perfect squares and stowing them in the outside pocket of her purse for easy access. Ray's eyes follow the glance.

"Alma, would you mind helping me grab coffee for all of us?" he asks. When they are outside he pulls the latch closed behind them and lowers his voice to a whisper. "Now, without upsetting your grandmother, what did you hear?"

Alma sighs and forces out the cook's words about Murray and Dennis and Kozinsky, while Ray leads the way down the hall. She can feel herself flush as if this is her own confession. "I don't know if it's true, what he said about Murray, but it sounds true. The home place was one of the last things she had left to bargain with." Alma raises her eyes with effort to his. "She wouldn't have done it lightly."

If Ray is surprised by what Vicky was involved with, he doesn't show it. "Murray Donner. His name came up already in interviews. We've got an outstanding warrant on him for a second offense of criminal possession. But this doesn't really turn Murray into a suspect, does it, even if it turns out to be homicide? Sounds like he had a pretty good setup and now it's messed up. Unless—"

"Unless there's more going on there than we know." Alma follows Ray into the break room.

"Exactly." Ray fills three unmatched mugs with weak coffee out of an industrial-looking machine and hands one to Alma. "I'll have to get out there and see what's going on, pick him up if he's dumb enough to be hanging around. Can you give me directions?"

"We're on our way out there now. I could show you." Alma sips and makes a face. This is her fourth or fifth cup of lousy coffee since the plane touched down. The Itching Post, to give proper credit to Pete, is fully up to Seattle standards.

Ray is contemplating the two mugs in his hands. "It's out of Billings PD jurisdiction. I'll have to touch base with the Big Horn County sheriff," he says, more to himself than her, "but yeah, let's do that. I'll follow you out." He looks up and nods with new enthusiasm. "What else can you tell me about her ex, Dennis? He's the father, right?"

"Yeah, Dennis Willson. They got together in high school. After Brittany was born they lived together for a few years but never got married. He comes across nice enough, but he drinks. He had bad problems with depression when they were together. He'd go to bed and not get up for days. She supported him for a while before she finally dumped him. From what I hear he hasn't been reliable about child support, but I don't think there's any conflict between them." Alma leans against the counter and resigns herself to the coffee, tipping the mug up for a longer drink.

"Does he live here in town?"

"The last I knew he had an apartment near the ballpark."

"Any known association with criminals, drug use, that sort of thing?" Ray opens a cupboard above the coffeepot. "Does your grandma take cream or sugar?"

"As much as possible," Alma confirms. He doctors Maddie's coffee, then offers packets to her, but she waves him off. "Drug use definitely. Vicky started smoking pot with Dennis in high school. She used to giggle to me about it on the phone, how they'd get high behind the gas station between classes."

Ray chuckles. "Time-honored tradition."

"For sure," Alma agrees, "but not for me. My parents would've grounded me until college if they ever thought I went near drugs or alcohol. It was different for her."

"Your parents treated her differently?" Ray asks.

Alma is startled at the reminder that Ray doesn't know the essential family history. They amble toward the break room door as a uniformed officer approaches the coffee machine with a mug, exchanging nods with Ray. "Didn't anybody mention the accident to you? Our parents died when Vicky was twelve and I was seventeen."

Ray stops moving and looks down at the coffee. When he looks up, his expression is abashed. "No, nobody mentioned it. I'm so sorry for your loss. Both times." He holds the door for her. They're quiet for a few paces before Alma swallows another mouthful of scalding coffee and goes back to her original reply.

"Anyway, I don't know what she might have been doing these days, and I don't think Dennis is in the picture much anymore. The break was pretty definite." The screaming fight they'd had when he dropped off Brittany for Grandpa Al's funeral felt definite, all right. Still, Alma can't imagine Dennis doing Vicky harm, if that's what they're talking about. He's too passive a personality, too absorbed by his own navel.

"I'll look into it. Anyone else?"

Alma opens her mouth to speculate, then shuts it just as quickly. Something lawyerly in her counsels caution when talking to the police. "You said, 'even if it turns out to be homicide.' Do you really think it might be murder?" The mug is still very hot, and she's having to hold it with both hands to keep the coffee from sloshing out as she says these words.

Ray breathes in and out before answering. "We need to wait for the autopsy. The coroner should be on it today. We have to treat it as a homicide because—"

"Yes, I get that," Alma interrupts, impatient. "Because it was an unattended death. But what do you *think*?"

"I think . . . I see too many people die in stupid ways around here. You know it's bad when it's not just Indians anymore. Nice local white girl like your sister—we'll hear from the council about that." He grins. Alma freezes for a moment at his words, then relaxes as she realizes that Ray is joking. She likes him too well to be offended, but Ray takes in her reaction and shakes his head. "Batting a thousand here, aren't I? Chief Rains on Parade rides again."

"Rains on Parade?" Alma starts to laugh in spite of herself. "I can't believe you just said that."

"Old family joke," Ray says, picking up the pace as they move down the hall. "I always know the wrong thing to say."

"No, it's okay. I'm just wound up tighter than a drum right now." Alma sips at the coffee again. Somehow it tastes better this time.

"To tell you the truth," Ray says in a more conversational tone than he's used until now, maybe trying to make up for his remark, "I've been thinking that there's something suspicious about it. I've seen deaths from exposure and there's just something off about this one. But I can't put my finger on what exactly strikes me as odd yet." They're back at Ray's office.

Alma pauses before pushing the door open. "So we'll know by tomorrow?"

"We'll know whatever the autopsy can tell us," Ray answers, then moves briskly into the office to give Maddie her coffee and sit down behind his desk with greater formality. "I'd like to ask both of you some questions, if you don't mind."

Alma goes to stand behind Maddie's chair and lay a hand on her shoulder.

"This isn't a formal interrogation," Ray continues. "I just need some background about . . . the deceased. I'm talking to people who were close to her, trying to gather any important information about her situation at the time of death. Just to be sure we're covering all possible areas of inquiry." Ray's careful detours around Vicky's name finally register with Alma. Like a traditional Crow, he is deliberately not speaking the name of the dead.

"Grandma probably knows more than I do," Alma says. "Vicky and I haven't been close for quite a while."

"Do you mind if I record this?" Alma and Maddie give short, indifferent headshakes. Ray taps a few times on his mouse and advances a tiny microphone toward them on the desk. "When was the last time you talked to her?" he asks Alma.

"Oh, it's been months. Vicky and I had a falling-out years

ago. She didn't trust me with personal things." Alma shifts but keeps her hand on Maddie. The thin shoulder is tense but steady.

"And you, Mrs. Terrebonne?"

Maddie resettles her purse on her lap and clears her throat. "The last time I saw her was Friday. She was going to work a late shift, so she dropped off Brittany with me."

"A late shift? Where?" Ray asks. The question surprises Alma, who moves to Maddie's side, to see her face better.

"Why, at Denny's, of course," Maddie answers. She looks to Ray for support.

"No, ma'am," he says. "She lost that job a few weeks ago."

"But she told me . . ." Realization comes over Maddie's face and her shoulders droop. "Oh, I see. I see." Alma thinks back on her interactions at Denny's. Now the use of the past tense makes more sense.

"How did she seem when you saw her Friday?" Ray asks.

"Energetic." Maddie isn't looking at Ray anymore. Her eyes have fixed somewhere on the linoleum floor. She looks embarrassed by Vicky's lie. "She was just racing around, talking a mile a minute about some class she wants to sign up for at the college this semester. I remember thinking it was good she had so much energy, working hours like that and going to school too."

Ray pulls a small pad from the pocket of the jacket hanging on his chair and makes a note. "Do you know anyone she confided in? Friends?"

"There's her brother, Pete. He watches out for her. He ought to"—Maddie pauses and lifts her head to give Alma a heavy glance before collapsing even further into her chair—"he ought to know more than I do."

"Alma, you talked to Pete about what happened Saturday night, isn't that right?"

"Just briefly yesterday after I got in. I don't think he knows much. Brittany called him, but he didn't go over, like I said."

"Anyone else she was close to?"

"Brittany, of course," Alma answers, "but I don't know how aware she was of her mother's life. Vicky lived with Helen and Walt for four years, until she got pregnant and dropped out of high school, but she wasn't close to them either." Alma puts both hands on Maddie's shoulders. "Ray—Detective Curtis—I think this is too hard on Grandma. Maybe you and I could talk more later."

Ray nods, but Maddie rallies and sits up straighter. "Vicky has some girlfriends from high school around town. There's a Tonya that she mentions sometimes. Tonya Schiff. And Vicky used to spend time with her cousin Emma Townsend, before she moved to Roundup. They might still be in touch. We have so many other cousins, but I haven't heard her talk about any of them in years. A lot of them are much older."

"Thank you, Mrs. Terrebonne. That's very helpful." Ray writes down the names in a tight script before folding the pad back into his coat pocket, but Maddie hasn't finished.

"And then there's this land agent who's been harassing us. Rick Burlington. He's been trying to get me to sign away mineral rights to the home place, near the Harmony mine. I've been afraid that one day Vicky might cross the wrong person. You hear stories about those coal people doing whatever it takes to get those leases. I worried for her and Brittany while they were living out there alone without a man."

"Without a man!" Alma can't keep herself from scoffing. "Grandma, Vicky knows how to use the shotgun as well as I do. She can take care of herself."

"Not if somebody got the drop on her," Maddie insists.

Alma smiles at Maddie's turn of phrase, but Ray sits back with a more serious look. "Now, that's interesting. I've heard stories lately about tribal landowners being threatened when they refused to sign over mineral rights. You say Vicky had been talking to the land agent?"

"While she lived out there, he kept showing up at the home

place, she said." Maddie leans forward, eager to tell. "He was pressuring her to come get me to sign. I guess he thought she'd have more luck with me. When that didn't work, he came right to my house and tried to wheedle me into it! Well. I wasn't born yesterday. I told him what he could do with that lease and to stay away from my grandchildren."

"And what did he say?"

"Oh, he was nice and polite sitting in my house in Billings, but I didn't like him. He said he'd be back and I told him there was no point, and then he told me that things change and he was sure one day I'd change my mind. It wasn't what he said, but the way he said it. There was a—a viciousness to him. But I don't scare easy. No, sir. My grandmothers faced down worse than the likes of him." Maddie is bracing herself on the arms of the chair, sitting bolt upright. Alma lowers her head to hide the smile of pride.

After handing over names and phone numbers for everyone Ray wants to reach, Alma asks for the addresses where Vicky had been living and where they found her, several blocks down. It's a street she doesn't know well, south of Minnesota Avenue in the wrongest part of town.

When at last they go, collecting Brittany along the way, Ray helps Maddie to the car, then goes back for a vehicle. Alma, drained as an old woman after the interview with Ray, lets the girl walk her to the car. Brittany watches her the whole way but never says a word. When she's sitting again, Alma rests with her eyes closed for several minutes, practicing the relaxation breathing she learned in yoga. Brittany and Maddie sit there with her, without a sound, watching their breath fog the windows. At length, Ray's police Suburban pulls into the lot and Alma gathers herself enough to put the key in the ignition.

CHAPTER 8

Alma is grateful to be heading toward the home place at last, with a police escort no less. Murray may be out there. She takes the interstate straight east, pulling into the steady traffic of semis and pickups, signaling by force of West Coast habit—nobody signals here but the professional drivers. Maddie has taken off her bright red hat and folded it in her lap. One small gloved hand rests on the door, up against the window, as she stares out onto the land with immense interest.

Alma's traveled this road a thousand times. Usually it makes little impression. She'll be thinking of something else, listening to the radio, talking to someone in the car or on the phone. Once in a while, though, the texture of the place comes upon her as a physical experience. All the stories, all the history, everything she knows about every point on the landscape envelops her, and the only word that can express anything about what this place is to her is *texture*—like running her hands over a variegated rock face or smooth birch bark, embedding them in dough, palming handfuls of red clay mud, sinking her feet into the pebbles in the creek bed, lifting a slick live trout with both hands, lying on the rocky earth, rubbing her horse's sweaty neck. Her body is part of the texture, made of this land and the good, sweet water, healed by the herbs, raised on the stories, grown on the plants and animals, quickened by the air. Her body knows textures here that her mind can't hold consciously all at once.

Maddie lived more than fifty years on the home place. Coming back to it lights and expands her like a hot air balloon taking shape. She tells stories the whole way there—homestead stories of unexpected delight, near-death, and triumph over the harshest survival conditions. The low-slung car takes the unpaved country roads more slowly than the pickups Alma remembers driving out here as a kid, though with Ray behind her she can't speed the way she normally would, either.

As they approach the home place, Maddie is buoyant, warmed from within. She gestures at every variation in the bare white landscape. "Look," she says, "the Thompsons painted their whole place yellow. Doesn't that look nice! It used to be kind of a beige, you know, just blended right in."

Then farther along, "Isn't that a new fence on the Birney place? My my, what do you suppose they're running that they need something like that?"

She speculates on the current value of properties and who must have inherited, who must have sold out. "They never were much use as ranchers," she comments gently about old friends whose house now stands abandoned, "but they used to have a barbecue every summer that was the event of the year in three counties! Oh my, it was fine. Three kinds of homemade potato salad, these old German recipes, and cider from their own trees—and he was a fiddler. We young people would dance the night away."

Maddie comments on the quality and quantity of livestock visible from the road, the number of cow-calf pairs these big acreages can carry, and the diminished amount of forage available after recent fires, twisting in her seat to see more as they pass. Like her voluble tongue, her eyes never rest.

The home place is just off the county road, sheltered on both sides by groves of pines and from behind by a low hill, with a dry irrigation ditch running by in front before passing under the drive in a huge steel culvert. The barns and corrals are behind and to the left, while in front of the house a large patch is fenced in—or more precisely, the antelope, deer, raccoons, and rabbits are fenced out—for a garden. When they pull around the house, they find an old maroon sedan parked in back in the only place it wouldn't be visible from the road.

"Do you know whose car that is?" Alma asks Maddie.

"I've never seen it. I used to know all the neighbors' cars around here." Maddie looks around 360 degrees, owl-like, and pulls her purse closer. "You think it might be that fella Detective Curtis is looking for?" She waves at Ray pulling in behind them.

"I'll go see if anybody's around. It could just be a neighbor, checking on things."

Alma leaves the car key in the ignition and crosses the broad porch to the back door of the house. All the curtains are shut and the blinds pulled down. Ray jogs over and steps up to the door in front of Alma. He unzips his coat and unsnaps his shoulder holster, then shrugs at Alma's obvious surprise. "You never know."

Ray gestures Alma over to a place to his right where she won't be immediately visible when the door opens. She holds out Maggie's key. He takes it, but first opens the storm door and knocks. When he gets no response, he knocks louder.

Something bangs inside and a shuffling noise reaches their ears. After a few minutes, a thin, long-haired man opens the door about a foot. He looks unarmed. Ray pushes the storm door open a little farther and Alma moves forward. The man could be part Hispanic, or Italian, or even some flavor of Asian—Alma's Seattle friends might take him for native, especially out here, but she knows the difference instinctively. He wears a hooded UNLV sweatshirt and a pair of wrinkled warm-up pants. He's barefoot and covers one foot with the other when the outdoor chill hits him.

"God, early enough for ya?" he says, blinking in the brilliant light off the snow. "How much you want?"

Alma stares at him. "Who are you?" she demands.

The man shields his eyes with one hand and peers back at her. "I'm Murray, who are you? What do you want?"

"I'm Alma Terrebonne. This is my grandmother's house. What are you doing here?"

Murray takes a step back from the half-open door and begins to close it, but Ray's boot is in the way. "I got a right to be here. Vicky gave me the key."

Alma feels bile rise, and raw anger. She wants to shove open the door and shout *You're selling drugs! Out of my grandmother's house! I'll bet my ass you've got a meth lab in the barn!* She looks Murray up and down, crosses her arms, and turns her glower to Ray. "This isn't Vicky's house. It's not hers to make deals with."

"It ain't none of your business," Murray retorts in a sulky tone. "If you don't like it, why don't you talk to her?"

"I would. Trouble is, my sister died yesterday. This is Detective Curtis from the Billings PD."

Murray's head snaps toward Ray, whose plainclothes hadn't triggered Murray's cop radar. Then the police markings on the Suburban catch his eye. Full comprehension strikes, and Murray bolts. He ducks between Ray and Alma to take the back steps two at a time. Ray jumps the staircase in one bound and leg-tackles Murray. Alma pulls the door shut before following.

"Get off me!" Murray is howling. "You split my fucking lip, you asshole!"

"And you just ran from a lawman conducting a homicide investigation. Smart move." Ray cuffs Murray with plastic ties, jerks him up to his bare feet, and walks him to the caged back-seat of the Suburban.

"I don't know anything about that! I saw her alive Saturday night!" Murray isn't fighting the march to the Suburban, but his protests are loud and frantic, directed back toward Alma as if she can change this unwelcome course of events. Ray helps him inside, locks the door, and turns back to Alma.

"I might as well clear the place while I'm here," he offers.

Before Alma can answer, Maddie swings open the car door. "Who is that man?" she demands. "What was he doing in my house?"

"Some friend of Vicky's," Alma replies. She moves to block Maddie from getting out of the car. "Don't worry, Grandma. We'll make sure there's nobody else around. You and Brittany stay in the car where it's warm."

Maddie reaches up to grab Alma's arm with surprising force. "You have to take care of the home place," she says. "We can't abandon it!"

Her delicate little grandmother is suddenly larger, stronger than Alma can remember seeing her for many years. Alma wonders if Maddie has left a bruise on her arm. "I will, Grandma," she says, surprised at the answering strength in her own voice. "I'll come back out and take care of it. I can spend a few days and make sure everything's okay here, maybe find a decent tenant so that somebody's keeping an eye on it. Don't worry."

Maddie settles back into the front seat, but Brittany pops out of the back as if Alma had pushed a button. "Brittany, I said stay in the car," Alma tells her firmly, but Brittany pauses her video game and hands back Alma's phone with finality. She steps up to Alma's side like she's made a decision.

Before any of them can make another move, the roar of gravel out on the county road draws their eyes. "Sheriff Marx,"

Ray says, nodding. "I told him we were coming out. He had a domestic violence call to finish up first." Alma remembers her mother volunteering for the Domestic Violence Crisis Center, shepherding wives and children to a safe house, digging new belongings for them out of trash bags of donations, how quietly the manless families bore it all, as if relishing the peace. The hierarchy is flatter out in the rural counties—no big-city police department like Billings or the resources of the Yellowstone County Sheriff's Office, just a handful of law officers trying to cover an area the size of Connecticut.

Sheriff Marx leaves his diesel idling and takes a good look at Murray as he strolls by Ray's outfit. "Doesn't surprise me," he's saying as he comes around the corner of the house. He's a heavy man with eyes watery and too white, perhaps the beginning of cataracts. Just what you want in a man with a sidearm, Alma thinks, sidling closer to Brittany. "We get all kinds of drug activity going on any time a place is left alone. Power, water, and all the privacy in the world—what more could they want? Have you cleared the place?"

"Just about to," Ray answers. "Detective Ray Curtis. I'm the one who called." He turns and offers his hand. Marx stops a few feet short of him and takes in Ray's appearance, the braid that fell over his shoulder in the scuffle with Murray. Something passes across Marx's face before it clears and he accepts the handshake. Alma wonders what kind of handshake Ray gives a man like Marx.

Marx jogs up the steps, unholsters his Glock, and enters the house without further preliminaries, moving quickly for a man with such a big belly. Ray moves behind him, taking more time to examine the mess Murray left behind.

Alma and Brittany step off the back porch into the kitchen together. Brittany slips her little hand into Alma's. "I'm glad we came back here," she says, squeezing Alma's hand.

Alma's knees nearly fold with relief. "Baby!" she cries, pulling Brittany into her arms. "I'm so glad you finally said something! Are you okay?" She puts a hand to Brittany's face to tilt it back and look at her.

Brittany nods. "I'm okay."

Alma presses an impulsive kiss to her niece's temple and hugs her close again. "I'm so glad. I love you." She rocks Brittany back and forth and sets her loose only when Brittany starts to wiggle. Of course this is where Brittany would take her first step out of the valley of the shadow of death. For a Terrebonne, the home place is the safe haven, the convergence of waters, the place where the beloved dead are as real as the living.

Brittany steps farther in and starts to look around. She stacks a few empty beer cans on the kitchen table.

"Yep, nothing here but a mess," Marx declares, returning to the kitchen with a printed plastic bag under one arm. "And a little meth stash I bagged as evidence. You planning to stay out here?"

Alma presses her lips together as she takes in Murray's detritus, but she gives Marx a firm answer. "Yes."

"You can bolt these doors from the inside while you're here, you know, but you'll have to change these locks," Marx observes. "You still got a phone hooked up out here? Cell reception's lousy."

"Everything should be shut off but electricity," Alma says. She picks up the receiver of the old black phone on the wall, just to check. Nothing.

"I'll call a locksmith for you," Marx offers. "You got a gun, then?"

"I think so. Hang on." Alma walks through the kitchen to the big pantry and kneels in front of the back wall. She feels below the bottom shelf for the hidden latch. A panel in the beadboard opens under her fingers. From behind it, she pulls a well-oiled shotgun and a box of shells. Smiling at their weight in her hands, she kicks the panel shut and returns to the kitchen to display them to the sheriff. He nods and holsters his own gun, satisfied.

"Okay then. We get weirdos wandering the county sometimes. Be careful by yourself. Let the neighbors know you're around, and don't leave anything valuable if the place is going to be empty. Times have changed." Marx is gruff but solid, a lot like her father. It's harder to suppress the memories here. Every time she rests her eyes some new place, there's Dad—sitting at the kitchen table showing her and Pete how to tie flies, letting her ride the back of the tractor pulling the haying rig through the big meadow beyond the barns, or leading them out on the back steps in pajamas to watch the Perseids. Alma sets down the shells and puts a hand to her throat, where the air is oddly constricted. Marx opens the back door and gives the Mitsubishi a long look. Maddie waves at him from the front seat, and he smiles and strolls down to her.

"How've you been, Mrs. Terrebonne?" Marx's gruff tone has changed to graciousness. Alma and Brittany trail after him down the steps, followed by Ray.

"Oh fine, thanks. Alma was sweet enough to bring me back out. We're going to stop by the cemetery." Maddie gestures toward the hill. "I miss it all so."

"You would, wouldn't you, a place like this?" Marx looks out over the yard, barns, and corrals, the double rows of sheltering pines and the icy bare country beyond. "I don't know how folks can leave. This is God's country right here." This last comes aimed at Alma.

Alma ignores it and asks, "Would you mind walking the barns with me too?" She looks from Marx to Ray for guidance. Ray moves toward his vehicle, showing clear deference for Marx's jurisdiction now that he has his prisoner in custody. Marx doesn't glance at Ray again, just leads the way to the nearest barn. Alma brings the shotgun and tows Brittany, not ready yet to leave her alone.

In the near barn—the livestock barn—the debris of Murray's meth operation is everywhere: empty Coleman fuel cans, soda bottles, plastic tubing, a few broken glass pipes. Marx scoffs. "Strictly small-time. I wouldn't worry much about this guy. The ones with brains go big-time pretty fast. We've come across industrial-scale operations you wouldn't believe. There was a guy last year managed to steal a whole trailer load of anhydrous from the co-op. He was supplying every meth head from here to Idaho before we busted him. Quite the entrepreneur." Marx's voice carries a note of admiration for a criminal mind clever enough to offer a challenge.

Alma lines up and connects a booted toe with one of the soda bottles in a smooth punt that sails to the other end of the barn. "Son of a bitch," she mutters under her breath. She's picturing Murray out here, taking his chances with blowing bits of the barn across the county, but Vicky is there too, moving the home place around her childish game of Chutes and Ladders. Fall in a hole, use the family's irreplaceable heritage to climb out, as if it's hers alone. Being angry at Vicky is more familiar, less painful, than the waves of guilt and grief, but Alma doesn't like it any better. She spins away from Marx, rubs at her eyes as the light hits them, and strides out of the barn with Brittany trailing after her.

After confirming that the second barn is empty, doing a quick tour around the small bunkhouse and corrals, and poking his head into a pair of abandoned outbuildings and the museum-piece outhouse itself, Marx heads back to the first barn to collect and tag the evidence of Murray's operation. By this time Ray is waving goodbye and turning around in the yard. Marx hands Alma a printed card with county emergency numbers and takes off too. As the dust vortices snaking behind their vehicles come to rest, peace descends. Alma and Brittany lean against the warm hood of the idling car, watching a jet contrail take shape.

After several minutes, Alma stirs to check the gauge on the propane tank. It's more than half full. She says a quick word to Maddie, snug in the car, and descends to the basement to check the furnace, which turns out to be clean and humming. Murray must have had his own crazy reasons for keeping the place so cold. Back upstairs, Alma ratchets up the thermostat and finds a few delinquent bills on the counter that she stacks and stores in the dish towel drawer. The store of firewood is almost untouched—Murray must not have known how to get a fire going. Alma drums her fingers on the cast-iron woodstove. Vicky sure found some winners. Brittany comes in the front door before Alma has finished building the fire and starts to stack newspapers in a corner.

"Brittany, we're going to be here a little while. Would you please help your great-grandma in and get her settled by the fire?" Alma asks. She pulls out her phone before remembering with an inhaled curse that it's no use to her here. She drops it on the floor next to her purse and turns her back on it. Brittany is already moving toward the door, but she looks back with a small, sly smile when Alma's phone hits the floor.

Once Maddie is settled inside and the stove has started pumping heat, Alma heads out for a closer look at what kind of mess is left in the outbuildings. Brittany follows her back to the livestock barn and stands beside her, looking up into the templed space and dusty light. They both played in these stalls as children. Alma remembers driving cattle into the sturdy corrals beyond as a teenager, then hauling whatever was needed, voices shouting for her all day long as the loud, smelly business of castration and branding went on. The space is empty now, the livestock sold off. There was discussion after Grandpa Al died of renting out the home place, but there were no takers for a place with no modern bathroom. Instead Maddie has rented the grazing land and hired a neighbor to mow the hay meadows as a stopgap until the day when one of the grandchildren is ready to take over. She maintains an earnest faith in that day.

Brittany walks from stall to stall, running her hands over the smooth wood. "I like it here," she says, to the air rather than to Alma.

"It's not too bad in the house," Alma answers. "Mostly a lot of trash to throw out. Do you want to stay out here with me for a few days and help get the place in shape?"

"Yes!" Brittany answers, the first sign of positive emotion she's shown since Alma's arrival. "Burro will love it!"

"Burro?" Alma suddenly remembers Brittany's invisible animals, her elaborate imaginary-creature world. A few years ago, Brittany created and presented Alma with an invisible finned flying horse. *He can fly along with you when you ride your bike,* Brittany told her, *and when you're busy at work he'll go down to the water and guide the ships in and out of port.* The animal came with detailed care and feeding instructions. He was Alma's to name. She never did.

"My invisible Newfoundland. He likes the barns because they smell like animals," Brittany says. Alma hasn't heard Brittany mention the invisible animals in years. Their invocation is like a small bird alighting within arm's reach, risking its delicate being to be near her.

"I see." Alma smiles as she turns fully to Brittany. The mention of Burro tracks her thoughts away from meth labs and prostitution, drawing them to higher ground, a place where her breath comes more easily. "You've had him for a while, haven't you? How old is he?"

"Almost four," Brittany says without having to reflect. She turns to Alma. "I know what we should do. We should live here, you and me, on the home place. And I'll have room for Burro and all my invisible animals."

"How many are there?" Alma asks, smiling. "These barns aren't that big."

"Oh, not that many. And maybe I could get a real animal

sometime." Brittany gazes fondly at the place where Burro would be visible, if Alma could see him.

Alma walks up to Brittany, shifts the heavy shotgun to the other shoulder, and puts an arm around her niece. "Honey," she begins, preparing herself to tell Brittany that this is only for a few days, to get the place cleaned up in the optimistic expectation of new tenants, that there's no way they can stay here, how impossible that is. But right here, in this moment, the words stage a sit-down protest and won't come out. "We're here today. And we'll figure out tomorrow."

Brittany hears the evasion and turns to Alma with the skeptical gaze she's recently acquired. "Mom and I lived out here for a few years. I know the kids. There's lots of room for you to have an office."

Alma eyes the heavy rafters, looking for the deus ex machina that can get her out of this one. "We'll talk about it later, babe."

Brittany isn't quite done yet. "She likes to come out here," she says, startling Alma.

"Who? Your mom?"

"Mm-hm. Out to the barns. She likes to sit at the back door and watch the clouds in the summertime. Over there." Brittany points to the far end of the barn, where another great door is shut tightly against the invading winter. "She tells me about where the clouds are going."

"Where they're going?"

Brittany smiles—another of these simple, joyful smiles that illumine Alma's heart—and takes a few steps toward the back door. "She has different stories every time. Like she'll point at one she says looks like a guitar and say, 'It's going to Chicago and on to Nashville, and there'll be a singer who'll look up and see it.' And she tells me all about the singer, how she comes from a little town and writes all her own songs and one day somebody important heard her sing on the radio."

"Are all these stories about people she made up?" Alma

traces Brittany's steps, drawn into her story, letting Brittany's galloping imagination carry away all that weighs on them.

"Well, not always. Sometimes she tells me stories about you. You know, 'Alma's going to argue a big case' or 'Alma's going to Japan to negotiate a deal.' Just made-up stuff, like that."

"Really? But she was so angry with me the last time I saw her. I'm surprised she'd tell you stories about me."

Brittany makes a gesture that might be a shrug but comes across as only a shift in her oversized coat. "I mean, I know she gets mad at you sometimes. But she wants to be like you. She says things like, 'There, now Alma will be proud of us when she comes home.'"

The sunlight razoring through the cracks in the barn walls goes blurry for a second and Alma blinks hard. "I never knew. I thought she hated me."

Brittany laughs. "But you're sisters. You always love your sister." Humming Patsy Cline to herself, Brittany turns and strides with her loose, little-girl walk out of the barn. Alma can almost see Burro at her side, the great, protective creature padding beside his small creator.

Outside, Brittany breaks into a jog in the direction of the swing set south of the house. She brushes snow from the higher swing, kicks her legs out, and begins to pump the swing. Alma joins her and sits to dangle in the second swing. From the beginning she expected tears from Brittany, not the disturbing silence and now the even more disturbing hints that Brittany has repressed Vicky's death entirely.

It cannot last. Alma half expects Brittany to be crying when her face swings back into view, but the face that meets the horizon now, in violent motion, is dreamy, not weepy. Brittany moves higher and higher until the chains slacken for a long second at the apex of her swing. In an instant, they're back in Billings, Alma and Vicky, on the night when Vicky fell from a swing. Alma jumps from her swing in a sudden panic to stop Brittany, bring her down to safety, but Brittany is far from her control. Her hair flies wildly, one direction then the other, a maelstrom around her face.

"Stop! Stop, Brittany, come down!" Alma pleads. Brittany drops her feet to drag herself to a halt on the frozen dirt below, looking up at Alma in surprise. "We have work to do," Alma says, to hide her embarrassment, and leads Brittany inside.

As Alma searches for cleaning products, she peeks through the doorway into the wide front room that runs the width of the house, lit by big west-facing windows onto the front porch. Brittany and Maddie are together in the rocking chair, arms tight around each other, heads tucked close, almost exactly the same height. Their strong, high cheekbones and wide-set eyes are nearly identical. Brittany's dark hair hangs limply down her back and Maddie's is dyed lighter and styled, but other than that they could be two ends of a set of time-lapse photographs. Brittany has lost so much so early, and yet, still to have this—her great-grandmother, her home place—these are priceless. Alma shuts her eyes and allows herself to know, just for a moment, how much she's missed these things, this place. Then she hangs up her coat, unfolds a rag, and gets to work.

Tossing out the first bag of trash, Alma screws up her face in disgust when she realizes that the frozen two-liter soda bottles in a long row on the back porch are full of urine. "Oh, God help me," she mutters as it occurs to her to wonder if Murray made it to the outhouse with the rest of his output. She takes out a long-handled broom and tackles the cobwebs hanging from drapes and moldings in the front room, cleaning up first for Maddie, who let out a small shriek when she stepped into the kitchen.

"Give me a hand with the dusting?" she prompts Brittany with a rag and spray can of polish. Brittany pops up and begins to work earnestly at the hand-lathed rails of the banister. When they've cornered the worst of the dust, Alma and Brittany stop to take in the room. As carefully insulated, sided, roofed, and weather stripped as Alma's father and grandfather left the house, the elements have made very few inroads all these years later. Within is a pine-scented serenity of stained wood and smooth, varnished edges. At the back, the big kitchen and pantry anchor the whole house. The wide staircase rises up the southern end of the front room to the three bedrooms, the steps worn but not bowed, the precious circular window a porthole in spring onto a greasy-grass sea. Alma looks out one of the front windows onto the long, deep porch and feels the same sense of time travel she's always experienced here. This house was built to endure.

"The house smells funny," Brittany says, her first words since coming inside again, "but it still feels the same."

"Yes," Alma answers with pride. She didn't build it, she doesn't technically own it, but it's hers in every way that matters, right down to the feeling they all get coming inside—a shrug and a sigh, a lifting of burdens.

Alma's great-grandfather Charles Terrebonne married the only daughter of a struggling family of Yankee homesteaders who, upon losing the family matriarch, decided to give up on their gorgeous spread of harsh land and move to town. Together with the daughter, Eliza Stoddard, and some of his hardworking French-Canadian and Métis kin, Charles razed the leaning, drafty homesteaders' cabin and from its strong foundations built, with traditional carpentry tools he'd carried from Québec, this house. He learned the cattle ranching business from Eliza and took a while to master it. Eliza was the hardheaded one, the cussed youngest child who refused to sell out and go to town, who knew with an unpopular certainty that she could make a go where her father and brothers had failed. Charles was in love with her as only a sentimental, superstitious Frenchman can be. He followed her willingly into the unknown. For her part, Eliza loved him all her life with the earnestness of a sweet, smitten young bride—but she loved her land more.

The house has begun to have a museum feel, so disinclined has been every single Terrebonne generation to change anything about their surroundings. Although running water and electricity arrived at last on the home place, there is still no indoor bathroom, because the only obvious space for it was the kitchen pantry, with its elegantly executed bins and nooks, or the upstairs linen closet, with its glowing cedar cabinetry. The basement, from the original cabin, is no more than a low-ceilinged root cellar. Al and Maddie made do with an outhouse and chamber pots rather than remove a nail that Charles had hammered or mar the strong lines of the house with some abomination of an addition.

More than a hundred years later, the double-hung windows move soundlessly and shut out the fiercest winds. The drawers roll effortlessly in built-in cabinets throughout the house. The floors don't creak. There is art to each room, and a clarity of purpose that makes the very air a comfort to breathe.

"Look at that." Alma gestures to the soft pine floors where Murray has been extinguishing cigarettes. "I should've kicked his butt when I had the chance."

"You?" Brittany giggles.

Alma gives her a sidelong grin. "I have moves you know nothing about."

They work in silence. Maddie sits where she has a view from the front window, looking across the porch to the small square of lawn and the much larger garden enclosure beyond. Alma and Brittany are in the kitchen when a scraping noise becomes audible out front, like clumsy footsteps, or something being dragged. Alma snatches up the shotgun and makes her way to the window next to the front door. Maddie is frozen in her chair and says nothing. When Alma peers out, the yard is full of antelope, scratching through the snow to what's left of the grass. Alma waves Brittany over. Their muffled laugh is a relief.

Pronghorns, she should say, but *antelope* is her father's word for them. He had a gift for spotting wildlife from absurd distances—the slightest movement on the landscape was enough to draw his eye, then he'd pull Alma to stand under his arm and look until she saw. Alma remembers vast fleets of pronghorns spread out over the high pastures in her childhood, before there were quite so many fences. Where deer jump like gazelles, pronghorns pull up their cheetah sprints to turn or even try to duck under the barbwire. Up close to the house like this they seem frail and goatlike, pawing through the snow cover at the tender grass, tossing black horns, flashing white-blaze necks. And there, hanging from the whitewashed porch rail, is Grandpa Al's cane, the one he used the last dozen years of his life, a presence and a talisman, alive as the antelope.

When at last the antelope move around the corner of the house, Alma turns, feeling lighter, and goes up to the bright southeast bedroom to make Brittany's bed with flannel sheets, wool blankets, and a heavy quilt out of what's left in the linen closet. They never really emptied the home place. No one could bear to do that. Alma smoothes the corners, arranging the scene with precision, fluffing up the pillow, thinking how the room will look to Brittany when she sees it again. Its shabbiness hurts her—the vertical tear in the handmade yellow curtains, a slight peel of paint where the morning sun hits the far wall. A maternal protectiveness steals over her: *Brittany will have what she needs. She will be cared for and loved. She will not be hurt, not here.* She is beginning to comprehend the oceanic nature of her feelings about Vicky's death, sometimes a smooth surface Alma can easily cross over, then welling up like a tide, something that could take her altogether if she's not careful. Alma's hands fall still on the double wedding-ring quilt, paralyzed momentarily by the totality of grief, how bodily it is, and the accompanying terror that honoring her sense of duty to Brittany will end her own life as she knows it.

The sound of Brittany jogging up the stairs shakes Alma into movement. She turns around with a smile as Brittany enters the room. "How does it look?" she asks.

"Nice." Brittany smiles back and comes a few steps closer. "I haven't had my own room since we lived out here," she admits.

"Well, this is all yours." Alma squeezes her shoulder, leaving alone the temporary nature of the arrangement.

Brittany's fingers fall to the tiny stitches on the quilt. "Mom is here, you know," she tells Alma in a softer voice.

Alma snaps around to look at her. "Oh?" Her forced calm makes the question come out like a half gulp.

"She's trying to make me feel better. She's glad you and Great-Grandma are here. Burro saw her first, but he didn't want to tell me." Brittany looks down with sympathy at Burro, stroking his invisible head, which hits nearly at her elbow.

"Why not?"

Brittany shrugs and moves away from Alma toward the east-facing window, overlooking the outbuildings. She fingers the disintegrating curtains. "He was afraid it would hurt me. But it doesn't. I'm glad she's here."

"I know she loved you very much." Alma swallows. If there are ghosts anywhere, there ought to be ghosts here. The home place would hold a potluck and dance for ghosts if any were out there to attend. And whether Alma believes or not, what harm can it do to let Brittany believe that her mother is present to comfort her? Alma backs out of the room, leaving Brittany to watch a few antelope cross in front of the barns as she whispers occasionally to Burro.

When the locksmith arrives, he scares off the antelope. Alma comes out to greet him as he hops out of his pickup and approaches at an energetic pace.

"You're Al's granddaughter, ain't you?" The man pulls the leather work glove from his hand and grips hers. Even in this cold, there are proprieties. He will not shake a woman's hand with his glove on. She introduces herself. "Hank Olson. Al and I were in the Masons together. When I got the sheriff's message I came first thing." Hank is a bustling little Swede, the runt of some robust litter, several inches shorter than Alma, with a walleye that gazes distractingly to the left behind thick glasses. He looks in the direction of the retreating antelope. "It never lets go of you, does it, no matter how far you go? When your family goes back as far as yours and mine do, this land is like your mother. My friend Ed up the road says he don't know if that's a blessing or a curse." Hank gestures in the direction of the Murphy place, just out of sight.

"So about these locks—" Alma attempts, but Hank is far from done talking.

"How long you been gone then, Alma?" Hank asks, hands on hips, getting to the important information first.

"About five years, this last time. Since Grandpa's funeral." She says these last three words slowly, trying to draw his attention back to the house.

"Oh right, right. It was a shame to lose him. He knew his way around an engine better than any man I've ever met."

Alma stands quite still. Hank's supportive hand squeezes her elbow.

"I'm sorry," he says. "I didn't mean to upset you."

Abruptly, Alma shakes his hand off. "I'd like to change the door locks," she says in a loud voice, turning away from him. "Come on, I'll show you."

As he works, Hank obligingly fills her in on all the local news without her asking: weddings; divorces; babies; deaths by old age, suicide, and accident; and of course the occasional and richly cherished victories of the local high school teams. The new mine going in. The fiasco with the unused jail. He's midway through the story of Chance Murphy's big-city wife and how any fool could have seen that wasn't going to work when Brittany steps out on the porch where Hank is fitting a dead bolt. Alma doesn't see her at first, fixated as she is on the horizon in an effort not to react to Chance Murphy's name in a way that will restart local gossip.

"Well hello there, young lady," Hank greets Brittany with a nod over his busy hands. "Are you Alma's daughter?"

Brittany pauses for a long moment, gives Hank a considered nod, and hurries back inside.

By the time Hank has changed all the exterior locks, told all his stories, tried unsuccessfully to pitch Alma an alarm system his nephew sells, and completed a long and friendly goodbye, Alma can barely feel her fingers and toes, and the noonday sun has passed them. Like on one of her long days at the office, she's lost track of the last time she ate, drank, went to the toilet. She braves the outhouse and hurries back inside. Hank has hardly been gone long enough for Alma to start to warm up near the stove when the gravel drive alerts again.

"The peace and quiet of the country," Alma mutters and stalks to the back door, where everyone seems to pull up. A new white Ram extended-cab pickup—clean like no Big Horn County vehicle ever is—hums just beyond the back porch. Out comes a tall, broad fellow in a shearling coat and a beautiful gray felt cowboy hat that doesn't fit quite right. His smile matches the shiny white paint job.

"Well hello there!" he booms, leaning across the hood of the pickup the way ranchers do, secure behind their 6.7-liter Cummins. On him the move looks practiced. "I heard in town that some of the family might be out here. I'm Rick Burlington. I don't believe we've met."

"Alma Terrebonne. Just a second." Alma goes inside, shuts the door, and sees Brittany standing in the doorway to the front room, watchful. "Do me a favor—go upstairs and turn on some lights, make some noise, okay, like there are more people here. It's the mine guy outside and I don't like the looks of him."

Without question, Brittany turns, and as Alma reopens the door she hears heavy footsteps pound up the stairs.

Rick looks a little taken aback by Alma's lockjawed welcome, but he wraps the smile back around his face and comes out from behind the pickup. "Sorry, don't mean to interrupt anything. I just wanted to welcome you back to the neighborhood. You finding everything you need out here?"

From upstairs, a noise drifts down like something heavy being dragged. Alma looks down to hide a smile. "We're doing fine, thanks," she tells Burlington as she shuts the door and steps out onto the porch. "You live around here?" She eyes his Colorado plates.

"Billings, temporarily. I'm from Denver, but work has me up here in this neck of the woods. I just love it. God's country for sure, as they say." Burlington hikes up the steps without invitation to stand a little closer than Alma likes and thrust his gloved hand at her. She steps away to put herself directly in front of the doorknob.

"What kind of work?"

"I'm a landman for Harmony Coal. It's a great company. I tell you, Alma, they do so much for the community. Just last year they contributed—"

"What's a landman for Harmony Coal doing on my porch, Mr. Burlington?" Alma interrupts the litany of Harmony's service to humanity, putting on her most lawyerly tone of cross-examination, but Burlington doesn't seem to be the sort of man who's put off by a less-than-enthusiastic welcome. She'd almost say he expects it.

"Like I say, just welcoming you back. We're working on tying up some mineral leases in the area and I like to make sure I know all the landowners. Am I right that Maddie Terrebonne is still the landowner here?"

Alma pulls her head back and looks at Burlington with even

less warmth. Her first thought is to tell this glad-handing prick to do his job and look up the land records at the courthouse, but some vestige of Maddie's hospitality, or professional prudence, restrains her. "That's right," she says.

Rick pulls a folded document out of an inside pocket of his coat. "This is the mineral lease I need her to—"

"No," Alma snaps.

"I beg your pardon?" Burlington feigns surprise, then continues in a wheedling tone. "I think you'll find that it's a very—"

"No." Alma takes a step forward to get into Burlington's personal space. See how he likes it. "We're not interested in any lease. Get off our property."

Brittany chooses the perfect moment to clatter back down the stairs in what sounds like Al's old steel-toe work boots. Burlington glances at the house, then out toward the barns, where Alma has parked the sedan out of sight. No telling how many people might be here. He knows it and she knows it. His face reflects a quick decision.

"Well sure. I didn't mean to cause any offense. Just doing my job, ma'am. But you know, in the next stage of mining, this place will be surrounded on all sides, blasting and hauling going on three hundred sixty degrees around you. Folks who hold out always regret it, and later the money won't be so good. If you want my advice—"

"I don't. And I asked you to leave. I'll post the place and call the sheriff if I see strangers on our land again."

"All righty then. See you later, Miss Terrebonne." Before heading back to the pickup, Burlington straightens to his full height, at least six two, and allows Alma to take in his size. The smile is gone. Then he jogs to the pickup and loses no time spinning snow and gravel down the drive.

"Perfect," Alma growls before going back to Brittany. *This is all we need.*

"What did he want this time?" Brittany asks from the bottom of the staircase, stepping out of Al's trashed old boots.

"You know him?" Alma's voice lifts in surprise. But of course Brittany must have seen Rick many times.

"He always used to bother Mom. She was afraid of him." Brittany grabs the worn newel-post with both hands and swings on it a little, nervously.

"Why would she be afraid of him?"

"She says he gets people alone and threatens them. She says that's how he gets people to sign." Brittany is talking to the newel-post now, refusing to meet Alma's eyes, getting quieter and quieter.

"Well, I was just alone with him and he didn't threaten me. And why would he threaten your mom? She didn't own this place."

Brittany casts her eyes around the living room, where Maddie is still watching rapt from the front window as if a Shakespeare company is playing on the lawn. Her hearing aid is off and she seems to have caught none of the conversation. "He wanted her to get Great-Grandma to sign. He offered her money if she could."

"What did she say?"

"Mom?" Brittany knots her fingers together around the post and stares down. "She kept promising we'd move out, like, every day. So I thought maybe—" She jerks her head toward the back of the house where Burlington's pickup had been.

"Oh, sweetheart." Alma crosses the remaining space between them and folds her arms around Brittany. "Your mom loved you and she loved this place. I'm sure she was trying to do the right thing."

"Alma?" Brittany's voice is muffled in Alma's sweater.

"Yes, honey?"

"Did somebody kill her?"

Alma swallows. In her own tragedy at least she was spared

this, but the news will be all over Billings with the morning paper. She can no more protect Brittany from this truth than she can stop the sun breaking immense across the eastern plains. "I don't know, baby. We'll find out."

Brittany is not a child given to tears or hysterics. Her arms tighten around Alma's waist, but she gives no other sign of distress. Alma has a detached, clinical feeling that they both ought to be crying, and hard, but neither of them was raised on emotion. Their ability to endure lies in a steely core of reserve, handed down from Eliza and the ancestors.

The home place is peaceful around them. A log snaps in the woodstove. Alma breathes in the strength gathered in the quiet. She holds Brittany as she remembers their elders' embrace, still and calm, all of them in this room even now, the ancestors around them, maybe even Vicky, beyond words but not beyond reach.

After a very long time, so long that Alma's toes are beginning to feel warm again inside her boots, Brittany speaks in a still, small voice. "Can I sleep in your bed tonight?"

Alma nods against the top of Brittany's head. "Yes, sweetheart. Of course you can."

CHAPTER 9

Delivering Maddie back to Billings, Alma takes the road past the Murphys' Little m Ranch, just to see how the place looks these days. She recalls old Ed Murphy lecturing at the table about how once you let the little things go, the whole place is on a quick slide to ruin. Sure enough, the property remains unchanged: no sagging fences, no broken siding, all the out-buildings in good repair, even a new prefabricated house set well back from the road, with a tidy apron and a small deck. All clean and well-maintained, from the outbuildings to the house to the cattle themselves, who still seem to stand a little straighter than the average black Angus, while the Terrebonne clan has packed up and let meth dealers and antelope move in. Alma blushes and drives by, feeling the full length of the fifteen years since she was last here trailing out behind her.

The driver of a pickup coming the opposite direction down the two-lane dirt road spots her and slows down. Murphy's Law rules in this valley: it has to be Chance, and it is. He stops the pickup even with her and rolls down the window. "Well, I'll be damned," he says.

Looking up at him in his heavy Carhartt jacket and black wool Scotch cap, Alma grins involuntarily out of sheer discomfort. "Bad penny," she smartasses back.

Chance stares at her, then slowly leans over to turn off a radio crackling with the farm report, contemplating. Finally he says, "Come on up to the house. Mom and Dad will want to see you."

Alma is glad for her gloves so that Chance can't see how badly she's white-knuckling the steering wheel. She wants a nice chatty coffee with the Murphys about as much as she wants to see that asshole landman again, but there's no civil way to say no. "Yeah, okay, just a quick visit. I've got Grandma with me."

"Who is it, honey?" Maddie tries to lean over far enough to see who's at the high pickup window.

"Chance Murphy, Grandma."

"That nice Murphy boy who used to take you out?" Maddie says at such volume that Chance must be able to hear.

"Yes, Grandma." Alma's face grows warm even in the bitter cold of the open window.

"Hello, Mrs. Terrebonne," Chance shouts down, then pulls forward to lead the way on to the Little m headquarters.

Alma spins the car to follow him. In front of the main house they get out and go through the motions of getting Maddie out of the car, Chance welcoming her and Brittany. They've both been at the home place much more recently than Alma. They greet Chance in a comfortable, neighborly way, while Alma stands back and observes, trying to keep her body language more relaxed than she feels. When last she saw him, he was a high school rodeo star bent on breaking as many bones as possible. He has the same lean, narrow frame, the same low-heeled roper's boots and jeans, the same brown eyes. Intriguing. The misalignment of his nose was new then. Now it fits the maturity in his face. For once Maddie doesn't stand around chatting for half an hour in the cold, but leads Brittany toward the house. Chance turns to Alma.

"Al." Chance doesn't look at her as he shuts the car door. There it is, the endearment, the name only he has ever called her. "It's a terrible thing," he says. Alma bows her head: he knows. She blows out the breath she's been holding.

"I'm glad I don't have to break that one to you. Exposure, they think. She was drunk." No reason to advertise the homicide investigation. "It's good to see you." Alma smiles and feels the unaccustomed movement in her frozen, tense cheeks.

Chance just looks at her, not unfriendly but not smiling either. Awkwardness overwhelms Alma and she looks away. Some kind of a tank with pipes sits behind the cab of the pickup. "What's that?" Alma asks, just to have something to say.

"Biodiesel, and a tank and fuel line warmer so it doesn't jell in the cold. I brew it right here out of used cooking oil. Just got another batch in town." As he explains, he adopts that slight, thoughtful stoop so many ranchers have as they discuss their pet projects, she notices, hands in his pockets, making only the occasional economical gesture. When he's done, he straightens. Unlike Burlington's, Chance's mannerisms are natural, unselfconscious.

"Biodiesel?" She's heard about biodiesel in Seattle, but of course it would have come first from the people who've spent a century cooking up every imaginable way to survive in a business that sometimes seems invented to destroy them.

"Almost free fuel, and nobody has to drill my backyard for it." Chance steps back and glances off to the east, frowning toward something beyond their line of sight.

"I haven't seen drilling rigs around here."

"Just wait. They're coming, that or the mines."

"We just had a visit from Harmony Coal." She gestures

with her own head back toward the home place, unconsciously mimicking his economy of movement.

"That's them. Subbituminous coal." Chance says the words like vulgarities.

Alma nods at the snug prefab uphill a few hundred yards from the old place. "Is that new place yours?"

"All mine," Chance confirms. "We put it in when I came back after Dad got cancer, about four years ago, not long after your granddad passed."

"I was so sorry to hear about your dad. Is he doing better?"

"According to him, never better." Chance casts a dubious glance at his father's low, sturdy ranch house. "Everything all right up at your place?"

"We had a little trouble. There was a meth head up there we had to get rid of."

Chance rubs at his clean-shaven jaw. "I've noticed movement up around there, but I thought it could be one of you. Didn't want to pry. If you want me to keep a closer eye on the place, I will. You be careful, though. That guy's not gonna be nice people."

"No, he's not, but the cops took him. Grandma wants me to stay out here for a while and get everything cleaned up."

"By yourself?"

Alma shrugs. "Don't worry, I can take care of myself." Her words strike the wrong note. Chance turns away and moves to the front door.

The warmth of the house has broken Maddie's unusual silence outdoors. By the time Alma and Chance step inside, she and Jayne are back in the middle of a conversation that seems to have carried on for years. Jayne has risen from the table where she and Ed have been going over accounts near an ancient potbelly woodstove. He is broad and well mustached, while she is small and neat, with hair in a tight perm and reading glasses on a chain. They welcome Alma with hugs and exclamations.

Maddie is looking wonderful, far younger than her years, they insist, and Brittany is growing well, but Alma is too thin, looks tired, needs pie. Jayne moves more slowly than Alma remembers, favoring the hip she broke years ago barrel racing, but she bustles quickly enough as she puts on a kettle and starts extracting cookies from jars. She offers her guests chairs and covers the near end of the table with food in a few minutes. Alma recalls being a teenager in this house, the extravagant welcome, like the warm, cozy pot where the lobster luxuriates before the water starts to boil. They wanted her comfortable, at home, so that she'd settle in and stay.

While Jayne and Maddie keep up a rapid exchange, Chance turns Alma toward the coat closet. She glances at his hands as the gloves come off. No ring.

"I don't know what to say about Vicky," he offers with a headshake. "I'm sorry. Word travels fast. Mom's trying not to say anything that will upset you, and she's had a speech waiting for you for years. She's liable to strain something."

Alma looks over to where Jayne is oversugaring Maddie's coffee while tracking Chance and Alma in her peripheral vision. "I guess this was never going to be anything but awkward," she says. "I had to come home. The police called early yesterday about Vicky. How did you know?"

Chance jerks his head toward his father. "Cowboy telegraph. Dad has coffee with the boys in town every morning."

"Ah. Has Vicky been out here lately?"

"Not much. Jesus." Chance reaches up to rub his face with his hand. "She hasn't looked good the last few times I've seen her. I wish—" Chance silences his wish. Alma knows why. There is too much to wish for and nothing to be done.

Quiet settles, then Chance says, "When's the funeral?"

"Wednesday, one P.M., at First Church in Billings."

"You mind if the folks and I come? I know Mom and Dad

will want to pay respects. She and Brittany stayed at your place up the road for a while, you know."

"No. No, I don't mind, I mean. You should come. Everyone remembers you too." The Murphys are old family friends, and how could the Terrebonnes not remember Chance? He was the love of her life senior year, starting the summer before. During so many summers, weekends, and holidays, Alma, Pete, and Vicky were out at the home place, wandering the land with neighbor kids like wild things. That last warm season of peace before her parents died, Chance got up the nerve to ask her to a June street dance in Hardin. After that their paths were like waters come together. They rode across the vast grazing lands, along cool creek bottoms, and onto buttes that lifted them up like demigods above the magnificence of a high plains universe. They groomed their horses outside the big Terrebonne barn, set the gleaming animals loose in the corral, made out behind sage-scented hay bales, then went inside for Maddie's mint-flavored iced tea. It was the sort of paradise that people move through unconsciously before they understand that what you love can whiffle away like a dandelion bloom, beyond your reach in the length of a breath.

Chance was moving into Billings to live with cousins that fall to take Advanced Placement classes. His parents wanted him to have opportunities he wouldn't have in a small town. Even now, Alma notes, Jayne watches her son across the kitchen, concern moving over her face like a weather pattern at seeing him with Alma again. She saw the aftermath of their breakup—Alma never did.

With his move to town, what would've been a short summer fling between them turned intense. When she shuts her eyes, Alma sees Chance's face in every memory of that year—flashing glimpses of his hand loose and confident on the reins of some green horse, the back of his head in calculus, his flannel shirt under her cheek at some sweaty school dance, the shortness of breath she felt around him.

The accident threw everything off. It sped up and then annihilated their relationship. The weekend after her parents' funeral, on an unseasonably bitter March night, Alma found herself out at the home place with the whole family in a sort of survivalist retreat, cooking and eating and watching television in silence, huddled together because nobody knew what else to do. Then Chance came by, and after the enthrallment of the summer and the excitement of the fall—homecoming, horse shows where he rode up smelling of horse and sweat and leaned over to kiss her in front of everyone, cold evenings in the warmth of his pickup where she girlishly pushed away his hands—her desire for him now was almost as strong as her desire to get the hell out of Montana. She didn't tell herself that she loved him—she felt she had no more heart to give—but she needed the aliveness of him like she needed oxygen.

As she looks at him now, that's the moment her mind homes in on, mercilessly, them in his pickup out by the cemetery that night, Alma craving his touch as the only possible balm to her wound. Before, she'd been so skittish, so virginal, but that night she was demanding. He took some convincing under the circumstances, but he was male. He loved her. He caved. It felt as if they were deciding something permanent that night, but even after that, Alma's desire to get out, leave Montana behind her, was an urgent biological need, stronger than her hunger for Chance or the tie to the home place.

When Alma awakes from her reverie, Chance is looking at her like she's a manuscript in some dead language that he must decipher. Jayne calls over that coffee is ready. Alma pushes her hair back from her face and tries to shake off all this unwelcome emotion. To orient herself, she thinks of Seattle, the quiet calm of her office, and Jean-Marc. The reason she agreed to date him in the first place was that out of the blue during a colleague's networking cocktail party, he started to tell her about his family back in Québec. A farm family, with goats and big dogs, he said. The picture of Jean-Marc, the smooth investment banker, at the heart of such a family, warmed her. She began to be able to picture him, alone among his board-stiff peers, as possibly able to survive without an Armani suit on his back. Now she is startled to realize that the farm home she'd pictured for Jean-Marc is actually the Murphys' house. She's been remembering and longing for all this without realizing it. How extraordinary, she reflects, that she fooled herself that way.

As their elders continue a long and caloric coffee that's expanding into late lunch, spreading out photos from a trip Jayne and Ed took to Alaska a few years earlier, Chance rises. "I need to check on a few things, if you'd like to see the place," he offers to Alma.

Alma looks up the table at the expectant faces. "Sure," she agrees with false energy. There's too much to remember, too many unwelcome surprises from her unconscious mind. She must get away from here before her control slips and she starts telling Chance secrets he must never, ever know. Brittany makes no move to follow them back into the cold, so Alma leaves her.

Chance, as always, sets off to display his land and animals with a quick step and a voice like a kid reading his Christmas list. He shows her his quarter horses—he always did treat them like his children, spoiled them really—and a few pregnant heifers he's keeping a close eye on in the barn, Jayne's chickens, a few greenhouse experiments he has going in darkest January, how he's taken his prefab house off-grid with solar and a geothermal heat pump. He asks her legal advice about conservation easements, something she knows nothing about, and wonders about her work in Seattle. He's proving something to her, she realizes. He's fine, he's moved on, she didn't break him. As they walk back from Chance's house toward Jayne and Ed's, he clears his throat.

"You know how I used to mess around with engines?"

"I remember," Alma says. It was the best way to get him talking, while he was buried to the torso in the engine compartment of his pickup, his face hidden and his hands occupied.

"I got a little more serious out in California, in college, and after."

"California? I thought you went to MSU." Alma is cold in the wind, shifting from one foot to the other.

"I transferred to Stanford sophomore year. Played football. I'm surprised you never heard." Chance stands a little straighter when he mentions Stanford.

Alma shakes her head but keeps her eyes on him. She's avoided hearing anything about Chance. She has too much to keep from him to risk knowing him again.

"Anyway, I kept at the tinkering. Even make some money at it these days, but it's mostly for fun. I have a workshop in the old barn, if you want to see." He throws all this at her fast, with a casual gesture toward the shed, already turning his shoulders toward the house. His casualness betrays him. This is important.

"Sure, I'd love to see." Against her better judgment Alma wants to keep talking to Chance, so she prepares herself to say something encouraging about a few bizarre Rube Goldberg contraptions. The Chance she knew back then wasn't an inventor. He took machines apart and put them back together the way a child plays with blocks, moving the parts through his fingers without looking, learning them, testing their secrets as he carried on a spirited debate about whether or not *Hoosiers* was the greatest movie ever.

When he rolls back the heavy door to the old wooden barn, a long row of skylights illuminates a sea of projects piled on every surface and hanging on racks and hooks from the ceiling. Robots, model helicopters in forms she's never seen full-size, several types of antiquated farm machinery merged Frankenstein-like with photovoltaic panels—is that a traction engine? Is that a still? Alma turns in a circle, trying to take in everything at once.

"What the *hell*?" She starts to laugh. "Have you gone survivalist?"

Chance chuckles and folds his arms. "Let me give you the tour." He motions with one hand and starts to walk her around, starting up the repurposed water heater that is his biodiesel refinery, showing her how to use the remote to the hexacopter, drawing a quick schematic for the photovoltaics integrated into an old pump head for watering cattle remotely in cold weather. Alma can't stop asking questions, picking up parts—answering Chance's questions without reflection, until she realizes that he has her talking about Vicky. Did he do it on purpose, or is it the only thing she can talk about?

"I'll tell you one thing I've been thinking about the last few days," Alma tells him as she climbs up to the high, wide steel seat of the traction engine and situates herself with a view of the whole operation, Chance below her, one foot resting on the great heavy wheel, watching her, she knows without looking. "She was always a daredevil. When we were little, Vicky was the first one to go off the high board or jump the horses over something too high. She'd be screaming at me over her shoulder to follow her and I didn't know whether to save myself or try to stay with her. I could barely keep her in sight and I'd be shrieking at her to slow down, but she'd just go faster."

"I remember her running the horses. She loved speed. Though you liked it pretty well yourself, as I recall." Chance turns his back and leans against the big wheel. "When you three used to stay out here I remember thinking Vicky was the definition of cocksure. I'd never met another girl like her. Boys, yes, but not girls. Things were either going to turn out very well or very badly for her." His face is hidden, but Alma hears Chance's little sigh, as if he's back there for a moment with young Alma, little Vicky, all of them happy and whole. "But you only really

see patterns looking back, after you've lived them. All I knew
was what I saw—you and Vicky were a lot alike, but it was like
you and I had known each other forever, and there was so much
I never understood about her. She was all instinct, and eventually instinct isn't enough."

Alma feels too high suddenly on the big tractor and slides
down to lean against the solidity of its huge barrel. "I remember
wishing I could be more daring, more of a smartass, like she
was. She lit the place up. And I wished I had her hair." Alma
laughs, then swallows quickly.

"You had the luck," he says.

Alma pauses and looks deliberately at Chance. There's so
much he doesn't know, and still, he's right. She moves to sit
cross-legged on the dusty floor. Chance joins her. They sit side
by side, leaning up against the incredible bulk of the tractor's
rear wheel, its immutable mass. Alma looks around the barn for
a few minutes before she can begin again.

"That summer, when she was learning to walk on the prosthetic, I prayed that it be me instead. I prayed so hard—God,
take my leg and give Vicky's back, or give me crooked teeth,
or pimples, or mean girls at school, whatever she was going
to suffer. Whatever it was, I knew I could take it, and I knew
it would destroy her. *I knew.*" Alma takes a long, shuddering
breath. "There was a night that summer when she went so high
on the swings that the chain disconnected and she took this
awful fall. I thought she must have broken something. I ran
over, ready to carry her home. But she was just lying there on
the grass, looking at the stars. I was so upset, and she just said
to me, 'Oh Alma, don't you get it? Nothing can hurt me now.'
After that, it was like she believed it."

Alma shuts her eyes and sees, for just a moment, her
own body lying on the gurney, zipped into the shroud. Hers
is the unlikely life. The honors, the ambition, the fire for
independence—none of that makes any sense in the context of

her down-home upbringing. And Vicky's life—the starfall of it, the rush of beauty and sudden darkness—that is what belongs here. She hears Chance's voice now, far away, a round tenor that makes the air vibrate and brings her back.

"When I won the scholarship to Stanford, Mom told the reporter who called, 'Things like this don't happen to people in our family,' and that's what he printed. You know my mom— she always worked like hell to give us kids every opportunity, but she didn't quite believe she could change anything for us. She and Dad never got to college. There was just too much work back on the ranches. It's easier to believe Vicky's story than yours or mine." Chance studies his hands. Just as he used to, he's spoken her thoughts.

"You know Mrs. Jordan at Senior High told me outright that I probably wouldn't make it at Bryn Mawr and I should try a few years at Eastern or Bozeman?"

"That old hack? I'm glad you didn't listen to her."

"Yeah. Then a few years ago, my therapist told me I should cut off communication with my family, to give myself space to develop an 'independent ego.'"

"What's that supposed to mean?"

"I don't know. I stopped seeing her after that." Alma pauses, then adds, "It's always death that changes things in my family, isn't it? That's what it takes to get through to us. I'd like to tell death it can't have any more of us. It's too much." This time, she takes herself deliberately to the accident fifteen years ago: the black ice on I-90, the terrifying trip across the median, the semi, the explosion of light, sound, and pressure, and the sudden silence, sitting stunned in the backseat and realizing there was no front seat anymore, wandering concussed and disoriented down the ditch, trying to remember where she was. That sequence of events was missing entirely for months after the accident, and she can still repress it successfully for long periods of time. When it returns, it's involuntary and traumatic. The images come unwanted, disabling her power of speech, leaving her staggering like the first, fatal impact. To draw it up as an act of will is new to her. She has never believed that she can control this memory.

Chance's eyes are on her as all this passes across her face. "I remember the day," he says. "It was a little before St. Patrick's Day."

"Yes." Alma is up in the rafters somewhere, looking down at herself next to Chance. "I've never gotten over the feeling that everyone blamed me but wouldn't say so."

"Nobody blamed you, Al." Chance's voice reverberates.

Alma can't halt the words that have to come. "I could see it in their eyes at the funeral. They blamed me for walking away while Mom and Dad lay there dying, Vicky mutilated. Not a single person ever asked me what happened, and the story was all over town. Even you never asked me. All of you figured I just walked away instead of trying to help them. And then I kept on walking." There. The words are out. What a relief to have said them.

Chance gives his head a rueful little shake, as if he's heard this sort of grim alienation out of her before. "Do you think people might not have asked just so you wouldn't have to talk about it?"

"Some people, sure. But there were others, I knew what they were thinking. People are afraid that grief and death are contagious, and they wanted me to be something I couldn't be. They blamed me even more for going ahead and leaving for college. I went and violated the greatest and oldest taboo around here—I struck out for myself."

"You think you were responsible for taking over for your parents, at the age of seventeen? What about Pete? He must have been, what, twenty? What about the rest of the family?" Chance objects. His words anchor Alma back on the ground. Yes, this is exactly what she thinks. Nobody else was fit to do it.

"Chance, you know as well as I do that Pete was such a drunk back then it was a miracle he got out of the Marines with an honorable discharge. Walt's been a wreck as long as I've known him. And you knew my parents. They had their flaws, for sure, but the only proof I need that the family couldn't get by without them is probably on an autopsy table having her brain weighed as we speak." The words come out guttural like they're dipped in something dark and oily, offered up as cold and ugly as anything that lurks in Alma. She is sorry to say them but glad to have them outside her, away.

Chance shifts and looks sideways at Alma as if he isn't sure he should say what he wants to say. "But your parents didn't really hold everything together, did they?" he says at last.

Alma can't hold back an angry glare, even after all these years. "It was all a big mistake, what happened with the business. They would have worked it out." This belief is part of the architecture, the mental construct she maintains of home and history. She leans forward to pick up a small, serrated spruce cone that has found its way inside, a prickly thing, imperfect but as omnipresent as the sky. "Anyway, they didn't and here we are. And the way it works is if I don't take care of things, then I'm the one who cleans up afterward. That's what I'm doing now."

"So you're dealing with it by not dealing with it." Chance has an ironic half smile. "Same old Alma."

Alma jumps up. This is the conversation every boyfriend for the last decade has wanted to have. She gives Chance her profile. "Maybe so. Pete used to tell me that when things go wrong I handle them by pushing them into a little black box with everything else I don't want to look at, tighter and tighter, and one day it's going to explode." She pockets the spruce cone with a dry little laugh.

"Pull your hat down tight and just LeDoux it?" Chance looks up at her.

Alma's laugh expands to take her whole body with it. She tosses the spruce cone at him. "Good one, cowboy."

Chance's face opens into a full smile for the first time. "You carrying all the guilt doesn't do them any good," he tells her as he stands.

"Maybe I deserve it," Alma says. She hesitates, not sure if she wants to make this personal, then decides what the hell. "I'm sure you've wanted to punish me now and then."

"Maybe." Chance shrugs. "Just a little. Or maybe I pushed you too hard and got what I deserved." He straightens to his full height and pulls the cap back on. Alma glances up to take the measure of the adult Chance, all broad shoulders and eyes that take in everything, then she thinks better of it and returns her gaze to the flying machines.

"I owe you a huge apology," she says, with what little voice she can summon.

"Water under the bridge." He clears his throat and shuffles in the dust.

"All this." She gestures, lifting their eyes, lightening things. "You have a gift."

He bows his head, almost bashful. "I'm glad you think so."

"What are you working on now?"

His head comes up. "You won't believe it, but I've been restoring that old Chevy pickup to its original glory."

"I wouldn't believe that the Murphrod had glory days," Alma says. Chance's old pickup, the Murphrod she called it, to tease him—the scene of way too many high school memories. "It was trashed twenty years ago."

"I'll show you next time you're over. It's in the machine shed."

"Next time? Isn't there a Mrs. Chance around here some-where who's going to mind an old girlfriend hanging around?" Whatever Hank Olson and Chance's bare ring finger might say, surely there's a woman.

"There was. Not anymore. Just me and Mae." Chance scoops up a couple of screwdrivers left out on a workbench and shoves them back into their brackets on the wall with a little more force than necessary.

"Mae?" Alma inquires.

"My daughter." He stalks to the door and holds it open for her. This conversation is over. Chance's stride is long and he doesn't pull it in for her. Alma increases her pace and stretches out her legs to match him. This is where she learned to stalk Seattle's broad sidewalks at a speed that makes her male associates break into a jog.

At the house, Alma opens the storm door and they stand facing each other in the blinding afternoon sun. She has half a dozen questions about Mae—*How old is she? Where is she? Does she look like you?*—but she can't force out even one.

"You want to come out tomorrow morning and ride? I'll bring Mae, you can bring Brittany. I want to show you something." He jerks a thumb toward the corral. The look on his face is reluctant, but he won't change course. She sees his conflict. Part of him must want to order her off his land, and part of him is still the soul that knew hers the day they met, small children saving nightcrawlers from the road in a warm summer rain. He thinks she'll beg off, so that their rift can remain her fault. This is a dare, the sort of thing they used to do as kids. *Race you to the creek!* He's trying not to make eye contact, but she catches his gaze and holds it. She won't give him the satisfaction of seeing her back down.

"Sure," she says, like it's no big deal. "First thing tomorrow morning. I've got to spend some time at the home place or Grandma will have a panic attack."

CHAPTER 10

As soon as her cell phone starts to pick up a signal again, nearing the interstate, Alma finds a message from Ray Curtis, along with several from Amanda and one from her supervising partner, Louis McBride. The sun is nearly gone. Alma feels fatigue in her stiff neck, her hips and back conforming unnaturally to the driver's seat. To be eligible for a bonus at her firm, she must bill an annual minimum of 1,950 hours. This sort of late-afternoon malaise is entirely familiar. She could work another six hours, easily. She calls Ray first.

"I've been trying to talk to Walt, but your aunt says he's gone out to a cabin past Nye. Have you heard anything from him?"

"Not since I saw him last night," Alma admits. "He wasn't very friendly."

"Not friendly how?"

Alma is very aware of Maddie and Brittany's presence. Almost nothing Walt said is repeatable in front of them. "Could I call you back later?"

"Sure. Or come by City Hall. I'll be here until late. Just call my cell and I'll let you in. We got the autopsy results back. I'd like to talk them over with you."

"Sure," Alma agrees. "I'd appreciate that."

Back in Seattle, Louis is furious at the mere sound of Alma's voice.

"What are you doing out there at a time like this? This deal is closing by the end of the week and I need you here. Duncan's turning himself inside out to cover everything on the closing checklist."

"Louis, I know it's terrible timing, but it's a family crisis. My little sister just died. I have to be here. I'll do as much as I can remotely and I'll be back in Seattle by the weekend."

"Look, I won't drag you into my personal problems if you don't drag me into yours, how about that? If you need some leave time go ahead and take it," Louis snaps, "but if you're still handling this deal, then I need to see your face the minute you get in from the airport. Otherwise I'll have to pass it off to Duncan, and there will be consequences."

Duncan Moi is an associate three years Alma's junior who drives a Porsche Carrera or a BMW motorcycle, depending on the weather; has dated half the paralegals in the firm and a few of the clients; and happens to be the nephew of one of the name partners. He's been looking for a chance like this to move in on Alma's practice, and Louis has been looking for a chance to help him. Bolstering Duncan's career would have the double benefit of endearing Louis to the managing committee and undermin- ing Alma, who intimidates him. Louis, a proud University of Washington law grad, falls bitter whenever any graduate of an East Coast law school succeeds in the local market. The fact that Alma is neither a UW grad nor a Washington native is a perennial topic of sarcastic conversation around Louis. He talks over her, edges her away from the head of the conference table, makes re- marks about her hair or clothes instead of responding to what she's saying, and likes to invite her clients on men-only golf outings.

In what she hopes are diplomatic, conciliatory terms, Alma has spoken to Louis about his behavior, but he's a lateral hire who brought a significant book of business with him and feels no need to get along with her. She doesn't dare seek help from a partner—it would be perceived as weakness. Her choices are unattractive. Either she can make a major issue of the situation and diminish herself in the eyes of the firm, or she can switch practice areas or perhaps even firms to distance herself from Louis. Running from a bully does not appeal, but Alma has begun talking discreetly to headhunters while scouting for ways to bring down Louis or Duncan—or both.

Making the most of her functioning cell phone, Alma calls ahead to the funeral home. Hills' on Central has been burying her family's dead for as long as anyone could say. Maddie has already set the funeral date and time with old Jack Hill, but he wants them to come in and decide on details. Yes, he says, now is a great time. When Pete picks up the phone on the eighth ring, he makes work-related excuses.

"Just let me know what my share is," he tells Alma.

Jack welcomes the three of them at the front door and offers to take their coats, but Alma declines and leaves hers buttoned to her chin. The place holds a chill for her that no form of mechanical warmth can dispel.

"I don't tend to see people in the best circumstances," Jack says, "but it always is good to see them. You're just the picture of your mother, Alma."

"That's what everyone says." But there's something creepy about it, Alma thinks, coming from the man who embalmed her mother and prepared her body for viewing.

"It was a beautiful service," he continues, as if he's read her mind. "So many people. So many friends." He offers Maddie his arm.

"Yes, I remember," Maddie agrees, stepping up to walk

beside Jack while Alma and Brittany follow, staying close to each other. Jack turns to talk to Alma as they move down the hall.

"You were back for Al's service a few years back. I saw you then."

"Five years ago. It doesn't seem that long." Alma takes in the innocuous Pottery Barn landscapes on the walls and waits for the chitchat to die. Jack Hill's life is measured in the pauses between one funeral and the next, like an alternative calendar. Solar, lunar, dead people. Why not? To her it feels like half a lifetime since Grandpa Al's funeral, but to Jack it's the last landmark they passed together.

"You still working for that same firm in Seattle? Corporate law, wasn't it?"

"That's right, same firm. I'll be up for partner soon." Her voice holds the correct animated tone for talking about her brilliant career, but her face can't maintain the show. She sees reflected in Jack's expression how stricken she must look. He reaches back and pats Brittany's arm, closer to him, as a proxy for hers.

"And that young man who was with you, name of Severson, wasn't it? Did he come this time?" Hill looks around as if Greg Severson might appear behind Alma, carrying a few small children. Greg was the last in a succession of men who became unsatisfied with Alma's evasions about her family and inability to say "I love you." The words—the genuine emotion itself—came so naturally to him, and filled Alma with a sense of claustrophobia so intense that she nearly hyperventilated when his mother asked if it was serious.

"We're just not compatible," she told Greg. "It's convenient, but it's not right."

"You might not accept it from me," he told her before he left, "but you've got to get help from somewhere. It's not healthy to keep so much locked up." Alma can still hear the echo of the door she slammed on him.

Now Alma turns her attention back to Jack with a forced smile. "Wow, I'm surprised you remember that. No, we broke up. He got a job in Singapore."

"Anybody new then?"

"Yeah. His name is Jean-Marc, but he's back in Seattle."

Only a day after touching down, Alma already has that Billings feeling, like no matter how far she goes, this town will always know her business. As high and mighty as she might get, here they will always remember her braces, her unfortunate junior high mullet, her air guitar band, or the church ski trip where she got busted for drinking wine coolers and skiing the double black diamond summit bowl at Big Sky, both of which were strictly off limits. The anonymity of a big city can be a blessed relief.

"It's funny, I saw Vicky just a few weeks ago," Jack is saying as he leads the way to his office, and Alma's mind wanders. "That Holiday station up on Grand. She was fighting with somebody. Long-haired guy."

Alma clicks back to attention. "Do you remember what they were fighting about?"

"Well . . ." Jack hesitates, then nods and lifts a finger as the memory returns. "That's right. I thought they were maybe housemates. They were arguing over a house. She wanted him out and he was angry. Told her she'd be sorry. That's not— important, is it?"

Alma's memory of the office they're in suddenly looms around her. This is where someone led her when she started crying hysterically at her parents' funeral. Was it Chance? She can't remember. "I— I don't know. Probably not."

"I'm sorry." Jack looks horrified. "If I'd thought it meant anything at all, I would have called the police."

"It's okay, I'll tell them. Don't worry about it."

Jack pauses long enough to bring out a florist's brochure.

The next question is already on his lips. "You must be enjoying Seattle," Jack continues. "Got a nice place, view of the Space Needle?" he says with a gentle chuckle. Ah yes, the financial evaluation.

"I rent a little room from an old lady with a lot of cats." Alma tilts her head at Jack with childlike sweetness. "It's all I need." Maddie casts her a severe look but says nothing.

At Al's funeral, Alma ran into a high school classmate who had acquired the chipper married name of Kirsten Kitchen and couldn't wait to tell Alma about her real estate developer husband (who owns Maddie's "mobile home lifestyle park"), their five-thousand-square-foot ski cabin, her exhausting home decorating project, her three stairstep children (with a conspiratorial "and another on the way!" as she patted a flat belly), and her many "prestigious" (yes, she used that word) volunteer obligations. Alma had liked Kirsten reasonably well in high school, didn't really have anything against her, but as the ladies-who-lunch résumé multiplied, she began to have the evil urge to come up with something that would truly, deeply shock her. When Kirsten paused to take a breath while describing her family's recent Disney World vacation, Alma leaned back and sipped her coffee out of the church's thick ceramic cups. "I donated all my eggs," she said with a shrug. "Let someone else raise the little buggers." The look on Kirsten's face was worth it. Alma finds herself half hoping that Kirsten will show up at Vicky's funeral. She has a few more whoppers ready to go. High school–style competitiveness brings out the worst in her.

After she consents to Maddie's modest flower choice, Alma must walk through a room full of caskets and come up with the name of a preacher.

"It has to be Leslie Kemp," Maddie declares. "She'll remember Vicky, and she's head pastor now, you know. You just get the cheapest of everything, Alma. I know all this stuff costs a fortune and nobody knows the difference once you're underground." This is typical Maddie advice and she means it, but even Alma can't bring herself to go for the cheapest coffin, which looks like flocked cardboard and would probably disintegrate in a hard rain. She upgrades slightly to a more elegant varnished pine with brushed nickel hardware.

Back in his office, Jack pulls out a map of the cemetery and points to the family plot to ask where in it they would like Vicky buried. The names are all there, Alma's parents among them. She has no memory of making these choices for her own parents. Al and Maddie must have done it, in this same room. Alma glances over her shoulder at Maddie, who sits attentively on the edge of her chair with a look of painfully forced interest. Brittany is hunched over, staring at her stained off-brand sneakers. Alma can't imagine which grave Vicky would want to be near—she never got along with any of them. Even their parents were sparring with her the winter they died, over Vicky's nascent interest in makeup, boys, and high school parties—a stage Alma skipped the way she skipped second grade. Maddie folds her hands over her mouth and sits back in her chair, as if this decision more than any other is too much.

"On the edge." Alma points. "She liked it there."

For the stone, they consider the first lines of Psalm 121, "I will lift up mine eyes unto the hills, from whence cometh my help." The psalm is Vicky, all right, stuck in these hills, longing impotently to get out, destined to lie forever in Mountain View cemetery and dream the same girlish dreams of escape and rescue. But when Jack explains that you pay for every letter and calculates the cost, it seems absurd for a single verse whacked into stone. Alma decides on the family name in big letters and Vicky's full name, Victoria Rose, beneath it with birth and death dates. Simple, dignified, cheaper.

After Alma has handed over the credit card, Jack walks them to the car. He's gracious in all these things, the little humiliations and difficulties that must be smoothed over with each untimely passing, yet he hesitates and stares at the ground, shaking his head, before he finds the words to farewell them. "It's too much for one family," he says at last. "I never thought I'd be here to bury another one of you kids. You just take care of yourself, Alma. I'll make sure everything turns out right at the funeral." With old-fashioned gallantry he helps Maddie into the car—assistance he probably requires more than she does—and stands at attention, waving a final salute as they pull away.

Alma drops off Maddie before the second trip to the police station. Brittany dozes in the backseat. She opens her eyes to ask, "Are we going home now?"

"One more stop, babe," Alma promises. Parked across the street from City Hall, before calling Ray, she lets the car idle through a series of awkward phone calls to administrative staff at her client's anticipated merger partner. *Anything unusual happen lately? Any new paperwork coming through?* With the rumors of layoffs, they can't wait to spill their suspicions. Alma scribbles page after page, flipping through her legal pad with one hand, taking improvised shorthand. Nobody wants to be recorded or quoted—but boy do they want her to know what crooks their bosses are, how little is left in what should be a fully funded pension fund. It's terrible news, it will sink the deal . . . and with it Duncan, who will never bother to consult the peons except to ask if they're single. In spite of herself, Alma is smiling as she leans into the backseat to give Brittany a gentle shake.

Ray meets them at the front door and takes Brittany back to the conference room with the television. Brittany ignores the remote and heads straight to the small couch against the back wall to curl up. Alma takes off her own coat and spreads it over Brittany before following Ray to the break room.

"How's she doing?" he asks.

"A little better, I think," Alma says. "She started talking again, out at the home place."

Ray nods. "That's a good place for her. And you?"

Alma has only the hint of a smile to reassure him. "I'll manage," she says. Ray himself is showing a few small signs of strain, she notices. His face is shiny and there's a faint coffee stain low on his pressed shirt. He pours coffee for both of them, and they walk to his office without preliminaries. He gestures her into the chair opposite him. Alma sits.

Ray drums the fingers of one hand and pushes aside his coffee before clearing his throat. "Well, provisionally it looks like exposure, but that's just preliminary until the tox screens come back. She took a hard fall on the ice, for sure, but that may just have been an accident, and it didn't kill her. She stopped breathing, and she had a few fibers from some kind of wool garment in her nose and mouth, even down into her bronchial passages, like she'd breathed them in hard, but no wool scarf or anything on her or back at the house, and no sign of the blood from her nose on her sweater. The coroner says there's not enough evidence of suffocation to make it the official cause of death, but he thought it was important enough to mention."

Alma focuses every functioning synapse on not spilling her coffee. *Exposure, unless it was drugs or suffocation? What kind of bullshit homicide investigation is this?*

Ray continues without looking at her. "That's not to say that she might not have died of exposure anyway. It's hard to say whether she would have been capable of getting up after the fall in her condition, but there was nothing about the fall itself that should have been fatal. And then all evidence indicates that she laid there until someone found her in the morning. No sign that she was moved."

"Okay." Alma manages to settle the coffee mug on the narrow right arm of her chair, held loosely by one hand. "So now you're looking for something made of wool with Vicky's blood on it, right? You're searching?"

"Yes. We will follow through on all avenues of investigation. That's still the official position. There's a possibility that it was just a terrible accident, but personally, it doesn't sit well with me. She was young and healthy. There was no physical reason she should've just laid there and died, and no good explanation for the wool fibers. The department's not going to want to put much more into this unless something more turns up, but I have some latitude to investigate further."

Alma plants her feet on the ground and her left hand on the chair arm with the firm intention of standing, but standing is somehow harder than expected.

"I'm sorry. I'm very sorry," Ray repeats. "Would you like me to call somebody, give you some time alone, anything—"

"I'm fine," Alma cuts him off. "Brittany and I need to get going. It's a long drive home."

Ray rises as if to see her back to the front doors, then drops back into his chair. "There's something I forgot. Before you go, there's something else the autopsy turned up."

"What's that?" Alma is glad she took off her coat. The office is too warm. The high collar of her sweater is strangling her.

"Your sister was fourteen weeks pregnant." Ray's knuckles press against the desk. Alma feels her own fingers curl around the chair arm, tighter and tighter.

"I see." She longs for this conversation to be a phone call, on a heavy old phone, where she could now set down the receiver, not hard, just rest it in the cradle, a subtle click. It's all she can do to keep sitting, eyes ahead, breathing in and out. Everything that's normally automatic has become an extra burden on her decompiling brain. What is she supposed to do with this unwelcome information?

Her mind seeks practicalities. The details of the death will come out in the paper—she hasn't looked, they're probably there already—but surely not the pregnancy. Does anyone know? Does she tell anyone? Does she keep the secret locked up in her soul like the proverbial worm in the apple? That would be the family way all right: keep it hidden, let the time bomb tick. Alma feels as if Ray has pulled the pin on a live grenade and handed it to her. She is holding it now, its malevolence like searing heat in her chest. Either she throws it away and hurts other people, or she clutches it to herself and takes all the shrapnel when it goes off.

Ray takes the teetering coffee mug out of her right hand. She never saw him move, but there he is.

"Thanks," she acknowledges. Then, in a monotone, she delivers the information she's gathered since this morning's interview: Rick Burlington's visit, what Brittany said about him, the encounter Jack Hill described between Vicky and Murray. Ray is back in his chair, taking notes, asking questions until she's told everything she can remember.

"This is all very helpful," he praises her when she's done. "Please don't talk to anyone about anything we've discussed here. We're still interviewing persons of interest, and it's easier for us to start with a blank slate. We'll have the ME run a fetal paternity test in case we need to compare suspects' DNA later. And please keep in touch if you hear anything more I ought to know. I may need to talk to you again."

Alma nods with the barest movement of her chin as she stands.

Ray tilts his head toward her. "I really am sorry, Alma. If there's anything I can do, maybe somebody I can call to come take you home—I know this is all a terrible shock."

"You're very kind." Alma's face contracts in a flinch she hadn't intended to show him. "I'll just go sit with Brittany for a minute before I go, if that's okay."

"Sure. I'll make sure you have some privacy." Ray tucks her hand into the crook of his arm, just as he did with Maddie, to walk her to the conference room.

CHAPTER 11

It doesn't matter how early the next morning comes. Alma hasn't slept. Chance is in the horse barn polishing a saddle when she spots him, after leaving Brittany with Jayne to get bundled up properly. As she waves at him, something fluttering beyond the barn catches her eye. She walks around to the back of the barn, facing the crenellated butte. This entire back wall, hidden from the farmyard and the road, is an elongated fishbowl view of Eighteenth and Castro in San Francisco, looking toward the Castro Theatre as if through a peephole. A rainbow flag waves in the foreground and the street is filled with people. The flag is real, hung from the barn on a long loop of rebar. Smaller flags populate the ground in front of the mural, dancing out of the painted scene to dissipate onto Montana prairie, getting smaller, randomly appearing to the fence line and beyond. They're faded and tattered now. Soon they'll be gone.

"Damn," Alma mutters. She backs up to take in the whole of the mural: the scope, the detail, the movement, the difficult perspective made convincing. "This is amazing." Morning light illuminates the colors, inhabits them. Alma can see the delicacy of the brushstrokes, the fine shading and textures. She moves forward to put her fingers on the rough surface.

"Beautiful," she whispers. These old places can be mirages one day, oases the next, and always they hide secrets. Beyond her line of sight, quick, light footsteps run across the yard. Alma moves to see. Outside the horse barn is a small child in a red snowsuit. "Daddy!" she cries when Chance steps to the door.

Chance lifts her to his chest with one arm. "Good morning, sunshine. Did Grandma give you breakfast already?"

Mae nods and twists her head around to look at Alma walking toward them.

"Is this your friend, Daddy?"

Chance's eyes follow Mae's and Alma wonders how he'll respond.

"This is my old friend Alma," he tells Mae. "Say hello, sweetheart." He sets Mae down and she marches up to Alma. Her skin glows café au lait and dark curls escape from her knit cap. She is breathtakingly like Chance.

"Hi. My name is Mae. I'm three." She holds up fingers but her mittens conceal them.

Alma squats to eye level with the little girl. "Hello, Mae. Are you coming riding with us?"

The girl opens a big, baby-tooth smile and nods. "I'm gonna ride with Daddy," she says, looking back at him with adoration.

"I'd better take her back across before she gets into the corral." Chance gathers up Mae from behind and heads across the snowy yard, starting to jog a little as he gets closer to the house. Alma stands in the aperture of the barn door, watching. She's able to turn away only when the door of the ranch house slams behind him.

When Chance returns she's working at Jayne's saddle, lengthening the stirrups. She's dying to ask about the mural, but something about him is so stiff, so distant, that she keeps quiet.

He starts setting out tack—blankets, bridles—and digging in bins for heavy clothes. He piles an old down coat, gloves, and scarf next to her. "What, you don't like the cashmere coat?" she teases.

"I don't want you to hurt my mother's horse when you freeze to death and fall off her," he answers in his most laconic tone.

"When did you turn into such a tough guy?" Alma asks, laughing.

"When did you cut your hair?" Chance counters.

She thinks for a minute. "Sophomore year. I started rowing, and it was always in the way. It's grown some since then, but nothing like all that hair I used to have." Rowing was transformative in its elitism, an outlet for too much light and heat. She was unrecognizable in the long boats, wrapped in bright Lycra, unlocking silent flight with each click of the oars, a fleeting classical figure in early mists. The home demons would never find her there.

"Goes with the power suits, I bet," Chance says.

Alma isn't sure that this is a compliment. She stiffens and says, "Thank you."

There's a moment of silence, which Chance breaks. "So is the funeral still on for tomorrow?"

"Yes, as long as the coroner releases the body in time. They did an autopsy."

"And?"

Alma grips the latigo in both hands and wills herself to tell him. "Exposure is the preliminary finding, but they're still investigating. It was . . . suspicious."

"And?" he prompts, cocking his head to get a better look at her face, to read her like he always did. Alma looks away, unwilling.

Chance shrugs and whistles. "I can't get over how much things changed with her. I should have done something."

"You? Why would you be responsible? I'm the one who blew it."

"You think you should have given up your own life to stay here and babysit Vicky?"

"Isn't that what you think? You stayed. You're taking care of the family."

"I didn't stay. I came back." Chance moves away from her, picks up the tack, steps outside. She follows. "There's a difference, you know that. There are the ones who never leave, and the ones who leave for good, and the ones who choose to come back. I have an electrical engineering degree from Stanford, Alma. I understand the leavers better than I understand the stayers. But I'm needed here like I'll never be needed anywhere else. Sometimes I think it's duty and destiny and all that, and some days I think it's just my own brand of quiet desperation. But if I don't honor something that important, what kind of man am I?"

"More important than your wife?" It's a harsh thing to say, and Alma immediately wishes she could take it back. The ties of his home place, the deep roots, the land itself, are inexorable to a man like Chance. She can no more blame him for that than she can blame herself for putting her career in jeopardy to take the first flight to Montana when Curtis called. "I'm sorry, I didn't mean that. It's not like I've been holding up my end around here."

Chance doesn't look offended. He tilts his head away from the sun and the shadow of his brim falls on his face. "No, you're right. When it came down to it, I couldn't leave for her. I guess the hard truth is, this ranch and I are a package deal. She knew that when we got married. And I was too weak a man to do what it took to keep my family together." The last words are low and bitter as they step into the corral and the remuda ambles toward them.

"That's not weakness, Chance," Alma says in a voice meant

for the horses, soothing. "It's who you are. The Little m is who you are. I always knew that."

"Well, you did, but it's damn difficult to explain to an outsider."

A flicker of the old connection passes between them as they stand at their horses' heads, rubbing manes, slipping on halters with gentle fingers. Alma inhales warm, grassy horse breath and wonders if love doesn't die of time and distance, but of little daily slights and brutalities, the sort of thing that has never passed between her and Chance. What existed between them is preserved under glass. It would have to breathe and live again, here and now, between their adult selves, for her to know if it was ever real.

Chance's hands are steady and his voice is low as he brushes out the horses' heavy winter coats, cleans their hooves, lays blankets and saddles across their broad backs. He never stops speaking to the horses, answering their contented nickers. Alma knows men out here who never speak to another human except out of necessity but regularly carry on extended conversations with their horses. Yet here Chance is, talking to her about the past, about duty and pain, like few men she knows can. "How long do you stay?" he asks from the far side of Jayne's mare.

"My flight's midday Friday. There's a lot going on at the office. It sounds like I'll be well and truly aced out of the deal I'm working on by the time I get back."

Chance stops arranging tack and walks up to wrap the scarf more snugly around her neck, matter-of-factly, as if she were Mae and had forgotten to zip up her coat. "Somebody's doing that to you when your sister just died?"

Alma nods.

"Nice bunch of people," Chance remarks. He sets down a blanket to snap the outer closures on Alma's coat where she's missed them. She reaches to pull his earflaps down where they've slipped and exposed bare skin. They used to do this so naturally, these intimate gestures. It takes conscious effort to stop. Her hands pause in an awkward pose between them and she crosses her arms.

Alma stretches her left foot up to the stirrup Chance brings near her. She waits as he checks the girth on this unfamiliar old saddle. Chance speaks a few words to the horse and smiles up at Alma. "This is Lulabel, Mom's horse," he tells her. "She likes to run."

Alma grins and guides Lulabel a few feet away to give Chance room to open the gate, lead out his horse and another, and mount up. Chance is on a big sorrel quarter horse that dances sideways away from the gate and eyes Alma and Lulabel with open curiosity. "Oscar, meet Alma. Let's see if the girls are ready," Chance says, wheeling back toward the main house. Alma follows.

When the horses approach the house, Jayne emerges with the heavily bundled toddler, and Brittany in more of Jayne's cold-weather gear. "This will do them good. Everyone's been so cooped up," Jayne says, then spots the third horse and beams. "Oh, that's perfect. El Dorado is just right for Brittany." She locks eyes with Alma as she hands up Mae to Chance, then leads Brittany to El Dorado and links her fingers to help her step into the stirrup.

"El Dorado?" Alma raises an eyebrow at Chance. The horse he's leading couldn't be mistaken for golden.

"'Cause he steers like a Cadillac," Chance explains. "Takes him five minutes to turn around. Bombproof, though. Good for kids."

Mae settles in behind the saddle horn, holding it with both mittened hands.

"When is Mama gonna come?" Mae chirps. Chance's eyes meet Alma's over his daughter's head.

"We'll go see Mama in California in a few weeks, baby," Chance answers, settling Mae into the crook of his left arm as he draws the reins across Oscar's neck and nudges him forward.

As Jayne steps back inside and the horses begin to move, Alma prompts, "Tell me about her."

Chance looks over, examining Alma to see if she can be serious. She nods to encourage him. The thought of Chance with another woman has been with her for fifteen years, ghost pain from a lost limb. Better to hear this from him than from everyone else who will want to tell her.

"Okay." He leans over to unlatch the rear gate out of the yard. "Hilary is a painter from San Francisco. I met her while I was working in Silicon Valley after college. She does street murals and installation work, incredible stuff. I was blown away because she knew Banksy." Chance's eyes are on the clean line of light breaking across the buttes, but he glances over to see if Alma is following him. She nods.

"When did she do the mural?"

Chance turns back to take in the fading mural as Alma relatches the gate. "First month she was here. She'd come out and sit in front of it, for hours, in all weather. I knew then that she was going to leave me."

El Dorado and Brittany are walking out ahead of them, taking eagerly to the trail. Alma shakes her head and stares at Chance as they turn to follow. "I don't mean to pry, but how on earth did this person"—she gestures at the mural—"get here?"

Chance shrugs. "What can I say? I have a gift for falling for women who can't accept what I have to offer." He glances at Alma, then says, "But yeah, there were at least a few months where I didn't think we were making a huge mistake. I was a fine arts minor at Stanford—there's something else you didn't know. It was like a graduate seminar, hanging out with her. She introduced me to people, other artists—every color, but all out of the same rural experience, all trying to say something that can hardly be said in modern urban America. When we tell the truth about the present, everyone thinks we're talking about the past. Or they want to pretty it up into something out of the movies. They have no context for us."

"Nobody from outside ever has had any idea what I come from," Alma says, concentrating on how the zipper pull of Chance's jacket reflects the white sunlight, shimmering above Mae's head. "There's no way I could explain." It's never occurred to her that it's possible to communicate between those two worlds.

"That's just it. How can you show what our lives are without demeaning the struggle people go through every day to keep one of these old places together, keep food on the table? How do you show how hard it is—not romanticize it—without discounting the richness? Or are we just an anachronism, like the Amish? The most important thing to me was just to know that there are other people out there, thinking about rural art and culture along with agronomy and what the land will bear, reading guys like Wendell Berry and Wes Jackson. Those books saved my life the last few years." He turns his head to look straight at Alma, his eyes lit with the sort of excitement he used to reserve for a great saddle bronc. Alma leads Lulabel in step beside him, drawn in by this person she never knew, grafted onto someone so familiar. She opens her mouth to answer, but the words form slowly.

"What happened?" She can't stop listening now. She wants this pain, needs to feel it at last.

Chance has a very firm grip on Mae and the reins. "When Dad had the heart attack and I had to come back, she said she wanted to come too, try to puzzle it out for herself. It was supposed to be temporary. She came out here to paint and then all of a sudden she was pregnant. I got this crazy idea that we'd get married and raise the baby here, so we flew to Vegas." His smile is less amused than rueful. "Mom's still sore about that. Then after Mae came it was like Hilary never recovered. She could hardly get out of bed for months, couldn't work, hardly talked.

I understand about postpartum depression, but it was more than that. The isolation wore her down. Plus she was scared of the horses. She's a city girl to the bone, and all this is . . ." Chance gestures with his head toward his land.

"She had no idea what she was getting into," Alma says without emphasis. It's too obvious. City people come and go, fall in love with Montana like Steinbeck, then find the big sky oppressive, the reserved people and their closed-off culture too difficult, the winters too long, the great spaces perversely claustrophobic. They leave as precipitously as they came.

"You know what it's like," Chance says. "You work your tail off twelve months a year and live or die by three hours at the livestock auction in February. Normal people can't take it. Eventually she blamed me. So she went back to San Francisco, Mae splits her time between here and there, and life goes on. It's been a couple years now. We visit. It's a shame you won't get to meet her. You'd like her, when she's herself."

Alma hunches her shoulders. How little men understand about women. She needs to know about Hilary, but she'd like to meet her about as much as she'd like to put her tongue on the pump handle. It's her own job to break Chance's heart. Alma tries to conjure up a picture of a San Francisco installation artist living out here, miles from town, with right-wing talk radio on the only stations that come in and no cell phone coverage. She's grateful to Hilary for taking over the top spot on Jayne's list of people to push off a ledge, but that's it.

"How long does Mae stay with you?" she inquires, to distract Chance from the nervous energy of her own body—fingers twitching, toes wiggling in her stirrups. This will have to be a short ride, she thinks as the cold grows sharper.

"We're going month on, month off right now. She changes so quickly that if we make it any longer, we miss too much, but it's a big expense taking her back and forth. And it'll all have to change when she starts school."

Brittany looks back for directions and Chance waves her onto the trail that winds up to the top of the butte. "How about you? Man in your life?"

Alma nods. "Jean-Marc. He's an investment banker. Spends a lot of time doing deals in Asia."

"Is that what you went looking for?" Chance asks.

"I didn't go looking for anything." Alma's voice is so quiet now that she's not sure he'll hear her, and not sure she wants him to. "I just went."

The horses take off at a trot up the switchback trail, out of the quiet valley and up onto a windy ridge. Alma examines the sky, watching for the red-tailed hawks that swoop down the air currents to fall on whatever small creature ventures out. This is the landscape she longed for in Seattle. It gives her a winged feeling, like Vicky's tattooed wings soaring on high, knowing the breadth and space and texture of air that is like the air of no other place on earth, leaning into it, uplifted and at peace. She turns to look back over the valley, past the Little m to the home place in the distance, almost hidden by a small hill but visible from this aerie. "Have you ever seen anything more beautiful?" she says.

Chance comes alongside her to stare out at the bare, icy landscape. He lifts his chin slightly. "There's nothing like it."

Chance strikes out to the east along a path Alma remembers, taking them toward another vista from which she knows the ranchland will unroll for many miles, unbroken to the brown horizon, heart-stopping at sunrise. The horses jog along, breathing steam like dragons. Mae chatters at her father about a fox that crossed their path on the last ride. Now Brittany lags behind, watchful.

Alma and Lulabel gain the viewpoint first. Alma raises her eyes from her horse to the eastern horizon and cannot stifle a sharp shriek. "Chance!" she cries. *"What is that?"*

In the middle distance, a black crater covers several square miles of the ranchland Alma remembers. Machinery moves across it so visibly at this great distance that it must be Brobdingnagian up close. Great clouds of black dust rise and float on a northwest wind, dark portents over spoil piles extending south along the valley in knobby, regular hills. Haul roads trace the land like new, dirty veins. The creek and trees that used to traverse the valley are entirely gone.

"This is what's been going on the last two years." Chance turns his back into the wind to shelter Mae. "They're trying to expand in our direction. Sometimes we can feel the blasts all the way over at our place."

"Whose land is this?"

"Most of it that they're on now is either BLM land or the Gingrich place, who got it from the railroad. It had all passed to the kids out of state, so they just sold off the mineral rights. Never even talked to the neighbors. And the feds don't care what we think. Now the landmen are leaning hard on folks who own the next tracts they want, so they can mine straight across to tribal land. It costs them a fortune to dismantle those draglines and start up on a new site."

"The Crow are letting them mine?"

Chance squints in the direction of the reservation, to the southwest, and nods with cold eyes. "Tribal government can't sign the contracts fast enough. All they see is dollar signs, and the historic preservation office is as crooked as they come."

Alma is trembling. She turns her face away from the view and nudges Lulabel back down the trail, the others descending with her out of the wind. As they step down onto level ground again, she feels Lulabel straining at the reins, wanting to run, and Alma opens her arms and lets her. She knows how wrong, how rude it is to ride away from the others, but her whole soul is stretched out in flight like Lulabel's, unharnessed, unhinged. Together they flee the horror behind them, stretched out, hearts pounding, Lulabel answering the tremors in Alma's body with flight, with blessed escape, running flat out for both of them on the smooth old stock trail, light hooves skimming the frozen earth in a cadence like skin drums. They flee together as Alma weeps, back toward the Little m—Chance, Mae, and Brittany trailing far behind. A quarter mile or so short of the barn, Alma reins in Lulabel. It will never do to let her run all the way in. Alma glances over her shoulder at the others far off up the ridge and drops her head, mortified at her loss of control.

When Alma arrives back at the barn, she brings Lulabel inside, out of the wind, carries the saddle to its stand and braces herself against the wall. The sobs that wouldn't come at the morgue, or as she and Brittany held each other in the kitchen at the home place, have arrived. Alma fights them hard, but it's several minutes before she can raise her head, take a steady breath, and let go of the wall. At last, a little better composed, she stows Jayne's clothes, reaches for grooming tools to carry back to Lulabel, then takes a big step back and nearly falls over Chance.

"Steady there," he says in the voice he uses with the horses, taking her elbow to turn her around. She looks up at him, her face icy with frozen tears. The girls have dismounted and run in for Jayne's hot chocolate. Chance holds the horses' heads and they observe from his shoulders like a pair of nosy aunties. His heavy wool cap with earflaps pulled down looks a little silly, but his brown eyes are bright in the dim barn as he leans down to brush her lips with a light, tender kiss. He moves away without a word to tend the horses.

If Alma was unsteady before, now she's legless. She reaches behind her for something to fall onto and comes down safely on an old wooden tack box just below knee height. The strain of the hard ride home is still in her arms and legs, her heart beating as fast as Lulabel's.

Chance's kiss takes her places she can't afford to go. She is back at the street dance in Hardin that was their first date, two-stepping awkwardly with a boy who's between hay and grass, all long legs and broad cowboy hat, with such a big rodeo belt buckle that it might pull his pants down. Her parents are dancing together on the far side of the dance space, glancing over now and then, trying not to hover but not altogether hiding their anxiety about Alma and the Murphy boy. Anne in particular has no intention of letting anything distract her daughters from the goal of college, the security of an education. After the accident, Alma will adopt her mother's ambitions for herself, but for now she ignores them and focuses instead on Chance's hand at her waist, her hand on his shoulder, their sweaty palms together for the first time under yellow streetlights.

The end of the song, and Chance doesn't release her hand, but walks her toward the quiet south end of the street where the lights high above them at the top of the grain elevator are the only illumination. They sit on the curb. He asks if she's thirsty, and when she looks up at him to say no, he takes off his hat, leans in, and kisses her, just like that, no warning. She's a skinny sixteen-year-old who's only just begun to notice the way Chance lays himself flat on the back of a good saddle bronc in flight, all unleashed muscle and sweat as the small-town crowd screams, or the way he lopes to retrieve his hat afterward, surreptitiously spitting in his palm and trying to make his cow-licked hair lie down. She doesn't know what to do with his sweet little closemouthed kiss. She stares like she did the time he handed her a live tiger salamander. Chance laughs and stretches out his long legs.

"Look," he says. "Orion."

That at-sea feeling she had then, on the curb, hoping she wouldn't have to stand up soon, wondering nervously if that brief encounter of lips really counted as a first kiss—it's back full force as Alma sits on the tack box in the Murphys' barn and tries to steady herself enough to stand. It is damned unfair that

Chance should still have this effect on her. Did he teach her this reaction to him, back when she didn't know any better? How does a person go about unlearning a thing like that?

When Alma regains her feet and leaves the barn, Chance is still brushing the horses, fussing over something knotted in Lulabel's tail.

"So you know a little about what's been going on with Vicky? Anything that might help figure out who did this?" Alma asks as she picks up a comb from the fence rail and starts on Lulabel's tousled mane, trying to mask her compulsive eagerness to get at the truth and hoping Chance won't say anything about the way she ran.

Chance shakes his head. "I doubt it. I knew more when they lived out here. I've been checking on them now and then when I go into town. I'm teaching an agribusiness class at the college Thursday afternoons. One of those landmen I told you about, he's been coming after Vicky, trying to get to your grandma through her."

"Brittany told me. I told you one of them stopped by yesterday—Rick Burlington?"

Chance snorts in the general direction of Lulabel's tail. "That's his name. We usually just refer to him as 'that asshole.' Your grandma told them to go to hell, which was a lot more polite than what I told them. But Rick gave Vicky a copy of the lease and offered her some kind of deal to get Maddie to sign it. She's been carrying that thing around, scribbling notes on the back of it. Last time I saw her we argued about it. I told her to burn the damn thing and she gave me some song and dance about how much the money would mean to Brittany and what a dilemma it was. Dilemma my ass. She owed money to everybody in town, including me, and she just needed time to work on Maddie." Chance pauses in his brush work and stands up to look Alma in the eye. "You don't know what she was like lately. She would've sold her soul for the next fifty bucks to get high."

Alma's never heard Chance speak so harshly of someone. It's wholly unlike the Chance she knows. A defensive instinct warms Alma against the creeping cold in her hands and feet. "She might've been having a hard time, but she would never have let them mine the home place. It means too much to all of us. Why are you so angry at her? What did she ever do to you?"

Chance's lips pull in tight and his eyebrows go up.

"What?" Alma repeats.

Chance sighs and leans on Lulabel's smooth back. "For one thing, when they were living out here, she kept bumming money off me. Every time I saw her, some damn thing. Brittany needed lunch money. The car needed tires. She couldn't pay the electric. She thought I was the First Bank of Murphy."

"You're mad because she owed you money? How much was it? I'll write you a check." Alma claps the comb back onto the rail and stands facing him, hands on her hips in the same challenging stance Pete favors.

"No, Alma, it's not like that. I didn't really care about the money." Chance stops and chuckles. "Okay, I did care about the money. I wouldn't be my father's son if I didn't worry night and day about the finances on this place. But it was more that she thought she was playing me. If I hesitated at all, she'd start talking about you, memories she had of you, or things your grandma told her about what you were doing out in Seattle, like she thought that would soften me up. And then . . ."

Chance stops talking and wind fills the silence. Lulabel twitches at the tension and moves away.

"Then?" Alma prompts.

Chance moves to El Dorado, rests his hands on the horse's back and speaks directly into it, his face turned slightly away from Alma. "I got back to the house after chores one night a few months ago and her car was out front. Mae was already asleep. Vicky was on my couch in a low-cut dress with a bottle of wine. Terrible wine, she must've stolen it from the C-store.

She said she wanted to talk, but as soon as I set down my glass she reached over and grabbed me."

"*Grabbed you?*" Alma's hands drop and she takes an involuntary step toward Chance. "What do you mean, grabbed you?"

"Just what I say. One minute I was trying to choke down a swallow of that wine and the next she had her tongue in my mouth and her hand down my pants. I was so surprised it took me a second to push her off." Chance glances at Alma as he speaks, gauging her reaction.

Alma tries to force down the blinding wave of hot jealousy rising behind her eyes before Chance can see it. Vicky kissing Chance—suddenly Alma wants to kill her sister herself. "Why?" she manages.

"That's more or less what I said. She's like a little sister to me. She started running her hand up my leg and said something about how she wanted me to know how much she appreciated me." Chance's face contorts in disgust. "I know a business transaction when I see one. I told her to get out before I threw her out."

Alma doesn't know what to say. This new image is worse than Vicky's sordid commerce with Kozinsky or Murray or Dennis. For her to go to Chance that way was abandoning old bonds of family and friendship. It was utterly debased—and particularly sinister in light of her pregnancy. Was that Vicky's plan? To rope in Chance? "Thank you," she offers at last.

Chance's head comes around quickly. "You think I did it for you?" He starts to laugh but catches himself. "Hell, maybe I did." He moves past her, gathers the tools from the fence rail, opens the gate, and snorts. "Ain't that a laugh. Just a pathetic cowboy who can't get quit of you." He strides off to the barn.

Ten minutes later, Alma wonders if the kiss and the awkward conversation ever happened. Over Jayne's hot chocolate and sandwiches, Chance chats easily about high school and makes Brittany laugh with funny stories of Vicky as a junior high kid, crashing parties and making a spectacle of herself screaming at basketball games, bouncing out of the seat between her parents, huge basketball fans themselves. Did Chance really pay that much attention to her family, watch out for her little sister too? Alma is touched. She's deliberately forgotten a lot about Chance, but there's even more she never knew. The idea of him pushing Vicky away fills her with gratitude. Finally, somebody in Vicky's life who did what a man's supposed to do.

Jayne offers to keep Brittany with her and Mae for the day and Alma eagerly accepts. She needs to see the place where Vicky was living, the place where she died, and have some hard conversations with people like Kozinsky and Dennis. Brittany cannot be present for any of it. "That would really help," she tells Jayne. "Pastor Kemp was wanting to talk to her when I called, something about reading a psalm in the service if she wants to. I said I didn't think so, but could you give her a call?"

"Of course. We'll work it out," Jayne promises. When the cocoa is gone, Chance walks Alma outside. Stopping at her car door, she turns to him with an urge to give him back his own honesty.

"Listen, I don't want to give you the wrong impression. I'm with someone back in Seattle and I shouldn't—" she begins.

"I'm seeing someone too," Chance tells her before she can finish. "Let's just call it one for old times' sake and forget about it, what do you say?"

"Sure," Alma agrees with less certainty than she felt a moment ago. "But you said yesterday—" She cuts herself off, struck by how jealous she sounds. Of all the foolish things to say, she chides herself, after she just reminded him about Jean-Marc.

"Shoot, Alma, I said I wasn't married anymore. I didn't say I was a monk." Chance's face goes red before her eyes and she feels hers respond.

"Right. Of course. I'm sorry, it's none of my business."
Alma hurries into the car, now thinking only of her getaway. "I
have to head into town," she explains, "see Pete again, get some
things for the house."

"Go on then." Chance nods, backing away. "We'll be here."

CHAPTER 12

TUESDAY, 9 A.M. MOUNTAIN STANDARD TIME

Alma heads for the interstate. As soon as she has reception she calls Amanda, who answers as if she's been waiting for days and reels off a list of frantic messages from colleagues, a few from clients. "Alma, you've got to get back here. Every time I turn around Duncan's trying to get into your office or go through your files. I'm pretending I don't have a key. Louis is about to hand over the deal to him. You've done the hard part and they're going to let him take the credit." Amanda's voice is oddly muffled, suggesting that she's cupped a hand over her mouthpiece and is trying not to be heard by others in the office. Alma can barely hear her.

"I'll do what I can. Tanaka knows who's running this deal. There's more going on that I haven't told you yet. We have an ace left. If Duncan tries to take over now, he'll just look like an idiot. More than usual, anyway." The only saving grace with Duncan is his fundamental laziness. Alma has always believed that it's only a matter of time until she traps him in such grievous negligence that it will finish him, but the stakes are getting higher. She'd better hurry.

"I'm not working for him. He's an asshole. If you leave, you have to take me with you."

"Who said anything about leaving?" This is more worrying than Amanda's panic about Duncan.

"Guess who. Duncan thinks you're a threat to him and Louis has always been scared of you. Watch your back."

"Thanks, Amanda. I will. Thanks for watching out for me. But you watch out for yourself too, you hear? Even if they somehow manage to roll me, there's no reason for you to lose your job."

"I wouldn't work here without you. The rest of them are undead. Just *get back here!*"

Alma reassures Amanda as best she can, then hangs up and dials Jean-Marc. He had a late work dinner the night before and is cranky and terse this early, so she just gives him the funeral details and apologizes—for calling, for taking so long to call, for being gone, for everything—and gets off the line. She is always apologizing to him. If it isn't for the hours and missing some important dinner or party or vacation, it's for her bad habit of delegating the most personal details of their relationship. A few months ago they had a huge fight when Jean-Marc realized that Amanda had planned every particular of his birthday weekend and handed Alma an itinerary as she left the office. He blew up and refused to drive down the coast with her to the bed-and-breakfast.

"Is there anything about our relationship that isn't . . ." He chose, as always when his emotions were aroused, the French word: "*arranged* by your assistant? I've never met the woman and yet I feel like she's an old-world matchmaker who will tell us one day that we're getting married and when to arrive for the ceremony. Does she tell you which nights we should make love?

Does she print out instructions on positions? How rude of me, I've never sent her a thank-you."

"You're overreacting," Alma had said, shifting her knees toward the door. "I just didn't have time. Amanda's good at this sort of thing. Why shouldn't I ask her to do it? Would you rather wind up at a Comfort Inn at the airport because I forgot to make reservations?" No previous boyfriend had complained. Greg called Amanda their concierge and tipped her handsomely at the holidays.

"Alma, I want to be in this relationship with you, not Amanda. If I wanted to know about her tastes, I would date her." Jean-Marc threw up his hands and glared at the steering wheel. "What am I saying? I do know her tastes. She buys our opera and theater tickets. She makes our dinner reservations. She chooses gifts for me. She sends me flowers. She plans our vacations. We're like actors who come in to read our lines at the appointed time!"

"You want me to spend my time picking out presents for you and planning our vacations?" Alma attempted, nonplussed.

Jean-Marc shook his head and waved his hands in another gesture she didn't understand. "I want you to . . . want to, once in a while. I would like to believe that you think about me from time to time, when we're not together."

She was torn between the pinch of conscience and the wish that he'd start the car and get moving before the traffic got any worse. "It's not like I'm spending time with someone else. When we're not together, I'm working. So are you. You don't spend your days picking out the perfect flowers for me." As soon as the words came out, she knew this was the wrong example.

They were parked at the curb on Madison Street, looking out through layered evening blues descending over the sound. Jean-Marc tapped his fingers on the steering wheel. His smooth leather driving gloves made a soothing staccato, like tabla drumming. "You remember the orchid I sent you a few months ago, when you closed that big deal in San Francisco?" He didn't look at Alma as he asked.

"Yes—of course, it was gorgeous." The plant had arrived in her hotel room. It was a ridiculous nuisance to get it back to Seattle—she had to carry it on her lap on the late commuter flight home—but it was a generous, thoughtful, beautiful gift.

"I ordered it specially. I got a book on orchids and chose the most beautiful one, in your favorite color. No one in town had it. It had to be shipped directly from Costa Rica." She never knew this. She never asked when she thanked him in the middle of a breezy rundown of her triumphant week's work.

"You didn't tell me." His words should have warmed her toward him, made her cherish his genuine thoughtfulness, but all she felt was the cold vacuum of space in one more disconnect between them.

"You were too excited. Everyone was celebrating. Where is the orchid now, Alma?" His voice was too calm. Then he looked over at her, waiting for an answer he must already know. Jean-Marc should have been a litigator. He was a master of the trick of never asking a question without knowing the answer.

Alma hesitated. After that late flight from SFO, she'd gone straight to the office to leave urgent documents for Amanda and a paralegal to start on first thing in the morning. The orchid went on her desk that night, and over the course of the coming days was relegated to a chair, a shelf, and finally Amanda's desk, where it had some hope of being watered but little access to sun. There it sat until the day when a partner from down the hall wandered by and expressed concern. He loved orchids, he said. Could he help her with it? Without a second thought she'd handed it to him and scooted him out of the office so she could prepare for a call. One thing less to worry about.

"It's at work," she said, with a confidence she didn't feel.

"It's doing fine." The fight had gone out of her side of the argument. She sank back in her leather seat and sighed. "All right, Jean-Marc. You win. I'm a shit, I don't deserve you. Let's go ahead and drive down to the inn, and when we get back I'll go to an actual brick-and-mortar store and buy you an honest-to-God present that I picked out, from me to you. Okay?"

Probably to keep the peace, Jean-Marc agreed. The weekend passed cozily enough, but now Alma can't remember if she ever bought the promised birthday present. Probably she forgot altogether, and so did he. Jean-Marc stages these sentimental protests once in a while about the speed and superficiality of their lives, but he loves it as much as she does, she's sure of it. If anything, he works longer hours than she does. After hanging up, she realizes that she doesn't know what his big dinner was about or what he's working on these days. These aren't things they talk about, not part of the script. She might like to know, but it's too late, Jean-Marc is busy, and she'll let it pass, like a hundred moments in the past when she wanted to reach out to him and drew back because it would be too much work to know, to care. There is never enough time.

Alma takes the Twenty-Seventh Street exit and heads into the south side. The neighborhood looks like 1940s Billings, untouched for seventy years except by the destructive hand of time. The houses lean at architecturally unlikely angles. The walks are unshoveled and broken, the hedges and trees untrimmed and taking over. The snow gives bad and nonexistent lawns a smooth, even appearance that improves matters somewhat, but slats are still missing from fences and porch rails. Windows are boarded up. Some houses and fences bear graffiti that is itself faded. Cars and the occasional large appliance sit in yards or on blocks, masquerading under snow as a giant modern art exhibit. Alma pulls up in front of the place where police have marked a big patch of windblown ice with a faint red stain at one end. The tape is coming loose and waves in the breeze.

Alma gets out of the car and goes around to stand on the unshoveled sidewalk. She recalls a Northern Cheyenne story she once heard, of an epidemic that took a number of babies, and the mothers walking single file down a trail to the burial place, each holding a dead infant. In her imagination the mothers are silent, wrapped up in the last moments with their precious babes before the time comes to place them—cradle boards, tiny beaded moccasins, and all—under big rocks near the river, safe from animals, as was tradition. Alma breathes in the quietness of those mothers, their anguish beyond words and cries, the strength drawn from the other mothers before and behind, walking the same path, carrying the same backbreaking burden of grief. Quite unintentionally, her arms come up in the age-old gesture of a mother holding an infant. She looks down. Feels foolish. Drops her arms. Shivers. Sighs. Snaps herself away from the sight.

Neighbors, paramedics, police, kids on their way to and from school have trampled the snow up and down the street—it's impossible to say whether anyone was near Vicky when she fell. What might it have been? A fight over money, drugs, land—or just an unexpected sort of bad luck? What made Brittany call Walt? They aren't close. Back when they were still talking, Vicky told Alma that Walt and Helen cut her off like a stranger when she failed out of college the first time and didn't repay the tuition they'd covered. Alma doubts the story—it seems like such an overreaction that it must be another of Vicky's embroideries, something she said out of a sort of misguided tact, to cover up the ugly stain of truth. Alma needs to talk to Walt again, as unpleasant as that can be.

Driving down to Kozinsky's house—that's how Pete referred to him, just "Kozinsky"—to fetch Brittany's things, Alma dials Ray Curtis and gets voice mail. If that clue about the wool fibers is real, not just some sick coincidence, then the killer must have suffocated Vicky with something that can be found, marked with her blood. And there must be more evidence, if she or Ray can just ask the right question, look in the right place. She leaves a message wondering if the keys and Vicky's nails have been swabbed for DNA evidence and how the search warrants are going. She feels a sudden frustrated impulse to go to City Hall, pull a chair up beside Ray's, and start reading over his shoulder. Whatever he's seeing, whatever he knows, she wants to know too.

Kozinsky is watching recorded basketball. From the top of the narrow, poured cement steps, Alma can see the big screen dominating the room.

"Come on in," he shouts when she knocks, after trying the broken doorbell. The hydraulic hinge on the storm door is broken and the glass in the bottom half has shattered from the force of the wind slamming the door against the house. The glass is half buried in snow beside the steps, only a few shards now visible. Alma steps over the threshold into the herbal aroma of the house. Kozinsky looks up from the Timberwolves long enough to see who it is.

"Who're you?" he asks the screen.

"I'm Alma. Vicky's sister." She steps up to the chair far enough to hit his peripheral vision. "I came for Brittany's things."

"I thought the cops cleared out all her stuff," Kozinsky says, trailing off as a player begins a drive down the court. The layup fails and Kozinsky swears. "But go ahead and look. Back there." He waves her toward the back porch and she willingly distances herself.

The living room is warm enough, but back here the temperature must be thirty degrees lower. Cracked windows meet the frames indifferently, missing most of the glazing. The old family house on Lewis had the same kind of maintenance challenges, Alma recalls, but her mother and father were up to it. After apprenticing at her parents' shoulders, she can spackle, grout, seal, glaze, and rewire anything. The rest of Brittany's clothes are where she said they'd be, in a torn suitcase under the open sofa bed. Alma pokes around the corners for anything else, but the porch is nearly bare. Even the overhead light fixture is missing from its dusty metal bracket and the bulb burned out.

Alma zips the suitcase and heads back to the front door. Kozinsky pauses the game and spins the chair to face her, taking a long swig on a fresh PBR from a half-full twelve-pack, in spite of the early hour. Mousy brown hair hangs around his face and the collar of his plaid flannel shirt. "Find what you came for?" He eyes the suitcase, unsmiling.

"You're welcome to search it if you're worried I'm trying to steal something," Alma retorts. As angry as she is after seeing where Brittany slept, she'd love to have a good reason to tell off Kozinsky. Shouting, angry words rise and fall within her. He's not worth it. Kozinsky might have been athletic once—he's got the height and build, hidden under at least fifty pounds he doesn't need. He might have had good hair, though what's left hangs limply around the growing bald patch on his crown. And he's clever enough to have a roof over his head and the cable turned on. But Alma doesn't believe he was ever kind, not with a face like that. He's just attractive enough to lure a woman in and shatter every illusion she has left. Alma could mention the funeral, could invite him. Then she thinks of the unheated porch and Vicky's body lying on the ice through that long, cold night, to be found by a stranger the next morning.

"So what do the police say?" Kozinsky ignores her provocation. "Did somebody kill her?"

"Do you think somebody killed her?" Alma throws back the question, moving toward the front door.

"I don't see how. Nobody but her left the house until morning. It wasn't exactly a night she was going to run into someone in the street."

Something about that sentence makes Alma pause. He's right. The only way someone who wasn't at Kozinsky's would have known that Vicky was wandering alone across the south side that night was if they got a call about it. "They arrested Murray," she tells him, just to see what he'll say.

Kozinsky snorts, which causes an unattractive rumbling of his belly fat. "If that guy were Indian, his name would be Outstanding Warrant. He was passed out right there"—he indicates a patch of stained carpet near the couch—"until somebody shouted police the next morning and he hoofed it out the back. Murray wouldn't kill anybody. He's just a jackass."

"So you think she just . . ." Alma can't finish the sentence, and Kozinsky doesn't help, just watches her struggling for words, as long as the game is stopped. "Just fell down and froze?"

Kozinsky finishes his beer before answering and tosses the can toward the kitchen arch behind Alma. "Look, sis, I'm sorry too. She was a nice chick, most of the time. Touchy about her kid. I told the police, I don't know anybody who'd want to hurt her. Her luck just ran out, that's all." He clicks the game back on and swivels instantly to it.

Alma grabs the doorknob and stalks out without a word. She's got another La-Z-Boy dweller to deal with.

She heads for the last address she knows for Dennis Willson, Brittany's father. It isn't far, a little fourplex off North Twenty-Fifth Street with missing shingles and a few bricks fallen from the front façade, the same apartment where he lived with Vicky before she got fed up. There's movement from the sheets over the windows upstairs in the place that was Dennis's. The downstairs door is open. Alma takes a chance, climbs to Dennis's old door, and knocks.

Dennis answers in green camo board shorts and a T-shirt featuring a huge marijuana leaf. His face softens in immediate recognition. "Hey there, Alma, what's up?" He greets her with some kind of hand jive she has trouble following, then hugs her with one arm and waves her in.

Dennis is fleshy like Kozinsky, shorter and hairier, with an untrimmed beard under the wide, ready smile that was always his best feature. The beard improves his appearance by hiding the acne scars on his neck, although he's doing something spiky and unappealing with his hair these days. The living room is mostly filled by a dilapidated sectional couch, a wide-screen television, and an expensive stereo and speakers, all supported by plywood planks and cinder blocks. Dennis has hung a black plush blanket with an Elvis graphic behind the couch, using oversized pushpins. In the adjoining kitchen area, dirty dishes are visible in the sink. A professional amp and three guitars are propped in the corner. Dennis can't pay child support, Alma notes, but at least he hasn't had to pawn the guitars.

"I'm here about Vicky."

"Join the club." Dennis chuckles with a nervous glance to one side, then opens the door further to reveal Ray Curtis standing near the front window, eyeing the street. He and Alma exchange amused nods. Ray moves quickly toward the door.

"I can come back later, Alma. You and Dennis go ahead and visit," he says, reaching for the doorknob as Alma steps inside.

"No, I don't mean to interrupt you," she objects. "It's nothing important."

Ray holds up a hand. "It's okay. I just got here. We'll talk later." And he is gone, the heavy door lock clunking into place. Alma turns to Dennis with her mouth open, but before she can speak, Dennis continues.

"Oh hey, listen, I don't know what she's been telling you, but there's no way I can pay her this month. I was out of work four months and I just got this job at the *Gazette*. My benefits don't kick in for another couple of weeks, I'm behind on my rent, and now they're garnishing my wages! Can you believe that shit?" He doesn't know. Ray hasn't told him yet. Alma hears Ray's unmarked car start outside, the police V8 purring to life. Her mind turns over. Ray made a split-second decision that he wanted her to tell Dennis about Vicky's death, alone. What is he hoping for? What does he think Dennis might reveal to her but not him? Dennis wanders into the kitchen and rearranges a few items in the fridge before emerging with a growler half full of dark beer and two fairly clean-looking glasses. "Check this out. We played a gig at Yellowstone Valley and they paid us in beer. Porter." He sets the glasses on the plywood coffee table and begins to pour.

Alma unbuttons her coat a little in the heat and stuffs her gloves in her pocket. She lets out her breath. "Dennis, Vicky's dead."

He sets down the growler with a heavy thump. The table wobbles. "*Dead?* What do you mean, dead? I just saw her last week. She was fine."

"It was in the paper."

"I don't read the paper." Dennis turns back to the beer, pours himself a very full glass, and starts to drink it in long gulps.

"You just said you work for the paper." Alma examines the other glass for cleanliness before pouring herself a few inches of porter, just to taste.

"That doesn't mean I read it. I do page layout."

"And you don't read the articles?" Alma is stuck on this point. She takes a tiny sip of the porter, then a bigger drink.

"A lot of times the articles come in at the last minute and we're just playing with blank spaces. It can be a real bitch." Dennis stares down into the dark beer at the bottom of his glass with a child's look of deep confusion. "What happened to her?"

"They found her frozen in a yard on the south side early Sunday morning."

"Whoa." Dennis stands still for a moment to absorb this,

takes a swipe at his wet eyes, then remembers his manners and comes around the low table. "Listen, you want to stay a little while? Have a pipe or something?" He gestures at the couch. He's wearing flip-flops in January, and the cracked plaster of the old walls drips a little in the humidity. Somewhere in here, she feels sure, there's a grow light. No wonder he was nervous around Ray. Alma remembers when Dennis was the white-hot star of the local indie music scene, such as it is. The heat seems to have slipped a few degrees.

No way is Alma sitting on that couch. "No thanks, I can only stay a few minutes. So you didn't get a chance to talk to Ray at all?"

"Ray? Oh, the Indian? No, he just got here. I thought he was trying to bust me."

Alma smiles a little at her beer. "I don't think that's his beat. He's investigating Vicky's death."

Dennis slumps onto the couch with a harsh laugh. "I guess the PD'll hire anybody these days." He takes a long sip, looking Alma up and down.

"Ray? I've known him since high school. He's sharp."

That same nasty laugh. "Yeah. Whatever. Probably didn't even make him take the exam, so they could fill their quota. Those guys off the res all think the world owes them a living. They don't lift a finger. I know, I've worked with 'em." The marijuana leaf has hitched up to expose Dennis's deep, hairy belly button. Alma sets down her glass and wipes the condensation from her fingers onto her coat. She turns her face away from Dennis. The professional habit of hiding her emotions is so ingrained that she practices it involuntarily, even when she might rather reveal herself.

"The beer's nice, thanks," she says.

"Told ya. So you still doing that law thing in Seattle?"

"Yep. Still doing the law thing. How's your band?" Are

they really going to do catch-up small talk, Alma wonders, like everything's normal?

"Oh, you know, ups and downs. We lost our drummer when she had a kid and we haven't been able to find anyone else the last six months or so. Can't seem to get ahead." Dennis sits back down and kicks up his feet on the block-and-plywood coffee table. Whatever his flaws, Alma remembers him as the guy who didn't ditch Vicky when the baby came. She wonders how he'll react to her main agenda item: parental rights.

"I'm sorry to hear that," she answers, almost surprised to hear her own sincerity.

"Yeah." Dennis sighs. "Just broke up with my girlfriend too. I mean, we still hook up once in a while, but she moved out. She wants to get married and have kids and I guess she finally decided I wasn't going to change my mind."

"That's too bad," Alma says, feeling a notch or two less sorry for him.

"Nah, not really. I'm happier on my own. I was never much for commitment. More of a loner, you know. Lone rider." Dennis pours another glass and holds it up to toast his words before sucking off the foam. "I'm thinking about getting a paternity test, you know. Friend of mine brought it up. I mean, how do I know if Brittany's really mine? Wouldn't it be the shits if Vicky's just been playing me for a sucker all these years? Women are tricky. That's what I've learned." He starts up to sit at the edge of the couch. "Wait, you're not here about that, are you? You don't expect me to take her? Look, no way I could do that. I'm never around. I practice all hours. Ask my new neighbors, they hate me. And sometimes I just gotta take off and be on my own. I'm not dad material."

"That's not what I'm here about," Alma says, resting her hands on her hips as what's left of her patience starts to go. "Nobody expects you to take Brittany. One of the family will.

But I'd like you to terminate your parental rights. Then we won't have to check with you every time she needs a tooth pulled. And you could stop worrying about child support."

Dennis sits back—way back, the couch moving with him—and takes a long slug of beer. "Well, I don't know. She's my only child. If I gave up rights, then you could just move anywhere with her and I'd never know what happened to her. I couldn't protect her."

"Protect her? I thought you hardly saw her. She hasn't mentioned you in three days."

"Hey, I have a life. Maybe if something went wrong I could do something. You know, someday. Not now, though. Now's not good. But you can't just expect to take my daughter away from me. That's not right. Besides, if you take her, you've got lots of money. You don't need any child support from me, so what's the difference?"

Alma makes an angry, slicing gesture with one hand and points a finger at him. "Dennis, the law says you have to support your child, and I can guarantee you that I'd be a lot more hardass about it than Vicky was. You do not want me going after you." She gives him her nastiest negotiator's glare across the table.

"So you're taking her?" Dennis leans forward, his expression almost hopeful.

"I didn't say that. Let's say I'm thinking on it. I wanted to know where you stand." Alma begins to button her coat, closing the negotiation.

"I guess we could work out a deal." Dennis stays in the same supplicant position in front of her, looking up meekly now. Alma feels a moment of guilt for intimidating him this way but shoves it aside. This is what the Bryn Mawr and Yale education bought. When something important, like Brittany, is on the line, Alma knows how to get her way.

Alma turns her back on Dennis. "All right then. Don't get

up, I'll let myself out." As she opens the door and looks back, Dennis hasn't moved. He sits staring at his half-empty growler with the same look of innocent confusion he showed her when she told him about Vicky's death. Tears are beginning to move down his cheeks. Alma almost goes back to him, almost sits on that couch stained with God knows what and puts her arms around him. Instead, she shuts the door and stands in the hall for several minutes, forcing herself not to cry too.

CHAPTER 13

Back at the Itching Post, tucked in behind the counter on a stool next to her brother so that they can talk while he keeps pulling coffees, Alma breathes several times and starts the easy way.

"We've been spending some time with the Murphys," she begins, describing their visits, picking up a teasing old conversation they used to have about Chance as if she's never been gone, the comfort of their familiar routine immense. "Brittany's out there today, playing with his little girl. His ex-wife is a big San Francisco artist," she says.

"That good old boy is into the art world?" Pete nearly loses his cap when he tosses his head back to laugh. "Sounds like a variation on 'Come up and see my etchings.'" Pete was always suspicious of Chance. After his time out working on the ranches, Pete will never think any former rodeo cowboy good enough for Alma. She knows what Pete would say—too rough, too egotistical, too closed off, no kind of decent husband. But he saw only the caricature, the silent man on the horse, the kid from up the road who gave him a hard time for being a city boy. Pete never knew the boy who saw her cry over broken robin's eggs the year before they started dating, and how she began to find eggs—wood, ceramic, glass, stone—in places only she would go, underneath things of hers left outside. Alma lined up the eggs on the front windowsill at the house on Lewis that last summer, when all other decoration was gone, and watched the light change on them, the only objects of beauty she owned. Now they're in a small box at the top of a closet in Seattle, out of sight but never out of reach.

"I thought we made a deal that you don't pick on my ex-boyfriends if I don't pick on yours."

They're surrounded by people at the bar. Pete gives her a look. "Louder, I don't think they heard you in Laramie."

Alma sets down a tin of breath mints she's been tossing and catching. "Why do you live like this, Pete? It's undignified. When are you and Shep going to go someplace where you can live like ordinary people?"

Pete leans both arms on the bar and bends toward her. "We do live like ordinary people, we just don't advertise. For the hundredth time, Alma, I'm not going to leave my hometown and go live in some queer ghetto. *That* would be undignified. And Montana isn't like it used to be. Do we have to have this conversation every time you visit?" He offers her his old, exasperated smile. "This is our home. All our friends are here, our families are here. I can drive an hour and be on my great-great-great-grandparents' homestead. If I have to be a little discreet about my private life, well, that's a price I'm willing to pay. It's not like people don't know. Some of them are just blind because they want to be, and that's fine by me. They don't ask and we don't tell and we all get along. You're the only one who has a problem with it."

"Walt has a problem with it."

Pete darkens. "Walt is an asshole. What else is new?"

"I don't blame you for keeping your distance from Walt," Alma assures him. But this is more than dislike of Walt talking. He's leaning over with his head down and his hands on his knees, rubbing his palms angrily on denim.

"It's not your fault, Petey." Alma grasps his heavy hand. "It was probably just a stupid, stupid accident. Even if you or Walt had gone, who knows if you'd have found her? Who knows if it would have changed anything?"

Pete looks up quickly, his eyes unfocused.

"That's right. It was nothing but a stupid accident." He squeezes her hand without meeting her eyes and hops up to serve another customer, then returns to her side to tamp down coffee for espressos and resume the conversation. "Whatever you might say about Vicky as a mother, and God knows she has her problems, she loves Brittany." His persistent meandering into the present tense for Vicky rubs at Alma, but she can't bring herself to correct him. "She would have done anything in the world to protect her from the dangers she understood. But the drugs weren't the only problem. She told me other things that would make your skin crawl. Under the influence, of course, so I could never be sure what was the truth and what was crazy talk. Vicky lies, you know that." Pete looks at Alma with these words.

"Yes, I know. She's lied to me many times. I always thought of her as not so much dishonest as . . . creative." Alma raises her voice a little over the hiss of the espresso machine.

"Yeah. She's creative, all right. Creative like a rug. Brittany's got a little of it too, you know, when she really wants something. But I never knew Vicky to lie about something that really mattered. It was more like—like embellishment, telling people what they want to hear. Making things more interesting than they are, or protecting someone. Do you know who Brittany's father is?" Pete lowers his voice so much that Alma can barely hear him over a noisy set of girls chattering at the pastry case.

"I always thought Dennis, but I just saw him and he says there was never a paternity test. Wouldn't there have been one for the child support order?"

Pete shakes his head and leans closer. "Not if he didn't contest."

"So then, you're saying you think it wasn't him?" Alma has never heard such a suggestion before this moment. Back when Vicky had Brittany, she was still in near-daily phone contact with Alma. Surely she would have said something about seeing a boy other than Dennis. "But she would have told me."

Pete shrugs. "Maybe."

Alma accepts the tea Pete's been brewing for her and puts the weight of her back against the counter, perplexed. She wonders for an instant if Pete has an idea of who else might be Brittany's father—why would he bring it up?—but dismisses the thought. They never kept secrets. Just like Vicky would have told her, Pete would tell her. Like she has to tell him the new and awful secret she's just acquired. She sets down the tea and takes his forearm lightly in her hand to draw his attention.

"I don't know who to tell this to, so I guess I'll tell you. It has to be a secret."

"I oughta be good at those." Pete flicks his eyes up and down the bar, but the patrons are all involved in their own conversations.

"Okay. Try this on: Vicky was three months pregnant," Alma says low into his ear.

Pete just stands there, rag in hand, leaning forward with the same contemplative expression, studying the pattern on the bar. Finally he nods. "I know."

"You little shit! How could you not tell me that?" Alma slams down her hand on the counter. "When did she tell you?"

Pete shakes his head. "She didn't have to."

"Look, Pete, she's dead. You're not betraying confidences if you tell me what the hell was going on with her."

Pete bends down to rest on his forearms. "I'm just glad you've been away from here, little sis. You've been safe from the shit that goes on in this town." He rubs his face with both hands before continuing. "I knew she was pregnant because I know she was raped three months ago, and I know what she's been acting like since. She's been sick and crabby, going on one bender after another like she was trying to kill herself, lost her job, got evicted, dragged Brittany all over the place. I wouldn't have been surprised if they'd said it was suicide. And you can keep a secret yourself—don't go telling your police buddy everything I say to you."

Alma sits back, stunned. "Jesus, Pete, you do know how to keep a secret." A moment later: "Did they catch the guy? Did she press charges?"

"No, there was never any talk about that. She wanted to forget about it. She'd been trying to get things together the last year or so. Things got rougher after—that happened, then it all just fell apart one day. She stopped going to work—I started getting collections calls because she wasn't paying the note on the car and I cosigned. I figure that's around when she found out she was pregnant."

"But she didn't end the pregnancy." Alma's face shows puzzlement.

"You know how many abortion providers there are in this state?"

Alma shakes her head.

"Two. The closest is in Livingston. It ain't easy even if you're firing on all cylinders. I don't know what went through her head, but she just fell apart."

"But it was *rape*." Alma objects like a lawyer who's identified the technicality that will get her client off and can't understand why the court won't sustain her objection.

Pete just looks at her and rubs his hand over his mouth as if holding in threatening words, words that might get out and harm all of them, even the dead. Alma blinks in the dust particles circulating under the blown-glass light fixtures. She has a strong desire to sneeze but holds it in.

Pete hunches even closer. Coltrane playing in the background and the click of pool balls hide his voice from the students embedded in soft furniture around them. "Vicky came to me and Shep for help the night it happened." Pete pauses and knots his hands in a gesture of grief and penitence. "I don't know if you realized, but Vicky wasn't doing so badly the last few years. She had a pretty good job at Denny's. She rented a little apartment near there. I cosigned for her on a decent car so she could get around. I thought things were shaping up for her."

Alma reaches out and puts her hand on Pete's as he continues. His hand, grasping hers, is sweaty.

"It was a Sunday night. We were both home for once. Shep was working on lesson plans and I was doing market research on this idea I have for a coffee brand. Man, that's all gone to hell the last few months. We heard a knock and Vicky stumbled in, looking like hellhounds were after her, blouse torn, shaky on her feet. We sat her down and gave her water and tried to get her to talk." Pete's eyes meet Alma's for a moment, insisting on his next words. "She was stone sober, but half incoherent. She kept saying over and over 'He did it again,' but that's all she'd tell us. 'I can't believe he did it again. I thought it was over.' She showed us a big horizontal bruise on her shoulder, but she wouldn't say who did it. Just stared at us with those crazy eyes."

Alma wants to put her hand to Pete's face to stop the words, but something in the truth he is telling acts like a force field. She can't move. She feels sure that if she shifts at all, they'll both break into a million pieces.

"I don't know what she expected us to do. For some reason she could never actually say it was rape, but I've never been so sure of anything in my life, Alma. I didn't know what to do. She didn't want us to call the police, wouldn't go to the hospital. I thought about calling you, getting legal advice, and then I thought, what if she doesn't want the police involved because she's lying again? What if this is a setup like all the stories she used to tell me about needing money, and she smoked it all?" Pete looks for a second as if he might drop his head into his hands and weep. Instead he steps back off the bar stool and takes a few deep breaths while staring at the ceiling. When he looks back down, his face is blank. "I feel like such a jerk. I just didn't know what to do, and if I had, she might still be alive."

Alma's limbs begin to work again as soon as Pete moves. She reaches out to grab his arm and pull him close. She wants to find something soothing to say. She wants to have been there and known and done something, anything, to make it all different for Vicky and Brittany. At the same time, an awful, subversive, cynical voice in her head is recounting the many lies and petty manipulations Vicky has used on them all over the years. Could this be one last master stroke from the grave? The lie that will reach out to lash them all, even after the liar is gone?

Pete holds Alma, rubbing her back. "We told her we'd be there for her if she wanted to press charges or get counseling or anything, but she would never even admit who it was." Pete's sigh is long and gravelly. "She was pissed. She said the law wouldn't do anything for her." Pete cuts himself off, biting back more words, and steps away from Alma. "It was more like she was hinting that if we were real men, we'd kill him, whoever 'he' was. Make it look like a hunting accident or something."

Suddenly, something in Pete's face makes Alma lean toward him. "So did you?" Her voice is a whisper, but Pete can't mistake her meaning. He recoils in surprise.

"Did I what?" It's a false protest. Alma makes an emphatic eyebrow gesture. He knows what she means. He looks away.

"Christ, Alma, no."

CHAPTER 14

The rented Mitsubishi has no way of knowing how to get to the house on Lewis, but still, it takes her there. Alma is in front of her parents' old house without any intent, idling under the streetlight, her mind empty. She hasn't been here in more than a decade, when she threw most of their possessions into trash bags to take to the rescue mission and the consignment shop. Except for the few things she, Pete, and Vicky chose as mementos, some camping gear, kitchenware, and a few useful dorm-room items, they loaded nearly everything into the back of Walt's pickup and watched it roll away.

Most of it wasn't worth saving—stained rugs, worn towels, secondhand furniture—but Alma remembers the weight and taste of the tears as she bagged up her family's possessions. She remembers the petroleum smell of trash bags filling the living room. It felt horribly cruel to dispose of her parents' personal things: if they came back now from the dead, there would be nothing to come home to—no shoes, no face cream, no electric razor. Walt—along with the IRS—insisted that there was nothing to do but sell the house for the little equity in it and dispose of everything inside.

"Sell everything," Walt told Helen as he strode out the front door, leaving the work for his wife, the Saints, and his orphaned nephew and nieces. "Clear it out and keep the receipts."

Alma was sleepwalking in her grief, unable to protest, but Pete fought Walt with all his youthful ferocity. "It's ours," Pete cried, standing on the threshold of their house in his military-issue long underwear, snow swirling around his feet. "We have a right to it!" It has never occurred to Alma until this minute how strange it was that Pete should follow Walt into the military. But of course, that was before the accident.

"You don't understand anything." Walt was angry and unwilling to give explanations. "Your parents' assets are forfeit. There's nothing left. The sooner you get used to that the better, 'cause it's all going." He stalked back to his pickup in the darkness.

Still, they remained family, locked together in a macabre dance over Mike and Anne's worldly leavings. The house was already on the market. By the end of his leave, Pete could turn to Alma and joke that at least they'd never have to look at that god-awful carpet again. Alma sits in the warm Mitsubishi now and finds herself longing for the good old days when all she'd lost was all she thought she owned.

The house is well kept. A young family lives here. There's a child's sled in the front yard and a car seat in the little Toyota in the driveway. They've planted shrubs that have grown large enough to hold snow. There's new siding, yellow instead of white. The walk is shoveled. Alma is strangely comforted. It's good to see the house cared for, when so much of their former life has grown weeds.

Alma last slept here the night before she left for Bryn Mawr, nearly six months after the crash. At that time, there was a real estate sign in the yard, only a few odds and ends left inside. Mercifully the market was terrible that year and the house took months to sell. The young IRS agent, who couldn't meet their eyes and scratched himself incessantly while talking to them, managed to forget that the young Terrebonnes still had the keys. All the government cared about, after all, was the money.

Helen stayed with Alma and Vicky until the mission sent a truck for the furniture, then went back to her house. Alma refused to leave, even after the beds were gone and she and Vicky were in sleeping bags side by side in the living room for a good five months. Helen didn't resist. As long as Alma was in town, there was an unspoken compact that Vicky belonged with her. Helen had suffered some early miscarriages, then became completely unable to conceive, the years accumulating dust in a home that could have functioned only with the distraction of children. Helen's mild alarm at becoming a parent after all those empty years didn't register with Alma until long afterward, when out of nowhere she remembered whispered stories of the unwelcoming home that drove Helen into Walt's arms at such a young age.

All that was only gathering clouds that last summer. Alma would finish her long shifts at Albertsons and walk home with a backpack full of groceries, then stroll the neighborhood with Vicky as she learned to use her prosthetic. Chance was working all hours on a friend's ranch to save money for college, but he'd still come in many nights. There was no television and they were half afraid that turning on the lights would bring down an IRS eviction notice, so in the evenings the three of them sat on the back stoop or walked to the playground or laid on a blanket in the backyard until the stars rose, Vicky fell asleep, and Alma and Chance rolled together like gravity had realigned. The girls drifted toward childhood haunts, places their parents used to take them: the park, the library, the soft-serve ice cream stand. They had a million things to talk about and only a few days left together, so naturally, they never spoke. They were together, that was the thing.

And then they were two. Alma remembers Chance calling over and over in those last days after she abruptly cut off all contact between them, leaving notes after the phone was disconnected, even showing up looking frantic during her shift at the grocery store, following her through the aisles while she mutely stocked shelves until the manager made him leave. There's nothing left to say, she told Chance as he pleaded with her, and she meant it. For the last few days she and Vicky sat for hours at the park, Alma feeling so disconnected to the ground, trees, streets, that she thought she might well float away. Alma pictured them that way in her head, floating through the streets almost invisible, the wraiths of Billings, half dead themselves.

Lying on the floor those late August nights with cicadas and crickets crying on the other side of the screens, Alma played with the zipper on her sleeping bag and felt sure that once she left, she would never be able to come back. Everything that made Billings her home had taken wing in the silent flight of rubber on ice. The last night before she left she lay awake in the evening cool, letting tears roll for Chance and waiting for the flight to Philadelphia like it was an evangelical resurrection. Vicky fell asleep quickly on the hard floor and didn't turn over all night, exhausted from struggling to master the prosthesis.

In the intervening years, Alma's regrets about those last weeks have become a sort of rosary, thumbed over in her mind until the worried beads are worn and familiar. *I should have found another place for you to live.* Click. *I should have taken you with me—impossible, impractical, but I should have found a way.* Click. And last but most awful: *I should have stayed, delivered you from evil.* There were only the hasty, inadequate words at the airport, as Helen hung back and Vicky clung to Alma: "It'll be okay, bug. You can call me anytime."

Alma reassured herself at the time that she was leaving Vicky in the best available hands. She wouldn't even have to change schools. Walt and Helen were family who would welcome Vicky into their home like the child they'd never been able to have.

"He's never rubbed my nose in it that I'm barren," Alma heard Helen say to her mother once when they thought Alma had stepped outside. "He deserves my loyalty for sticking with me." Helen had an autoimmune disorder that made conception and pregnancy difficult. Later this vague illness developed into full-blown multiple sclerosis. The specter of disease and disappointment walked with Helen at the best of times, and Walt drew further away as she grew worse. It was no secret that they'd never had anything to talk about. The day they got married, Walt shipped out for Vietnam. He never wrote his young, fearful bride, not once. She had to find out from other soldiers' families that Walt had been spotted alive, where he'd been stationed. Helen never reproached him for it in all the quiet years to come.

Maybe it's hindsight, but Alma still feels as if she should have known that there was never much hope for Vicky in that emotional vacuum, only a long descent toward the morgue, under a big sky full of a million stars, none of them lucky for her.

Really, Alma asks herself still, what alternative had she had but to leave Vicky with Walt and Helen? She and Pete were both so young, just starting to live their lives. To take care of Vicky would have meant sacrificing everything. And yet here in front of the old house, looking at the steps where she and Vicky played with sparklers on some long-ago perfect summer night, Alma condemns herself again. Whatever she could have done to save her sister, she didn't do it. There is no "working through" that. No amount of talking or Zoloft will make it right. It's an old-fashioned cross to bear. She'd better fit it to her shoulder and start down the road, beginning with finding Vicky's killer.

A half hour later Alma pulls into Maddie's carport. She wants to give Maddie a quick report on the home place before stopping by the grocery store and heading out to pick up Brittany. Before she's gotten around the car, a thin man steps out of the afternoon shadow of Maddie's small garden shed to stand in front of her.

In a stocking cap he looks different, but after a second she recognizes Murray. Alma rears back and lurches away from him, cracking her hip painfully on the side mirror. "What do you want?" she demands. She spots Murray's car parked out on the cross street, where he could see anybody pulling up to Maddie's.

"I want to talk to you," Murray says, stepping forward to close the distance between them. His hands are in his jacket pockets and there's sweat on his face in spite of the cold. He's not really bigger than Alma, but the way his eyes fail to focus properly makes her lace her fingers through her keys.

"I thought you were in jail," Alma says, taking a careful step backward.

"Made bail." Murray's smile reveals decayed meth teeth. "Girlfriend of mine helped me out."

Alma shivers. "So why are you jumping out at me like that? You couldn't just ring the bell?"

"I wanted to talk to you alone. I've been thinking about Vicky."

Alma wants to take another big step away from him, but holds herself firm beside the car.

"What about Vicky?"

Murray puts a hand to his head, as if he's in pain. "I don't want to get involved in what's going on. I don't know nothin'. I was passed out in the house the whole time. When I woke up in the morning I saw police lights, so I scooted out the back. I hardly knew her."

"That's not true. You must have known her pretty well. She let you use the house."

"All right, I know, but the cops don't know about all that.

I can beat this possession charge, but I can't do hard time. I'm a businessman. It'll fuck things up."

Alma sniffs. The cops arrested him at the home place. They know all about his connection to Vicky. Murray's not making sense. "You're dealing meth, that's what it'll fuck up. Why should I care? Why are you telling me this?"

"Because you know I knew Vicky. I want you to keep quiet about it. Just let things play out. I didn't kill her."

"I've already told the cops everything I know about you. There's nothing to keep quiet about." She glances up at Maddie's windows and catches the hum of a laugh track. Maddie won't hear anything coming from outside.

Murray's face loses its slack expression. "I'd say that was a mistake." He steps forward and brings his face a little closer to hers. Alma can't help but recoil. "I'm already out time and money because of you. My whole operation's got to relocate. You drag me into a murder investigation and I might start to get pissed off."

"Are you threatening me? Because if anything happens to me, you're going to be suspect number one." Alma's mind jumps to Vicky's last moments, bleeding in the cold and dark, with nothing but her keys as a weapon, and someone leaning over her, covering her face. She's frightened and furious all at once, and she wants to smack that smartass look off Murray's face. The *nerve* of this little prick. She's bested his professional kin, the toady corporate negotiator who thinks he can intimidate women with threats and never expects to eat his lopsided contract for lunch.

But Murray isn't finished. "I know your brother. The faggot. And the little girl too." He smiles a creepy little smile with only the edges of his mouth. His skin, so close, is rough and colored an unhealthy gray. "Brittany Terrebonne, right? Goes to Broadwater?"

Alma's anger overwhelms her fear. "If you go near that little girl, you'll have a lot worse than police to worry about," she hisses.

Murray takes a step back but the smirk doesn't change. "All I'm saying is, let the dead rest. No reason to get me involved, right?"

Emboldened by his slight retreat and the wobble in his gait, Alma takes a threatening step to look him straight in the eye. "I want you off this property and away from the home place for good. I want you *nowhere near* my niece or any member of my family. You want to be left alone, you leave us the hell alone."

Murray has turned and taken a few more uneven steps away, but at this he stops and glares back at her in the already fading light. The muscles in his neck flex and he shows his hideous teeth. "It's a deal, lady."

Inside the house, Alma checks all the locks and gives what sounds to her own ears like bland, unconvincing reassurance that she'll take care of things at the home place, that Murray has left there for good. Maddie is satisfied. Now that she's calmed down a little, Alma considers Murray's words further. If he's ceding the home place to her, that means he understands that Vicky's death has extinguished his claim. With Vicky gone, he has nobody to hide behind. That alone is a reason for him to want her alive. It's almost a shame. Alma frowns. Murray would make an ideal suspect. But he could have motives she knows nothing about. Back in the car, she calls Ray with the news about Murray's visit.

"Well that punk." Ray is indignant. "I'll send out a uniform to bring him in. We'll find some excuse, keep you out of it, don't worry. Sorry about that."

By the time she's filled the backseat with groceries and hit the interstate, Alma feels as if she's running down a street in London during the blitz, trying to get to the bomb shelter in time, frantic to reach the place of safety. The home place is the only refuge left.

When Alma gets to the Little m, Brittany is waiting at the front windows of the ranch house in a white sweater, a fetch to Alma's eyes in the gathering country night. She runs out and hops in the car. Jayne is at the door with Mae on her hip, waving a warm goodbye. Alma steps out to say a few quick words of thanks, but she is weary, desperate to regain the quiet of the home place. She settles back into the driver's seat with relief, throws the car into gear, moves them forward toward the road.

"Hi," Brittany says. "Did you know the Murphys have chickens?" Her tone is casual, as if Alma comes to pick her up every day and this is a conversation resumed.

Alma hesitates. "I know it's nice spending some time here, honey, but don't get too used to it. We haven't decided anything permanent yet."

Brittany's left hand starts to move out in a petting gesture, making Alma wonder if Burro is in the car with them, but just as suddenly Brittany withdraws the hand, as if she's remembered that this is a thing she no longer does. Instead she leans forward, watching for the evening star, taking in the shades of darkness on the land. "But this is nice, isn't it? Going back to the home place?" The road is pitch-black before the headlights in the dark before moonrise. The home place will have dropped to forty-five degrees, where Alma set the thermostat.

"Yes, babe. It's nice going back. But you wouldn't want to leave Billings and start all over out here, would you?" Alma attempts. "A new school, all that? Wouldn't it be nicer where your friends are? Your family?"

Brittany has one hand on the window ledge, peering out at the night as if there's something obscure and important to see there. "I went to school in Hardin when we lived here. I think my friend Mia is still there. And I like playing with Mae. She's nice."

"She's very nice." Alma fiddles with the instrument panel, trying and failing to make AM radio come in. "Brittany, honey, you never did tell me—what did you do that night after you talked to Walt and Pete?"

"I just waited for a long time. I watched out the front window and once I thought I saw a car coming up the street, but it didn't come as far as the house. The window was all fogged up and I couldn't see very well. I guess I fell asleep. I should have woke somebody up." Brittany's voice gets smaller and smaller before disappearing altogether. Alma steals a look at her and waits a moment before speaking again.

"What about Uncle Pete?" Alma offers a change of subject. "Wouldn't you miss him out here? And Great-Grandma, and Walt and Helen? And all your cousins in town." There's a raft of acknowledged and unacknowledged cousins, this and that twice removed, faces so like her own or some cherished ancestral photograph that to see them always brings a little chill, like someone walking over her grave. The living are the dead, and the dead aren't gone. Alma will eventually hear about everyone she hasn't connected with on this trip. One doesn't neglect the family with impunity. There used to be family reunions at the home place, daylong events with music and hayrides. After Mike and Anne died, not to mention the falling-out with Walt, Al and Maddie seemed to lose all heart for it. Is all that gone forever, or just waiting to live again?

"You told me that time that I could come live with you if I ever needed to." Brittany's lower lip is starting to project. This is true. At one point last year, after Brittany fought with Vicky over a school field trip, Alma tried to calm the waters by saying that Brittany could come to Seattle to stay for a little while if she needed to. The remark was meant to drive Brittany back to the bargaining table with Vicky. There seemed little risk that she would take the offer. But Vicky saw it as Alma's attempt to come between her and Brittany, steal her daughter even. As Vicky tended to do, she went for the jugular.

"Just because you can't find a man who's willing to give you kids—you probably can't even have kids, you're so tight and dried up—you think you can come out here and take mine! Well it ain't gonna happen, sister!" Vicky hurled the words at her before hanging up over the shrill sound of another wedge springing into place between them.

Of all of Alma's words that have come back to haunt her, these are some of the most ironic. A thoughtless phrase that she would have taken back mere hours after pronouncing it, and now a year later Brittany is throwing it back at her. This should teach her not to get involved in other people's arguments, she thinks, then remembers that interfering in other people's disputes is her chosen profession.

"I did say that, didn't I? You know you're always welcome at my house, but we also need to think about what's best for you." Alma pulls up behind the house. "I'd hardly be able to spend any time with you in Seattle. I work really long hours. But how about this: I'll visit you more often. You can come out for holidays. We can go on vacations together, things like that. And you'll still have your friends and family here. You'll be fine." She wants to fill up the yawning need behind Brittany's request with promises and reassurances, but nothing she can say is anything like enough. As Alma's mind thumbs frantically for options, there are too few functioning family members left on her list. Her mind drifts toward Pete and dredges up a call many months ago, maybe more than a year now.

"It's still one day at a time, Alma," he told her. "Sometimes Shep's like a big bungee cord holding me on the wagon. Everything's this delicate balance."

"But you're doing so well," she'd protested. "All that's behind you."

"No," Pete insisted. "It's with me every day. I look it in the eye every goddamn day."

A little electric fear traverses Alma's chest as she looks over at Brittany, who has taken off her mittens to play with the air vents, the door locks, the sound system controls. Alma wants to stop those nervous fingers before they break something. She clicks off the headlights but lets the car idle, thinking that at least she's won the argument for now, and reaches for her purse in the backseat. When she looks over again, Brittany is smothering sobs in her overlong dirty coat sleeves.

"Oh, sweetheart," Alma cries and grabs her arm. "It's not that bad. It's okay. It'll be okay."

"I want my mama," Brittany sobs. "I promise to be good." Alma reaches over to hold her small niece and stroke her head, as much for her own comfort as for Brittany's. It is truly dark now, high country dark, with only the stealth illumination of glowing dash lights.

Alma fixates on what she would say to Vicky if she were here in the car with them right now. *I knew how hard it was for you,* she wants to tell her sister. *Maybe didn't know exactly what you were feeling, but I knew you were drowning too. I just couldn't help you because I could only save myself. I selfishly saved myself. I'm so sorry.*

It's too late for Vicky, but as Alma's tears dry, the future seems suddenly like the open plains: empty, dark as a stage that lies waiting for the opening curtain, replete with possibility. At this moment, Alma and Brittany can choose paths that would not have been available to them a week ago.

Alma helps Brittany dry her face. "It'll be okay, honey. Whatever happens, I'll always be there for you. I will always take care of you." Alma finds herself saying more words she hadn't intended to say but now understands to be necessary. "Listen to me. I'll stay with you—I don't know where yet, but somewhere. I'll make things right, whatever it takes." These are the words she feared. They are true. They will change things.

Brittany's expression responds to the new sincerity in Alma's voice. She calms, brushes her hair out of her face, and looks up at Alma by the light of the stereo with eyes made transparent again by faith. "Okay," she says. "I'm all right now."

CHAPTER 15

Alma wakes up stiff and cranky in the same bed as Brittany, who kept her up half the night thrashing and now sleeps with limp abandon. She leaves a note for Brittany and drives over to Ed and Jayne's to use the phone. The first message on her voice mail: Jean-Marc will be on the first flight this morning, coming in for the funeral. Alma presses her lips together to stifle a sigh. He will not take well to conditions at the home place, but there's nothing she can do. Her first call is to Amanda, who is perfectly alert at this early hour and talking fast.

"Thank God. Alma, it happened last night. I went out for dinner, and when I came back past the building I thought I saw a light on in your office, so I came up. Duncan and Louis got hold of a key to your office. They were loading files on a cart and they took your hard drive. I'm sure they've had it hacked by now. They have everything, all your notes and contacts. They're meeting the client today—I got their calendars off the network drive. Alma, I'm so so sorry, I don't know what to say.

I tried to call you last night but you weren't picking up. Where have you been? Is everything okay?"

"No," Alma says, "everything is not okay. At this point . . . maybe I'm glad to have one less thing to worry about." She plants her forehead with a thump on the ivy-patterned wallpaper. Behind her at the stove, Jayne glances up in concern.

"Are you still coming back on Friday? I don't know if it will make any difference now."

"I think so. Everything's a mess here too. Are you going to be okay?"

Amanda's breathing sounds on the verge of hyperventilation. "Yes. I just need to breathe. I hardly slept last night. I'm just going to keep doing what I do."

"When I get back we can talk about what happens now. Over martinis."

"You're on."

When Amanda hangs up, Alma shuts her eyes and presses her fingers against them, a physical channel change. She can't deal with Seattle now. She opens her eyes and considers calling Detective Curtis and asking about the fetal paternity test.

"Ed and I are planning on coming in for the funeral too, if you don't mind." Jayne startles Alma with the quiet words and a hand on her shoulder. "We're all so very sorry."

Alma turns around to look into the lined, cautious face watching hers. Jayne's hair is completely silver now, nothing like the blond bob she used to maintain so carefully. Something— maybe Ed's cancer—has sped up her aging. The grace of Jayne's gesture floods through Alma as Chance enters the kitchen through the back door and grunts a good morning on the way to the coffeemaker.

"I'd like that." Alma's attempt to smile doesn't quite come off. Jayne reaches out and hugs her—really hugs her, like she used to before Alma broke her son's heart—then pulls away

with the same air of caution she's had since Alma came back.
The hug is a moment of weakness for Jayne, but its sweet gen-
erosity rests on Alma like a mantle, giving warmth. Chance is
blowing on his coffee and watching them.

"We wanted to invite you both to supper if you're coming
back out here tonight," he says, with a glance at Jayne that says
she's already approved.

Jayne nods. "Yes, we talked last night and we don't want
you having to go home to a dark house after the funeral. You
just come here and we'll make sure you get a hot meal," she says
with raised eyebrows and lowered chin, asking Alma to agree.

There is no refusing this invitation. Besides, the alternative
would be leftover funeral casserole or fast food off the interstate.
Dinner at the Murphys' will be good for Brittany, that's the
important thing. Alma nods. "Thank you, that would be very
nice. My—um—" She's trying to say "my boyfriend," but the
words sound ridiculous in her head. Chance and Jayne wait
for her to stop stammering. "Jean-Marc is flying in. He'll be
coming back with us tonight."

Jayne beams at this. "Your boyfriend?" she enthuses. "Oh
yes, bring him too!" Chance sets down his half-full cup and
stalks back outside.

Alma thanks Jayne and moves toward the front door. Brittany is ready and waiting when Alma swings by the home place
to pick her up. "First stop is the airport," Alma tells her. "You
remember Jean-Marc. He bought you that pretty umbrella last
time you visited."

"Why does he have to be here?" Brittany whines at the
ceiling upholstery. "He doesn't like it here."

"How do you know that? He's never been here. Besides,
he's here for me, and for the family," Alma answers without
taking her eyes off the road. "Be nice." She knows that Brittany
is remembering what Alma told her about why she doesn't visit

Montana more—Jean-Marc doesn't want to, and they have so little vacation time together. It seemed like a harmless admission at the time—true, even—but it will only come between Brittany and Jean-Marc now.

Alma glances over to see that Brittany has set her jaw in exactly the expression Maddie uses when she's made up her mind. Terrebonne women, she sighs to herself, just before a thud from the rear sends the car skidding full speed across both lanes of the county highway. Alma steers hard across the rumble strip, trying to straighten out before they head into the borrow pit. In her peripheral vision a white pickup speeds by. All she can do is focus on bringing them safely to a stop as the car fishtails and skids across the asphalt.

They shudder to a halt, half off the pavement. The highway is empty, the pickup already gone over the next rise. Alma gets out to check the damage. There are some scratches on the back bumper, but nothing that matches the terror she felt as the car slid out of control. Alma rubs her neck and takes her time walking back to the driver's seat, where Brittany leans toward her anxiously.

"Is the car okay?" she asks.

"It's fine. Are you okay?" Alma puts a hand on Brittany's arm and examines her face.

"It just scared me, that's all."

"Probably just some drunk." Alma shakes her head at the words even as she says them. Eight A.M. isn't a common time for drunk driving, but Brittany is prepared to believe just about anything about adults these days.

At the airport, Jean-Marc is settled in a chair near the baggage carousels, checking e-mail. He stands to embrace Alma. His hugs are real and warm, never awkward. There's a faint scent of cologne on him, not from actual cologne, but from an expensive body wash that Alma knows he likes and now buys for him in bulk when it shows up at Costco on discount. His face is a little red from the heat of the terminal and his wool topcoat, but he's smiling. He offers a firm handshake to Brittany, who shakes once and pulls her hand away.

"About where we're staying," Alma begins, looking for words that will prepare but not alarm. "It's a little rustic."

Jean-Marc raises a smooth eyebrow. "Ski cabin rustic or trailer park rustic?" he inquires.

"Homestead rustic," Alma says. "Outhouse. No cell service. No Internet."

Jean-Marc's face shifts into a thoughtful moue. "This is your childhood home?"

"My grandparents' home, yes." Alma watches him, awaiting a verdict. Jean-Marc is the sort of man who ponders a little, then decides for good. If the home place is unacceptable in his eyes, there will be no convincing him otherwise.

"I'm sure we'll manage." He shrugs and picks up his bag. Alma's shoulders drop in relief. They file out to the car and descend from the rims for a cup of Pete's strong coffee. Pete and Jean-Marc surprise her by falling into an easy conversation about international coffee markets, as if they're old friends. Something about Jean-Marc's impeccable topcoat, silk scarf, and shiny shoes has won Pete's confidence. She can see it as Pete smiles past Jean-Marc at her. *At least one of my sisters will be taken care of,* she can almost hear him thinking as he claps Jean-Marc on the shoulder. Her brother's satisfaction twists in her as she pulls at the sleeves of her sweater. She has never wanted to be taken care of. Let him worry about Brittany. The successful visit with Pete is followed by a long lunch of donated casseroles and pointed questions about Brittany and the home place at Maddie's. Alma hedges and Jean-Marc entertains with stories of Gatsby-esque parties in Singapore. At last, but still before Alma feels ready, it's time to go to Vicky's funeral.

The 1950s-era church is at the center of the downtown, on the foundations of the older church it replaced. Alma remembers attending with her parents, who bookended the family in one of the forward pews, a solid, united front. She drew on the walls in the nursery, and Pete once threw a Tinkertoy straight through a plate-glass window into the alley. As a child, Alma pictured prayers rising like smoke signals from the church's chimney into the unspoiled sky. For several years, she believed their white-haired pastor to be God.

When Alma walks into the church with Maddie, Jean-Marc, and Brittany, she finds Pete and Shep already inside, standing a little apart from the rest of the crowd. The Murphys come in soon after and greet them one by one. Chance asks after business at the Itching Post and makes small talk about the school board with Shep. Glancing at Chance's broad, flan-neled back, Alma imagines him chatting with gallery clientele in Denver, New York, anywhere. He seems to have absorbed Pete and Shep's relationship automatically and approvingly, his cowboy hat dangling from his fingertips as he nods at the taller man. Jean-Marc, on the other hand, stands apart from the as-sembled mourners, reading plaques on the walls and occasion-ally tapping out a text.

Alma glances away from Jean-Marc's blond head to notice the way Chance's dark hair curls onto his collar. He feels her stare and looks her way. Before she can break her gaze, he passes her the quick schoolboy grin that used to make her toes clench in homeroom, then turns back to Shep with a more serious expression. She turns her attention to Brittany, who sits alone at the end of the back pew. Alma sits, puts an arm around her, and looks for Walt, expecting his Obélix-like frame to fill the big sanctuary doors any minute. No Walt. What could he be thinking, disappearing for this long at a time like this? Is he punishing the family for something—the tense confrontation with Alma, perhaps?

Then Leslie—or Pastor Kemp, as everyone seems to be call-ing her these days—comes in from welcoming the small cast of mourners near the front door and bends down to embrace Alma and Brittany together. She takes Brittany's chin in her hand. "Are you ready for your part, honey?" Brittany sniffles, nods, and fishes a piece of paper out of her pocket to show Leslie, who straightens up to read it. Neither Brittany nor Leslie takes any notice of Alma's surprise. "This is very nice. It will be perfect," Leslie affirms and reaches over to hug Brittany again. "Do you want to come sit up front now?" Leslie looks down, inviting Alma with her expression to come forward too, but Alma shakes her head.

Leslie takes Brittany's hand and leads her to the front pew before beginning the service. Alma is left alone. The furious rush of words and emotion that hasn't stopped since she got off the plane comes to a halt for a few minutes. Vicky is dead. The knowledge comes upon her anew, like a revelation, and she's immersed again in the high school chem lab smell of the morgue, faced with Vicky's heartbreaking tattoos like they're on the undersides of her own eyelids. Vicky's life represents what would have—easily could have—happened to Alma had she stayed in Billings, had she not won the scholarship, had their parents died a few years earlier, had she had a baby too early, had any number of tumblers not fallen into place so that the lock opened and she was free. Vicky's face, so like her own, lies there in its last, chilly peacefulness, and Alma feels the chill run up her spine as surely as if Vicky had taken a bullet meant for her.

Chance, now a few feet away as Shep and Pete find their seats, notices her sway a little in her seat. He slips in to sit beside her and put his large hand over hers where her left hand grasps the edge of the pew for support. Alma looks up to see Jean-Marc moving toward her from the other end of the pew, looking at Chance, not her. She pulls her hand away. Jean-Marc sits and puts an arm around Alma's shoulders, snugging her to him.

"I don't think we've met," he says, leaning around her to look Chance in the eye. "Jean-Marc Lacasse."

"I told him about you," Alma attempts, but it sounds weak even to her own ears.

"Chance Murphy. Family friend." Chance offers a hardened hand to Jean-Marc's smooth palm and they hold the grip longer than necessary. Alma sits very still and wonders about the risk of a matter-antimatter reaction.

Neither Alma nor Brittany has any spirit after the funeral for anything but heading back to the Murphys', but here they are in the basement multipurpose room of the church, walking to a table with plates of pie in their hands. Maddie is surrounded by a phalanx of church women clucking over the tragedy. Helen sits at the same table as Maddie, with her but not with her, head down, poking her pie but not eating it. When Alma passes, she reaches out with a surprisingly strong grip on Alma's wrist.

"Have you heard anything from Walt?" she demands without preamble. "I haven't seen him since he left Sunday night. I—I had to ask a friend to come over and help me get to the funeral," she adds, dropping her voice as if the humiliation is too much to share with the table.

"No, Helen, I'm sorry, I haven't heard anything." Alma rubs her shoulder. "If he doesn't turn up by tomorrow, I'll drive out to the cabin and see if I can get him to come back. What can I do? I need to take care of things out at the home place, but is there someone who could come stay with you for a few days, until Walt's back? Would the ward secretary be able to arrange . . ." Alma trails off. The Saints will arrange everything, if only Helen asks, but Helen is too proud to ask.

"I'll be fine," Helen whispers.

Alma kneels beside her. "I'll call that fellow who came the other night, what's his name, Fred, Frank—"

"Fred Winters."

"I'll call him. He'll be happy to help out."

Helen hesitates, gripping Alma's hand, before nodding and turning away.

Pete, Shep, and Jean-Marc are at the next table and Alma moves to join them. Mae runs up and down a pew pushed against the wall, playing airplane and giggling at her father's admonitions to play more quietly. Even cousin Emma is there, looking heavier than when Alma last saw her, standing behind the table where pie is being served, putting slices on plates. She steps out from the table to give Alma a long, tender hug, leaving a small damp patch on Alma's shoulder. There are a few other cousins here and there from both sides of the family, familiar faces much aged. They come over one by one, patting Alma's and Brittany's shoulders in an uninterrupted susurrus of condolences.

"Vicky was such a pretty little girl," cousin Edna from Laurel sighs, only the third or fourth person to make that observation. Alma smiles to be polite. Brittany shrinks from the stranger's hand on her hair.

"Don't forget the casserole I dropped off with your grandma," Maddie's sister Bea urges as she squeezes Alma's shoulder much too tightly—the Vulcan mourning grip— before attaching herself to her husband's arm with the same claw and steering them both out of the room.

Kirsten Kitchen trails not four but five children through the maze of tables to express her condolences. She offers to take Brittany to an indoor water park over the weekend. Alma thanks her without telling a single one of the outlandish stories she'd concocted for the occasion. All of the concern is sincere, the presence intended as comfort, the gestures genuinely helpful and kind. Alma can't wait to get away from all of it.

CHAPTER 16

At last Alma and Brittany set off with Jean-Marc, who asks about the industrial neighborhood they're passing through: the oil refinery, the sugar beet refinery, the women's prison, the coal plant. As they pass out of the city, crossing the river in the lee of Sacrifice Cliff, moving out onto the high plains, he grows quieter. The dull sunlight shows no color but brown and white beyond the gray river of highway. At last he asks:

"How far out here are we going?"

"About another hour," Alma says.

Jean-Marc exhales a low whistle. "I brought cowboy boots."

"You did not. You don't own cowboy boots."

Jean-Marc smooths back his thin blond hair and beams his polished smile. "I do! A client gave them to me a few years ago. They're pure ostrich. Gorgeous. The most politically incorrect footwear imaginable. I hate to wear them and scuff them, but the occasion calls for it."

Alma shakes her head and laughs. "This I've got to see."

Jean-Marc slips off his soft leather gloves and slaps them on one hand. "And what's his name—Buffalo Bill—lives out here, punching cows and rescuing schoolmarms?"

Alma keeps her tone neutral. "His name is Chance Murphy, and yes, they're just up the road. Actually, he invited us all over tonight for dinner with his parents."

Jean-Marc makes a face. He dislikes social interactions with people too far outside his own cultivated world.

"I always annoy parents."

Alma rolls her eyes. "You can charm anyone you decide to charm."

"And this Chance—is he an old friend or an old boyfriend?"

"A little of both," she says, careful not to show any emotion as she taps the radio tuning buttons. She is glad she's driving and doesn't have to make eye contact.

Ahead of them on the black lanes of the interstate, a heavy snow has begun. The sun has disappeared and visibility is dropping fast. Alma takes a deep breath, turns down the radio, and settles her hands more firmly on the wheel. Jean-Marc is half-turned in his seat, watching Alma with an anxious expression as she takes the exit to the county highway.

From one instant to the next, the road becomes snow-swept black ice. At the same time, all three of them feel the car shimmy. Alma's instinct takes over. The car has antilock brakes, so she slams the brake down and opens her fingers on the wheel. The only way to drive a sheet of ice is to give in to it, let it carry you forward, force nothing. Alma's shoulders relax as the car flies down the off-ramp toward the stop sign. Together, all three listen to the brakes pump, eyes on the road, not a word spoken. The car shudders and stops just halfway through the empty intersection.

"Well done," Jean-Marc breathes.

Alma turns right onto the county road. "Just keep it between the navigational beacons," she says aloud, to remind herself more than Jean-Marc. Driving these icy roads comes from deep memory, a feeling of stepping into clothes older than her own, with ghosts riding shotgun. Roads like this killed her parents, mutilated her sister. Rather than anxiety, the loss of control brings her peace: if these roads want her, they will take her. Her breathing slows, her grip releases, her concentration becomes complete. They drive in silence over the long, treacherous roads to the home place.

"Impressive," Jean-Marc comments as he steps out and surveys the undisturbed horizon. "You may have located the actual geographic center of nowhere."

"Nowhere has a fine capital," Alma declares, following his eyes.

"I think I need a nap," Brittany says when they enter the dark kitchen at last. She heads straight upstairs.

Jean-Marc starts to assemble sandwiches out of groceries Alma picked up in Billings the day before, while she turns up the furnace and starts another fire in the stove. He'd carefully ignored the selection of Tater Tot casseroles and Jell-O salads at the funeral, and Alma had no appetite. Now they fall to their plates. After they've eaten, Alma checks on Brittany—sound asleep facedown, still wearing the woolly hat Maddie forced on her—then pulls out rubber gloves and attacks the fridge with a bucket of soapy water and a scrubbing sponge. She can think of nothing she needs so much in this moment, her sister's funeral hymns still resonating in her, than to see that filthy appliance gleaming clean again. After several minutes she hears a low chuckle from Jean-Marc and realizes that she's singing "Shotgun Down the Avalanche," rather loudly and very badly.

"I'm going to look around." He smiles and walks out of the kitchen. She hears him knocking through the house, opening doors, turning lights on and off, poking around upstairs. Finally he reappears.

"Where's the toilet, Alma?"

She knew this was coming. She points at the back door.

"I told you. Outhouse. About twenty yards that way."

Jean-Marc turns his head toward the door by which they entered the house. He knows what's out there. A smile sneaks across his face.

"I thought you were joking."

She fixes him with an exhausted gaze and drops her sponge in the bucket.

"Honey, I wouldn't joke about indoor plumbing. We kick it old school out here. Baths in the tub in the pantry, and the outhouse. And be sure to latch the door tight when you come out."

He gives her an even more astonished look. "Why?"

"Birds, bats, you never know. It's not a place where you want surprises, if you know what I mean." She ducks her head back into the fridge to hide how much she's enjoying his consternation. To him, the home place is beyond quaint. It's isolated, disconnected, abandoned—and she knows better than he does how many eccentricities it hides. Firearms and whiskey hidden in odd corners, violence and insanity just below the surface, the way that civilization can become nothing but a thin polish over the animal will to survive. Her belly clenches as Jean-Marc sighs, pulls his hat back on, and heads outside. He has no right to look into the family secrets. He's an outsider. Until now, she's never labeled him that way.

As the sound of Jean-Marc's footsteps on the back steps dies away, the realization simmers to consciousness that Chance shares the old desperation of the homesteads. His love of this place is as visceral as hers, maybe more so. For the first time, Alma considers how difficult Chance's homecoming must have been for him, and how far he might go to protect the valley from Harmony Coal. She scrubs harder at the layer of dried meat drippings on the bottom of the fridge.

Jean-Marc startles her when he comes back waving one gloved hand in the air. "So you weren't kidding about the phone either?" The level of frustration in his voice has increased.

"'Fraid not. But you've still got a calculator and a camera there."

Jean-Marc walks to the old black wall phone and picks up the receiver. Alma knows there's nothing but silence on the line. Jean-Marc's jaw juts out.

"Satellite Internet? VoIP?" he offers the last vestige of hope. Alma withdraws from the depths of the fridge and grunts as she stands to face him.

"No connectivity whatsoever, I'm afraid. The Murphys have a landline and a satellite dish if you need to reach somebody."

Jean-Marc shuts his mouth with effort before he shakes his head and hangs up the phone.

"What do you do in an emergency? What if you needed to call the fire department?"

Alma reflects. Québec, of course, would be a lot less rural than Montana. Even after her years of school there, she still has no instinctive grasp of East Coast geography, the closeness and connectedness of it all. Her default is Western vastness. "Aren't there places like this where you come from? On the farm? You mean to tell me the entire province is perfectly modernized?"

"No, of course not. The Nord-du-Québec is much rougher than anything here. But, Alma, the suburbs of Québec City surrounded our farm years ago. My parents' biggest complaint is that Montréal has two Ikeas and they still don't have one."

"But they keep goats." Alma clings to her cherished image of the Lacasses' rustic homestead. "It can't be all that urban."

Jean-Marc puffs his lips in a classically Gallic expression. "Listen, we're French, we value agriculture, *le terroir.* We like to think of ourselves that way, so we keep some animals in the suburbs and buy artisanal cheese. It doesn't mean that anybody would go five minutes without modern plumbing, unless it was for some kind of hippie experiment. Seriously, what would you do if there was a fire? Flee into the snow?" Jean-Marc eyes the crisply burning woodstove through the door into the front room.

"Well, let's see. There's a volunteer fire department based in Hardin, so odds are pretty good somebody within a few miles would see smoke, call it in, and come straight here with their gear. Or if not we'd drive to the Murphys' or toward the interstate until we got reception. I bet the response would be faster than in Seattle."

Jean-Marc rubs his jaw. "Okay," he says as he turns away, tension rising off him like steam in the chilly room. Alma stands and puts her hands on her hips, ready to challenge him, then shakes her head and drops back into her position in front of the open fridge. Jean-Marc's silence is resigned but angry, like he's being held hostage. The quiet of the home place absorbs the late afternoon as she finishes the fridge. Jean-Marc plugs in his laptop and taps at saved documents.

Twenty minutes later, Brittany gets up and comes downstairs with an old rag doll cradled in one arm. The doll was old when Alma was a child. She's surprised it's still in one piece. "It was on a shelf in the closet in my room." Brittany points above her head toward the southeast bedroom, which has traditionally been the girls' room. "That was my room when we lived here too. Is it all right if I go look around in the barns?"

"Sure," Alma says. "Just come in and tell me if you see anything strange. There could be chemicals out there still. Be careful. And take the flashlight out of that drawer there."

Brittany's smile still feels like a new thing. Alma has seen it so little in the past three days. The girl who pulls on her coat and mittens, grabs up her dusty new toy, and runs outside is something like the child Alma remembers herself being here.

Alma goes to the window over the kitchen sink to watch Brittany jog across the yard and disappear into the horse barn, then lets her eyes relax on distant hills until a new sound distracts her. A pickup is coming in from the road, humming on the snow-covered gravel. Alma hesitates only a moment between going straight for the gun, then checking the window in the front room to see who it is. The Murphrod. She relaxes. "Get a grip," she mumbles to herself, resting the gun on the wide molding above the window.

Chance pulls around and is up at the back door before Alma gets there. When she enters the kitchen, Alma finds the two men staring at each other, square-shouldered, the door wide open. "What's going on, Chance?" she interrupts, stepping in front of Jean-Marc to usher Chance in and get the door shut. "Not time for supper already, is it?" The sun is gone, it must be after five. At the home place, they read time based on the season and the position of the sun against the buttes. There has never been any need for clocks.

"Your grandma called. She couldn't get through to you so she called our place. She got a visit from Rick Burlington. Same day as the funeral, can you believe that?" Chance stands just inside the door. Although he looks at Alma as he speaks, his shoulders stay squared toward Jean-Marc, who has retreated only a few steps.

"What does he want?"

"Same thing as usual. The mineral lease."

"Did she sign?"

"Your grandma? No," Chance answers with the hint of a smile. "But she was upset. She says he threatened her. Threatened you, actually. Said a few things about you and Brittany out here by yourselves." Chance rubs his fist with his gloved hand and glances dismissively at Jean-Marc, as if his presence on the home place doesn't count as any sort of protection. "He said something about how she ought to sign so that 'all this will be over.' She thought he might be talking about what happened to Vicky."

Alma's hands are still cold as the chill of the house wears off, but that doesn't explain the shiver that trickles down her back.

She stuffs her hands in her armpits and stares back at Chance. "You think she might have just misunderstood him?"

"No, I don't. I've heard things like this from landowners, and others just won't talk at all, like they're scared. But that's how he works—he gets the old folks alone and says things they can't prove. It's all hearsay and he denies it. Once they sign, it's all over."

Alma paces into the living room, toward the warmth of the woodstove. This is Chance, of course. She trusts him. But the diabolical landman is too much of a stock character. Her lawyer's mind works at other explanations, other motivations. When he talks about Harmony, Chance's voice vibrates with his desperation to prevent their advance across the valley. What stories might he tell to accomplish that? What might he be willing to do?

She hears Jean-Marc in the kitchen. "Are you suggesting that this Burlington person would come out here and—what, try to kill Alma or Brittany?" His tone is incredulous. To Jean-Marc, this is one more note in a crazy tune that includes the outhouse and lack of phone and Internet. He's a sentence or two away from telling Chance to calm down, which won't go over well. In a flash, Alma remembers the speeding white pickup on the highway this morning.

Chance ignores Jean-Marc and follows Alma into the front room. "Why don't you just come with me now?" he says to Alma. "We've got satellite Internet. Brittany can play with Mae. We can talk this over while we get supper ready." He doesn't speak the subtext: *under my roof, you'll be safe.*

"Something happened this morning," she says in a voice Jean-Marc won't be able to hear. "I can't believe I forgot. A white pickup came out of nowhere from behind and rear-ended us while Brittany and I were driving into town. I nearly lost control. Barely got a glimpse of the pickup, it was moving so fast. Do you think it could have been . . ." Alma's question trails off as she realizes she's not quite sure what she thinks it might have been.

"To do with the lease?" Chance prompts. "You're damn straight I do. All the more reason—"

"What do you think, Jean-Marc?" Alma raises her voice to speak to him where he's come to stand in the doorway. "The Murphys have Internet. Should we just go over now?"

"Sure." His answer is terse.

Alma shouts Brittany in from the barn, then together with Jean-Marc they follow the Murphrod up the road and come into the house in the warmth of greetings from Mae, Jayne, and Ed. The old woodstove burns hot and the smell of bread baking fills the space.

Chance catches Alma's elbow as she starts to take off her coat. "I was just going to park the pickup in the machine shed to get it out of the wind. You might want to put your car in there too."

"Sure," Alma agrees. Jean-Marc is already peeling off layers to sit down and accept the cup of hot cider that Jayne offers. "I'll just go put the car away, Jean-Marc," she calls across the room to him, but whether he doesn't hear her or doesn't feel like answering, she gets no reply.

Chance and Alma slam the door and head back into the last light of a frigid day. Chance drives around to a newer-looking steel building, mostly hidden behind the older wooden house and barn. He shoves open a big, rolling door, pulls the pickup into its old spot, and gets out to wait for Alma to pull in behind him.

It's dark in the shed with only a few small windows, but warmer out of the wind. Dark outlines of impressive power tools and machinery line the walls. Chance leans against the pickup, arms crossed, in no hurry. His curly head is bare. Alma walks toward him. "I'm surprised you still have that old thing."

"She's a great old pickup. You like the new paint job?"

She nods and pats the shiny fender. "Beautiful."

"Just for chores these days, though," Chance continues. "I'll never get rid of her, not as long as I can keep her crawling along. Too many good memories."

Alma recalls a few of those good memories and blushes in the weak light. Chance sees where her mind has gone and ducks his own head to glance into the cab with a look that evokes the boyish shyness she remembers.

"May I?" She gestures toward the door.

Chance opens it, puts his hands on her waist, and lifts her up with a grunt. "I remember you right there," he says, resting a boot on the running board and filling the doorway, very close to her but looking down instead at the way the brown steering wheel has changed colors from weather and the oils from his hands.

"I remember being here. Those were good days."

"They were," he affirms in a low voice as she runs her gloved finger around the large circle of the steering wheel. The windshield reflects their nervous faces floating in darkness, linked to nothing.

"Come sit by me," she says on impulse. She moves over to make room for him.

Chance doesn't argue. He steps in, sits down, shuts the door, and puts his arm around her in the pose they used to hold on long drives to games, to town. Alma leans into his warmth without thinking. It's hard to remember that any time has passed. She reaches out to feel for the key over the visor. It falls into her hand. She slides in the key and clicks the ignition forward a notch, then pushes a button on the old cassette deck. Its heads whir to life and the sound of slow piano and Patsy Cline sighs into the cab. "Crazy."

In this darkness they could be parked down some abandoned country lane again, her hands in his hair, his lips on her neck. She lays her hand on his denim thigh, on the place where it used to rest while he drove. *Chance*. Good God. How can they be here again? How did she let this happen? She used to drive him crazy in this pickup, in the long months before they went all the way, and then after, in the distraught aftermath of the accident, crazy with each other's skin. He hasn't forgotten. His lips slowly settle on her hair, move to her jawline, and she cries out from a need indistinguishable from memory, a loud sound in the small cab, turning into his kiss as if she'd never turned away.

From that moment, neither of them hesitates. He puts a hand on her shoulder to pull her into his kiss. She grabs his jacket and leans backward, letting his weight push her down on the broad seat. He cushions her head with his thick gloves, then reaches a warm hand up under her sweater to push aside her bra. Her mind is unable to form a single consonant of resistance. Her hands are pushing aside the rough jacket, pulling shirts and undershirts out of his jeans, yanking at his belt. The light is off, the sun has set, the moon is barely visible outside the cavernous machine shed, and the darkness is nearly complete. Their hands move with rehearsed certainty. She gasps at the cold as her pants come down, then Chance's hand is on her. This much has changed: he's a man now. His touch is assured. The same frantic energy she remembers from high school is here, though, the same sense of needing all of each other right away, of being unable to wait. Chance moves over her, gentle, then urgent, then beyond control. The feel of him with her this way again releases years of pain. Alma clutches him and sobs as he climaxes.

"Alma—" His voice is soft, cautious in the silence that follows. "Did I hurt you?"

She'll have a bump on her head from the door panel. "No," she whispers. "I hurt you. I'm sorry." She feels for his face in the dark and kisses him.

It is too cold to linger half dressed. They sit up and pull

their clothes together blindly. Alma wants to say something but has no idea what that ought to be. Nothing with Chance or anything else is happening according to plan.

Chance pulls her against his chest and rests his head on hers. "Al, listen—" he begins, clearing his throat. "I know you're going back to Seattle. You know I can't turn it on and off with you. Just tell me goodbye this time. You owe me a goodbye."

Alma can't see Chance's eyes and she's glad he can't see whatever is on her face. "One for old times' sake?" she echoes his words from yesterday. "No, it's not that. I don't know what I'm doing. I can't believe we're here again."

"Me neither."

"I guess—at the time I thought you'd forget about me pretty fast. We were so young, and I never heard from you in college." Even in the darkness, Alma drops her head away from Chance. This is a lie. She remembers his letters. She told the student clerk in the tiny college post office some story about a stalker and persuaded her to return them to sender, unopened.

Chance's hand stops rubbing her arm. "Alma, you never gave me an address. I wrote a few letters to you addressed to the college, but they came back marked insufficient address. I'd run into Pete once in a while when he had leave. He said if you wanted to be in touch, you would be. He wouldn't tell me anything."

That was Petey all right, trying to protect her when he had no idea what was going on. Alma's eyes have adjusted to the faint light. She looks around the dark cab, remembering the tweedy pattern of the upholstery, the broken radio, the glove compartment that can be opened only with a flathead screwdriver. There's a new crack along the top of the windshield that has begun to stretch out horizontally. It's a fault line. The glass will have to be replaced. Even the trusty Murphrod is mortal.

"I know. I'm sorry. It was such an awful time. Right after they died I was just clinging to you. I'm surprised you even

wanted to be around me. I was this hideous, desperate person—"
Alma ducks her head against Chance's jacket, which smells like
cows and dirt and home.

"You weren't." His hand squeezes her arm.

"And then the way I cut you off that summer—I thought
you'd hate me." More than that, she'd counted on it. He was
supposed to get disgusted and give up, forget her.

"I could never hate you." That voice, so soft and sure, strikes
at her.

"Oh, never say never." Alma's whole body tightens around
the secret she's still keeping. "I was afraid I wouldn't be able to
leave if—well, you know what that summer was like."

"No, Al. I don't know anything. We were together every
spare minute, I was so— And then it was like a light went out,
sometime in July. You wouldn't let me anywhere near you. I
thought I was going to lose my mind." Chance reaches down to
the floor, picks up a screwdriver, and hands it to Alma. "As long
as we're talking about that summer, you might as well know
what I wanted to tell you."

Alma stares at him for a second before she remembers that
the screwdriver is for opening the broken latch of the glove
compartment. She wiggles it under the hardware until the
drawer falls open and the little light comes on. She pulls out
a pile of proofs of insurance, registration, a yellowing owner's manual, two pairs of snub-nosed pliers, and a wire cutter,
before she comes to a green velvet jeweler's box buried at the
bottom. She hesitates like Pandora at the moment of decision,
then takes out the box and stuffs the papers and tools back in.
"This? What is it?"

"It's what I wanted to tell you before you left. Open it."

The diamond inside is tiny and beautiful. One hand flies to
her mouth to catch her gasp.

"Oh, Chance."

"I bought it with my rodeo winnings that summer. It ain't

much. After you took off I never knew what to do with it." Chance opens the door. "We should be getting back," he says.

Alma puts the ring back in the glove compartment. "I'm sorry. It was wrong of me to cut you off like that."

"Why did you, Al?" Chance's voice is still soft, but the weight of emotion in it is planetary. She hears the door click back into place. He wants an explanation for the last fifteen years. He deserves one. This is why she's avoided this scene. She hoped never to have to give this explanation. Alma grasps his hand with both of hers, but it stays heavy and limp.

"What can I ever say? I behaved atrociously. I was afraid if we were together, I wouldn't be able to leave. I wanted to put everything about this place behind me. I tried not to think of you at all. Pete and Vicky thought I abandoned them. That's what I wanted everyone to think. I didn't want anybody coming for me. I was afraid if I came home I'd never leave again." She turns away and leans over on her knees, feeling again the hollowness and guilt of those lonely years. "You wouldn't have wanted to know me then, anyway."

Chance sits still. "I always wanted to know you, Al. That never changed. You planning to do that again?"

Alma lifts her head to look at him. "Run away? No. I can't now, not with Brittany." She digs her toe into a place on the floor where the carpet has ripped away to reveal the steel chassis. This is a night for revelations, for old, bare truths. "But there's something you need to know. When I left here that fall, there's something I didn't tell you. What happened in July."

She hears Chance shift to see her face better. The moon's subtle silver glow has begun to illuminate the dark machinery around them.

"You cut me off pretty hard and fast." He lays one hand on the steering wheel, wrapping his fingers tightly.

"I know." Alma is beginning to feel the cold now. She pulls her arms around her middle and plunges into the torrent of words that must come out all at once or not at all. Montana is starting to feel like a mountain of ugly, abandoned words. To deal with the past, she will have to clamber over every miserable one of them. No wonder she's avoided this.

"The thing I couldn't tell you was, I was pregnant. I know"— she hears the start of his protest—"I know we were very careful, but there was that time down by the creek, remember, when the condom broke?" She'd made him buy condoms in Billings, mortified at the thought of buying them herself and terrified that someone who knew them would see him doing it. She'd been such a child, and he'd been almost as nervous. She half smiles at the memory before she continues.

"I had no idea what to do. Mom and Dad were gone. Pete and Vicky had enough to worry about. I thought if I told you— it seemed like it would ruin both our lives. You'd think we had to get married, and it was—I wasn't ready. You were off to Bozeman. I thought if I could just get to college then everything would work out somehow. I'd be safe. It was stupid. I thought maybe I'd tell you once I was out there, and then, well, it just became impossible."

"What happened to the baby?" Chance's voice sounds piped in from a thousand miles away. The cold is getting more intense around her kidneys. Alma wishes Chance would put his arm around her again, but he's not moving.

"I got an abortion in New Jersey, a week after I got to Bryn Mawr." Chance's rough inhalation is loud in the small cab. "It happened so fast. I knew I had to do it, and if I waited or told anyone, I was afraid something would happen to stop me. I didn't want anything to show up on my college medical records, so I looked up a clinic across the river. I was in and back all in a day, only missed one class. Paid for it with my Albertsons money." It's a small, frightened, young girl's voice describing all this, trying to explain, looking for the absolution and understanding she's never been able to give herself.

"All by yourself? You went alone?" Chance's voice is unusually high. She would almost say distraught, but she can't see much of his face, can't be sure.

Alma nods, bent very low. "I didn't have any friends yet. Not like that."

"You never told *anyone*?" Chance has both hands on the wheel now, gripping it like the Murphrod's brakes have just failed going down Beartooth Pass.

Alma shakes her head. "My therapist. And you."

"And that's why you cut me off like that, because you were pregnant?" Chance's tone is twisted, tight.

Alma nods, eyes shut tight, shoulders hunched away from him over clenched hands. She's dreaded his next words for fifteen years. She braces herself for the mortal wound of Chance's judgment, the end of whatever light of young love he's held her in.

"Oh, Al. Oh my God." Chance falls silent and Alma doesn't dare speak. "He'd be fifteen this year. Or her."

"I know. I think about the birthdays too. I almost bought her a present once." She can almost smell the cold rain on the paving stones at the Ardmore pedestrian mall, feel the perfumed warmth of the baby boutique, touch the shiny frog print raincoat that drew her in, just the right size for the little girl whose birthday it would have been. *Stop it,* she orders herself.

Chance's breathing is still audible, his head low. Alma tastes blood and realizes that she's biting her cheek, hard. Her unbuttoned coat is letting in the cold and she turns her attention to buttoning up, straightening, giving Chance a few minutes to process.

"It'll take me a while to get my head around this. The way I feel about Mae—" Chance stretches his neck and shivers. "I'm gonna need some time. I remember even back then thinking about what our kids would be like. I remember thinking they'd be something special." Chance's voice lowers dangerously. "Listen to me. I'll shut up before I make it any worse."

Alma has migrated far enough from him that she can press her cheek against the cold glass on the far side of the cab. "You can't make it worse. Anything you could say I've already said to myself, believe me." She's no longer the girl he loved, and it was good to be her again, for a few minutes.

"I don't mean it like that. I just can't pretend it's no big thing, that's all. You've had a long time to get used to it." He meets her eyes and she shuts hers. "I'm glad I know what happened, even after all this time. At least I won't have to wonder when you go away."

Now he opens the door and climbs down deliberately, measuring his steps as if the earth might be uncertain under him. He does not reach to help her out. She reluctantly climbs down to follow him from the shed. They were children the last time they got out of this pickup together. Now he's a grown man with a child, someone who lost his wife to the big city, and she's presented him with a new, crushing loss he never knew he'd suffered. His posture is slumped, she notices as they step out into the moonlight—Chance who always stands so straight.

When they return to the house, a newer Dodge is parked outside. A school parking permit is taped in the windshield and what looks like a religious medal on a chain hangs from the rearview mirror. Inside, Alma finds a blond woman chopping vegetables at the table. Jean-Marc is sautéing something wonderful smelling while Jayne slices bread and Ed replenishes the woodpile. Only Jayne seems to have noticed Chance and Alma's long absence. She looks up with a watchful expression to read what's written all over them. "Everything okay out there?" she inquires, a little more loudly than necessary.

"Just showing Alma around," Chance says, shrugging off his coat and taking Alma's. He puts them on the same hanger and turns to scoop up Mae. He holds her smooth baby cheek against his and shuts his eyes. She starts to wriggle before he's willing to put her down.

"You haven't met Chance's girlfriend, Tiffany, yet, have you? She teaches second grade in Forsyth." Jayne advances on Alma to get between her and Chance, leading Alma to Tiffany by the arm. Alma smells an ambush and wonders if Jayne decided to invite Tiffany before or after she knew Jean-Marc was coming. Probably before. "Tiffany, this is Alma Terrebonne. Her family has the place just up the road. Old friends."

Tiffany rises and walks over to shake Alma's hand. Alma has been afraid they'll know each other, but she has never seen the woman who stands in front of her, tossing back a head of ash-blond hair over a well-filled-out snowflake sweater. Interesting. If Chance is a breast man, that's a new development. Alma sneaks a quick look at her own athletic proportions under a fitted cashmere sweater. Her bra strap is twisted where she pulled it up in the dark, but she doesn't dare rearrange it now. Tiffany's face is pretty and open. Alma looks in vain for something not to like, aside from the eighties mall-rat name.

"Nice to meet you. So you're old friends of Chance's, you two?" Either Tiffany is quite an actress or she knows nothing about Chance's history with Alma. She's young enough that she might have no idea.

"Chance and I went to high school together," Alma volunteers. "I live in Seattle now. We're just in town for a funeral." That nutshell version of events, she hopes, will hold off awkward questions.

"Oh, I'm sorry. Somebody in the family?"

"My sister."

"Oh my gosh! Your sister! Oh, what a shame!" After this exclamation, Tiffany is struck dumb by the information and retreats to the cutting board. Alma sympathizes. It's hardly a conversation topic.

Jean-Marc is humming French opera to himself, sipping at Ed's homemade hard cider and adding butter liberally to a pan of onions. As Alma approaches he looks up, smiles, and holds out the cider glass. "You've got to try this!" he enthuses. "Notes of oak." It's an inside joke, from a wine tasting they did at a Washington vineyard where the wine tasted like it had been strained through oak chips. The pushy winemaker kept referring to oak this and oak that until Jean-Marc and Alma turned it into a drinking game. Alma smiles and tastes the cider. It's better than the wine was, and Jean-Marc turns back to his pan in satisfaction at her approving nod.

As he turns away, Alma knows suddenly that their relationship has entered that twilight between the moment when it's over and the moment when she works up the nerve to tell him. It's impossible that what she and Chance have just done isn't written in neon on her forehead. If Jean-Marc were paying attention to her at all, her tension should be screaming at him. But he trusts her. She's never lied to him. She walks to the counter to pour herself a large glass of cider, aware of Jayne's wary eyes on her every step.

Dinner lasts too long. Alma doesn't know which way to look. Chance—situated by Jayne at the opposite end of the table, between Tiffany and Ed—drops the ceramic butter dish and spends what seems like a very long time on his knees beside the table, rubbing up the greasy butter mark and collecting shards of crockery.

"There were antelope," Brittany says when the conversation pauses. She's speaking softly to Mae, but everyone looks up. These are the first words Brittany has spoken since arriving at the Murphys' this evening, while Mae happily chatters enough for both of them. Her silence comes and goes now, a protective veil she puts on.

"Oh, right." Alma sets down her knife. "At the home place. Right up next to the front porch, close as can be."

"Some of them were going to have babies!" Brittany tells Mae, eyes full of excitement. "They were all big like this." She gestures with her arms and puffs out her cheeks to imitate a heavy antelope. The table dissolves into a common laugh of affection and relief at being able to laugh at anything. Brittany looks up with an expression of unalloyed, bright-eyed joy, taking in their pleasure. It comes and goes quickly, but Alma drinks it in, watching her niece long after the moment has passed.

There is discussion of Maddie's worried call, and the consensus emerges that Alma will leave the front porch light on. The light is visible from the Murphys', just barely, and in case of emergency she'll turn it off as a call for help. The plan suits Jayne, who bridles at Ed's suggestion that the Terrebonnes and Jean-Marc simply stay on at the Little m for safety. "There now," she says, taking a very firm grip on her husband's arm, "let's not go overboard. I'd be more worried about Maddie all by herself in town."

"That's right," Alma joins in, grateful that Jayne has moved the focus from her. "I should call Detective Curtis and ask him if someone can check in on Grandma, especially after this afternoon."

Tiffany stirs at the table, pushing her chair back. "I need to be up early for school. I'll call you tomorrow," she says, giving Chance a quick kiss on the cheek as she gets up. At her touch, Chance reddens and his eyes flicker to Alma, who picks up her glass of cider and bolts the rest. When Tiffany pulls away from Chance, eyes close to his face, she freezes for an instant, then continues farewelling the whole group as she moves for the door.

"I'm sure we'll all have an early morning," Jayne announces, folding her napkin and standing. "Alma, why don't I walk out with you to get the car, just to be on the safe side?" The offer is at once kind and inarguable. Before Alma can say a word, she's back in her coat and walking into the snowy night beside Jayne, who settles her shotgun against her shoulder. Alma is light-headed from the cider—good God, what must the alcohol content be?—and the intensity of the last two hours.

"You certainly lost no time getting reacquainted with my son," Jayne says. Her tone is not unkind, but the worry comes through powerfully.

"That wasn't my intention. It just sort of . . . happened."

Jayne takes this in as they walk. "Our Chance, he's a good man, and he's had such terrible luck with women, starting with you."

Alma presses her lips together to hide a wry smile from Jayne, who has shown her nothing but kindness since childhood. This is fallout she never considered—how much her actions would have hurt Jayne. Chance must know what his mother will say to her, must be stiff with embarrassment, but under the circumstances he can't prevent it. "I'm sorry, Mrs. Murphy. I never meant to hurt him. Or you."

Jayne moves the gun to the shoulder farther from Alma and reaches out to pat the younger woman's shoulder. "You know, back then, after you wouldn't see him anymore, he closed up so tight none of us could reach him. I think it's why he transferred to Stanford, to get away from everyone who knew him. Even after Ed had his cancer surgery and Chance came back here to help out, I worried to see him so alone. I asked him once, didn't he want to get married, have a family? You know what he told me?"

Alma doesn't dare answer that one.

"He told me, 'Ma, I'm not the marrying kind.' Can you imagine? After I helped him pick out that ring for you, telling him all the while you were both way too young. He finally stopped me and said, 'I love her, Mom. You understand that.' Alma, I can understand telling him no, but then just to break it off without even saying goodbye—how could you do that to him?" Jayne's eyes are moist and her question is plaintively stated, the cri de cœur she's held in all these years.

Alma stops walking and turns to Jayne. "I should have said goodbye," she begins. "It was wrong of me just to cut him off like that. I was . . . not myself. But you should know, he never proposed. I guess I didn't give him time. I didn't even know about the ring until tonight. He showed it to me."

Jayne sighs right down into her boots. "Tiffany is such a nice girl. I set them up, you know. I should have known it would never work out. There's no edge to her. Chance's been humoring us both, like he does." She lets the weight of the shotgun slip through her hands until the butt end rests on the ground. "So are you going to break his heart again? I'd like to be prepared."

Jayne looks so small and fearful and fierce, standing there in the snow with the barrel of the gun clenched in her hands, that Alma has to smile. "Jayne—" she risks. It's always been Mrs. Murphy, but for the first time they're speaking to each other as women. There is no room for falseness in the moonlight between them. "Would it be enough if I promise to give him a decent goodbye this time?"

"I guess that'll have to satisfy the mother bear," Jayne agrees and resumes their walk toward the machine shed. "Maybe I took it so hard because you broke all our hearts, Alma. You always fit here so well. We thought you'd be our daughter one day, we really did."

Tentatively, Alma reaches out to squeeze Jayne's hand. The snow has begun to accumulate, hiding ruts in the yard, smoothing over imperfections in the buildings and landscape, making the circle of light through which they walk as fresh and perfect as new creation, where all things are possible.

CHAPTER 17

WEDNESDAY, 9 P.M. MOUNTAIN STANDARD TIME

When Alma parks the car in front of the Murphys' and goes back in, Jean-Marc insists on driving home.

"You've had way too much to drink," he tells Alma, snatching the keys from her hand.

"Now hold on there," Chance interjects. "You've had quite a bit yourself. Why don't I drive you? I've had nothing but coffee all night."

"I've had about enough of your help for one day," Jean-Marc snaps in a voice just a little too loud for sobriety. He puts an arm around Alma and steers her toward the door. Alma looks back to see Chance's jaw clenched tight, but he says nothing as they follow Brittany into the night.

Jean-Marc relinquishes the keys to Alma without looking at her. The ride home is short and silent. The three of them wash up in the kitchen sink and tread upstairs, where the clanking radiators have raised the temperature enough that they can no longer see their breath. It can't be later than nine thirty, but Brittany falls asleep immediately and Alma can hardly stay awake to strip down to her long underwear and woolly socks. Jean-Marc sits on the edge of the bed, still dressed.

"So what were you doing out in the barn all that time?"

Alma dives under the covers and curls up facing the wall. "Just catching up. I haven't seen him in years."

"And he wanted to try your lipstick on his neck?"

Alma freezes. Of course, that too-dark shade she put on for the funeral. It would smear easily and show up on anything it touched, leaving traces even when wiped away. Back at the house she'd been too busy not looking at Chance to examine him for stray smudges. What a rookie error. So that's what Jayne saw—and what Jean-Marc eventually spotted too. She wonders about Tiffany's powers of observation.

"I'm sorry, Jean-Marc. We have a lot of history."

Jean-Marc waits. Minutes tick by and Alma says nothing. After this day, at this hour, she has no strength for confrontation. At last he sighs and pulls off his outer clothes. They lie on opposite sides of the bed and fall asleep without moving, like tired children.

Alma is walking along the creek, in among the water birches and black cottonwoods, their bark papery and slick under her hands as she moves from rock to rock, balancing barefoot like they used to, she and Petey and Vicky, playing in the creek bottom, running free as long as the sun stayed up. She's alone, but their laughter echoes in the water sounds. The sun lights on the water in golden currents, carrying off the mountain of words. They float away in foamy clumps, dissipating, dissolving into eddies, swirling around her toes, then breaking free, leaving her, washing her with the benediction of the waters.

From upstream, a smell begins to accumulate around her—natural, but nothing she's accustomed to. A smell of hurt. Standing bare-legged in the middle of the cold current, Alma feels an unexpected warmth. She begins to walk upstream, seeking the source of the temperature change.

As she comes around the bend, she hears an elk's cries, and then she sees it: in the shallowest part of the creek, a cow elk is down, under vicious attack by a pack of coyotes. Two are at her neck and two more at her belly, ripping at her, releasing her hot blood to the stream. Alma looks down to see that the warmth she feels is the elk's blood, coagulating around her knees, and what she thought was the dissolution of the mountain of words is in fact blood flowing out of them, blood flowing because of them, because of all she's done and hasn't done. When she looks back up, buzzards are descending. The coyotes have begun to tear at the elk's exposed viscera, and when her dying, glazed eyes meet Alma's, the eyes are Vicky's. Alma begins to scream.

Jean-Marc is shaking her. "Alma! Alma, wake up! It's just a dream, wake up!"

Alma throws her arms around his neck and hugs him close, breathing hard. The moon has risen and hangs so near it feels like a personal visitation. "Oh God, it was awful. It was Vicky. It's my fault. *It's my fault.*"

"It's not your fault." Jean-Marc shushes her and pushes her hair back. "It's not your fault. Calm down."

Alma relaxes onto her pillow as Jean-Marc rubs her back and holds her. She feels the tension still alive in him, set aside to comfort her. "I'm sorry about tonight," she says.

"Would you like to tell me about your history with Chance Murphy?" Jean-Marc's hand moves through her hair in a gentle, familiar gesture. He is not yet fully awake.

They are so close that any telltale movement could give away her racing thoughts, the foregone conclusion of the end of the relationship. Alma wants to save that for later, when she's gathered up the courage and the words to do it right. She forces her shoulders to wiggle a little like she's looking for a comfortable spot on the old, lumpy mattress.

"The oldest, most boring story around. My first love." The words are as laughing and dismissive as she can make them, a weak effort, but apparently enough for Jean-Marc.

"I think he still has plans for you." Jean-Marc takes the same amused tone.

"Maybe he did, I don't know. But not after tonight." Her mind goes to the jeweler's box, then to Chance's slumped profile outside the machine shed. She and Jean-Marc are looking back over an evening as they often do, mocking and interpreting, sharing anything the other missed. Normally she enjoys these conversations.

"No?" Jean-Marc's question is light, clipped . . . hopeful.

"No. I'm not quite the person he remembers." She feels the heat in her face, glad he can't see it.

"It was a long time ago. He couldn't possibly understand who you are now." Jean-Marc leans into her neck and laughs. Alma knows perfectly well that everything about Big Horn County is dangerously exotic to Jean-Marc. A safari trip. He's one of those who will never go back to the country, could never live here. She hadn't understood that about him until recently. He believes her to be like him.

Jean-Marc runs a hand up her body, settling on her breast in a gesture of ownership that, for the first time, bothers her. Yet she lets the hand stay.

"Jean-Marc, you and I have had a lot of fun," she begins.

"Past perfect," he notices. Every muscle in him goes taut. "Is that the tense we're in?"

"I'm sure we could go on having a lot of fun. It's just that—I'm starting to think that life will have to be about more than that."

"More than having fun?" Jean-Marc runs a finger between her breasts, down to her belly, then follows the line with his lips. "Like living out on the tundra with that cowboy, a thousand miles from a decent restaurant or a nice shoe store? Is that what you have in mind? Because it doesn't sound like you." His voice strains to hold the same unemotional tone, but his eyes are locked on hers as he moves down her body. This is the way he usually ends arguments.

"I know. Not the me that you know. But you don't know all of me. Maybe you don't know me very well at all." What she intends as defiant comes out instead small and sad.

Tugging at her long underwear bottoms, watching her sad expression, Jean-Marc changes. He looks down at her body and inhales. When he looks up, his eyes have gone dark and impenetrable. "And he does?" he whispers.

Alma's mouth opens. "I didn't mean—" She breaks off, afraid of what Jean-Marc might know.

Jean-Marc's jaw is set. He raises himself over her lower body on flexed arms. "Did you think I wouldn't be able to smell this?" he says in a lower voice than she's ever heard from him.

Of course. How could Alma have forgotten? She shuts her eyes and pulls her arms in tight, covering her breasts. "I'm sorry." She realizes that she can smell sex herself, all over her. It's impossible to miss.

"So am I." Jean-Marc moves back up to look at her eyes. "I don't know how I expected this to end—I guess I knew it would, but I never imagined it would be like this."

"You're right, you don't deserve anything like that." Alma squirms for a more comfortable position, but Jean-Marc is right on top of her, alive to every flinch and grimace. "Jean-Marc, it's no excuse, but these last few days, I'm finding out things I don't know how to handle. And in the middle of all that, I have to deal with him again. Last time I saw him, I was seventeen years old and knocked up. Seeing him—I kind of lost my grip on reality."

"Knocked up? You have a—"

"No. I . . . I didn't have it. He never knew."

Jean-Marc looks down into her face as if she's a total stranger. This isn't moral disapproval. She knows that he long ago abandoned his diligent Roman Catholic upbringing. The blow he's feeling is what she's hidden from him through all these months of intimacy, and what she did to him tonight, an arrow's shot from the ranch house. This is the person she's becoming—someone capable of brutal, almost sociopathic acts of detachment. This is what she will be, a few more episodes of serial monogamy down the road, never genuinely connecting, never allowing entry to the darkened sanctum. She sees her soul all at once as a snow globe balanced on a windowsill: something beautiful within, but sizzling with potential energy, so close to falling, shattering.

"So you told him tonight." Some of the tautness goes out of Jean-Marc's body, other emotions edging out his anger.

"I didn't mean to. I didn't mean to tell him *ever,* it just came out." How long has it been since she let a secret loose like she did tonight, just *told,* because the need to connect was stronger than her risk aversion?

"In the heat of passion." The dark, shuttered eyes are back, holding hers with their poorly hidden pain.

"It wasn't like that. Jean-Marc, you're heavy." She wriggles a little, trying to get out from under him.

"Am I? You never used to complain." His tone is singsong, his movements familiar, but their meaning has become different. Jean-Marc pulls her forearms up near her head with both his hands. The moves to propel him off her run through Alma's mind in crisp choreography, but she has no will to do it. She's betrayed him. She's let down everyone. Rather than indignation, she is consumed by despair, and a desire to bring punishment upon herself. She goes limp and turns her head to the side.

His lips come down on her neck as one hand shoves up her long underwear shirt. His head goes to her breasts and his body moves against her, going through motions they both know, automatic, a hand already pushing long underwear down her lower body and his, baring their middles. He has never been like this with her. He has never made her feel merely present, a prop in his act. She doesn't want him, not like this, not after Chance, but she doesn't resist him or say no. Her words to

Chance a few days ago come back: *Maybe I deserve it.* She lets Jean-Marc take what he wants—grunting at her, oblivious to her passivity, maybe enjoying it—then push her away as he gets up to jog downstairs and clean himself in the kitchen sink.

Her own reaction leaves her shaking more than anything Jean-Marc has done. She pulls her clothes over her bare skin, sinks into the blankets, and cries as quietly as she can, hoping Brittany can't hear. The soul-scouring thought that carries her to sleep is: *What satisfaction guilt takes in punishment.*

CHAPTER 18

When Alma awakens just before dawn and pads downstairs, Jean-Marc is sleeping on a nest of blankets next to the woodstove. She steps over him to run a hose from the sink to fill the low hip bath that resides in the pantry.

She's there, rinsing her hair with a dipper, when she hears Jean-Marc's footsteps. He steps behind the curtain over the doorway, still in rumpled long johns. His face is abashed. "I'm sorry," he says. "I don't know what came over me. I'll leave today."

Alma wants words to put some fitting end to this relationship of nearly two years that they just tore apart, but now, when she needs them, none will come. She can only nod as she reaches for the towel.

Jean-Marc looks down with a face full of regret. "Do you love him?"

She hurries to wrap herself in the towel. "I used to. We were high school sweethearts."

"But do you love him?" Jean-Marc isn't fooled by her historical summary.

Alma steps out of the tub, dripping, freezing, grabbing for underclothes, her sweater and jeans crammed onto a shelf. "This isn't about him. After what I told him last night I doubt he ever wants to see me again. This is about you and me hanging on to something because it's convenient, not because it's right." These are words she's used on other boyfriends, her nuanced version of *I'm just not that into you.* She's mastered this quick escape, plotted the moves and words that will create the cleanest break, not a single frying pan or set of high-end speakers gone astray when the split is complete.

"If that's the way you feel, I'll get my things out of the condo." The way he says the words—the flawless articulation— shows her how he must deal with a client who's become troublesome and must be dismissed. There is caution, firmness, even respect, over an impenetrable professionalism, like an air lock closing.

The condo is in her name. All their affairs are labeled. There will be no messiness in separating them. There has been genuine tenderness between them, but after last night they can hardly look at each other.

"I'll be back in a few days. Just leave the keys with the doorman."

Jean-Marc fixes her with one last resigned look and drops the curtain.

They stop on the way to Billings to leave Brittany at the Murphys' again, as agreed the night before. Jayne and Mae are waiting at the front door of Jayne and Ed's house with smiles. Jean-Marc stays in the car. There's no sign of Chance.

Jayne insists on giving Alma at least one cup of coffee and asks about what Brittany might like for lunch. As Alma turns to leave the cozy kitchen, another question for Brittany bubbles to the surface, now that she's talking more easily.

"Brittany, honey, did you ever see your mom with a copy

of the mineral lease Rick Burlington wants Great-Grandma to sign? Did she ever talk about that with you?"

Before Brittany can answer, Chance stomps in the back door with a rush of cold air, tracking snow onto the mat. "Ma, I told you, you're getting low on propane. When are you—" He stops short a few feet in front of Alma. "Oh, sorry. I didn't see the car."

"We're just headed into Billings. Jean-Marc is leaving." Her words get smaller as she goes, like they're disappearing down a drain. Alma gestures with a limp hand toward the front of the house, the rest of her frozen in place by Chance's sudden apparition.

"Nothing I said, I hope." Chance turns away stiffly and strides over to the coffeepot. Alma looks quickly to Jayne, who busies herself rinsing coffee cups, then turns back to Brittany, who has backed up against the wall. She's at another of her nervous mannerisms, playing with the ends of her long hair, trying not to be noticed. Alma gets that same prickly hair shirt feeling she had in the kitchen at Denny's, like she's about to hear things she'd rather not.

"Brittany," she says in a voice intended to be calm. "What is it?"

"I didn't know anything was wrong," Brittany says. "Mom and Rick fought every time he came over. There was nothing funny that night."

"What do you mean, that night? Rick was there that night?"

Brittany twirls a long lock of hair around her index finger and sticks the end in her mouth for a few seconds before spitting it out to answer. "Everybody else was asleep by the time he came by, trying to get Mom to promise she'd get Great-Grandma to sign, like he always did. I only called Uncle Walt and Uncle Pete because I saw Rick slip out and follow Mom."

Alma takes another cautious, stalking step toward Brittany. She can feel Chance tense behind her, hear his accelerated breathing as he sets down his coffee cup and turns with her toward Brittany. "You saw him follow her outside?" Alma asks.

Brittany studies the linoleum pattern. "I just wanted them to tell him to stop bothering us. You won't tell him I told, right?" Brittany's eyes sneak up at Alma, then shoot down again. "Mom was afraid of Rick. She wrote it all down on those papers, and I don't know where they went."

Alma turns her head and locks eyes with Chance. As the flash of realization passes between them, the sound of a big engine nears the house.

"That's not Dad," Chance says and moves fast to the front window, Alma right behind him. Rick Burlington's white pickup, getting dirtier by the day, is pulling in next to the Mitsubishi outside the front door. Chance has his keys out of his coat pocket, to open the gun locker next to the door and pull out his rifle.

"Mrs. Murphy, please take the girls in back," Alma directs.

"And call the sheriff," Chance adds as Jayne herds little Mae toward the hallway and Brittany follows, wide-eyed. "You stay inside," he directs Alma, who's hanging in the kitchen doorway watching Chance chamber a few bullets. The door of the back bedroom slams.

"No," Alma snaps, moving toward him. "She's my sister, and this is my valley as much as it is yours. If that son of a bitch did this, I want to face him."

Chance scowls and lets his hand hover above the knob for a second before pulling open the front door. "Stay behind me, then," he orders.

Chance pushes through the storm door as Rick gets down from the pickup. Alma notices Jean-Marc spot the rifle from his place in the passenger seat of the car and lower himself slightly, like he's not sure that Chance isn't coming for him. But Chance's full attention is on Rick Burlington.

"I thought I told you last time you were here to get the hell off my land." Chance raises his voice over the pickup's rumble.

Rick sighs and puts his hands up in a mocking gesture of surrender. "Murphy, like I told you on the phone, we can do this the hard way or the easy way. You think you're going to want to stay out here when the mine comes across the Guthrie place? You realize how close the blasting is going to be? You can't stand in the way of progress, son. Harmony is going to mine this valley from butte to butte, like manifest destiny, and the Murphys can't stop it. Why, I just spoke to Mrs. Terrebonne yesterday, and she's getting ready to—"

"Threatened her, is what you mean," Alma rebuts, stepping up shoulder to shoulder with Chance so that Rick sees her for the first time. "Or threatened me, might be more accurate. Is that how you do business? Terrorizing old people? Is that what Vicky found out about you?"

Rick's smooth reactions veer off balance for a second as he takes in Alma's words. There's a flash of fear, then the smile and the mocking little laugh return full force. "A misunderstanding, obviously. You've filled your grandmother's mind with such awful stories about me that I wish her good morning and she thinks I've threatened her. Harmony is a good member of the community, a good neighbor. I'm just offering Mrs. Terrebonne very good money to do what's in her best interest."

"That's not the way Vince Guthrie tells it," says Chance, knuckles white on the rifle. Alma feels anger radiating off him like electricity. She puts a hand on his forearm to ground him but he shakes her off angrily.

"Guthrie's embarrassed to tell his neighbors what a great deal he got." Rick crosses his fleshy arms across his chest. "He's made up this story so you'll feel sorry for him instead of being mad. Come on, I'm not such a bad guy. I'm just doing my job, for a good tax-paying company, so little Mae can go to a good school and—"

Before Alma understands what's happening, Chance has raised the rifle and blown out the right headlight of Rick's pickup. The deafening crack of the shot reverberates like a tympani while safety glass tinkles to the ground like sleigh bells.

Chance takes a menacing step toward Rick, the gun pointed down but still at his shoulder. From behind him, Alma can see that he's gripping the gun to hide how much he's shaking. Chance's anger, disgust, and fear roll over her like a speedboat wake as Rick scrambles back behind the open door of the Ram. She throws a wild glance at her car, where Jean-Marc has disappeared altogether.

"Jesus Christ! You'll pay for that, you crazy hillbilly!" Rick shouts.

Jayne comes running out of the house. "Stop!" she cries. "The sheriff is on his way. Just stop it, all of you!"

"This is not over! You'll get a bill for that, asshole!" Rick clambers into the cab and rolls down the window so he can keep shouting at them while he pulls away. His last attack is for Alma. "Don't you try to pin your sister's death on me, missy. That little piece of trash was just asking for what happened to her."

"That does it." Chance raises the rifle again as Rick reels the pickup toward the road, spewing snow across the yard as the big tires grapple for traction.

"No!" Alma snatches the gun away from him and slaps a hand onto the middle of his chest. "Enough! The sheriff will take care of him. It's okay. He's gone. It's okay."

Everything—*everything*—that's happened in the last few days hangs suspended between them, like they're standing on a rope bridge over a thundering waterfall hundreds of feet below. Chance is panting as if he's just gone a few minutes with a green saddle bronc, staring after the Ram with a panicked rage in his eyes. Alma hands off the gun to Jayne and wraps her arms around Chance. He leans heavily on her. Over Chance's shoulder, her eyes meet Jean-Marc's. In them, she reads anxiety tempered by compassion.

Sheriff Marx shows up barely fifteen minutes later. Alma and Chance have gone back inside to reassure Jayne and the girls. When Marx arrives, Alma hurries to the door in time to see Jean-Marc leap from the car to intercept the lawman.

"We had a report of a shooting," Marx says. "Who are you?"

"Jean-Marc Lacasse," he begins, offering his business card with two fingers and an air of authority. "I'm an eyewitness."

"Oh?" Marx examines the thick card with raised eyebrows. Jean-Marc puts his hand on Marx's shoulder and steers him toward the small pile of shattered safety glass. "Because first Mrs. Murphy called and then Burlington flagged me down on the highway just now wanting to press charges. What the hell happened? He claims Chance tried to kill him."

"That's nonsense," Jean-Marc answers in his most imperially dismissive tone. "This Burlington fellow was trespassing and we told him so, but he wouldn't go, so Mr. Murphy—the younger Mr. Murphy, that is—fired once in the air as a warning. Burlington was so agitated that he drove into this fence post—" Jean-Marc points at a post that is indeed within the spray pattern of glass—"and broke his own headlight. If anyone should be pressing charges, it's the Murphys. Burlington was very rude, and then he left this mess." Jean-Marc sighs and shakes his head with an expression that conveys all his genuine bewilderment at peculiar local behavior.

Marx looks back and forth from the glass to Jean-Marc, stumped for words.

"Is there anything further I can help you with?" Jean-Marc prompts, snugging up his gloves.

"I'm going to need to talk to Chance," Marx says.

"I'll just fetch him," Jean-Marc offers. He sweeps past Alma without a word and returns so quickly with Chance that Alma can't believe they've had any time to review this new version of events. Chance steps outside and faces Marx.

"I've got nothing to say," he declares, shoving his hands into his jean pockets. "You heard what happened." He gives a slight nod toward Jean-Marc. Alma sees how hunched his shoulders are, how much he dislikes blindly endorsing whatever story Jean-Marc has told.

"So you're confirming Mr.—ah—Mr. Lacasse's story that Burlington knocked out his own headlight?" Marx waves the business card between them, as if it represents the palpable lie hanging in the air. Chance lets the words settle, staring at Marx, then takes two long steps backward and reenters the house without saying another word. Marx throws his hands in the air and turns to Alma.

"What about you? Did you see what happened?" he asks.

Alma glances at Jean-Marc, standing at attention, ready to speak whatever words will get rid of Marx. She shakes her head very slightly. "He'll give you your statement," she says, and follows Chance into the house, a new knot forming in her gut at Jean-Marc's protective, generous, facile willingness to lie, and her own willingness to go along. Standing in the kitchen doorway, Chance looks back at her as she steps inside. They both look away, embarrassed at what they've just allowed.

Starting toward Billings with Jean-Marc plugged into his music in the passenger seat, Alma begins to take stock of all the things she hasn't yet told Ray Curtis, as a way of organizing her mind for the ride to come. The dark history with Walt, suspicions about who Brittany's father is and who was responsible for Vicky's latest pregnancy, worries about what's happened to Walt, Vicky's missing marked-up copy of the mineral lease, Chance's angry accusations about Rick and the leases, and Brittany's story about Rick being there the night Vicky died. She'll tell Ray what few facts she has. Much of the rest is private affairs, family matters, nothing she can be sure has direct relevance to Vicky's death—in her own mind, Alma still can't call it murder. Yet she feels unease at the imbalance, as if she's accusing Murray and Rick by keeping her own counsel in these other things. The family tradition of keeping secrets, protecting their own, is as real an honor code as the oath she took to uphold the Constitution and laws of the United States, but it's tightening around her now like a straitjacket.

Will Walt show himself? It's been several days. Maybe he's ready to come out of the woods and talk. Maybe he abandoned Helen to her fate after all these years. Alma has begun to sort relevant from irrelevant, wondering all the while if she's qualified to make that call.

Back on the interstate, she gets Ray on the phone.

"Well, no word on Walt." He knows somehow what she's after, a reassurance that the latest stray sheep has wandered back. "It's starting to look like something's happened to him. It's been over seventy-two hours with no withdrawals from any known account, no activity on any credit cards, and he didn't take much of anything from either the house or the cabin that we can tell. If he'd run, he'd have to take something, even if it was just something to pawn. From what I can tell, all he has are the clothes on his back. He took off from the garage and all he had out there were tools and sports equipment. At the very most he might have grabbed a fly rod or two. His pickup is at the cabin but hasn't been touched since before it snowed on Monday. We searched the cabin and the electricity is on, a few things in the fridge that might be new, but no sign of him. It's possible he took some camping gear from the cabin. We found a sleeping bag out there, for example, but Helen hasn't been out there in years, so she can't vouch for what should be there. She's pretty sure nothing is missing from the house."

"So you think he disappeared in the woods?" Alma asks.

"The only outcome that makes sense is that he's walked into the wilderness area and gone missing, one way or another. But before I jump to conclusions, I'd very much like to see a body. It's going on four days. If he had any camping equipment with him, he still would've had minimal supplies, so if he walked out of there yesterday morning at the latest, before we got there—"

"But if you saw no tracks he would have had to leave earlier, before or during the last snow. Sunday night or Monday."

"We can find out when the storm came through the canyon. So even earlier. That means if he's out there, he's been there going on three nights in subzero temperatures. There's nothing but thousands of acres of some of the least-used wilderness in the Lower Forty-Eight that direction. There's nowhere to go, and nobody to find him. Unless he managed a real Houdini of a getaway, I'd say he's lying dead somewhere. I'm sorry, but that's how it's looking."

"I see," Alma says, her hands beginning to shake as she struggles to hold the phone and the wheel steady. Her ability to absorb the death of another family member is redlining. Jean-Marc looks up from his e-mail.

"Now, the only thing we can do is send out a search party. Best-case scenario is he's bivouacked out there with a sprained ankle or something and we can still bring him in alive. You always have to hope." Ray pauses, his voice transmitting reflection and finally, decision. "But honestly, the chances of finding him out there at this point are probably slim and none. In the back of my mind is always the possibility of foul play; we have to consider it and investigate for it, but we just don't get strings of homicides around here, and I don't see much to indicate that in this case." Ray's voice drops out. Alma worries for an instant that she's lost the connection before she hears him clear his throat and begin again. "I hate to have to say this, but the fact pattern developing here is murder-suicide. Walt kills Vicky in some sort of family conflict, is overcome with guilt, and takes off for the woods to end it. So that's another reason to send out search parties. It may be the only way to collect evidence before it's destroyed by the elements or four-leggeds, so we can close the case. We've got a new forensics report back that I want to talk over with you." Ray delivers the news in a crisp, detached tone. He is telling her what she must understand, but his reluctance to say these words to her is like a crackling on the line. She feels it without him saying it again: he is sorry. For her part, despite Walt's misanthropic nature, she just can't picture the scenario Ray spells out. Walt is a crank, not a killer.

The cruise control is on, carrying the car forward, which is lucky, because Alma would like nothing better than to pull over, curl up, and stop drawing breath in a world where things like this can be real. Instead she shakes her hair off her face and lowers her chin with a determination that Ray can hear rather than see. "I'm on my way out there myself, if that's not a problem. If there's any chance he's hiding, he might come out to talk to me. I know where some of his stands are."

There's another heavy pause on Ray's end. "I'm meeting you out there, then. Don't go into the cabin, and don't touch anything. I have to take care of a couple of things here first, but just wait for me, okay? I don't want anybody else going missing."

Alma is nearly at the convergence of I-90 and I-94, the great roads rolling westward together like great rivers merged, a pioneer drainage snaking toward the Gallatin Valley along a path traveled by the Crow and Nez Perce. Ordinarily Alma loves the pulse of this fast, truck-heavy interstate, pushing toward the Bozeman Pass, or eastward to Sheridan or Bismarck. More than that, she loves the feeling of the great open lands, the ranges she's hiked and skied, the peace and isolation of the plains, the fortress of solitude. It holds the greatest safety, this land, once you know how to live on it. Nothing can come at you across the high plains that you can't see from miles away. But right now she notices none of it. She's shaky and perspiration is slick on her upper lip. Jean-Marc turns his head to look at her, then drops his head away to watch the billboards flash by.

After dropping off Jean-Marc with a few simple goodbyes, Alma rolls downhill into a space outside the Itching Post. She wants one of Pete's hugs and a few minutes of uncomplicated sibling irritation, along with Pete's take on what's going on with Walt.

"Hey there, kid. You know, I think one of my staff is wasting coffee in the espresso beverages," Pete says as he comes around the bar. "Either that or stealing it outright. We're using way more than we should for the number we've sold. Usually they don't use enough and people start complaining that the coffee tastes weak. I mean, I don't mind if the baristas drink a few, but they've got to keep a record. How am I supposed to keep inventory and write orders if—"

"Pete." Alma has to step into his path to get his attention, speaking low, close to his chest. "I understand you're trying to run a business here and I'm sorry I keep distracting you, but nobody's seen Walt in days. I'm about to head out to the cabin to look for him. He could've had an accident, I guess, but it seems like too big a coincidence, him and Vicky all at once, you know what I mean? It has to be related." She resists the words internally. Every step into this quicksand sucks her farther down into a life she's cast off with all her strength. Every muscle is taut with the urge to run, but she cannot abandon Vicky and Brittany, not this time.

Pete stares back coldly. "Whatever happened to Walt, he had it coming for years. It doesn't surprise me at all, and I don't give a shit."

This reaction slows Alma's enthusiastic exposition. She bends her head closer to his.

"Ray Curtis thinks maybe he killed Vicky and took off. You think that's possible? You think Walt could be on the run, trying to make us think he's dead? I mean, I know it sounds crazy, but I don't know what to believe."

Pete shrugs and glances toward the bar, busy with customers picking up large morning coffees. He reaches for a shelf and puts a few pound bags of coffee back where they belong, slamming them into place with unnecessary force. "Wouldn't surprise me if he had cash stashed somewhere. You know how paranoid he is. I'm just saying it would never surprise me if the universe or anyone else had it in for Walt Terrebonne. That man ought to just drop off the karmic totem pole. And that is for your ears only. I don't know what you're thinking, chasing around after Walt. What good will it do? Either he'll turn up or he won't, and either way, we have no way of knowing what's happened to him." Pete turns back to Alma with sudden intensity, even a hostile edge to his normally laid-back gaze. "Look, Ray Curtis is a smart guy in a small police department and he's looking for some excitement. I think you ought to go ahead and catch a plane to Seattle and let the dead lie in peace."

Alma stands blinking as Pete strides toward the front of the bar and snatches up his clipboard. She wants his advice about so many things. He knows Billings and Vicky and the family far better than she does these days. He'd reassure her that breaking up with Jean-Marc is obvious and overdue. But he's shutting her out and sending her away. Somewhere in the last decade or so, she became the outsider, and now her own brother is letting her know it.

CHAPTER 19

Alma is lost to her own daydreams, elbow up against the cold window as she turns the car out the Nye road at an inadvisable speed. She and Walt have never had much of a relationship, but who can claim to be close to Walt? Vicky is the niece he raised from the age of twelve. To any ordinary man she'd be like a daughter. He must realize that if he'd gone out that night he might have saved her, unless he himself . . . But Alma will not walk herself down that road yet. Not until she has no choice.

In spite of his gruffness, in her childhood Alma felt reassured by Walt's brick wall presence. The massiveness of him was a bulwark. Her mother never liked him. She didn't care for his silences and his way of disappearing. "He's hiding things," she would say, "and I don't think I want to know."

The two families hadn't been close—awkward holiday dinners, forced conversations at family and community events, and then all at once, in the absence of a will, Vicky was left alone with these arm's-length relations. Alma shivers at the memory of Vicky standing in the airport corridor, several feet away from

Helen, silent tears wetting her face as Alma turned to wave one last time, back when everyone still walked right up to the gate and watched the planes take flight.

At last Alma pulls into the long Forest Service road, over the frozen creek, toward the little cabin above the upper Stillwater. The scenery evokes late summer days floating the river on inner tubes with a contraband six-pack of beer tied on behind, swimming the deep holes, jumping off bridges and high rocks, all those things that everyone who grew up here has done.

Alma is so absorbed by memories that she misses the turnoff to Walt's cabin and has to go back. Ray isn't here yet.

The cabin is locked up tight and nobody answers her knock. The steps and ground are windswept with no trace of prints. The hiking boots Alma remembered to pack at the last minute scratch at the frost on the steps but leave no recognizable marks.

There's snow on the windshield of Walt's GMC and a trace of snow on the steps. He'd have to walk in or out of the cabin or he'd have to use the pickup. There ought to be footprints somewhere. Alma has never known him to camp so long, not in winter. She looks around her and starts to circle the cabin. Even if Walt were in a stand, it's not comfortable, especially in this weather. And he wouldn't pack in days of supplies. He'd come back for things, and he hasn't.

Alma's mind starts to tick over. What if Walt did come the night Vicky died? What if the killer saw him? Could someone— Murray, Rick?—have followed him all the way out here without Walt noticing? How would someone Murray's size overpower a man the size of Walt, or move his body? But Rick—Rick would be big enough.

On a rear windowsill is the Ace key copy that has always been there. The police have already searched the place and she'll hear Ray coming for miles. Alma wastes no time. She goes to the fridge—two six-packs of PBR, a stack of burger patties, a bag of buns. On the counter is a paper bag of canned goods. She turns the faucet—no water, but a coughing sound. Walt must have turned on the water and left it long enough for the pipes to freeze. He expected to be back.

She sits down on a folding chair next to the scarred card table in the main room that doubles as a kitchen. None of this makes sense. Walt knows how to handle himself in the woods. She gets up and paces a few times across the cabin with her hand to her forehead, breath billowing in the chill.

Forgetting her good intentions not to leave any sign of her presence, Alma flings open the front door of the cabin and runs down the steps. The nearest stand is less than a mile away. She has to look. Panic is on her like sudden sickness. Nausea rises. She rounds the corner behind the cabin and starts to run up the trail, taking in the stinging cold air with big, panting breaths. The elevation and the slope slow her, but she makes good time, powering through ankle-deep snow, following the terrain line.

"Walt, goddamn you, be alive," she mutters, pulling off her cap and stuffing it into a pocket, opening her coat as she starts to sweat. There are wildlife tracks and scat—some kind of big hare, squirrels, deer—but no human sign.

The stand appears in the distance all too quickly. It's high up, higher than a stand should be, but Walt liked the perspective and took pride in the difficulty of the project. Alma makes no attempt to hide her tracks or muffle the sound of her approach. "Walt!" she cries. "Walt, are you up there?" Her voice is shockingly loud against the winter quiet of the tall pine forest. She sees no sign of life above, but she's put her hand to the lowest grip all the same when an odd shape catches her peripheral vision. Perhaps ten feet away, even with the drip line of the tree, something pokes out of the light covering of snow.

"Oh shit." Alma steps back from the tree and regards the object in the snow for a long moment before moving to it. Her body knows and clenches tight before her mind admits what it sees. As she comes closer, the bottom of a boot, then the leg attached to it, reveal themselves under the light crust of snow. Walt's twisted body is sprawled on the forest floor, up against a decaying log that hid him at first. She knows him from his boots, his coat, his size. She comes near enough to see the white and red beard trailing from under his hood, then backs away, keeps backing until she smacks into the tree. She puts her hands behind her and clings to the trunk for support. "Dear God," she breathes.

The prayer is inarticulate, a plea for nothing more than the strength to turn around and put one foot in front of the other. This much she does, stumbling back down the slope, falling a few times, crying. At last the cabin appears, like a mirage in the desert. Just past it stands the Billings PD Suburban.

Alma's momentum carries her into the clearing. Ray is standing on the front steps of the cabin and bounds over to her. He grabs her by her upper arms to keep her from falling.

"Alma? Alma!" Ray guides her to the idling Suburban and helps her up into the passenger seat. "Just sit here, okay?" He hands her a small plastic package of tissues, fishes her keys out of her pocket, slams the door, and starts back up the trail with long strides, unholstering his handgun as he goes.

He is back in what feels like too short a time to Alma, but his face has changed. His jaw is fixed and the gun back in its holster. He climbs behind the wheel and sits for several minutes before speaking. Alma has stopped crying and blows her nose in the silence.

"You okay?" Ray asks.

Alma hiccups and forces a trembling nod. "I don't think I'll ever get that image out of my mind." She pulls out a fresh tissue and begins to tear it into tiny snowflake shreds. "I'm just not used to this much traffic in dead bodies. He's been up that tree a thousand times. I never thought he'd fall." Alma brushes the tissue flakes off her leg and starts with a fresh tissue, her fingers working the soft paper frantically.

Ray reaches over and takes the package back. "Seems unlikely," he agrees. "Also seems like a low-value way to kill yourself."

"He's armed like the Tenth Mountain Division," Alma observes. She looks down at the shredded tissue as if seeing it for the first time, then wipes her nose on her coat sleeve. "If he'd wanted to kill himself, he didn't need to jump out of a tree."

"So we're back to a double homicide," Ray replies, then waits to hear what she'll say. Alma leans back against the hard seat. She notices that Ray has locked up the cabin and wonders how long he would have waited until he followed her tracks.

"There's Murray," she begins. "But you arrested him Monday morning at the home place and he didn't post bail until Tuesday. And Rick. I can't be sure, but I think he might have forced me off the road the other day with his pickup. And this morning Brittany said . . . she told us that Rick was there that night, and he went after Vicky. So Walt could've witnessed something. And Pete told me"—another deep breath, preparing to let this burden go—"that she was raped a few months ago. That's why she was pregnant."

Ray exhales heavily. "Okay. I'll need your statements. You think Brittany will be willing to talk to me?"

"I hope so. She's been getting better."

Ray settles a hand on the dash and taps it in a slow drumbeat as he reflects. "I'm still working on Murray's motive. I don't think there's much there, but some of these guys will kill each other over what's for dinner. Everyone who was there that night claims that nobody left to go after her, and nobody has mentioned Rick being there. So now we've got Brittany telling a different and uncorroborated story. You're right that if Walt was an eyewitness, that could be a motive for coming after him. As far as I can tell, though, Rick had no relationship with Murray's crowd. How would he get them to lie for him, especially when it might mean casting suspicion on one of them instead? Nothing about that makes sense. If he'd been there, at the very least Murray would've tried to use the information to get leniency, and he never said a word."

Ray is thinking aloud as he tries to reassure Alma, but his words are only a reminder of the word they're both thinking: *murder*. Double homicide. Murder suicide. Not good options. It was easier to think of Vicky as a victim of the elements than to see her in the scene that now runs incessantly through Alma's mind: stalked, attacked, left for dead on a slab of ice in the fury of a January night. She would do anything to blot out that image, but instead her imagination is filling in the details, showing her how it's all possible, only blurring the murderer's face as he leans over Vicky. Facts would help, if there are any, but just when she thinks she has a handle on one, it runs like watercolor and changes into something less reliable.

"You were going to tell me more about the forensics report," Alma prompts.

"Right. The autopsy produced the gray wool fibers I told you about. We don't have any DNA and the blood work isn't back yet, but it's possible that somebody covered her nose and mouth with something like a scarf or a blanket. High quality, long fibers. She breathed in a few, and we didn't find anything like that on her or at the house. If we can match the fibers we'll be a little closer to building a case."

"Where are you looking?"

"We're executing search warrants for everyone connected to her recently."

Alma notices again how Ray avoids using Vicky's name. "I assume you talked to Dennis and Kozinsky?"

"Yeah, we talked to Kozinsky first thing and interviewed Dennis a few days ago. Kozinsky's best alibi is Brittany—she was sitting right there in the room with him until she fell asleep that night. Dennis was at the *Gazette* until nearly one A.M. getting the paper to press and then his car wouldn't start, so a co-worker gave him a ride home. Why, have you heard something we ought to check into?"

"Not really. Dennis sure doesn't live like he has any extra money lying around, but Vicky always said he put on an act so he wouldn't have to pay child support. And Kozinsky—I mean, sure, he's probably mixed up in the drug trade, but I don't know why he'd be more of a suspect than anybody else Vicky knew. They got along well enough to live together."

"They were in some kind of relationship," Ray acknowledges. "Although it didn't seem like much more than sleeping in the same bed."

"That's what I thought. And Brittany says he didn't like her, but you could probably guess that from where she was sleeping." Alma balls up the remaining tissue and stuffs it into her pocket so hard she hears the lining tear.

Ray pulls off his gloves to warm his fingers over the heat vents. "I hear from Sheriff Marx that there was an incident out at the Murphy place first thing this morning."

Now, sitting next to Ray, Alma feels unconflicted about Jean-Marc's lie. She nods.

"I spoke to a Chance Murphy by phone this morning after the run-in with Burlington—I take it he was a friend of both you and your sister?" Ray continues.

"Yes. A childhood friend."

"He seems to think that your sister was under some kind of pressure from Burlington. Would that be related to what your grandma says, about the mineral lease?"

Alma turns a little toward Ray in her seat. "Chance and Brittany both say that Vicky had a copy of the lease with notes all over it, things she found out about Rick's dealings with the landowners. Did you ever find anything like that?"

"No sign of it." Ray reaches between the seats and pulls out a notepad. "It could be an important piece of evidence, depending on what's on it, and the fact that it's missing may be important too."

"I've been starting to think it could've been a motive, but I couldn't figure out how Rick could've been there that night at exactly the right moment when she wandered out. And then this morning Brittany told us he was there. She said they argued and he followed Vicky outside. That's why we were all so upset when Rick showed up at the Murphys'."

Ray turns his head toward her and raises one slender black eyebrow. "It's sure inconsistent with all the other information we have. Rick's got an alibi from a woman in Billings he's been running around with behind his wife's back while he's up here from Denver. She says they were in bed asleep at her place. What do you think?" Ray flips through his notes. His tone is curious, not sarcastic. "Does Brittany lie? Why would she lie?"

Alma sits back. Pete's words rise up: *Brittany's got a little of it too, when she really wants something.* And her motivation to lie? It suddenly seems clear as the high country pools that gave the Stillwater River its name. Alma's eyes snap up to Ray's. "She'd lie to protect the home place."

"Hmm." Ray meditates over his notepad for a moment. "But if she's not lying and Rick was around, it opens up different possibilities. Your sister could have told Walt what she knew, and then he'd be—"

"No, that wouldn't have happened," Alma interrupts, pulling her arms in tight around herself.

"Why not?"

"Because Vicky and Walt hated each other."

Ray lowers his pencil. "Hated each other? Nobody's said that to me. Why would they hate each other?"

"Walt and Helen raised Vicky after our parents died. They never got along. Oil and water. She moved out as quickly as she could, and then they broke off contact a few years later, except for the way Vicky kept coming back to all of us, asking for help, playing games. When I saw him Sunday evening, he told me to go back to Seattle and leave them the hell alone."

"Wow." Ray sets his pad and pencil on the dash. "You never mentioned that. He's got an alibi from your aunt, but that doesn't sound very good for him. You think she'd lie for him?"

Alma rarely thinks about Helen, but now that Ray asks—of course Helen would lie for Walt. "I don't know," she tells Ray.

CHAPTER 20

Back on the road, there is nowhere to go but the Itching Post. Alma can't face Helen yet. She needs to talk to Pete, hear him tell her what to believe, what is real and what is insanity. An unholy instinct grips her as she pulls off the interstate. The way Pete reacted this morning, the unfamiliar hardness. Alma feels the clockwork pieces slip into place so that a mechanism comes to life with an evil hum and purr. Who else could have gotten close enough to Walt to do this? Who else could have found the cabin, let alone the stand? Her beloved Petey, her big brother, her protector, what has he done?

She parks and runs up the sidewalk toward the Itching Post without bothering to lock the car. Halfway up the block, she slips on black ice in the shadow of an insurance agency awning and falls hard on her left hip—the sound is the sort of crack that will mean a giant yellow bruise along the bone. She curses at herself and gets to her knees, then her feet. The pain is raw and deep. She is crying. Her hand is ripped open and bloody—she had her hands deep in her pockets and barely caught herself as she went down. Her coat is pebbled with sidewalk salt and gravel.

She staggers along the sidewalk, waving off an offer of help from the insurance agent who rushes out in shirtsleeves. She rubs desperately at her tears with the sleeve of her coat, trying to make it all go away, as she reaches the front window of the Itching Post.

Pete sees her from inside. He stops tamping down coffee for the next latte and races around the end of the bar toward her as she steps through the door. "Alma, what happened to you? Are you all right?"

"I'm fine," she protests. "I fell down. I just need to sit for a minute."

Pete helps her to an upholstered chair, gets her settled, then spots her left hand. He hurries off for the first-aid kit and orders Alma a coffee from the teenager who's busy clearing tables.

"Here we go," Pete says with calming authority as he opens the kit on the low table next to Alma. He's talking her through it, talking her down. "We'll just clean that off, get some Neosporin on it, bandage it up, you'll be good as new. You got any other wounds I should look at?"

Alma looks at him with eyes still full of tears and puts her hand to her heart. Pete makes a funny little pout, trying to make her laugh. "Problems with the boyfriend?" he inquires. He wipes away grit from her bloodied hand with a cotton patch soaked in alcohol.

Alma hisses at the pain, then leans over, still grimacing. "Pete, where's Walt?"

She can hear him swallow. "You think he ran?" he says, very quiet and still.

"No."

"Then what?" Pete puts the first-aid kit in his lap and starts to dig for antiseptic cream.

"Pete!" She grabs his shirt with her less fragile right hand and yanks him back to her. "I know!"

Pete looks her in the eye for only a second before bending back over her hand. "What are you talking about, Alma?" His Adam's apple bobs, the only sign of discomfort as he answers her.

"Do you want to have this conversation here?" she hisses.

Pete carries on with his first aid, spreading cream, measuring gauze. "What are you going to do?" he asks, still not meeting her eyes.

This sudden frankness drains her. Alma leans back into the chair, trying to come up with something that would explain Pete's actions. She winds up back at the home place, on a spring day when Pete was working with the ranch hands, branding and castrating. He hated it, but his way of dealing with the revulsion was to work harder than anybody, force himself to do better and faster all the ugly things that had to be done. He was up before dawn every day, pushing through, refusing to look at Alma. When he came in the door the last night, stinking of blood and dirt and sweat, she hadn't recognized him. He had transformed himself in the service of what had to be done. This capacity would have made him a very good soldier if it hadn't also driven him to drink himself half to death.

Pete swings his head around to take in the busy shop. "Come on," he says, and grabs her arm. He leads her past the bar to a small door into the windowless storeroom. He locks the door, overturns two buckets, and gestures for Alma to sit.

"It was you, wasn't it?" she whispers so softly that even Pete, crouched beside her in the tight space, can barely hear. "You and I, we're the only ones who could have found him out there."

"I did what I had to do," Pete says, moving on to Alma's less damaged hand. "This is a family matter." He tapes the last bandage across her hand with professional efficiency. She'd forgotten about his medic training in the Marines. His hands are steady, but just like that spring on the home place, he won't look at her face.

"Did he kill her?"

"Who else?" Pete's eyes come up for a second, not quite meeting hers, still hiding something. Her raw hand contracts painfully in his.

"But Petey, why?" It's a child's lament, a little voice crying out at the unfairness of it all.

Pete shakes his head in a gesture of futility she remembers from fights when they were kids, as if explaining things to his baby sister is beyond him. It infuriated her then too. "Jesus Christ. I don't know who I'm trying to protect anymore. Alma, don't you get it?"

"Get what?" Alma's indignation is the same instant heat it has been since childhood, when Pete refused to take her seriously. Will he ever give her credit for being a competent adult? "I am not now nor have I ever been psychic. You have to speak the words."

Pete sinks back against a set of steel shelves, pale. He looks at her blankly. "Alma," he begins, then looks down and rubs his brow. Suddenly he drops his hand in a gesture of capitulation and blurts, "Brittany's his. He had to cover it up."

As these words ricochet around the room, neither of them cries out or moves. Alma fixes her eyes on a deep fissure in the cement storeroom floor. Their breathing is loud in the small space. If this is what Vicky told Pete, then in her heart, Alma believes her. These are not the sort of lies that Vicky told. Vicky was wild, but not malicious, and Alma's memory of being in the pickup with Walt and being afraid, on top of the incident just a few days ago in his garage, now makes her very sure of what he did—what he would have done even to her, Alma the inexorable, had she lived under his roof. She wants to hurt him with her own bare hands.

But none of that makes him a murderer, necessarily. Alma's

mind produces a sudden, unwelcome recollection of a wooden train set Walt made for all three of them during one of those happy years of their lost childhood. She can see the carefully painted cars laid out around the Christmas tree and Walt standing at the door, embarrassed at the children's warm attention.

"How do you know?" She finds that her voice is weak but still present.

"Oh I knew," Pete says, still bent over, refusing to look at her. "I think I knew a long time ago. And then when I went out to the cabin, he told me."

"So you think he killed her." Alma's words are not a question.

There is no shadow of uncertainty in Pete's cold eyes when he looks up this time.

"Yes." Pete bites his lip and stares back without blinking. She reaches out her right hand and takes his left. They sit there together for several minutes with bowed heads, holding hands, staring into depths in the other that each has only begun to contemplate.

"You talked to the police," Pete says, dropping her hand and wrapping his arms around his middle. It's cooler in the storeroom than out in the shop.

"Yes. Ray Curtis came out to the cabin."

"What did they say?"

"He thinks it's suicide." Alma wraps her coat around her legs.

"And what did you say?"

"Not much. I didn't argue. I didn't figure out that it had to be you until I got back to town."

"How did you know?"

"You and I are the only ones who could have found him, and strong enough to hike out to the stand. And even if somebody managed to track him there, we're the only ones he wouldn't see as a threat. Besides, if Walt were going to kill himself, he'd put a gun in his mouth, not jump out of his stand." She chokes down a strangling feeling and reaches for Pete's arm. "God, Petey, he could've killed you too. How could you take such an awful risk?"

Pete relaxes, not entirely, but perceptibly. He takes Alma's hand again, rubs it. "Where's Jean-Marc? Was he there?"

"No." Alma swallows. "He went home this morning."

Pete lifts Alma's chin to get a better look at her face. "He just got here."

"Yeah, well, I fucked it up again." She pulls away.

Pete's face softens in a gentle look of recognition. He doesn't know the details, but he's familiar with the list of perfectly good boyfriends she's ejected at cruising altitude. He leans on the shelving again. "You didn't have to go out there and find him right away, you know. I was kind of hoping animals would get to him."

"Now you're scaring me." Her voice is low. What Pete has done is just beginning to come over her, like a chill, a fever, some illness that will never be gone. Of course she understands the impulse. It is such a human reaction to horrors, to lash out, to strike back. But animals obscuring the evidence? He's thought this through, maybe after the fact, but with a detachment that she feels right down to the ligaments holding her bones together.

Pete senses her unease and leans in to try to catch her eyes. Reluctantly she looks back at him. "Just to mess up the crime scene, I mean," he says with sad eyes and open, pleading hands. "There aren't any marks. No bullet hole or anything."

"Signs of struggle? DNA?" Alma sits up straight. He's right. Whatever Pete's done, there must be no loose ends. He must never be linked. That is the priority now.

"Don't think so. God, I wish this had never happened," Pete says.

"What did you see?" Alma realizes that she has a scene already drawn in her mind: Walt leaning over Vicky's body sprawled on the ice, and Pete watching from somewhere, witnessing the heartbreaking, unnatural crime, resolving to be the swift hand of justice.

Pete shakes his head. "Nothing. But I chased him out to the cabin Monday morning and he more or less confessed. Told me how she got what she deserved."

Alma hesitates. Her shoulder twitches under the bruise from slamming into Walt's garage door. "He said something like that to me, how he knew she'd end up like this. But Petey, why didn't you call the police?"

"I—I don't know." Pete takes his head in both hands. "I was beside myself. I guess that's what I thought at first, that I'd tell the police everything. But Walt just kept talking. She'd ensnared him, tempted him. He did wrong, but it was all her fault somehow. He said—" Pete's voice catches, and he starts again. "He said it was better this way. Vicky would be at peace, and he and Helen would get custody of Brittany. You hear what I'm saying? That son of a bitch would get away with murdering Vicky and then *he'd get Brittany*. I couldn't let it happen.

"I drove back down the road and parked out of sight of the cabin, waited for it to get dark. Walt was drinking, so I knew he wouldn't hear me come back. I got the key and looked inside. I was about ready to turn back then, but—God, I couldn't believe it—that bastard had a picture of her out there. Brittany. One of those posed school pictures. He must have gotten it from Helen. Right there on the window ledge, like he'd been out there by himself thinking about her." The contortion of Pete's face is alarming. He leans to one side and reaches for his wallet, pulls out the photo and shows it to Alma. Brittany is beaming at the camera, her hair glossy and her pretty face open like it hasn't been in all the time Alma's been back. "I couldn't leave it in that place." His fingers grip the photo so tightly that it crinkles at the edges. Alma unwraps his fingers and takes it.

"I thought I knew where Walt might have gone, just for a

night, if he didn't want to be found," Pete goes on. "I hiked out that way. I could tell I was on the right track. It looked like Walt did it on snowshoes, dragging a pine bough to cover his tracks. He always liked *Last of the Mohicans* crap like that. The snow was hard pack and I was almost on tiptoe trying not to leave prints or make noise. For all I knew, he was up in that stand, drawing a bead on me, and he's a good shot when he's sober.

"I get to the tree. No shots, no noise. I was starting to think maybe I was wrong, but the snow was knocked off the lower branches and his little hidden footholds. I climbed up. It's just this little platform, you know, smaller than I remembered it, and Walt's lying there all zipped into his mummy bag, sound asleep. I grabbed him by his feet and yanked them up so he was hanging upside down off the side of the platform. And he is a big fucking heavy man. I almost couldn't hold him. He woke up and couldn't get out of the bag, so he's going crazy, clawing at the bag and cussing me out. I think he thought I just meant to scare him. He was mad, not scared. I was shouting at him that I knew what he did to Vicky, and then he started saying, 'I didn't mean it. It was a mistake, I didn't mean it to happen.' Like he thought I would understand." Pete's face contorts and his fists clench. "There's—there's a bald side to the tree where it's a straight drop to the ground. I just swung him over that way and let go. Once he hit the ground, he never made another sound. Then I thought, well, he wouldn't commit suicide in his sleeping bag, so I took it back to the cabin and stowed it."

They sit in silence, staring at the floor, the reviving smell of coffee all around them. Then Pete stands and offers a hand to Alma. "Better get back to the front." She hears his double entendre.

Alma stretches her arms around her brother and hugs him tight. "I love you, Petey."

The road to the heights is clear and dry. Maybe Helen will be willing to say more about Walt, now that he's gone. There was always more to Helen than people saw. Next to Walt's intimidating size and intensity, she was the quiet wife who never demanded much attention. Her passive nature made room for the tortured past he carried. They fit together like jagged, deformed puzzle pieces.

To give her aunt some small measure of warning, Alma calls Helen as she drives along the rims. Helen picks up after several rings, there as always.

"Come right over. I didn't know if you'd make it back here. Maddie says you've been running all over, taking care of things. Did you go talk to Walt?"

"I drove out there, like I said I would. Listen, I'll be there in a minute and we can talk." Alma hangs up and tries to piece together words to tell Helen that Walt is gone, talking to herself as she drives. Then there are Pete's words about Vicky. If Helen knew—*she had to know, how could she not know?*—then Alma's sincere anguish at her aunt's loss is turned inside out. She can't do this. She can't face Helen and hear whatever she's going to hear. Navigating the suburban maze distracted, Alma finds nothing but dead ends. She's dry-mouthed and her heart is beating too fast. Helen has to have known something and kept quiet. Finally Alma stops, collects herself, and maps the route to Helen's on her phone, resolved to put on her most professional persona as armor.

Parked at last in Helen's driveway, Alma goes around to the sliding glass doors in back that stay unlocked all the time and finds Helen in a chair next to them in the weak winter sun. She gestures Alma inside without her usual greetings and inquiries. "You've been out there? Did you see him?"

Alma sits down in the chair next to Helen's. She nods.

"And is he coming back?"

Alma takes a deep breath and shakes her head. She leans over to take Helen's hand. "No. He's not coming back." She tries to invest her words with all the meaning they must carry, but Helen's eyes show no comprehension.

"How can he not come back at a time like this? He knows—I can't—" Helen makes a helpless gesture and stops talking, her hand picking at the afghan on her legs. Her eyes fix on Alma, who realizes that Helen's usually tidy hair is coming out of its braid, and her shoes are unlaced. *Why didn't Walt buy her slip-ons?* Alma asks herself first, then becomes aware, looking at Helen and her surroundings, of an unfolded basket of laundry at the bottom of the steps and the smell of the litterbox.

Alma puts the bookmark in Helen's Bible, sets it on the coffee table, and kneels to tie her laces. "Where's your hairbrush?" she asks.

"Upstairs in the bathroom, on the vanity." Helen gestures. Alma jogs up the stairs, wondering how Helen manages to get up and down on her own. In the master bedroom, the bed isn't properly made—a very un-Helen-like omission—but shows only a small disturbance on one side, as if she's tried to slip in and out without mussing the covers too much.

Alma straightens the bed. In another moment, she's back down with the brush, smoothing Helen's hair back, reweaving the long braid. Standing out of Helen's view helps Alma gather herself for what she's decided to do.

"Vicky didn't have a very happy adolescence with you and Walt, did she?" Alma asks. In spite of the shell now before her, she cannot afford to see Helen as only an object of pity. The abuse that devastated her sister's life and ended in her murder began in Helen's house, where Alma left Vicky for safekeeping.

Helen's almost transparent hands lift to temple in front of her. She turns her head to gaze out the glass doors toward the squirrel examining the snow-covered deck. "Well no, I suppose not, but nobody has a happy adolescence. After what happened, I don't think we can be too surprised that she went off the tracks."

"After our parents died, you mean?" Alma's hands keep moving, finishing the braid, knotting the elastic, brushing out the tail.

"Yes." Helen's response hangs in the air, as if there's more to say but she won't let it out.

"What about what happened at your house?" Alma sets the brush on the side table. The little *clunk* is loud in the quiet.

"What happened at my house? What do you mean?" Helen's confusion is feigned, Alma is sure. She doesn't try to turn to get a look at Alma's face, but they can see each other in the glass, frozen reflections of blank stares. Helen holds her posture, staring out the window, allowing no movement—lying with her body. Alma knows that one.

Alma pauses and grips the back of Helen's chair. It's the cruelest possible thing, what she's about to do, if Helen really knows nothing. If she's somehow unaware, Helen ought to be left with whatever happy memories she might have, whatever ghost of kindness Walt may have left. She can't have long to live, a few years at most. But something pitiless is working in Alma, maybe Vicky's ghost at her shoulder. Helen has to have known, she tells herself, and because she failed to spare Vicky, Alma will not spare her now. She looks at Helen's stiff back, which waits for Alma's words, dares her to say them, and Alma finds at last that she has no heart now to forgive Helen. That part of her compassion lies dead and frozen like her sister's bruised cheek in some mortuary freezer, awaiting the spring thaw.

Alma squares her shoulders and smoothes Helen's braid against her back with one hand. She comes around the chair so that she'll be able to see Helen's face. Standing between her aunt and that damned squirrel she considers so important, Alma clasps her hands behind her back and speaks.

"Walt abused her, starting after Mom and Dad died. Brittany was his. Then he raped her again three months ago, and that's why she was pregnant again when she died." It's like pulling a knife out of a fresh wound, worse than the pain when she first heard the words. *Get it out. Say everything.*

Whatever Alma expected, Helen's expression isn't it. Her face changes so quickly from puzzlement to a mask of contempt that Alma can hardly accept the change. There is no shadow of surprise or shock, just this stunning transformation. Helen looks like a different person—hardly a person at all, but a dark and angry apparition. Alma recoils, bumping into the glass door and falling against it as her legs give way.

Helen leans forward with hostile energy. "She said that, did she? I was glad to have her out of my house, that little slut and her nasty slurs. She deserved what she got. She deserved it. She'd been looking for a bad end for years and finally it came for her." Helen pushes herself out of her chair to stand over Alma, who has slid down the glass to sit with her knees hunched in front of her. "I would have kept quiet. You didn't need to hear the truth about your sister. Nobody needs to hear that sort of thing. But if you're going to come into this house with her lies, you're going to hear, all right. She was nothing but a no-good piece of white trash and we're lucky she's gone, all of us. And you, you're just the same. Drying up, no husband, no children, just whoring it out there with one man after another. *Trash.*" Spit collects around the edges of Helen's mouth.

"She told you—" Alma chokes out. She can't decide if it's worse to know how much Helen knew or to slam that door for good, but something in her is calling out for answers, whether she's prepared to hear them or not.

"Oh, I heard it all," Helen spits out. "She liked to tell me her sick little stories, blaming Walt for getting her pregnant when she slept around with every man in town. She taunted me with it. But I knew what she was—a liar and a whore."

"A liar?" Alma clutches at the cramp in her stomach. The words hit her like physical blows. *"He raped her.* She was sixteen when Brittany was born. How can you say—"

"Well, she would say that, wouldn't she? Everything was always somebody else's fault. Then she came here one night several months ago, talking about bringing charges and claiming child support. Walt took her out to the garage to talk some sense into her. Then later he told me he'd heard from her, she was pregnant again, and I just knew she'd start the same lies about him." Helen uses chairbacks—carefully placed, Alma now realizes—for support as she walks to the small coat closet behind the front door. Before reaching in, she pauses and turns back to Alma, who is still sitting half collapsed against the sliding doors, staring after her in shock.

"What are you doing?" Alma asks.

Helen's voice projects across the vaulted living room. "I have to show you something. I want you to defend me."

"Defend you?" Alma's legs are sprawled at painful angles. She can't seem to untangle them, and she can't understand what Helen's talking about.

"Yes. You're the only one who will understand what I had to do. You know what she was. You'll be my lawyer."

"What are you talking about, defend you? What did you do?"

Helen reaches to the back of a closet shelf and pulls out a soft, wadded object. With a sigh, she straightens herself against the frame of the closet, then walks back to Alma. As Helen approaches, Alma sees more clearly what she holds in her hands: a gray wool scarf. Helen stops, standing over her, and drops the scarf in her lap. Its folds are stained with something dark that can only be blood.

"Oh dear God," Alma croaks. "You. No." One hand flies to her mouth. With the other, she braces herself on the carpet. She looks around the room, working at breathing. Helen stands unmoving, her feeble, knotted hands at the height of Alma's head.

" 'Anger assists hands however weak,' " Alma recites, fixing her eyes on her aunt's vengeful features. The words rise out of some black gulf of memory, some dozy afternoon Latin class at Bryn Mawr, offering an explanation her conscious mind can't yet accept. Alma knows that Helen's passivity hides the same thing that led the wagons westward, the same nerve and sense of duty that drove her great-great-grandmother away from the fire on cold winter nights to midwife new mothers up and down the valley, riding into bitter storms on a great draft horse, never failing, never brought down by the fear and fatigue that rode with her every mile. The years of deprivation and isolation made the women like winter aspens—bare of ornament, stark, giving the appearance of death, yet green and resilient at the core, and tied to the place and the people with a vast network of unseen roots. Eternal. The men have always been strong, but the women have been steel.

She's half afraid that Helen will somehow manage to hold her down and use the scarf on her. Hard-wired instincts for self-defense buzz like fried circuits. "How?" she asks in the same strangled tone.

"Oh, it wasn't hard," Helen says, her voice steady, lacking inflection. "Brittany called that night, another one of these helpless princess calls, oh come save us, Mommy wandered out in the cold. Walt would have gone, of course. She had him wrapped around her finger. But I thought, this can't go on. There will be this new baby and it will never be over, they'll have their claws in us forever. So when he went back to sleep, I drove down there to find her."

Alma clutches the scarf against her chest with one arm. The fabric is stiff with more than blood, as if wrapped around something. Alma shifts a few feet farther from Helen, seeking for logic, a way to dissuade Helen from the story she's telling.

"But you're— How did you—"

"I'm so weak, you mean?" With effort, Helen draws herself

to her full height, staring down at Alma. "I had strength enough for this. It didn't take long. And wasn't I clever to take the lease too? I bet they're hot on the trail of that landman by now."

Helen, who can hardly lift a forkful of broccoli? Alma can't believe it. "You're lying," she attempts. "You're lying to protect Walt." Anything would be easier than this. And why not? Helen is dying. Then Alma realizes that she hasn't yet told Helen the news that seemed so all-important just a few minutes earlier. "I went out to the cabin this morning," she begins.

"Did you talk to Walt?" Helen lowers herself back into her chair, showing the strain.

"No. He wasn't at the cabin."

"Not at the cabin? But where could he be? It's too cold to camp and it's not hunting season." Helen's voice is back in its normal register, conversational. This is even more chilling than that awful, vengeful face she showed a few minutes ago.

"I hiked out to his tall stand."

"And he wasn't there either?" Helen's voice rises on a note of panic. The terrifying show of strength and anger was fleeting. Helen is small again, diminished by the thought of Walt disappearing.

"He was." Alma grips the scarf tightly and finally gets her feet under her.

"Well, why didn't you just say so?" Helen slumps a little against the chair. Her relief makes her face less fearsome. "When is he coming back?"

Alma doesn't want to see Helen's reaction to the next words. Delivering them gives her no pleasure. "Helen, I found his body."

Helen's hands on the chair arms grow rigid and her face lengthens. Instinctively Alma takes another step back, feeling for the door latch with one hand, but abruptly, Helen begins to wail. It starts high-pitched, emitting straight from Helen's lungs like a ghost sound, ventriloquized from some spirit in the room.

The sound surrounds Alma, dropping to a low, chilling register that ought to frost glass, she thinks. All Alma can do is hold still, keep her feet steady on the floor, and try not to distract Helen as this emanation moves through her, hollowing out the space between them until Helen's eyes open and she gazes up at Alma with a sort of bereft innocence.

"Who did this?" Helen asks in a hiss.

"The police think it was a suicide," Alma says. "He fell from the stand." She has one hand on the door handle.

Helen has enough strength left to bark a laugh. "My Walt would never commit suicide. A person who takes his life will be in the telestial kingdom throughout all eternity. It's a terrible sin."

A terrible sin. With more effort than it ought to take, Alma rolls the door along its track. The rush of cold air feels good. She is exhausted. "Believe whatever you want. It doesn't matter now."

"He would never do that. It has to be—it's you. *You* did it. You took him by surprise somehow." The vengeful look is creeping back.

Alma puts one foot outside the door. "No, Helen. I didn't kill him. It must have been an accident. That stand was way too high."

This thought gives Helen pause. "It's the judgment of the Lord upon me," she says at last, reaching out with both hands to pull the Bible back from the table into her lap, all her angry strength dissipated. "What I told you—"

"You asked me to represent you." Alma hears the echo of her own voice as she acknowledges the significance of their conversation. "Everything you told me is privileged."

Helen smiles, but her eyes fix Alma coldly. "I thought so." Helen leans back against the chair and shuts her eyes. "I learned a thing or two doing prison ministry. Now get out."

"I'll send someone to look in on you," Alma says as she pulls shut the sliding door, unable to take her eyes off Helen, half afraid to. She staggers down the back steps and around to her car, the scarf clutched in her hand. It's wrapped around something else. Alma can hardly force her hand to touch the scarf, to pull it back to reveal the lease, with Vicky's insectile handwriting all over it.

For perhaps the first time in fifteen years, Alma doesn't know where to go. She drives away from the heights, circling a few times in the suburban maze, dazed and unwilling to face another human being. In the back of her mind is a nagging memory, something Chance said about teaching an agribusiness seminar at the college. Was it Tuesday afternoons or Thursday? At last she finds herself at MSU-B, pulling into the small faculty parking lot behind the business building, and there's Chance's Silverado, collecting a light snow at the back corner of the lot. Night is falling. Class must be over soon. Alma pulls in next to the pickup, shuts off the car, and pulls her coat around her.

"Alma! Alma!" She startles awake with a small shriek to Chance calling her name, knocking hard on the window as if he's already tried knocking softly. "Open up!"

Her arm is very heavy as she pulls at the latch to let the door fall open.

"Are you okay?" Chance pulls the door farther open and leans in to get a better look at her. "I was shouting at you several minutes to wake you up. You're— Alma, you're freezing cold. How long have you been here?"

She shakes her head and shuts her eyes. "I don't know."

Chance reaches across to unbuckle her seat belt. "Come on, get up. We'll go get you something hot to drink. Come on."

At Chance's insistence, Alma unfolds herself and climbs out, stumbling, hands and feet numb from cold, then lets Chance hoist her into the pickup. He tosses her purse and keys up to her. The pickup is cold too, so Chance pulls an old Pendleton blanket from behind the seat and tucks it around her legs. Five minutes later in the drive-through lane at the Itching Post— because of course, her wandering mind is telling her, this is

Billings and there's a drive-through lane even at the gym—he orders her a chamomile tea and folds her hands around it. Then Pete's voice is at the window.

"What's going on?" she hears her brother say, his face blocked by the big side mirror. "Is she okay?" She's missed whatever Chance said to Pete.

"She's right here." Chance leans back to let Pete see Alma. "She came by the college. I'm going to get her home. I just wanted you to know she's all right."

Pete leans out the window to take a good look at Alma, bundled in the striped blanket, barely able to raise her eyes to his. "You don't look all right," he says with a suspicious sidelong look at Chance. "You want to come inside? I'm short-staffed. I've got nobody to cover the till."

Alma can only give a small, forlorn headshake. Pete swears and fixes a fierce glare on Chance. "You take good care of her, you hear me?"

"I will," Chance answers with his most sincere nod.

"Okay then." Pete stares at her another long moment, then withdraws and slams shut the little service window. Chance's shoulders relax and he puts the pickup back in gear.

"Do you want to tell me?" he asks once they're parked out front, the diesel engine finally pouring out heat.

Swaddled in the blanket, Alma breathes in the fragrant chamomile steam and wags her head a tiny bit. *No.*

"Did you find Walt?"

Alma nods. *Yes.*

"Alive?"

Alma shakes her head. *No.*

She hears Chance inhale and exhale. "I had that feeling." He pulls off his cap as the cab starts to warm up. "How did Helen take it?"

Sleep and cold have allowed Alma to push everything out of her mind but a primal urge to get warm. Now that she's awake and the tea is thawing her hands and nose, Helen's name cracks open her mind like falling through ice. Alma is with Vicky again, bloodied after a hard fall on ice, reeling, drunk, and the face that bends near hers, the rescuer, the comforter, the mother, is instead the merciless specter of death. She drops the tea, throws her hands to her face, and begins to sob. Chance scrambles to grab the covered cup and shove it in a cupholder. He puts a hand on her shoulder and lets the sobs play out. When she calms enough to start hiccupping, he says: "Okay if I take you home?"

Alma nods, wiping at her nose and eyes with a gloved hand. As the pickup pulls out into traffic, she curls up under the blanket, unable to keep her eyes open.

When next she wakes, Chance is shaking her shoulder. She's been asleep on the seat of the pickup with her head propped uncomfortably on the console. She sits up and sees Ed and Jayne's house.

"I slept all the way here?"

"Yep," Chance confirms. "I don't mind saying you're scaring me, Al. Come on, let's get you inside."

The smell of food is still in the air as Chance leads Alma to the couch. Jayne hurries forward with questions. Out of the corner of her eye, Alma sees Chance silence her with a look and a gesture toward the liquor cabinet. As Chance stows Alma's coat, Jayne appears before her with a water glass half full of whiskey and ice.

Alma takes the whiskey and sips. Low conversation moves away from her, into the kitchen. She hears Brittany's and Mae's animated, chattering voices come closer, then move off together, on the trail of invisible house dragons. She drains the glass, sets it on the floor, slips off her shoes, and curls up on the couch.

The house is dark and quiet when she wakes up again, feeling a prickling new alertness, like a spell has worn off. Someone has tucked a blanket around her. The fire in the stove burns low. She lifts her head to see Chance lying under a blanket in the extended recliner a few feet away. Her stirring rouses him.

"You feeling any better?" he asks through a yawn.

"I don't know." She sits up and looks around. "Where's my bag?"

"Right there on the floor, next to you."

Alma reaches down and snatches the leather purse to her chest. Chance observes without moving. "Whatever it is, we can deal with it," he says. "Talk to me."

Alma unfastens the latch and looks into her bag. "I'm surprised you want to hear another word out of me."

The glow from the window of the wood stove lights Chance's half smile. "You say that like I have a choice in the matter."

"Don't you?"

Chance just gives her a look.

"I'm sorry," Alma says.

"Let's not do apologies now." Chance yawns and rubs at his face. "You were honest with me. Most people wouldn't have been, in your situation. Let's take that as a place to start. That's the Alma I remember."

"Okay." Alma looks around the room, wondering where Jayne stowed that whiskey bottle. Chance catches her glance at the liquor cabinet and gets up to retrieve the bourbon and another glass.

"So what's in the bag?" he asks as he pours them both a generous double shot.

With one hand, Alma lifts first the scarf, then the lease out of the bag and sets them on the small oval table.

Chance kneels on the other side of the table, staring at the display between them. "What is this?" he says.

"Evidence."

"Of what?"

"Ray says that Vicky might have been smothered with something made of high quality gray wool, long fibers." Alma lays her hands flat on either side of the scarf and the lease.

"Where did you get this?" Chance's eyes grow wide and alarmed. "Walt?"

Alma shuts her eyes tight and shakes her head. She hears the sound of the table shifting. When she opens her eyes, Chance is leaning on the other side of the table, looking more closely at the bloodstains on the scarf without touching it. "Then I don't understand— Who— But that doesn't make any sense, not after what Brittany said about Rick. Not . . . *Helen?* But why? *How?* And if she killed Vicky, then what happened to Walt?"

"I think what Ray believes," Alma begins, then pauses to throw back a sip of bourbon before continuing, "the conclusion he'll come to, is that Walt killed Vicky, then committed suicide. There's too little evidence to support any other conclusion. And that's what we need him to go on believing."

"But that's not what happened." Chance has abandoned his examination of the scarf to look at Alma as if she's a wounded animal, capable of anything.

"No."

"Alma—what happened to Walt?" There is an awful, careful blankness in Chance's face. Alma lifts her eyes, lets him look into them and see the truth.

"No, it wasn't me. He fell from his tree stand. He was"—Alma can't meet Chance's eyes anymore—"thrown from his tree stand."

She sees Chance studying her face, the heartbroken sound of her voice, the anxious way her hand is reaching toward him across the table—Chance who understands animals without benefit of words, who always knew which songs she hated just by watching her. She pulls her hand away, but it's too late. "Pete," he says.

They sit in excruciating silence. Chance downs his whiskey.

After several minutes, Alma offers the only change of topic she can think of, then regrets it the moment it's out. "So, I, uh—broke up with Jean-Marc this morning."

Chance nods. "Tiffany dumped me over the phone," he replies. "Something about you and me sharing the same taste in lipstick."

"Ah. I'm sorry. She seems nice." Alma risks a look at Chance, but he's observing the fire with an embarrassed expression.

"She is. Mom's been trying to get us together for months. First time I've ever been called a two-timing son of a bitch." Chance's boot leather creaks as he levers himself to his feet.

"Your mom wasn't too happy either."

"I knew the minute she took you outside." Chance cracks a smile as he opens the stove and throws in another log. His gaze falls on the hard-scribbled lease. "Have you looked at what Vicky wrote?"

"No." Alma brings her head up and sniffles with renewed energy. "I should read it."

"Do you mind if I look?" Chance puts out a hand but waits for permission.

"Go ahead."

Chance sits on the floor, settles his back against the couch next to Alma, and unfolds the four-page document, so light and harmless to the eye for all that it conveys and condemns. The firelight is very dim. Alma clicks on the floor lamp beside her and leans over Chance's shoulder. Vicky's script looks like ants crawling across the page, tiny and wound in on itself. The notes are in no particular order, connected with arrows and lines in some places, heavily underlined and circled in others. Family names figure prominently, people Chance and Alma know, tied to home places in this valley and beyond. Vicky has been busy.

Chance reads for a few minutes before glancing over his shoulder at her. "This is incredible. It's every family Harmony has contracted with since they started mining the valley. Some of them went for the money, but look—" Chance points a finger at Vince Guthrie's name. "Burlington threatened to turn off his oxygen!"

"Renata Byer." Alma points too, tracing a wavering line of print along the side of the page. "He forced her pickup off the road with her infant granddaughter in back. She signed standing on the side of the road, 'shaking so hard she could barely hold the pen.'"

"I don't get it. How'd she get these folks to talk to her? I've asked them the same questions and they won't tell me anything," Chance says. "She's got numbers, dates, what Burlington threatened them with—everything. Can this be true?"

"More importantly, can it be admitted into evidence?" Alma picks up the first page to see if the second is scrawled as thoroughly. It is. More names. More numbers. "Unless these people will testify, it's all hearsay. Even we don't know whether to believe it or not. We need affidavits."

"But now we know where to get them." Chance's voice takes on a tinge of excitement. "Somehow she got them to talk. Maybe I can use it to get them to go one more step."

"How are you going to explain where you got it?"

Chance considers. "Nobody knew for sure Vicky had it that night, right? It could have been with Brittany's things. It could have been anywhere."

They sit for a few minutes, letting the patterns in their minds metamorphose and realign as they skim another page of Vicky's notes.

"How long are you staying?" Chance asks when they've turned the last page, deciphered the last of Vicky's hieroglyphs.

"My flight's tomorrow at one thirty. I wish I could stay longer, but my job is in meltdown." Alma presses fingers to her temples. The whiskey is moving in her blood, blurring the edges of her compromised brain.

Chance's own hand is shaking as he holds the paper. "What

did we do to bring these people here? This used to be the most peaceful place in the world."

"That was only a veneer, wasn't it?" Alma sits back. "Scratch a few layers in the dirt and there's violence all around us. Blood feuds and massacres."

"Vicky was trying to fight it." Chance turns a little to look up at Alma. "At least you know this about her. You know she was fighting to save the home place."

Alma feels more tears slip down her cheeks. She's given up holding them. Vicky was fighting the coal company, and her own family did her in. "That's my little sister. That's what we'll tell Brittany." She stretches out a hand and this time Chance takes it.

"What are you going to do with this?" he asks, gesturing with the lease toward the scarf.

"I don't know. I don't know if I even believe Helen, but she was pretty convincing. She scared the hell out of me."

"Will you tell Curtis?"

Alma stretches her neck, still trying to work out the crick from sleeping in the pickup. "Chance, I can't. That's what you have to understand. She asked me to represent her. What she told me is privileged. I could be disbarred for telling you. And now I'm tampering with evidence, which is crossing over from unethical to criminal behavior." She gestures at the scarf in frustration.

"But couldn't you mail the pages to the county attorney or something? Somebody ought to see this."

"The one thing we can't do is show this to anyone else. Helen gave it to me as her attorney. We can ask more questions, but this is our secret." She tugs at Chance's hand until he looks up.

Chance rests his hand on his chest with hers held tightly under it. "I promise."

"This might sound awful, but we need the case to close as a murder-suicide. If it wasn't, they might start looking at Pete.

Helen will be gone so soon. She's no danger to anybody else, and I don't want Brittany having to think of her . . . doing that, on top of what she's going to find out about Walt. Let it all be Walt. I don't want a trial. We need the investigation to end now."

Chance stares down at the small hand in his, considering. "I know where to hide this," he says, rising. He gets his coat, gingerly dumps the scarf and lease into a big Ziploc bag, and disappears out the front door. Several long minutes tick by. A log snaps in the stove and Alma startles.

When he comes back, Chance sits down hard on the couch beside her, as if his task has exhausted him. "I'm sorry I brought all this into your life," Alma says in a voice barely audible above the crackling of the reinvigorated fire.

"Your life is part of my life," Chance answers. "I never had much choice about that. I guess I'm glad I got to share a few more days of it." It's not quite bitterness she hears in his voice, but deep frustration.

"I've been thinking about Seattle." Alma is cautious now, trying not to do damage with her ragged, unpolished words, torn from a place in her that doesn't speak, not anymore. "While I'm out there, it's like things aren't happening in real time. Here, every little wide place in the road from Sarpy to Three Forks has some memory attached to it, some family story or something. All our ghosts. All our kin. I get this feeling when I'm away like I'm . . . like I'm . . ." Alma gropes for words and fails.

"Like you're a desperate woman. Like you're underwater, trying to get back to the surface to breathe again," Chance says with certainty. How does he do that? It's damned irritating. No way should he be able to escort her into his parents' living room after all these years and casually tell her what's in her soul. Maybe this is why she's been with Jean-Marc. All this time, she's be-lieved that if she stays at the office and scorns the closest kinds of human contact, she'll be safe from the kind of pain she left in

Montana. Now it turns out that the pain was with her all along, padding along invisible like Burro, waiting to be cared for.

"Oh, I don't know." She pulls the blanket snug around her. It will never do to let Chance know how he gets to her. "I don't know about desperate. But I'll tell you this. Sometimes out there I just stand up against a building, something big enough to block out the sky, so I can pretend that on the other side there's open plains, and the Big Horns in the distance."

"Did that in San Francisco a few times myself." Chance smiles and there's a hint of the shyness Alma remembers, a peek behind the steady man he's become, into the skinny high school boy who carried pictures of his horses and her in his wallet and had problems with premature ejaculation. "I'm glad you're back, even if it's just for a few days." He waves a hand, open-palmed, releasing.

Alma had forgotten about Chance's hands, how much she likes them. Heavier now than she remembers, they are chapped and hard, hammers forged by the perpetual hard work of ranch life, old-fashioned hands, with fingers as big around as quarters. *Tus manos son dos martillos que clavan y desclavan alegres la mañana.* Your hands are two hammers that joyfully nail down and pry up the morning. She settles down on the couch again and pillows her head on his leg. His hand smooths her hair and settles on her shoulder, the kind of anchor that holds ships in a storm.

Jayne finds them that way in the earliest morning light, the room cold, the fire out, Chance's head nodding at an awkward angle against the back of the couch, Alma coiled under his arm. "Damn," she whispers.

CHAPTER 21

The flight touches down early at Sea-Tac. Downloaded work has kept her busy the whole way, while Brittany thumbs video games and watches the clouds. The distractions were almost enough to keep Alma from thinking about the hiss of wheels leaving asphalt, wings banking west, the stark outlines of cliffs and river, the stretch and break from home. As the plane slows in a classic Puget Sound drizzle, she rotates her head and takes a long swig of cold coffee.

When she takes back her phone from Brittany, there's a voice mail from Ray Curtis. "Alma. Ray. Just wanted to update you. Walt's autopsy indicates death on impact after falling head-first out of his deer stand. No sign of foul play. BPD executed a search warrant on the Terrebonnes' house and found nothing significant. Barring anything unexpected in the remaining tox screens, we plan to close the investigation fairly soon. Murder-suicides are all too common in this part of the world." Ray's digitized voice descends as he speaks. "I'm very sorry it played out this way, but frequently there's a family member involved.

At least you can go back to Seattle with some closure." Alma shuts her eyes and clicks Delete.

She takes a cab straight to the office, working through another set of auctioneer-speed voice mails from Amanda while Brittany presses her cheek to the glass and stares at the sodden city, drawing graffiti with her finger in the condensation. Alma's floor is buzzing with the sound of Louis shouting and junior associates running up and down the halls. Duncan's due diligence review failed to discover some dubious offshore transactions in the accounts of the merger partner, revealed by Alma's phone interviews. At best, it's minor financial information that should have been in the dealbook. At worst, the target is hiding assets and the whispered rumors about money laundering are true. When Alma steps out of the elevator, pulling her suitcase and leading Brittany, Duncan is chasing Louis up the hall, whining about everything he did that should have turned up the Cayman transactions and didn't.

"There was no trail!" Duncan protests. "We went through everything, every last document. We were in a warehouse for six weeks. You know that! This isn't my fault." He spots Alma and points to her. "She set me up!" With a quick, whispered word, Alma sends Brittany down the hall to where Amanda is waiting.

Louis marches straight to her. "How did you find this? Where did this come from?" he demands, waving a printout.

"I interviewed their administrative staff by phone earlier this week. They were very forthcoming once they heard about the layoffs." Alma keeps walking toward her office, pulling off her coat.

"She just got lucky," Duncan snarls. "I suppose I could have spent my time chatting with the secretaries, but I was busy with actual legal work."

"It was your job!" Louis stops to shout into Duncan's face. "You can't pass the buck on this one, Duncan. You knew there were questions about the status of the pension fund. Why didn't you talk to these people Alma found? Where were they? You're just damn lucky she covered your ass on this, in the middle of her sister's fucking funeral, or we'd all be up shit creek. I ought to fire your ass right now!"

"You can't fire me." Duncan lets out a little laugh. There it is—he's playing his trump card. Alma smiles as she turns on the lights in her office. Louis is still a junior partner, and Alma is getting close to partnership review. Both of them stand to lose big in a standoff with the entrenched powers of the firm— people like Duncan's uncle.

Louis's and Alma's eyes meet behind Duncan's back. They openly dislike each other, but the stakes have gotten too high. Duncan's amateurish error could have brought down both of them. He's a third-year associate. He should know better. Louis and Alma both know that Duncan didn't bother interviewing the administrative staff because he's been busy romancing one of them and billing their dinners as business expenses.

With the slightest nod to Alma, Louis turns back to Duncan. "Clean out your desk," he says. "I've had it with you."

"*What?*" Duncan starts a hiccupping, hysterical laugh. "You know you can't do that. You don't have the power!"

"I'm an equity partner in this firm, Mr. Moi." Louis returns to old-fashioned lawyerly formality, to emphasize that he knows what he's doing, and to whom. "We'll find out if that's still worth something around here. Now clean out your desk, give me your key card, and get out. I give you fifteen minutes. Alma, go with him and see that he doesn't touch his computer. I want all the files as they are, especially the e-mail."

Alma escorts an explosive Duncan Moi—although not explosive in the way she'd expected, simmering rather than erupting—to the bright, wide office he's enjoyed since his earliest days as a new associate. Without speaking, he grabs a few document boxes and fills them with whatever comes to hand:

framed photos of his boat and Porsche, glass tchotchkes from major deals, office supplies, a PlayStation, an assortment of silk ties and pill bottles from a lower drawer. Alma watches to prevent the escape of work documents and client files, but Duncan's drawers are mostly devoid of work. He shoulders his golf bag, piles one box on the other, and turns on Alma. "This isn't over, you bitch," he snaps. "I'd watch my back if I were you."

Alma watches Duncan's retreat to the elevators, then walks back to her desk, fingering the key card, lost in thought. Louis, hurrying back from the kitchen with a glass of water, runs into her, spilling it all over both of them. They stand in front of Amanda's desk, flicking water from their clothes and shaking it off their feet.

"I'm sorry, Alma." The words sound awkward coming out of Louis's mouth, but he manages them. "We should've gotten rid of Duncan a long time ago."

"Don't worry about it." The apology, so long owed, torn from him at such obvious cost, would have thrilled her a week ago. Now it falls through a void, touching nothing. She looks him fully in the eyes for the first time in months and is surprised to discover that she's several inches taller than he is. Louis's face looks small and lost behind frail designer glasses as she pushes past him. He flutters out of her path like a pile of fall leaves— weightless, insubstantial, as he always has been, she realizes now. Her future here is before her on a platter, now that Duncan is gone and Louis at least temporarily defanged, and she sees like coming to the crest of a long-building wave that she wants none of it. A few feet into her office, she stops. "Louis?" she says without turning around.

"Yes?"

"I quit." She starts walking to her desk, winking at Brittany, who sits cross-legged in one of Alma's leather chairs, abusing a stress ball.

"You—you can't quit! We're about to close a deal!" Louis

steps into the doorframe, grasping it on both sides, enlarged and irate. Brittany stands and moves to put the desk between herself and Louis.

Alma steps behind her desk and looks up at him in amusement. "Oh, you might be surprised what I can do," she tells him. "I've finally got it worked out. There's somewhere else I need to be." She opens a drawer and begins to pile personal items on top of her desk: dark chocolate, ibuprofen, hand lotion.

"Alma, what are you doing?" he shouts. "This will affect your bonus!"

"Excuse me," a voice says behind him. Alma looks up to see Amanda smiling at her. Louis lets her pass and Amanda calmly shuts the door in his face.

"You quit?" She grins. "For real?"

Alma grins back and waves a toothbrush at her former assistant before tossing it in a banker's box at her feet. "Looks that way."

"Well happy independence day. Good for you. Where will you go?" Amanda drops into a chair and kicks her feet up onto the desk for the first time.

"You're going to think I'm out of my mind."

CHAPTER 22

SIX DAYS LATER, 1 P.M. MOUNTAIN STANDARD TIME

The U-Haul grinds up the last rise in second gear. "Hey, I see them coming!" Pete shouts from the passenger seat.

"Who?" Alma asks, peering into the side mirror.

Brittany, squeezed between them with coats on her lap, cranes at the mirrors. "I can't see anything!"

"It's Chance and Mae, and I think— Oh yeah, Jayne's there too, holding something on her lap."

Alma slowly takes the turn into the drive and now sees the Murphrod cresting the last rise on the snowy road, bearing a well-wrapped welcoming committee. Alma would bet money that Jayne is carrying baked goods. She pulls in behind the house and backs up the truck to the steps, then they all jump down and come around the side of the house to meet the visitors, shrugging on coats, laughing and gasping as the wind catches them hard beyond the lee of the house.

Alma watches the truck advance cautiously on icy gravel, smiling at the sight. Pete puts an arm around her and they stand together while Brittany runs down the drive, coat open, hair flying, a native-born Montanan heedless of the cold. The pickup rolls in as Brittany holds the gate, then Jayne opens her door for the girl to jump up. There is still no cell phone coverage. There is still a huge coal mine a few miles up the road, its land agents circling like buzzards. There is still only an outhouse. Vicky and Walt are dead, Pete is a murderer, Brittany is a liar, Helen is a creature beyond Alma's capacity to comprehend, and all this Alma carries up against her own skin, her own flesh the poultice that will draw out the poison for as long as she is strong enough. There's a pain in her stomach that hasn't gone away in days. Montana has drawn her close to whisper in her ear that evil exists, even in places of great beauty. Even in the people you love.

But evil is not the end of the story. Her arm is tight around her big brother and the land rolls out beneath them. The home place rises solid beside them, Charles and Eliza's deep roots spreading above and below, intricate, textured, real. *Everything changes. Nothing perishes.* Alma is not whole, she is not healed, she is not everything the family needs. She's an escape artist run out of tricks. All she has to offer is that she's here. It will have to be enough. The effort of holding life at arm's length is more than she can sustain, so here it is: the biggest risk, the act of commitment.

The heartbreaking arc of big sky unfolds over a landscape imprinted on their souls, repeated in their DNA, generation after generation, past and promise, curse and catalyst. Chance stops and Brittany leaps out with the Murphys to hike up the last curve of the drive, red-cheeked and smiling, Mae's hand in hers, the girls' hair blowing like festival flags. Alma lifts her chin and faces into the wind, and the wind smells inexpressibly sweet.